ON THE
EDGE OF
TRUST

Books by Patricia Bradley

Logan Point Series

Shadows of the Past
A Promise to Protect
Gone Without a Trace
Silence in the Dark

Memphis Cold Case Novels

Justice Delayed
Justice Buried
Justice Betrayed
Justice Delivered

Natchez Trace Park Rangers

Standoff
Obsession
Crosshairs
Deception

Pearl River

Counter Attack
Fatal Witness
Deadly Revenge

On the Edge of Trust: A Logan Point Novel

ON THE
EDGE OF
TRUST

A LOGAN POINT NOVEL

PATRICIA BRADLEY

Revell

a division of Baker Publishing Group
Grand Rapids, Michigan

© 2025 by Patricia Bradley

Published by Revell
a division of Baker Publishing Group
Grand Rapids, Michigan
RevellBooks.com

Printed in the United States of America

All rights reserved. No part of this publication may be reproduced, stored in a retrieval system, or transmitted in any form or by any means—for example, electronic, photocopy, recording—without the prior written permission of the publisher. The only exception is brief quotations in printed reviews.

Library of Congress Cataloging-in-Publication Control Number: 2025007953
ISBN 9780800747008 (paper)
ISBN 9780800747398 (casebound)
ISBN 9781493451395 (ebook)

This book is a work of fiction. Names, characters, places, and incidents are the product of the author's imagination or are used fictitiously. Any resemblance to actual events, locales, or persons, living or dead, is coincidental.

Cover design by Mumtaz Mustafa.

The author is represented by the Seymour Agency.

Baker Publishing Group publications use paper produced from sustainable forestry practices and postconsumer waste whenever possible.

25 26 27 28 29 30 31   7 6 5 4 3 2 1

In memory of Bryan Byars, the love of my life,
and Mavis Alexander, my big sister in Christ.
Your encouragement pushed me to write the best book I could.
To God be the glory for lives well lived.

1

A ding from her phone jerked Jenny Tremont from a sound sleep on her den sofa. She hadn't been able to sleep and had come down to the den to watch her favorite Friday night show.

Her phone dinged again. The security camera. She grabbed her phone and clicked on the video but didn't see anything. Maybe an animal?

She replayed the video, looking closer. This time Jenny saw it. A shadow. And it wasn't an animal. Her sins had found her out—wasn't that what her mother always said? That her sins would be exposed.

Whoever it was hadn't gotten in the house yet. She could grab her go-bag, find the intruder's location on her cameras, and go out on the opposite side of the house.

Jenny raced for the stairs. *Wait.* The back door. She'd locked it and set the alarm . . . hadn't she? She always did, even before she had reason to fear, since Logan Point, Mississippi, was next door to Memphis. But sometimes she forgot.

Was there time to check? She couldn't risk not checking and changed direction. At the back door, her shoulders sagged. She hadn't locked it. Dumb mistake.

Jenny threw the dead bolt. Getting caught had always been a possibility—she'd even prepared for it. But she'd never really believed it would happen. And she hadn't thought it would happen when she couldn't get to the money. She couldn't go to Zack Mitchell's house in the middle of the night—he would want to know where the money came from. *Think.*

Zack's son. Drew would bring it to her, no questions asked. Jenny's thumb hovered over the phone. But not here—that might put him in danger.

Quickly she punched in his number as she hurried to her bedroom. Once it started ringing, she laid the phone on the bed while she changed from her pajamas to a pair of jeans and a T-shirt. By the third ring, she'd yanked on a pair of Nikes and grabbed the phone again.

"Come on, Drew, answer!" she muttered under her breath.

On the fifth ring, he picked up. "'Lo?"

Thank God. "I need you to bring me something."

"Jenny? What? I can't hear you." He sounded half asleep.

"Drew!" she hissed and pressed her hand to her head. "Pay attention and don't ask any questions, just do what I ask."

"Huh?"

"Please, just listen. I have to leave town. I hid a package in that place you showed me back when your mom was sick. Get it and bring it to the house on Winslow."

The house was on her way out of town, and meeting the boy there shouldn't put him in any danger.

"I don't under—"

"Please. Drew, just do what I said. I need it now."

Silence stretched for five seconds. "Okay . . . it'll take me a little bit," he mumbled.

A board creaked outside her bedroom, and she snapped her head toward the door. Was it the old house settling? Or had the intruder found a way in without alerting her?

"Just hurry," she whispered.

Jenny disconnected and eased to the door, holding her breath as she pressed her ear against the wood. Hearing nothing, she exhaled quietly. She was on edge. That's all it was.

Even so, she tiptoed back to her bed, where she grabbed the go-bag. As an afterthought, she silently opened the drawer on her night table, where she kept the Beretta that Zack had given her.

No gun.

It had to be there—she never kept the gun anywhere else. Jenny quietly burrowed through the drawer.

It wasn't there.

Had she accidentally put it in the lower drawer? The gun wasn't there, either.

When had she last seen the Beretta? *Think.* Jenny pressed her fingers to her temples. Maybe Zack had taken it the last time he was here, when he installed the security cameras. He wouldn't have done that without telling her.

Earlier this week, people she worked with had dropped by for her birthday, including—

Her cell phone buzzed. Drew. She punched the answer button. "What is it?"

"Where did you say to meet you?"

"The house on Winslow. I'm leaving now."

Jenny hung up, crept to the door, and stood stock-still. Her breathing and the grandfather clock ticking off the seconds at the end of the hall were the only sounds in the house. If anyone was here, they weren't moving.

She waited. An eternity passed, and she checked her watch. *Five minutes?* Time she needed to be on the road.

Jenny calculated how long it would take Drew to get to their meeting place . . . the same amount of time it would take her to drive there. Would he wait around if she was late? Probably not. Knowing Drew, he would come check on her. And that might put him in danger. She had to leave now.

Jenny cracked the door just as the grandfather clock chimed

the two o'clock hour, masking the creak of the door. Ignoring the pounding of her heart, she stepped into the hallway and looked both ways. Empty.

Encouraged, she eased to the top of the stairs. No one hid at the bottom. Treading lightly, she descended the steps. Front door or back? She'd parked her car at the back . . . and probably there was no one in the house anyway. She couldn't believe she'd let a little creak put her in such a panic. Except it hadn't been the creak. She'd seen someone's shadow—that's what set her on edge.

She had to leave. Now. Jenny tiptoed down the hall to the dark kitchen. She should've put alarms on her doors, but she'd thought the cameras were enough. An intruder could've gotten in before she locked the back door and be hunkered down behind the island. Or under the table. Impossible to tell in the dark. Did she dare risk turning on the light? Even though she'd almost convinced herself no one was in the house, the hairs on the back of her neck stood on end.

Jenny hesitated. If someone was in the house, they would expect her to go out the back door to her car. She backed away and hurried to the den with its sliding doors. It wasn't much farther to her car, anyway.

If only she had the Beretta. Jenny knelt and removed the security bar from the track. The steel bar felt good in her hand. At least she had a weapon now.

Light flooded the room. Jenny whirled around, and her eyes widened. The intruder stood just inside the door to the den. "What do you want?"

"You know why I'm here."

Jenny tried to swallow, but her tongue stuck to the roof of her mouth. "I-I don't know what you're talking about."

Cold eyes stared at her. "Come on, Jenny—I'm tired of paying you."

"What you're giving me is only a fraction of what you've stashed away." She needed the money to help her dad start over.

"Wrong answer. I'm tired of you holding that data drive over my head."

"You should've thought of that before you got your hands dirty with drug money."

"That's rich, coming from you. You were the one snooping on my computer."

And found an encrypted account on the computer that she'd hacked into. "I thought you were embezzling, not putting dirty money in an offshore account."

Jenny hadn't shared the file with anyone since she didn't know who else was involved in the scheme. A gun raised level to Jenny's chest.

She gasped. It was the Beretta Zack had loaned her. "How did you get my gun?"

"That part was easy—like most people, you are so predictable. A key under the flowerpot on the front porch—although I didn't need it since you conveniently left your door unlocked. As for the gun . . ." The intruder shrugged. "It was where I expected it to be. Why couldn't you have been that predictable with the data drive? Hand it over."

"I don't have it." Jenny gripped the cold steel bar. She wasn't a fool. If she gave up the drive's location, she'd be dead. Jenny tightened her hand around the bar and edged closer to her intruder. She'd never tried to kill anyone before, but there was a first time for everything.

"Where is it?" Impatience rang in the voice.

She didn't have much time. "I . . . I mailed it to Victoria Mitchell two weeks ago."

No! She'd just put a bull's-eye on Victoria with words that weren't even true. But they were believable—everyone knew she was close to the Mitchell family. She would just have to survive to keep Victoria safe.

The intruder fixed her with an intense gaze and seemed to be considering the possibility that what she'd said was true. Jenny was almost within striking distance. "But we can work this out. Just turn around and leave. We'll pretend this never happened."

"Not without the drive."

And that would seal her death. Jenny swung the bar, knocking the gun to the floor. She scrambled to reach it first.

2

What was going on with Jenny? Drew had never heard his mom's friend scared like that. And when had she put something in his secret hiding place? He'd forgotten he'd even shown it to her.

Drew checked his phone: 2:00 a.m. He hoped his dad was asleep. Jenny had said to come as soon as he could and to bring the package she'd hidden. It'd be hard to explain what he was doing if his dad caught him.

Drew grabbed the jeans he'd dropped to the floor a few hours ago and pulled them on, then tugged a T-shirt over his head. As an afterthought, he slipped on a hoodie—even though it was mid-May, nights had been cool this week. His grandfather said something about it being blackberry winter, whatever that was.

He had no idea what Jenny could've hidden, but it couldn't be bigger than his backpack, so he grabbed it. The house his grandparents had lived in until his dad bought it after Drew's grandmother died was old, like nearly a hundred years old. He walked lightly to his closet and knelt, pushing aside a pile of dirty shirts.

His aunt Tori had shown him the hiding place when he was a kid, and he'd never told anyone else about it except Jenny. After his mom got sick, Jenny had practically moved in to take care of her, and after she died, Jenny had been there for him. Not like his dad, who cared more about drinking than about how Drew felt.

Even now she came every couple of weeks to make sure he had clean clothes to wear to school.

Jenny understood him, and he'd told her a lot of things, like about the secret compartment and how he figured it had been used to hide money a long time ago. She'd thought it was cool.

Quietly, he opened his pocketknife and slid it between the boards, triggering the spring on the hidden compartment. His eyes rounded. "Whoa," he muttered.

Inside the compartment was money.

Where had it come from? *Duh*. Jenny put it there, but where had she gotten so much money? Questions whirled through Drew's mind. He bit his bottom lip, hesitating until he remembered she said to hurry. He stuffed the bundles in his backpack. He would ask her when he handed it over.

Drew picked up the last bundle and flipped through it. So many hundreds. Money that would go a long way toward the medical bills from his mom's cancer. Drew figured that the stress of those bills was one reason his dad drank so much.

He glanced into the backpack. If Jenny was hiding this money . . . was it even legal? And there was so much here that Jenny probably wouldn't even miss one bundle . . . Drew stared at the money in his hand a little longer.

It wasn't his, no matter where it came from. And what she'd done for his mom when she was dying . . . he owed Jenny a debt he'd never be able to repay. He stuffed the last bundle into the backpack. The last thing he picked up was a small box with a string tied around it. The contents rattled when he shook it.

Hurry.

Drew laid the box on top of the money and zipped the bag, then checked the time again. A little after two. Time to go.

He eased down the stairs, hoping not to awaken his dad, but when he passed the den, he frowned. His dad's snores usually raised the roof, but now only silence came from the room. Drew tiptoed into the den far enough to see that his dad's recliner was empty.

No wonder it was so quiet. Drew checked his parents' bedroom, not really expecting to find him—his dad hadn't slept in the bedroom since Drew's mom died. A sigh escaped his lips. He knew where he was. McKay's, the local watering hole for drunks that didn't close until two.

So much for his dad's promise to quit drinking. Drew slammed out of the house, climbed into his pickup, and peeled out of the drive. He would be eighteen next year, and he wasn't staying here one day past it. He was going to be like his aunt Tori—leave and never come back except for short visits.

Ten minutes later, he parked in front of the vacant house on Winslow. Drew had expected Jenny's car to be in the drive. Where was she?

Maybe she'd parked somewhere else and walked over. Drew grabbed the backpack and climbed out of his truck. He jogged to the back door and entered the house, using the key she'd given him when she hired him to clean the windows. Jenny had been looking after the house while the owners were out of the country and had hired him to do odd jobs like the windows and mowing the yard.

"Jenny, it's me," he called out. "You here?"

Silence answered him. He tried to phone her, but it went to voicemail. He hung up without leaving a message.

Drew paced the darkened kitchen, waiting for her to show. Maybe he'd gotten it wrong—why would she ask to meet him here? He *had* been sound asleep when she called. Or maybe something happened to her car. He ran to his truck and hesitated. Her house was only a few streets over. He could leave a note on his windshield and run over there. That way if she came after he left, she'd see the note and wait.

When Drew reached Jenny's house, he paused at the back door. The lights were out. It looked like she'd already left, except her car was still in the drive. Something weird was going on.

Drew tried the door. Locked. He used his key to unlock it, stepped inside, and turned on the light. She wasn't in the kitchen.

"Jenny?" he called softly.

No answer. Maybe she was in the den—that was where she stayed most of the time. In the den, he flipped on the light switch, but nothing happened. Oh yeah, sometimes it didn't work—his dad was supposed to fix it, but as usual he hadn't gotten around to it.

Drew crossed the room to the lamp by the sofa. A coppery odor filled his nose, just like when he'd field-dressed a deer back in the winter.

Goosebumps raised on his arms. Something wasn't right. He fumbled for the lamp switch, and light filled the room. Drew's breath froze in his chest.

Jenny lay on the floor in front of the sliding doors, with blood pooling under her body.

No . . . Shaking his head, he squeezed his eyes shut. Maybe he was seeing things. Drew opened his eyes again, but nothing had changed. His gaze fastened on the gun beside her body, and his gut tightened.

His dad once had a Beretta just like that . . .

Drew knew his dad had a thing for Jenny but that she didn't feel the same way. Had his dad—

He jerked his head toward the street at the sound of approaching sirens. Someone had called the cops. They would think he killed her. Or worse, if the gun was his dad's, they would think *he'd* killed her.

Drew grabbed the gun and stuck it in his belt, then turned and bolted out the way he'd come. He sprinted through the same yards he'd crossed earlier. Had to get as far from the house as possible. When he reached the street his truck was parked on, he dashed across.

A horn blared, and he looked to his right. Oncoming lights flashed in his eyes. Tires screeched as the car skidded toward him.

At the last second, he jumped sideways, and the car barely missed him. The driver lowered his window. "Are you crazy?"

He'd heard that voice before. Drew ducked his head and kept running. *Have to get out of here. Have to find my dad. Ask him if the gun is his . . .*

He reached his truck and jerked the door open, practically falling inside as he shed the backpack. His hand shook so hard, the key missed the ignition the first time. Once he was rolling, he pointed the truck toward home.

Someone had killed Jenny. Was it his dad? No. Even drunk, his dad could never do anything like that. But if the gun was his, the police would never believe he was innocent.

So who did it? Drew gripped the steering wheel. What was he going to do with the money in the backpack? And the gun? The questions chased through his head in a never-ending circle. He needed help.

Tori. He'd call his aunt—she solved crimes, she'd know what to do. Then he shook his head.

No way—Tori would make him take the money and the gun to the police.

3

"Live in five, four..."

Tori Mitchell nodded at her friend and producer, Amy Bradsher, then took a deep breath. When the count ended, she leaned closer to her mic.

"Twenty years ago, the state of Tennessee incarcerated Huey Prescott for the murder of businessman Walter Livingston. Yesterday afternoon Prescott walked out of prison a free man almost a year to the day after *Dark Deeds Unraveled* highlighted irregularities in the case. It had taken that long for the courts to order a new trial, where he was found not guilty."

She paused and then leaned into her microphone. "I'm Victoria Mitchell, coming to you from Knoxville, Tennessee, and this is 8:00 p.m., Saturday, May 16. You're listening to a live broadcast of *Dark Deeds Unraveled*. Tonight, we'll be discussing the closing chapter of Huey Prescott's wrongful conviction for murder. Later in the podcast, I'll be deviating from my normal format and taking calls from listeners."

Early on in her podcast career, Tori had patterned hers after a top true-crime podcast that was broadcast live, mainly because she liked giving her listeners the transparency being live brought. But now she mostly prerecorded them due to the ease of taping.

But tonight was different. She was doing the podcast live to celebrate Prescott's release and was taking calls at the end. The calls had been Amy's idea, not Tori's. The idea of taking calls on-air made sweat break out on her palms, and she swiped them on her pants. "After we pay the bills, I'll give a brief overview of the case. For an in-depth account, check out the previous episodes of *Dark Deeds Unraveled* detailing how we uncovered evidence not presented at Prescott's trial. Now for a word from our sponsor . . ."

Tori killed her mic and rocked back in her chair to rest her eyes while the sponsor's ad ran. Four hours of sleep didn't cut it anymore. She was still dragging from the six-hour drive from Knoxville to Memphis and then another six hours back.

Prescott had agreed to a brief interview for the Knoxville TV station where Tori freelanced as a reporter only because she'd been instrumental in getting the DA to reopen his case—he'd turned all other interviews down. But he'd insisted the interview be at his sister's house in Memphis and in person.

Amy doubled as her videographer, and they'd made the trip, arriving late yesterday afternoon. When the interview was over, Prescott wanted to take them to dinner, so it'd been close to two this morning when they rolled back into Knoxville.

She hadn't worked late nights in a while, not since she'd opted to only work special assignments at the TV station after the *Dark Deeds Unraveled* podcast took off, and normally would have slept in since her time was her own. But her old producer had called at 7:00 a.m. requesting that she appear on *Good Morning Knoxville* during the 9:30 segment of the program. It'd been too good of an opportunity to pass up, but now she was paying for it.

"You look like you could use coffee."

"Definitely." Tori opened her eyes and smiled at her best friend since first grade. They made a good team, and there was no way the podcast would have taken off like it had without Amy as the producer—if a problem popped up, she had a work-around.

"You didn't get a nap this afternoon?" Amy handed Tori a mug.

"Thanks, and no." She cradled the warm cup in her hands and took a sip. "That's good, but I might need a Red Bull too."

"That bad, huh?" Amy asked with raised brows.

"Yep." Tori eyed her friend. "How do you look so fresh? You made the same trip I did."

"I made time for a nap," Amy said with a laugh and checked her watch. "Thirty seconds until you're live."

Tori gulped another swallow of coffee. "I'm still not sure we should take calls. I wish I hadn't agreed—"

"Stop worrying! The call-ins are a good idea—it's a reward for all those listeners who've followed the case. Gives them a chance to chime in with their two cents. You'll see."

"I hope you're right." Tori adjusted her earpiece.

"I'm always right . . . and I think you need to make the podcast a vodcast—let people see you."

"No way—I can only do one change at a time!" She wasn't about to do a video podcast. Period.

"We'll see," Amy said as she walked back to her microphone.

There was nothing to see. Tori liked the anonymity the podcast gave her. Answering questions and comments on her social media or the website was infinitely better than call-ins—gave her more control. And if there was one thing she liked, it was being in control. The die might be cast for live questions from her listeners tonight, but nothing else.

"Ten seconds." Amy's voice came through the earpiece. "And you already have two callers lined up to ask questions."

Two? That shouldn't be too bad or take too long. With a fortifying breath, Tori sat straighter. She'd found that her voice followed her posture. Straight spine with her shoulders back pumped energy into her words.

"Five, four, three, two, one." Amy pointed at Tori. "Go," she mouthed.

Tori leaned toward her mic. "Welcome back to this episode

of *Dark Deeds Unraveled* where we're discussing the release of Huey Prescott for his wrongful conviction in the murder of Walter Livingston. But first a brief recap of the circumstances around Prescott's arrest."

Tori knew the case by heart and had no need for notes. "Twenty-two years ago, on January 6th at 5:00 p.m., Walter Livingston, philanthropist and co-owner of the Livingston Oil Corporation, was in his Memphis, Tennessee, condo when his doorbell rang. When he opened the door, an unknown assailant fired four rounds and fled. Unfortunately, when the police arrived, they found the businessman dead.

"The condo was one Mr. Livingston used when he worked late at the recently opened Memphis branch of the Livingston Corporation. Their primary base of operation was and still is in Logan Point, Mississippi, half an hour's drive across the state line and where Livingston primarily resided."

Logan Point was also Tori's hometown. She paused to sip her coffee before continuing. "There were no witnesses to the shooting, but in August of that year, an informant steered authorities to Huey Prescott, a part-time bouncer at The Bluer Rose strip club and a low-level drug dealer with a rap sheet of twenty-five felony charges and ten convictions. Prescott was arrested a short time after the murder for drugs and weapons charges after an informant called in a tip. Jailhouse informants who claimed he confessed to them that he'd killed the businessman came forward, and Prescott was indicted for Livingston's murder in February of the next year, thirteen months after the slaying.

"At the trial, Prescott couldn't pinpoint where he was the night of the murder other than he thought he'd had dinner with friends. However, no one corroborated his statement. The prosecutor presented the four informants who swore under oath that Huey confessed to them he'd killed Livingston," Tori said. "All four testimonies were identical, and it wasn't a simple, 'Yeah, I did it,' but a detailed description of how he did it. And that bothered me—four people telling the same story almost word for word?"

She glanced at Amy to see how much time until another break. Two minutes. Tori turned back to the mic. "The jury deliberated less than two hours before returning with a guilty verdict even though no one put Prescott at the scene of the crime and the gun used was never found.

"What the DA didn't present was a pawn ticket found in Huey's wallet, showing he pawned a set of tools ten minutes before Livingston was gunned down. I'm not saying the DA deliberately withheld the information. Maybe he and the public defender both overlooked it, which isn't out of the realm of possibility since Huey didn't remember the pawn ticket—he was too wasted. An hour after pawning the tools, he was arrested for DUI with a blood alcohol content of 0.32. Folks, that's almost four times the limit for driving under the influence. None of that was ever brought out at the trial.

"He spent the next twenty years sitting in a prison cell for a crime he did not commit. That means whoever killed Walter Livingston is still out there."

She paused for dramatic effect. "So, if the killer is listening to this podcast . . . know this: the Memphis Police Department is reopening the case, and I will use every resource I have to help them find you."

4

Tori glanced toward Amy and touched her watch. Her producer held up both hands. Ten seconds. Tori turned back to the mic. "I hope to have Mr. Prescott as a guest on *Dark Deeds Unraveled* in the near future. Right now, he's adjusting to being a free man. But you can check out my TV interview with him. The link is in the comments. When we return from a short break, I'll take questions and comments—whatever you want to say as long as it's clean."

Once her mic was silent, Tori blew out a breath and turned toward Amy. "How do you think it's going?"

"Great. Your first caller is Jackson, and there are now ten waiting behind him. I'll cut it off at those ten, and you can wrap up the session." Amy grinned. "Save something for the next podcast . . . oh, and be sure to mention next week's segment on domestic violence."

Tori nodded. She was looking forward to starting the series on women in abusive situations. Her first guest was someone who'd gathered her courage and left the abusive relationship and who wanted to encourage others to do the same.

Just before the ad finished, Amy's voice reminded her of the caller's name and where he was from before starting the countdown in her earpiece. When she hit one, Tori's mic went hot. "Welcome back to this segment of the podcast where I'll take calls. First up is Jackson from Ohio. Welcome to *Dark Deeds Unraveled*."

"Thank you for taking my call, Victoria." The caller's smooth baritone carried well over the air. "I've only listened to the last few episodes. What got you involved in this case?"

She smiled, even though no one other than her producer could see it. "Two things, Jackson. Almost two years ago, Mr. Prescott's sister, who lived here in Knoxville at the time, called the TV station where I worked as an investigative reporter, claiming her brother had been railroaded. The station gave me the assignment, and it intrigued me. She'd hired a private investigator, who dug into the trial transcripts. He was the one who discovered the pawn ticket that had been entered into evidence along with other miscellaneous objects in Mr. Prescott's possession at the time of arrest. The ticket had been 'lost in the shuffle' so to speak.

"The more I dug into the case, the more convinced I became that Huey Prescott was innocent. And if he was innocent, that meant whoever killed Mr. Livingston had gotten away with murder."

"So, why do you think the police missed the pawn ticket?"

"That's a good question, and an even better one is why didn't the lawyers involved find it?" Both questions she had to be careful answering, because while she thought all the parties involved had been lazy, she didn't want to make enemies in Memphis.

"It's my understanding that the year Mr. Livingston was killed, there was a shortage of police officers in Memphis, while at the same time the city experienced over a 10 percent increase in homicides. I personally believe the detectives had tunnel vision and confirmation bias. They were slammed, and the four jailhouse informants—plus the fact Prescott couldn't account for his time the night of the murder—made for a closed case. They could move on to the next homicide. Same thing for the DA and public defender."

"Do you think the detectives did a sloppy job?"

Tori paused for a moment to collect her thoughts. "First of

all, Mr. Prescott didn't remember the ticket, and while I didn't walk in those officers' shoes, or the DA's and public defender's, I can imagine how overwhelmed they were by the explosion in the murder rate."

And that was twenty years ago. Her research showed it was even worse now. And not just in Memphis. From what she'd seen in her job with the TV station, Knoxville wasn't much better.

"Yeah, I see your point. One more question—what's Huey Prescott's next step?"

"To get back to a normal life," Tori said. "And to find his daughter. The first time he was arrested for drug possession, the girl's mother moved away from Memphis, taking their unborn daughter with her. He never knew he had a daughter until the detective tracked down the town the mother moved to and neighbors confirmed she had a daughter who was conceived during the time she was with Prescott. But it'll take a DNA test to prove paternity."

"I hope he finds her," Jackson said. "Be sure to post when Mr. Prescott will be on your podcast. Thanks for taking my call."

Amy spoke into the earpiece. "Line two is Paul from Mississippi."

Tori punched the second line. "Thanks for calling, Paul. What's your question?"

"I've enjoyed following this case," he said, his Southern accent thick. "What made you think Huey Prescott didn't confess to the four inmates?"

"Another good question," Tori said. "I had several reasons, the main one being how identical their stories were. I can't see four different men reciting the same details unless they got together first and rehearsed what they were going to say. And then the vendetta they described Prescott had against Mr. Livingston's neighbor because the neighbor failed to pay the defendant a drug debt. The neighbor in question vehemently denied he owed anyone a debt, much less one for drugs, but he was never called to testify."

"You're kidding," the caller said.

"Afraid not." She held that prosecutor in disdain, and if he were still alive, she'd go after him, but he'd died years ago.

"Yeah . . . I get you. I read a copy of the trial transcript online and told my wife I didn't believe the jailhouse snitches. Like you, I thought their testimony sounded rehearsed. Why didn't his public defender contest their statements?"

"I'm afraid we'll never know the answer to that question since he died not long after the trial in a tragic hit-and-run, a case the police never solved, by the way."

They chatted a few seconds more, and he signed off. This wasn't going half bad. Maybe Amy was right. In fact, this was kind of fun. It might even be a good idea to go live again and take calls more often. Her friend's voice sounded in her ear. "There's a caller on line two. John Smith from Kalamazoo."

"Welcome to *Dark Deeds Unraveled*. Do you have a comment or question on the Prescott case?"

"Yeah."

The person sounded like they had a bad cold. "Go ahead."

"What if getting Prescott off puts you in the killer's crosshairs? You or someone you love could pay for your meddling in the case."

Meddling? "Excuse me? Is that a threat?"

"Of course not. Just an observation on my part—people have been known to get killed for less."

She did not like the caller's tone. "I suppose my investigation could be called meddling, but I hardly think Huey Prescott would look at it that way."

"If I were you, I'd watch your back."

"Thank you for your call."

Tori looked over at Amy, whose eyebrows were raised in alarm. The words hadn't necessarily been a threat. It was the way the caller had said them that sent a shiver running down her spine.

5

Tori Mitchell was infuriating.

The AirPods bounced when they hit the table, the tinny sound of the podcast continuing from the earpieces.

If Victoria Mitchell was dumb enough to tell the world her plans, it made sense to take advantage of her stupidity. And at least the last call had been interesting—it sounded as though not everyone agreed with Ms. Mitchell.

"What if getting Prescott off puts you in the killer's crosshairs? You or someone you love could pay for your meddling in the case."

Interesting choice of words, and if something happened to Mitchell, those words spoken live on air would send the police in a different direction. An excellent red herring. But was Jenny telling the truth when she'd said that she mailed Victoria Mitchell the data drive? It was hard to know, but it was very possible she was.

Jenny. Life turned on a dime . . . or ended. Had it really been less than a day since Jenny had died? Killing someone didn't leave one as dispassionate as TV would have their audience believe.

It left extremely tight muscles in the neck. Massaging the tense jaw muscles felt good until a sharp twinge shot from a pressure point. Even moving on down into the muscles in the neck and shoulders didn't bring relief.

Victoria Mitchell had to be dealt with. There was a chance she had the data drive. And that blasted *Dark Deeds Unraveled* podcast would put Livingston Oil Corporation on the news and on every social media platform. What if the offshore accounts were discovered?

But how to shut the podcast down? It had a huge following. Cases that might fall through the cracks were pursued because her rabid fans stirred up so much publicity the cops were forced to investigate.

The podcaster lived in Knoxville. It hadn't taken a private investigator to find that out.

What to do next? Listening to the podcast had given insight into the way Mitchell's mind worked. It didn't take a degree in psychology or any other degree for that matter if you had street smarts and you knew people.

Before ending the podcast, Victoria Mitchell always teased her audience with the general topic of her next podcast. While she didn't always follow through on the teaser—often something else caught her attention—Mitchell had been pretty vocal about investigating Walter Livingston's death.

The decision now was whether to kill her before she left Knoxville or wait until she was in Mississippi. She would probably make Logan Point, Mississippi, her base—it's where she'd stayed while investigating the Huey Prescott case.

Much smarter and stronger people than Tori Mitchell had been crushed when they stuck their noses where they didn't belong.

6

Tori's first instinct was to not alarm her listeners. Maybe she could put a lighter spin on the call.

"Well," she said, forcing brightness in her voice, "as you heard, not everyone is happy with Prescott's release. So, if something should happen to me, the police will have a phone number and know who to look at first."

Except the caller probably used a prepaid cell phone—but unless it was an old one, the police might be able to trace it. While the newer burner phones still didn't provide an identity, they did have GPS and the call could be traced to the cell tower it came from.

When Amy didn't give her a new caller name, she glanced toward her. Her producer was giving Tori the throat-slash gesture again. Instead Tori shook her head and spoke into the mic. "I'll be right back after a word from our sponsor."

As soon as she was off the air, she removed her headset. "That was weird."

"It was more than weird," Amy said. "That man threatened you."

"Not in so many words. And I'm not certain it was a man." Tori shot Amy a determined look. "I'm not about to let a caller with an ax to grind dictate my podcast. Who do we have next?"

"Line one. Mary from Texas."

She'd never heard Amy's voice tremble before.

"And I think after this call, you should end the program."

"We'll see." *Saying* she wasn't going to let someone dictate to her didn't quell the dread in her stomach. She sipped the cold coffee. Amy gave her the countdown, and Tori leaned toward the mic, waiting for it to become hot. "Welcome to *Dark Deeds Unraveled*, Mary. What's your question or comment?"

"The way that person sounded made me start praying a hedge of protection around you, Victoria," Mary said, her voice strong and sure.

For a second, Tori was too stunned to get words past the lump in her throat. Those were the very words her mother always said as Tori walked out the front door to return to college after a weekend or a break. "Th-thank you," she managed to get out.

"I know you're a believer from different things you've said on your podcast," Mary continued.

She couldn't deny that, but what Mary didn't know was how shaky her faith had been since her mother's death, and then her fiancé's murder two months later when a teenager on drugs killed Michael in a robbery gone bad. Both were deaths God could have prevented.

Before she responded, Mary said, "And he'll protect you from callers like that last one. Keep up the good work! And that's all I had to say."

"Thank you again. Your words have encouraged me," Tori said.

She managed to get through the next two callers and wrapped up the program. "Be sure to tune in to the next show when I'll be interviewing a victim of domestic violence—the time will be posted on my website. The woman I'll be interviewing wants you to know you don't have to stay in a dangerous relationship, and she'll be sharing tips on how to safely escape. This is Victoria Mitchell signing off from the *Dark Deeds Unraveled* podcast."

As soon as her mic was dead, Tori released a hard breath, but the tension didn't dissipate.

"Good job." Amy sank in the chair across from Tori. "And you were right to continue."

"I had to. I wasn't about to let some crank caller mess with my podcast."

"What if it wasn't a crank caller?" Amy chewed her bottom lip. "What if the person who called is Livingston's killer?"

"I'm not sure the real killer would throw out a veiled threat like that, but if it was, then I'd say we struck a nerve. At any rate, I'd like to be instrumental in putting his murderer behind bars."

"Figured you would feel that way. Do you want me to call the Knoxville PD? They might be able to trace the call."

Tori doubted it, but then again, killers usually weren't as smart as movies made them out to be. "It's not a bad idea to have a report about the call on file with the police, but it can wait until Monday morning."

"That's a good idea," Amy said. "I'll call the detective we've reported threats to before. Even though it wasn't an out-and-out threat, the call made me uncomfortable." Amy stared down at her folded hands on the table, then she cleared her throat and looked up.

When she didn't say anything, Tori lifted her brows. "Okay, spill it."

Amy leaned forward. "Do you really think it's a good idea to broadcast your plans to investigate Walter Livingston's death?"

"Probably not. Sometimes my mouth works faster than my brain." Tori blew out a breath. "You don't need to come to Memphis with me. I don't want to put you in danger, and it could mean an extended stay there."

"You mean Logan Point, don't you? That's probably where whoever killed Walter Livingston lives, unless it *was* a random killing, which neither of us believe." Amy's lip twitched. "But if you're determined to go, you could stay with your sister."

"You gotta be kidding." The words shot out of her mouth before she could catch them. Stay with her sister? No way. Then Amy's lips quirked up in a "gotcha" grin.

They both laughed, and Tori said, "You had me going there for a minute. Erin and I would be at each other's throats in two days."

"I'll check with Aunt Rainey and make sure she's not expecting any of her kids or grandkids. Maybe we could stay with her. Any idea of when you plan to go?"

Rainey Bradsher was Amy's aunt on her dad's side and a hoot. Maybe staying in Logan Point wouldn't be so bad; at least the times they'd stayed with her before hadn't been. "Not right away. I want to wrap up the series on domestic violence first."

"I'll let my aunt know we're looking at being in Logan Point in . . . what, two weeks from now?"

"Sounds good."

"Maybe you can connect with your high school sweetheart."

"Eli Livingston? He's probably married with six kids by now." She rubbed her jaw. "Not interested, even if he's still single."

A hush fell between them, and Tori shifted her gaze away from Amy. The pity in Amy's eyes was the last thing she wanted.

"It's been seven years since Michael died." Her friend had gentled her voice. She was quiet for a moment before smiling and adding, "Well, I never thought you and Eli were suited for each other, anyway. How about that guy you crushed on after graduation? You know—the one Kate Adams brought to church."

The image of that boy popped into Tori's mind. "Scott Sinclair?"

"That's the one."

Tori shook her head. "I'll be too busy to reconnect with guys from my past. Besides, I doubt Scott would remember me, anyway."

"Come on, Tori. Michael would've wanted you to embrace life again, not bury yourself in work. It's time to rejoin the human race."

Bringing up Michael wasn't fair. While she'd never been in love with Eli and Scott had just been a summer crush, Michael had been different. Tori had loved him fiercely, and no way was she *ever* opening herself up to the risk of losing someone again.

She palmed her hands. "I'm happy just the way I am. And even if I weren't, I definitely wouldn't connect with Scott."

"Come on, Tori," Amy said. "Not every recovering alcoholic goes back to drinking."

"Can't prove that by me." She shook her head. "Besides, Scott probably doesn't even live in Logan Point anymore."

7

Tuesday night, Tori checked her watch. Ten minutes until her podcast interview with Megan Russell, the woman from the battered women's shelter, who had yet to arrive. They were back to prerecording, so if worse came to worse, she could scramble for another interview. Her phone rang, and Tori hoped an emergency hadn't come up and her guest had to bail.

She checked the ID. It was even worse. The call was from her sister.

Tori thought about letting it go to voicemail, but then she would have to deal with the call after the podcast. Might as well get it over with. She motioned to Amy that she was stepping into her small office and closed the door behind her before she answered. "Hello?"

"Oh, good," Erin said. "I caught you. I was afraid I'd get your voicemail—that you never respond to."

Tori ignored the dig. "I can't talk long." She checked her watch. "I have a podcast starting in less than ten minutes."

"This won't take a minute. Just reminding you I'm having a party for Dad's birthday next Saturday, and I wanted to make sure you—"

"I'm not coming."

"What do you mean, you're not coming? You have plenty of time to arrange your schedule. Besides, it's his sixtieth birthday."

A birthday Mom will never see, thanks to him. Tori paced the small room. She should have stepped into the hallway that led to her apartment for more room. "I'm sorry, Erin, but I just can't."

"Can't or won't?" Her sister's voice rose an octave on the last word. Silence stretched between them. "Come on, Tori, it's time you forgave him."

"It's not that easy. I've tried, believe me." She didn't understand how Erin could forgive him so easily.

The office door opened, and her producer cleared her throat. "Our guest has arrived . . ."

Worry bled through Amy's voice, and Tori nodded before turning her attention back to the call. "Look, I have to go—"

"Come home, Tori." When she didn't answer right away, Erin said, "At least think about it. Please."

Tori didn't have time for this. "Okay, I'll think about it. Gotta go."

With a sigh she ended the call and took a second to bury her past and focus on tonight's podcast. When she stepped back into the studio, she looked for Amy. Her friend was always the calm one, so Tori was anxious to discover why she'd sounded so concerned, but Amy was on her phone.

She scanned the room for her guest, Megan Russell, and instantly understood Amy's concern. The middle-aged woman had the look of someone who'd just seen police lights flashing in her rear mirror.

Tori hurried over to her. "Megan, I'm sorry I had to step into my office before you arrived. Are you okay?"

"I-I don't know if I can do this."

Tori's heart sank. Megan had been so excited about the podcast, but Tori had seen last-minute jitters before. "Is it nerves or something else?" She squeezed Megan's hand. "Because if it's nerves, it won't be nearly as bad as a root canal."

A startled chuckle escaped the woman's lips. "I am nervous. My tongue feels like it's stuck to the roof of my mouth."

"Don't worry. The podcast will be prerecorded, so I can fix any blunders."

"Good to know." Megan sighed. "It hasn't been the best day of my life."

"What happened?"

"The divorce was final today, and Cal was furious at the courthouse—I don't know what he would've done if my lawyer and the bailiff hadn't been there."

"I'm so sorry." Tori gave her a hug. "You want to reschedule? It's not like we have to do it today."

"No." Megan lifted her chin. "I want to do this now. If I can help even one woman . . ."

Tori nodded her understanding. "You don't think he followed you here, do you?"

"I took an Uber and watched behind us, and I didn't see anyone tailing me."

"Okay." Tori gave Megan a reassuring smile. "Let's do it, then, and when we finish, Amy and I will take you home."

"Thanks, that would be great."

Tori turned to Amy. "Give us five minutes to get settled in, then we'll start recording."

Amy nodded, and Tori turned back to Megan. "Your nerves will quiet down as soon as we start talking, and if either of us messes up, Amy and I will fix it." She pulled out the chair on the guest side of the table. "This is where you'll sit."

Megan hesitated. "I know it's not live, but I'm still nervous."

"Sit down and take a slow, deep breath—that'll help."

Megan did as Tori suggested, her chest rising as she sucked in air and released it. Better, but still nervous. That should change once they got into the interview. Tori handed her a headset and showed her how to put it on, then sat on the other side of the table.

"Speak into the mic, but don't get too close," Tori said and slipped on her headset.

Megan nodded, and Tori glanced over the podcast script in front of her one last time. It was a simple outline of questions that kept her from waffling and repeating herself. It also kept her *ums* and *uhs* to a minimum. But it didn't keep her sister's request from intruding into her thoughts.

"*Come home.*" Erin didn't know what she was asking. It'd been seven years since she'd been home to "visit."

She'd been in and out of her hometown several times since her mother's funeral while investigating Huey Prescott's case, but her time with Erin had been brief, usually at the local coffee shop or in Memphis. Her brother, Zack, was always too busy to meet with them, but Tori made it a point to spend time with his son, Drew. And her dad hadn't been invited.

There was no way in God's green earth that she was making the trip to Logan Point for her dad's birthday party. Period.

"Five, four, three, two, one . . ." Amy flipped the switch, and Tori's mic was hot. Everything but the show faded from her mind.

"Welcome to *Dark Deeds Unraveled*. I'm your host, Victoria Mitchell, and tonight we'll be talking with a survivor of domestic abuse. I won't mention her name because she is still in danger from her abuser. How's it going?"

"It's g-going." Megan frowned.

You're fine, Tori mouthed.

They spent a few minutes discussing the prevalence of domestic violence, then Tori segued into Megan's life. "I understand you're living at a safe house. Tell me about that."

"Well, we . . ." She swallowed hard and leaned in closer to the mic. "Right now, there are ten other women and their children, but I understand the organization has received a grant to build a larger place."

"That's awesome." Tori gave her a you're-doing-great nod. "Tell our listeners a little about living at the safe house."

"First, besides a safe place to live, they offered me hope and encouragement. A lot of women second-guess their decision, and I was no different." She paused for a moment. "Did you know that abuse survivors return to their abusive partners on average of seven times before they leave for good?"

Tori cocked her head. "Why do you think that is?"

"It's complicated." Confidence built in her voice. "The world can be a scary place, and for me, sometimes it seemed easier to go back to what I knew. Especially when I remembered the good times with my ex. The counselors at the safe house told me that what I was feeling was normal and that it takes time to adjust. This is where the organization that's helping me excels. They're so good at reinforcing my sense of self-worth and confidence that my ex destroyed.

"Once I was settled, they provided me with job training. Some abused women don't work outside of the home and some have had to relocate and might need to learn new skills. Two of our current residents have returned to college to get teaching certificates."

"That's amazing," Tori said. "I realize volunteers have to pass a background check, but if someone listening wanted to help, what can they do?"

"Right now, we could use someone to teach computer skills ... and if anyone would like to volunteer to teach a craft like art or ceramics, or knitting and crocheting, that would be wonderful too." Megan was warming up. "When new women arrive at the home, most of the time they don't believe they can do anything right—I didn't. There's an artist who comes twice a week to teach painting. I discovered I have a talent for it, and when I saw I could create something beautiful, my self-confidence grew."

"Okay, listeners, here's an opportunity to help someone. I'll put a link to the organization in the chat if you want to volunteer," Tori said. "And now we have to take a break, but don't go away. When we come back, we'll discuss how to recognize if you're in an abusive relationship, because sometimes women don't see themselves in this situation until it's too late."

Tori signaled for Amy to stop the recording, then turned back to Megan. "You're doing great. I'll give you a few minutes to catch your breath. When we start back, we'll talk about your story, and how to recognize an abusive relationship, and any advice you might have for our listeners."

"If I can help just one woman get to a safe place, telling my story is worth it."

"Good. Take this time to drink some water and relax."

Tori glanced at Amy as she turned toward the door and frowned. "Everything okay?" Tori asked.

"I thought I heard something outside." Amy cocked her head, listening. "I don't hear it now, but I'll check it out, unless you want to get started again?"

"I'm ready," Megan said.

Tori nodded for Amy to hit the record button. "Welcome back to our program with a survivor of domestic violence who hopes to help other women in such situations. I want to discuss with our guest how someone can get out of an abusive relationship." She smiled at Megan. "What's your first suggestion?"

"The main thing is to have a safety plan in place before you leave," Megan said. "But first, I want to address women who are in a relationship with an abuser and who are hoping the abuser will change. That's what happened to me.

"Every time my husband hit me, the next day he always apologized and acted sorry . . . and every time I thought he would change. Over time I started to see the pattern—it always started off with him getting more and more tense until I did something wrong. It was never anything major—things like not enough salt in the beans or the coffee was too weak. That's when he would explode and hit me. Afterwards he was always contrite and so sweet—treated me like a queen—it was like our honeymoon until the next cycle started and—"

Three shrill beeps blasted Tori's ears followed by three more. She jerked her head toward the only entrance. Smoke curled from under the door.

Megan's eyes widened. "He . . . he found me!"

Was it possible? Tori locked gazes with Amy.

"I'll call 911," her friend said, keeping her voice calm. "We need to get out of here."

Tori agreed. But how? They were on the first floor of her garage apartment, and there was only one door out of the studio. It led into the hallway where the smoke was coming from—the flames could be out of control already. "The window."

She stood and motioned for Megan to follow, but she didn't move. Tori grabbed her hands and pulled her up. "Let's go!"

Megan shook her head as smoke filled the room. "It won't do any good," she wailed. "Cal will be waiting for us to come through your front door. I know him—he'll kill us."

"We're not going out the door," Amy said. She ran to the window and unlocked the bottom and raised it. "Come on. Now!"

Megan's feet seemed to be rooted to the floor. Tori pulled her toward the window. "I'll go first, just in case he's out there," she said. "Once I give the signal, Megan goes next."

She climbed out the window and scanned the back parking lot. "No one is out here. Come on!"

Once they were out of the building, the wails of emergency vehicles reached her ears.

Two hours later, a chill raced over Tori as she stared at the charred boards of her garage apartment. At least the damage was limited to those outside boards. The studio itself and her upstairs apartment only received smoke damage.

A neighbor's security video had shown someone in a ski mask dousing the side of the house with liquid from a gas can. Even though the intruder was about the same height and build as Megan's ex, there was no way to be sure, or to even know if the fire was aimed at Megan. An officer had taken her back to the safe house.

"I hope whoever it was doesn't come back," Amy said beside her as she crossed her arms. "That caller was right Saturday night—you need to watch your back until the police find whoever did this."

8

"Eleven. Twelve." Scott Sinclair clenched his jaw and lifted the eight-pound weight in his right hand three more times. That was five more reps than the physical therapist said. He set down the weight and reached for a towel, the muscle in his arm quivering.

Scott wiped his face, then rested on the workout bench at the rehab center he came to every Wednesday and Friday. Today was his tenth Wednesday appointment and six months after getting shot. Rehabbing his shoulder was taking way too long—at this rate he'd never get his old job back. At least he'd lived. Andy hadn't, and Scott still couldn't sleep at night because of it.

"Sinclair, tell me I did not see an eight-pound weight in your hand."

Busted. The statement came from his physical therapist. Scott swung around on the bench, ignoring the way his right arm trembled when he used the towel again to wipe sweat from his face.

"It's only three pounds more than I was using last week." He grinned at Joe Green, who was the toughest PT at the center. "I thought you'd be proud of me."

"You know you're not to lift more than five pounds. Your arm isn't ready for that much weight, even if it's only three additional pounds." Joe shook his head. "I don't know which is worse, a patient who won't do anything or one who ignores the rules and overdoes it. You'll be lucky if you didn't tear something."

Scott flexed his right hand, mentally willing his fingers to make a fist, but there was little response to the command, thanks to the bullet that had plowed into his shoulder and damaged the nerves and tendons running to his hand. "What are the odds of getting the use of this hand back?"

Joe stared at him a minute and rubbed his jaw. "Probably fifty-fifty—if you don't overwork the muscles and nerves."

"You really believe that?"

Joe didn't respond right away.

"Tell me the truth."

"I don't know what the truth is. If it was just determination on your part, I'd say you'd be back on the shooting range within three months with your right hand. But the bullet wasn't the only reason for the damage to your arm—cutting it out of your shoulder took a toll on the muscles—it's going to take a lot longer—possibly even a year."

Not what he wanted to hear. Scott flexed his left hand.

"How's your aim with that hand?" Joe asked.

"Not good enough to qualify on the shooting range and get my job back." Returning to the FBI as an undercover agent was his top priority.

"If you practice as hard at using your left hand as you do at rehabbing your right, you'll get there a whole lot quicker."

"I don't know. It takes more thinking to use my left hand."

"That'll get better with practice." Joe cocked his head. "Do you fly fish?"

"Fly fish?"

"Yeah. It'd be a great exercise for your left hand to learn accuracy and dexterity."

"So, you *don't* think I'll regain the use of my right hand."

"I didn't say that. But it's always good to have options. I've had patients who actually had better accuracy when they switched to their left hand . . . and some who didn't. But they were the ones who didn't—"

"Practice," Scott finished for him, and they both laughed.

"Have you ever tried it, fly fishing?"

"Yeah, when I was a kid." For years, his brother, Nick, had set aside the second Saturday of the month to spend time with Scott. When he was old enough, that Saturday was spent fly fishing, and once he got the hang of it, Scott had enjoyed it. And with Logan Lake so close, Nick might even have a fly rod at the house that he and Taylor had remodeled.

Joe held up a tennis ball. "I'm adding a new hand-eye coordination exercise to your home program."

He led Scott to a wall and demonstrated the exercise before handing the ball to Scott. "Bounce the ball against the wall—five times to start with overhand, then underhand, and then switch hands and repeat. After that, repeat the process but with one eye closed. Start with your left hand."

Scott had been a Little League pitcher, but that'd been with his right hand. Still, how difficult could it be? He missed the ball the first catch. "This is harder than it looks."

"Right."

Determined to do it, Scott concentrated and managed to not drop the ball until the fifth throw. He could see how this would increase his dexterity.

When he completed the exercise, Joe said, "That's a wrap for today. Keep doing the home exercises, and I'll see you Friday at ten."

After rehab, Scott stopped by Two Cups, the local coffee shop, for his reward—a venti caramel latte—before he drove to his brother's house. The sweet drink was his one concession to avoiding a routine, especially since it gave him a boost after the pain he'd endured. At least the physical therapy practice was in Logan Point and he didn't have to drive the twenty minutes into Memphis for therapy. For a small town, Logan Point had a good medical center.

He opted to drive through the quaint town with the two-hundred-year-old courthouse in the center of the town square and storefronts still in use. Stores like the hardware shop on the corner where you could find just about anything you wanted. Or the drugstore across the street that, according to the sign over the door, had been there almost as long as the courthouse.

Soon he was on the road out of town and turning onto Coley Road, which would take him to Oak Grove, the house that had been in his sister-in-law's family for over a hundred years. Taylor and Nick had done a great job with the remodel.

He passed by the sign advertising Kate Adams's pottery shop and almost turned in. It'd been at least a week since he'd seen her. If it hadn't been for Kate, Scott might still be wandering around seeking answers to questions that only God knew. He smiled. Kate never pulled any punches. She called a spade a spade whether you liked it or not.

But he needed to find a fishing rod, and Nick was leaving soon. He drove on to his brother's house a quarter mile up the road. When he turned into the drive and parked, Nick left the wheelbarrow he'd been pushing and walked to the car.

No one would ever mistake them for brothers, and it wasn't just the ink on Scott's arms. Nick looked just like his dad—black hair and olive complexion on a runner's frame whereas Scott had his mother's brown hair and his birth dad's muscular build. A dad he barely remembered, but Nick's dad had taken him in and raised him as his own, even giving him the Sinclair name.

Their deaths in a plane crash and then a generous allowance from a trust fund from his grandfather on his mother's side had sent him in a direction he never hoped to go again. Scott rubbed his jaw. As a recovering alcoholic, he knew that even with a ten-year sobriety pin, he was only one drink from throwing it all away.

He climbed out of his pickup and waited for Nick to reach him before nodding at the wheelbarrow. "I thought you had a deadline."

Like his previous books, his brother's last release was a *New*

York Times bestseller, and the one he was working on would be as well.

"Finished it, and now I have a wife who wants a row of miniature marigolds across the front of the house before we leave for the book tour in the morning."

Taylor loved her flowers. Scott glanced around—his sister-in-law was usually the one with her hands in the dirt. "I'm surprised she's not helping."

"Ben called a little earlier and asked her to do a profile on a victim."

Taylor freelanced as a victim profiler when she wasn't helping at the Walls of Jericho teen camp she and his brother started years ago. Scott questioned Nick with his eyes.

"Jenny Tremont's murder Saturday morning," Nick said.

Scott still couldn't wrap his mind around Jenny's death. She was the last person he expected to be murdered. Scott rolled his shoulders, and pain stabbed his arm, making him wince.

"How'd your session go?" Nick asked.

"Okay."

Nick studied him. "You don't sound like it went okay."

"Joe doesn't think I'll regain the use of my right hand."

"Did he actually say that?"

"Not in so many words."

His brother lifted an eyebrow. "In other words, no."

Scott stared at the ground. "Then why is he pushing me to learn how to do things with my left hand?"

"Would being proficient with both hands be a bad thing?"

Ever the encourager. "You sound like Joe, and you're right, as always. Hey, do you still have those fly rods?"

Nick blinked. "What?"

"The fly rods we used back in the day."

"I guess—they should be around here somewhere. Why?"

"Joe said fly fishing would help with hand-eye coordination."

"Good idea." Nick thought a minute. "They're in the basement. Walk with me to the house, and we'll see which one you want."

The basement could only be accessed through the house, and they climbed the steps and entered through a large hallway that ran the length of the structure. It still surprised him that Taylor even wanted to fix up the house after the terrible memories she had here. "You two did a great job of restoring this place."

"Thanks. It has good bones."

It was also on the National Register of Historic Places due to its age and the tunnels that led from the basement to the nearby lake and river that enslaved people had used to escape to the North.

In the basement, Nick flipped on a light switch, revealing a computer in the center of the room, a whiteboard like detectives used, and a corkboard with photos. Nick's man cave where he churned out his mysteries.

Scott knew better than to bother Nick when he was writing and could count on one hand the times he'd been down here in the basement. "You have a good setup here."

Nick chuckled. "You think? It's my favorite place to write—plenty of solitude and room."

Scott glanced at the door across the room. More than a century ago, the house had been a stop on the Underground Railroad, and the door opened to the network of tunnels.

Nick nodded toward the far wall. "The rods are over here."

Scott followed him to where several rods and reels were mounted. Nick lifted one off the rack and handed it to him.

"This is the one you always used."

Scott held the rod and flicked it back and forth, memories of their times together bombarding him. "In case I haven't said this enough, thanks for being a brother when you didn't have to be. Couldn't have been easy having a little kid follow you around all the time."

"It wasn't so terrible, since you weren't a bad kid."

"Maybe not then . . ."

Neither of them spoke for a minute, the bad times filling the space. But that was then. He liked to think he'd redeemed himself as an FBI undercover agent.

He nodded at the rod in his hand. "This one will be fine."

"Take this one as well. That way if the line gets too tangled, you'll have a backup."

He took the second rod and reel. His brother knew him too well. "Thanks. Hopefully this will help me to qualify on the shooting range with my left hand. Then I'll get my old job back."

Nick opened his mouth as if to say something, then closed it. He rubbed the back of his neck, and then he pinned Scott with his gaze. Scott steeled himself for what he knew was coming.

"I know I shouldn't say anything," his brother said. "But would not going back into undercover work be so bad? It almost killed you the last time."

At least he didn't mention Andy, but it was the same song and verse Scott had heard from the time he'd woken up after surgery. His brother just didn't get it. *Do not lose it.* "It's who I am, Nick," Scott said evenly.

"It is not who you are."

That's where he was wrong. If Scott wasn't an FBI undercover agent, then who was he?

9

At ten on Wednesday morning, the odor of charred wood still hung in the air, burning Tori's nose as she once again surveyed the damage that was limited to the outside wall of the studio. She couldn't wrap her head around the fact that someone had set fire to her home and recording studio. And that someone was probably Calvin Russell.

Megan's husband hadn't been found yet, and a chill raced over her body. She scanned the street for the six-three former professional football player. Was he hiding in the shadows, gloating over his handiwork?

"You okay?" Amy asked.

Tori nodded, not trusting herself to speak. Amy had refused to hear of her going to a hotel last night, and Tori had crashed at her best friend's house. "We worked so hard on that studio, and now—"

"Stop worrying! It's not that bad, thanks to the fast response of the fire department." Amy squeezed her shoulder. "The insurance adjuster called, and he'll be here tomorrow morning. As soon as the check arrives, we can start the remodel."

Ever the optimist. Only Amy could look at what had to be done and call it a remodel.

"Have you called the reno guy yet?" Amy asked.

"Not yet. I will now—might as well see how long his waiting list is." Tori fished her phone from her jeans pocket and scrolled to the contractor she'd used before.

A couple of years ago, she'd had the opportunity to buy the garage apartment she lived in when the main house burned and the owners hadn't wanted to rebuild. Thank goodness she'd kept the insurance premiums current.

He answered on the first ring. "What can I do for you, Ms. Mitchell?"

Tori explained about the fire. "The outside wall sustained the most damage. The rest was caused by water and smoke. Mostly smoke."

"Hate that for you."

"Me too, but it could've been much worse," she said. "How soon do you think you can get to me?"

"I'll try and get by there tomorrow to look at it. I'm working on a big job right now, and it'll be three weeks before I can even think about starting on yours—and that's putting you at the top of the list."

That's what she'd been afraid of. "I appreciate it. Do you know what time tomorrow?"

There was silence on the line, then he said, "How about eight, or is that too early?"

"That will be perfect." Especially since the insurance adjuster was coming at nine.

"Of course, you know that the estimate won't be written in stone."

A chuckle escaped her lips. "I know, but I trust you."

"You and my dog."

She smiled at the laughter in his voice.

"See you then," he said.

She disconnected and turned to Amy. "Guess you heard?"

Her friend nodded. "You'll stay at my house until the job is completed."

"No . . . it'll be weeks before he can even get started. Insurance will pay for a hotel room, or maybe I can find a place to rent." Tori appreciated Amy's offer, but her friend was used to her solitude. Tori wasn't going to impose.

"Not happening. You are staying with me." Amy's voice was firm.

"You sure?" Tori's cell rang and she glanced at the caller ID. Erin. *Again?* She didn't have time to argue with her sister about coming home.

"Are you going to answer that?" Amy asked.

"Not now. It's my sister. I'll call her back." She let it go to voicemail.

Thirty seconds later, Erin phoned again.

"Answer it," Amy said. "It might be important."

Tori handed her the phone. "You answer it and tell her I'm too busy to talk right now."

Her friend reluctantly took the phone and slid the answer button while putting it on speaker. "Erin, this is Amy. Tori is, um, tied up at the moment."

"Tell her to call me right away."

Tori stared at the phone. Was Erin crying?

"What's wrong?" Amy asked.

"Jenny Tremont was murdered Saturday morning and—"

Tori grabbed the phone. "Jenny's dead?"

"Yes. And Sheriff Ben Logan is questioning Drew—he thinks Drew killed her. He's going to arrest him, I know he is. Tori, you have to come home."

Tori chewed her thumbnail. Her nephew wouldn't kill anyone. "Why is Drew a suspect?"

"Someone saw him running near Jenny's place around two that morning—about the time the medical examiner says she died."

"What does Drew say?"

"That's just it—he won't say anything except he didn't do it, and he won't say why he was out at that time of night or what he was doing in Jenny's neighborhood."

Regret swirled through Tori's mind. She'd been close to Drew when he was a kid, and while she still kept in touch, either texting or calling, she should've come home more, especially after his mom died and her brother buried himself in a bottle. "How about Zack? He can't get Drew to talk?"

"Our brother is no help at all. He and Drew barely tolerate each other, mostly because of Zack's drinking," Erin said. "You two have always clicked . . . I think he'd talk to you if you were here. And you know how to dig up evidence—you talk about it on your podcast, how you've found evidence when the police didn't."

Erin listened to her podcast?

"Please. Come home—it doesn't have to be long, and you can stay with me."

Tori turned and stared at her apartment, warming to the idea of Erin's offer. It would solve one problem—getting away from whoever set the fire. Maybe while she was gone, the police would find and arrest the culprit.

While she hadn't planned on starting her investigation into Walter Livingston's death this soon, a quick trip to support Drew would also give her an opportunity to talk to some of the people in town who knew Walter. And she could stay with Erin this trip since it would only be for a few days. Build bridges there. As for her dad . . . she could find ways to avoid him, and if she didn't, Tori knew how to be civil.

"All right, I'll come," she said. "But I can't get there until tomorrow, probably late afternoon."

Her sister's sigh was heartfelt. "I'll put fresh sheets on the guest bed."

"I'll call you when I leave Knoxville." Tori disconnected and turned to Amy. "I guess you heard . . ."

Amy nodded.

"You want to come? I'm only staying two days, max."

"What about the podcast? Do you plan to continue with a temporary studio? I don't think the equipment was damaged, just the wiring that was in that outside wall."

Tori considered their options. "I hate that we don't have one to post in our regular spot Saturday night. And I'm sure not going to ask Megan to finish the recording from last night."

"I agree." Amy tapped her finger against her mouth. "But I think I can edit that one, cut it off before the fire alarm sounds, and have you do a voice-over with additional info we want listeners to know."

Tori slowly nodded. "That would work. It's definitely a message that needs to get out."

"Why don't we plan on setting up in one of my bedrooms, like when we first started?"

"Sounds good."

"I'll take care of that while you're gone." Amy cocked her head. "Or if you have to stay longer than two days, I can bring the equipment to my aunt's in Logan Point. Her basement would make a great studio, and we can stay on schedule."

Tori considered Amy's suggestion. "You wouldn't mind?"

"Of course not. I love being in Logan Point. I'd go with you tomorrow except I'm meeting with a potential sponsor in the afternoon."

"I'd forgotten that."

Amy grinned. "If I come to Mississippi, you can stay with my aunt too—if Erin's house gets too small."

A good option to have if the trip stretched any longer than she expected. *No.* She'd make sure it didn't.

Tori hugged her friend. "Thanks. There wouldn't be a podcast without you."

"Get outta here."

"No, seriously, you keep the wheels turning."

"I enjoy what we do, and I think the podcast is important," Amy said. "But returning to Logan Point to help your family is important too. If Drew gets arrested, they'll need you to find out who really did it—your nephew is no killer. Erin was right about you knowing how to dig into a case."

Tori closed her eyes briefly. What if she failed and Drew went to jail?

10

Thursday afternoon, the closer Tori got to Logan Point, the more her stomach churned no matter how many times she told herself this was going to be a fast visit, in and out. She'd already decided not to jump-start the Livingston investigation. No, she'd drive to Erin's house, talk to Drew—she was convinced it wouldn't take long to get him to tell what he knew—and then return home to Knoxville. Wherever home was going to be.

The insurance adjuster had arrived promptly at nine and had given her a rude awaking. Evidently there was wiggle room for the company not to pay for the repairs since the fire was caused by arson. She'd spent the last five hours fretting over whether to use her savings for the repairs based on the contractor's estimated costs.

The adjuster said the insurance company would get back to her in a week or so. Then there was the problem of when the contractor could get to the remodel. Insurance or no insurance, the repairs had to be made. He'd assured her that he would start in three weeks, but she'd dealt with his assurances before when she'd converted the downstairs garage into a recording studio.

And that meant she'd probably take Amy up on her offer to move in with her until her apartment was livable again. She blew out a breath. No probably to it . . . at this point, insurance living expenses coverage was not looking good.

At the turnoff to Logan Point, she left I-40 and drove away

from the sun beaming directly into her windshield. It was almost five when she hit the Bradford County line. Erin had texted that she'd had to run errands and Drew was with her and wouldn't be home before six. Tori's mood lightened. She had plenty of time to make a stop at the lake.

She hesitated as the crossroads approached. Should she just go on to Erin's and get settled? No. Tori turned right—she needed the calming influence of the lake before walking into the turmoil at her sister's. The circuitous route took her over the bridge that spanned the dam over Little Wolf River.

A quick look in the rearview mirror brought a frown. A gray pickup had made the same turn to the lake that she had. And it wasn't the first time she'd noticed the Dodge Ram behind her. She'd seen it, or another one just like it, when she pulled off I-40 to fill up. And then again when they slowed for road construction.

She eased off the gas to see if the vehicle passed her. When it sped up to pass her, heat crept up her neck to her face at her reaction. The fire on Tuesday night had her paranoid.

Tori glanced to her left. Didn't Mississippi pass a law against tint that dark? She couldn't tell who or how many were in the vehicle.

Once it passed, she released a shaky laugh. What had she expected? That the driver would try to run her off the road? She really needed to get a grip.

Half a mile farther, the road curved upward to the bridge. As she crossed the river, Tori glanced to her left again, and memories of being at the lake with her family hit her. Back then, they'd been the perfect family, and she'd had an idyllic childhood. No major traumas . . . she hadn't even known her dad was a recovering alcoholic. How she wished they could go back to that time.

A text dinged on her phone, and she glanced at it in the cup holder. A text from her sister.

Thought I'd better tell you. Dad's here.

No. Tori clenched her jaw. She should've known her sister would force the issue of their father. Or maybe it was her dad who was doing the forcing.

Tori took a breath. Two days. That was all the time she was spending in Logan Point. She could do this—her mom always said a person could endure just about anything if they knew the starting and ending date of the problem.

The side road that led to the lake approached. She really needed the calming effect of the lake now, for sure. Tori flipped on her blinker and whipped her Toyota GR86 off the main road onto the narrow two-lane road. She wound around to the picnic and beach area and parked a few yards from a pickup. Another Ram? At least it was an older model and dark red, so it couldn't be the one that passed her.

After texting Erin that she would see her a little around six, she walked down to the water's edge to a huge oak tree, where a light breeze cooled her face. To her right was the Point where they'd picnicked and swum, and a little farther down, where they'd fished. She shaded her eyes with her hand. Looked like someone was there now, and the way he was throwing his arm, it appeared he was fly fishing. Not a threat.

The man glanced her way, then went back to casting and not very well. He must be new to fly fishing, especially since he didn't know it was the wrong time of day to catch fish.

She shrugged. *To each his own.* She turned her attention back to the lake. It was amazing how blue the water was—how had she forgotten that? As she looked toward the horizon, the lake seemed to touch the sky.

"God's beautiful creation." Another of Mom's stock phrases, one she used every time they came to the lake. "He loves us so much he created this for us to enjoy."

Tori crossed her arms over her chest. If he loved them so much, then why did he let Michael get murdered? Or let her dad drink and then drive her mother to the doctor with a hangover so bad he couldn't keep the car on the road?

The crunch of tires pulling into the parking area caught her attention. She flicked her gaze toward the vehicle and froze.

The gray Dodge pickup.

Move. She couldn't—it was like her feet were anchored to the ground. Her mind whirled with possibilities. Possibilities like Calvin Russell or whoever set fire to her studio had come to finish what he started Tuesday night . . . or someone else her investigation had put away.

The truck idled in the parking lot. She took a deep breath, telling herself it was a coincidence. The lake was free for anyone to enjoy, and there were a lot of gray trucks around, especially in Mississippi. It didn't have to be the one that passed her earlier.

Slowly the driver's dark window lowered. The barrel of a rifle pointed toward her. Tori scrambled to hide behind the oak tree just as a bullet plowed into the tree trunk, the report echoing in her ears.

What if the shooter came after her? She had no place to run. Tori had a concealed carry permit, but her Glock was in the gun safe in her car. Another bullet knocked the bark off the tree right by her head.

A gun report from the Point ratcheted her heart even more. Tori looked over her shoulder. *The fisherman?*

Maybe she wouldn't die . . . She jerked her head toward the pickup as the driver fired again. If the fisherman had been aiming at the shooter, he'd missed.

What if she got an innocent person killed?

11

Scott's shot had gone wide. He gritted his teeth to keep from swearing. He'd come running after the first shot and fired two more shots as he dove behind the tree with the woman. They missed their mark as well. "You okay?"

She nodded, fire glinting in her eyes.

The lady was one cool cucumber. She looked familiar in a distant sort of way, but he didn't have time to figure out how he might know her. "Right now, we're okay here, but if he changes position, we'll be an easy target."

"I know."

Scott glanced around for another place to hide. It was the tree or the water.

"Let me have your gun." She held out her hand.

Was she kidding?

"We can't afford another miss," she said, not moving her hand.

Before he could formulate an answer, the shooter revved the motor and the pickup shot forward, speeding away from them.

Scott dashed after the truck, trying to get the tag number as he dialed 911. When the operator answered, he identified himself and explained what had happened.

"Is the shooter still there?" the operator asked.

"No. He's driving a late-model gray Dodge pickup."

"Did you get the tag number?"

"Sorry, the truck was too far away."

"Is anyone with you?"

Scott glanced back at the woman. "He wants to know your name."

"Victoria Mitchell."

Her name definitely had a familiar ring to it. He relayed the information, and the 911 operator told them to stay put until a deputy arrived. After disconnecting, Scott turned to Victoria. "Why was he shooting at you?"

"Good question."

His face warmed as her gaze took him in, and he returned the favor, quickly snapping a mental picture of her beautiful features. Scott would've checked her out anyway, committing her to memory out of habit. Again, he felt he should know her, especially in his line of work where he always had to be on alert to running into people who might blow his cover.

Victoria was definitely easy on the eyes. About five-two, straight blond hair that framed a heart-shaped face. Petite and compact. Earlier he'd noticed well-defined biceps when she asked for his gun. The lady worked out.

But it was her cornflower blue eyes framed with thick lashes that made him forget to breathe. Scott shook himself mentally. The way she looked was the last thing he needed to be paying attention to.

"Nice tat on your arm." She nodded toward his left arm.

It took a second for her words to penetrate his thoughts, and he glanced at the inked road that wound around a mountain on his left bicep. "Thanks." He pointed to his right arm. "You don't like my rose?"

"Yeah, but I like the mountain better." She held out her hand. "Call me Tori instead of Victoria. And thank you, by the way. You probably saved my life . . . even if you missed the guy."

He supposed a backhanded compliment was better than none.

Scott hesitated, then used his left hand to shake her hand. "I have a bum shoulder and haven't regained the strength in my right hand. I'm Scott Sinclair."

Her eyes widened. "Scott? You've changed."

"Do I know you?"

"You should. We went to church together a hundred years ago. Granted, it wasn't for long, but still, I would've hoped you would remember me."

Heat crawled up his neck. While not a hundred, it must have been at least ten years ago, and anyone who knew him then would not have a favorable recollection.

Scott rolled the name around in his brain. The image of a skinny girl with curly blond hair and a smart mouth segued into a memory of that same girl gracing him with her beautiful smile when most of the other people at church had avoided him like the plague. He cast a skeptical glance at the woman standing in front of him. "You can't be Tori, the girl with the curly hair?"

"Have you never heard of a flat iron?" She stood straighter and lifted her chin. "I was almost eighteen, and old enough to have a huge crush on you."

Tori'd had a crush on him? He stared at her as sirens sounded in the distance. And she was twenty-eight? He would've guessed nineteen, max. "Have you ever thought about doing undercover work in the high schools?"

"Excuse me?"

"Never mind. Sorry if I've insulted you, but give it a few years and you'll be happy if people think you're ten years younger than you are."

Tori didn't respond for a second, then she burst out laughing. He joined her, then shook his head. "I can't believe we're standing here arguing about age when someone just tried to kill us."

She sobered. "I know, but you wouldn't believe how many people dismiss anything I do or say because they think I'm so young."

The sirens grew closer. "You have no idea who shot at you or why?" he asked.

"Unfortunately, there's a big pool to fish from."

"What do you mean?"

Tori took a deep breath. "There are a couple of people who would like to see me dead . . . or at least out of action."

That didn't make sense. Tori Mitchell didn't look like the type of person someone might want dead. "Why?"

Before she could answer, two cars with Logan County Sheriff's Department logos on the doors pulled into the parking lot. One was the sheriff, Ben Logan, and the other was Wade Hatcher, his chief deputy.

Ben and Wade were some of the first people he'd met when he came to live in Logan Point, and over the years, Scott had kept in touch. The lanky sheriff hadn't changed much, maybe gained a few gray strands in his dark hair. The same couldn't be said for his chief deputy.

Wade had always been a big guy, mostly overweight, but evidently in the past few years he'd started working out, and now the fat was muscle—Wade's biceps and shoulders would rival his.

Ben took the lead. "Scott, Tori, although I wasn't sure when dispatch said it was a Victoria Mitchell."

"That's my professional name—guess I was in reporter mode."

What did she mean by that? Scott cast a glance toward her, information tugging at his brain.

Ben took out a notebook. "What happened?"

Scott gave Tori a "you want to tell him?" glance, and she squared her shoulders. "Erin summoned me home—she's afraid you're going to arrest Drew for Jenny Tremont's murder. I decided to stop by the lake before I drove to her house. A gray Dodge pickup that I'd noticed earlier pulled into the parking lot and started firing. Scott, here"—she nodded toward him—"fired back, and the truck took off."

Ben turned his attention to Scott. "That about what happened?"

"Yeah." Tori had succinctly summarized the incident, and he was surprised she hadn't mentioned his bad aim. She got points for that. But it was news to him that Ben might arrest Tori's nephew for Jenny Tremont's murder. Town gossip indicated Drew had been seen near her house at the time. Even so, he couldn't see the boy killing Jenny.

"Did you recognize the shooter or the vehicle?" Wade asked.

"Afraid not," Scott said. "I didn't get a good look at him."

"Did you?" Wade turned his gaze on Tori.

She shook her head. "The glass on his pickup was tinted so I didn't see him at all until he lowered his window, and then he was sort of in the shadows. I think he might've had on a ball cap and aviator shades. I was mostly focused on the rifle pointed at me."

Ben scribbled something in his notebook. "Any idea who it might be?"

Tori chewed her bottom lip. "Probably whoever set fire to my studio Tuesday night. Knoxville PD are investigating."

Ben stopped writing and looked up, concern in his eyes. "What happened? Any suspects?"

She shrugged. "I have no proof, but I believe it was connected to the person I interviewed that night. She's a survivor of domestic violence. Escaped her abusive husband a couple of years ago and is still living in a safe house with other victims. I believe he followed her and set fire to my studio and apartment. We were lucky to get out alive. Unfortunately, whoever it was got away."

Scott was relieved that the shooter didn't seem to be someone from *his* past.

"Does this ex-husband have a name?" Wade asked.

"Calvin Russell. But I didn't get a good look at the driver of the pickup, so I can't swear that's who shot at us."

"Any particular reason this Russell would want to kill you?" Ben asked.

"I helped his wife get away from him."

"Can you give me more details?" he asked. "You gave me the who, now give me the where, what, when, and how."

"I interviewed her while I was a reporter for the local TV station in Knoxville. That was three years ago, and we became friends. From the start I tried to get her to leave him if he wouldn't agree to get psychiatric help, but it was only after he put her in the hospital that she finally left him and went to a safe house."

"Why did he wait this long to come after you?" Scott asked.

"The divorce was final this week. I think that's what set him off. You can probably get a photo of him from the Knoxville police."

Ben instructed Wade to check out the information, and the deputy walked to his patrol car. The sheriff turned to her. "How long do you plan to be in Logan Point?"

"I hope no longer than two days." Tori lifted her chin. "*Are* you going to arrest Drew?"

12

Ben's response was slow in coming, and Tori figured she wasn't going to like his answer. "It's a yes or no question," she said.

"It's not that simple," Ben answered. "And your nephew isn't helping matters by refusing to talk."

"What do you mean?" Even though Erin had said the same thing, Drew never had a problem with talking before, but then, no one had ever accused him of murder, either.

Ben shrugged. "He won't explain what he was doing near Jenny's house around the time she was killed."

She crossed her arms. "It wouldn't matter if he was seen coming from her back door—Drew isn't capable of killing anyone. Do you have any other suspects?"

"Not yet." Ben eyed her. "And don't get it in your head that you can investigate Jenny's murder on that *Dark Deeds Unraveled* podcast."

"Wait . . ." Surprise laced Scott's voice.

Tori shifted her gaze to Scott. She'd been so intent on questioning Ben, she'd almost forgotten he was there. He stared at her, recognition dawning in his face.

"Tori . . . Victoria Mitchell from *Dark Deeds Unraveled*?"

"You've listened to my podcast?" She couldn't suppress her proud grin. It always amazed her to meet a listener.

"It's one of the few I listen to," he said. "Most of the true crime podcasters don't care whether they get their facts straight as long as their ratings are good."

Ben tapped his pen on the notebook. "I will agree with him on that—you don't spout off just anything."

"Thank you." Tori prided herself on providing accurate information on the cold cases she discussed on the podcast. However, one look at Ben's face dampened her enthusiasm.

"But, I'm warning you again—I better not hear one mention of this case on your podcast."

"I've never investigated an active case, only cold cases, and if you listen to the podcast, you would know that."

Ben narrowed his eyes. "None of the other cases involved a family member."

She crossed her arms. "You don't know me at all if you think I'd cash in on Jenny Tremont's death and my family's connection. Besides, I only plan to be here long enough to get Drew's side of the story—two days, max."

She could hope. But if Ben arrested Drew, all bets were off—she'd be investigating the case whether the sheriff liked it or not. At least investigating as much as two days would allow.

A text dinged on her phone, and she glanced at it. Erin. She'd gotten home early and wanted to know where she was. "If you're done with me, I need to leave. My sister is wondering where I am."

Ben gave her a curt nod. "Mind giving me your cell number, in case I have questions?"

She didn't normally give out her number, but being cooperative might win her points, and she rattled it off.

"Mind if I put it in my phone too?" Scott asked.

"Why?"

A flicker of surprise crossed his face. With Scott's good looks, she didn't imagine many women questioned his request for their phone number.

"I like to keep up with the women I rescue."

"Yeah, right." The way he missed the target, she was the one who would've had to do the rescuing if their assailant hadn't fled.

Scott had the grace to redden. "No, really. Besides, I'd like to talk to you about your podcast."

Was he putting her on? She eyed him, her heart skipping a beat when he didn't look away. He looked nothing like the skinny Scott Sinclair of her teen years. The man was . . . Tori didn't quite know how to describe him. Eye candy, that was what he was in his sleeveless tank top that showed off muscles any body builder would envy. And those smokin' brown eyes that she could easily get lost in. Except after Michael, she wasn't interested in dating . . . and if she were, there was no way she'd ever date a recovering alcoholic. That's what he'd been when she met him at church—a nineteen-year-old trying to get sober.

"I'll repeat it in case you missed a number." Tori managed to get the number out without stammering. A few seconds later, her phone dinged with a text.

"Now you have mine," Scott said. "In case you need rescuing again."

She managed not to roll her eyes at him and turned to Ben. "Mind giving me your cell number?"

When he hesitated, Tori said, "I'll have it anyway if you call me."

Ben laughed and repeated Scott's action. When her phone dinged, she saved the contact information, then did the same for Scott's number. "Thank you, gentlemen. If there are no more questions, I'll be on my way."

Tori climbed the hill to where her Toyota was parked and looked back at the two men. They appeared to be in deep discussion, about her, probably. *Get real. Everything's not about you.* Shaking off the thoughts, she climbed in her car and called Amy to fill her in on the shooter.

Twenty minutes later, she pulled onto her sister's street, hoping the delay had sent her dad on his way. Her heart sank when she pulled into the drive and got out. A late-model, green Chevy Blazer sat parked between a Honda Civic and an older Toyota Tacoma pickup. The last time she saw Erin, her sister drove the tan Civic, and Tori had helped Drew buy the silver Tacoma. That meant the Blazer belonged to her dad, who had a fondness for Chevrolets.

Just keep your cool. Don't let him get under your skin . . . Erin's front door opened, and her sister hurried out to Tori.

Erin wrapped her arms around her. "I was getting worried. What happened?"

Always the mother hen. Tori guessed that came naturally to Erin as the older sister. "I stopped at the lake for a few minutes," she said, hugging her sister back.

Tori wasn't ready to tell her about the shooter. Actually, she'd never be ready and prayed the three men who knew about it wouldn't say anything.

13

Tori looked toward the house. "Where's Drew?"

"Inside. He seemed glad to know you were coming."

That was her Drew. Her nephew had always gravitated toward her, probably because there was only eleven years difference in their ages. He had always seemed older than he was, and she figured it was because of what he'd been through with his mother dying and his father's drinking—something they had in common. "Has he told you anything?"

Erin's shoulders dropped. She shook her head. "But I'm hoping since you two are close, he'll talk to you."

"Give me a little background first. Why was he at Jenny Tremont's house that time of the morning?"

"I don't know. But they were tight after Jenny was there for the worst of Beth's cancer." Erin glanced toward the road. "After she died, it was Jenny he turned to."

Instead of Tori. She hadn't been here, so he turned to his mother's best friend, who had been. Maybe she could make it up to him. Tori grabbed her computer. "Let's go talk to him."

"You want me to take in anything?"

"I'll get it later." She turned toward the house, and her sister placed her hand on Tori's arm, stopping her.

"Thanks for coming home. I know it's hard."

She gave her sister a curt nod. Erin had that right, and Tori didn't want to discuss the reason why.

"Look, not talking about the issue with Dad isn't going to make the problem go away. Will you at least be civil?"

She turned and studied Erin. "When have I not been?"

"Oh, you're polite enough, but one look at your face tells everyone how you really feel."

So now she had to wear a mask as well?

"He's really struggling. He can't forgive himself."

"Good."

"Tori!" Erin shook her head. "Can't you remember all the years he stayed sober? We had a great childhood."

"A great childhood doesn't erase the fact that Mom died because of him."

"I don't know why you say that. He wasn't drinking the morning the accident happened."

"But he had the night before—got roaring drunk, somebody said."

Erin caught her eye and held it. "You act like you've never made a mistake."

"At least my mistakes never killed anyone."

"Don't be so quick to say that. You don't know what the future holds." Her sister took a deep breath. "Please . . . your forgiveness would mean so much to Dad . . . and it would set you free—'cause don't tell me you have any peace with all that anger in your heart."

Tori hadn't had peace in seven years. Anger was better than the overwhelming grief that swept over her when she thought about her mother. She turned as Erin's front door opened and the object of her anger appeared.

"Y'all going to stand out there jawing all day?" her dad yelled, teasing in his voice.

He didn't look or sound like he was struggling to Tori.

"Coming," Erin called back. Then she turned to Tori. "Please don't ignore him like you usually do."

"No promises." When they reached the door, she managed to nod at him, but she couldn't bring herself to speak and especially to say *Dad*. That didn't stop her father.

"Victoria," he said. "I'm so glad you came home."

She bit back the "whatever" on the tip of her tongue and gave him a smile she knew didn't reach her eyes. "Where's Drew?"

"In the den."

Tori followed Erin and her dad to the back of the house. Drew sat in the small, darkened room, the glow from his phone the only light. Erin flipped a switch, dispelling the darkness.

He looked up, and Tori saw desperation in his eyes. "How're you doing?"

Her question brought a grimace, then Drew shifted his gaze back to his phone. "Been better."

"Me too." She'd had to strain to hear his words. This was the Drew she remembered from after his mom died. Tori glanced at Erin and her father. "Mind leaving us alone for a few minutes?"

"I don't think—"

"Sure," Erin said, overriding their dad. "Dad, you can help me make us a snack."

Once they were alone, Tori sat on the sofa, catty-corner from Drew, their knees almost touching, and waited. At first the silence was tense, but as the seconds passed into minutes, he relaxed. After five minutes, a smile quirked Drew's lips.

"I know what you're doing. You're waiting for me to start talking."

"Always said you were a smart kid."

He actually laughed. "I don't know about that. If I was, I wouldn't be in this mess."

"Want to talk about it?"

"Not really."

"I don't think the mess is going away," she said. "Let's start with something easy. Why are you staying with Erin instead of your dad?"

He made a face. "Me and Dad had a big blowup after he had to go with me to the sheriff's office Sunday."

No surprise there. "So you came here instead of going home?"

"Something like that."

Talking to him was like digging a ditch in concrete. "What were you doing in Jenny Tremont's neighborhood at that hour?"

His mouth twitched. "I couldn't sleep."

She waited for him to say more. When he didn't she said, "So you walked over to her house?"

He shrugged.

"You're telling me you walked over two miles and just ended up at her house because you couldn't sleep?"

Drew gripped the arms of the chair as Erin's grandfather clock ticked the seconds into minutes. Tori waited, and when the silence grew longer, still she waited, fearing he'd shut completely down if she pressed him harder.

"Drove my truck part of the way." He chewed his thumbnail then locked gazes with her. "How long are you staying in Logan Point?"

Tori hadn't expected that. "My plans are to leave Saturday."

"No!" He jumped to his feet, his hands spread. "You can't leave that soon."

Her heart sank. "I—"

"Please! You can't leave." Drew paced the den then stopped in front of her. "If they arrest me, you're the only one who can find out what really happened. I . . . I need you."

The fear in his voice ripped her heart out. Tori and Drew had always been close, so close he'd never added Aunt to her name—it'd always been Tori. Her mother had taken care of Drew when Beth had complications from the C-section, and eleven-year-old Tori suddenly had her own real-life doll to love.

She stood and put her arms around his tense body. "It's okay," she said, trying to calm him. "I can't promise how long I'll stay, but to help you, I need to know what happened."

Drew collapsed in the chair and held his head in his hands. She couldn't make out what he was saying. "You want to talk about it instead of muttering words I can't understand?"

He shook his head, wiping the tears that leaked from the sides of his eyes.

"Like I said, if I don't know what happened, I can't help you."

"But you got that other person out of jail."

"I had something to work with there. He told me his side of the story, and if I'm going to help you, Drew, you'll have to tell me what happened."

He turned his gaze toward the fireplace. When he looked at her again, he said, "I didn't kill Jenny, but I think I know who did . . ."

She gave him a minute to finish the thought. When he didn't, Tori leaned forward. "Who?"

For a second, she thought he would answer, but then he shook his head. "I can't."

14

"Nice rod and reel," Ben said.

It had surprised Scott when the sheriff offered to walk with him around the Point to retrieve his tackle. "Yeah. It's the one I used when Nick took me fishing when I was a kid. My physical therapist said casting might help me gain accuracy with my left hand."

Ben winced. "The rehab isn't working on your right hand?"

He shook his head. The sheriff was one of the few people in town who knew that Scott had been an FBI undercover agent. "After ten weeks of therapy, I've probably gotten as much strength and accuracy as I'll get, and that's not enough to qualify at the FBI gun range."

"You'd make a great teacher," Ben said.

The thought of never going undercover again ratcheted up his anxiety a notch. Being out of the action . . . Scott stiffened. He lived for that action. "I, uh, wouldn't make a good teacher."

"I think you're wrong about that."

A Jet Ski raced by on the lake, and they both turned toward the water as the wake rippled toward them. A call came in on Ben's phone, and Scott waited as the sheriff walked a few yards away to answer. It hardly seemed polite to leave until he finished.

Ben pocketed his phone and walked back to Scott, a frown on his face.

"Anything wrong?"

"Could be," Ben said. "You in a hurry to leave?"

Scott laughed. "I have all the time in the world . . . as long as I make my seven o'clock AA meeting."

"This won't take long. I have a favor I'd like to ask."

Those words rarely preceded anything Scott wanted to do. But Ben was the sheriff and a friend. "I'll do whatever you need if I can."

"Good. Hand me your tackle box, and I'll fill you in when we reach our vehicles."

They retraced their steps around the Point, then climbed the hill to the lot where Scott's pickup and Ben's SUV were parked. "Nice truck," Ben said. "2018?"

"Yeah. I bought it from a friend." He glanced at the deep-cherry-red pickup. Actually, from Andy's family after he died from a gunshot wound that should've been Scott's.

"I'm a little surprised you don't have a new one."

The sheriff was also one of the few people in town who knew about the trust fund his grandfather had left him. "This one gets me where I want to go."

"Gotcha." Ben handed him the tackle, and Scott stored it in the box attached to the bed. He cocked his head. "What's the favor?"

"That call was from Wade. He talked with a detective in Knoxville. They haven't been able to locate Calvin Russell. He's six-three, played a season or two in the NFL, and video from a neighbor's security camera showed someone about his size dousing the side of Tori's studio. He also has a late-model gray Dodge Ram registered to him."

"So, more than likely, he was the one who fired at us."

"No way to be sure without a description of the driver or a tag number, but you both said the pickup was a gray Dodge." Ben rubbed his chin. "The thing is, Russell isn't the only enemy Tori has. She's a good investigative reporter—she's dug up dirt on more than one person. According to what the detective told Wade, a suspicious call came into the podcast last Saturday."

Scott had been listening to *Dark Deeds Unraveled* since he'd been laid up with his shoulder. "I bet I know which call it was. It wasn't so much what the caller said as how he said it."

"I usually catch the program," Ben said, "especially when it's live, but I missed that episode."

The podcast had made the major news outlets a few times because of evidence Tori uncovered. During one case, her research unearthed a man with motive, means, and opportunity that the police had missed.

"She's definitely put a bull's-eye on her back. Like I told Tori, she's a good investigator, and she gets her facts straight." Ben rested his hand on his service pistol. "The thing is, I'm afraid she'll try to investigate Jenny Tremont's death, and that may put her in the crosshairs of whoever killed Jenny . . . and at odds with my investigation."

Scott wasn't sure where Ben was going with this. "I only know her from the podcasts and for a brief time ten years ago, but I get the impression that once she sets her head to do something, nothing will stop her."

"Yeah. That's where you come in. I'd like you to unofficially shadow her."

"She needs a protector, not a shadow."

Ben grinned. "You catch on quick."

Scott shook his head. "You have the wrong man. I can't use my right hand, and when I fired at whoever attacked us with my left, I didn't even hit the truck."

"I get that." The sheriff shrugged. "But, I don't have anyone to spare. And seems like she kinda liked you, so maybe you can influence her to keep her nose out of the investigation."

"Let me get this straight—you want me to go undercover for you to protect Tori without her knowing that's what I'm doing? And at the same time steer her away from the investigation?"

"That's about it." Ben raised his eyebrows. "You up for the challenge?"

Am I? "Sure." Anything was better than sitting around half the day—there were only so many hours he could spend learning to use his left hand. "But from what she said, I don't think she'll be in Logan Point for more than two days."

"I hope you're right, but I figure that nephew of hers will change her mind."

"Do you really think Drew Mitchell could've killed Jenny?"

Ben shrugged. "At this point, I honestly don't know. I do know he was seen near her house around the time of her death. He swears he didn't kill her, and I can't find a motive to tie him to the case. He also didn't appear to be on drugs when I talked to him, but that was a day later, after a witness came forward and put him near the scene of the homicide about the time it happened."

Scott nodded. "His dad, Zack, has attended a few of the AA meetings I go to, so the tendency could be there. That said, I've seen the kid around town, and I've never gotten the sense he's doing drugs." Scott chuckled. "I have a sixth sense about those things."

Ben grinned. "I agree."

Scott thought a minute. "I'll call her, but Tori is going to be focused mainly on Drew, so I need a better reason for calling her than to just ask her out for coffee."

"I'm sure you'll think of something."

"Maybe she'll settle for my good looks."

"You wish."

They both laughed, then Scott sobered. "What can you tell me about the case?"

Ben hesitated. "We're just starting the investigation . . . in fact, the judge hasn't even granted a search warrant for Jenny's bank accounts. I do expect him to rule on a search warrant for Zack's house sometime today. Unfortunately, at this point, Drew is the only suspect we have."

Scott turned that over in his mind. "You found his prints in Jenny's house."

"Afraid so. The man who saw Drew near Jenny's house was his baseball coach—that's why he recognized him. He intended to ream him out when he saw Drew again for being out so late, but at church, he learned Jenny had been killed and he came forward. I had Zack bring Drew down to the sheriff's office Sunday afternoon, offered him a Coke, and got his prints off the can. They matched prints we found in the house."

"But you don't know when he left them," Scott pointed out.

"True. The prints don't mean he killed Jenny, but I want to bring him in for questioning again. Probably tomorrow."

Scott raised his eyebrows, surprised Ben wasn't bringing him in today.

"I know what you're thinking, but he's not going anywhere. One of my deputies is tailing him, and Drew is staying with Tori's sister," Ben said.

Scott knew Tori's sister. Erin Mitchell owned a cybersecurity company, and Nick had hired her to install an antivirus software security system she'd developed onto his computer. "Why is he staying there?"

"My son TJ says he stays there sometimes, especially when his dad is drinking. They have a lot of blowups." Ben paused. "I don't believe he killed her—the crime scene is too tidy for someone Drew's age, but I believe he knows something. His coach said he seemed to be in a panic when he ran in front of him. I thought if he stewed about it another night, he might share what he knows."

"You know teenagers," Scott said with a chuckle.

"Yeah, well, TJ's seventeen, same age as Drew, and the two have been friends since TJ came to live in Logan Point."

That's right. Scott had almost forgotten that Ben hadn't met his son until he was almost ten. "How is TJ? I haven't seen him since I've been back."

"He's good, staying busy. This is exam week, but his grades have exempted him from finals—Drew as well—they're both in the running for valedictorian next year." Ben beamed like any proud daddy.

Scott nodded. "Where's TJ going to college?"

"Mississippi State University, I hope. Leigh drove him to Starkville this morning to check out my alma mater—even though he has another year, I wanted to get my bid in first."

He liked Ben's wife, Leigh. She was a doctor at the local hospital and an all-around kind person. "How about Drew? Do you know what his plans are?"

"He talked about getting a criminal justice degree . . . like TJ, his counselors are talking about a couple of academic scholarships he can apply for. I hope this doesn't mess up his plans."

A timer beeped on Scott's watch, and he glanced at it. Six fifteen. "I have to get ready for the AA meeting." He opened his door and climbed into the truck. "I'll let you know how it works out with Tori."

Scott wasted no time getting home and changing for the meeting. A little before seven, he climbed into his truck and called Zack Mitchell. He'd halfway agreed to go to the meeting, and Scott was supposed to pick him up. The call went to voicemail. Didn't surprise him. He'd seen Zack's car at McKay's the last few days when he passed by.

But maybe this gave him an excuse to call Tori. The woman was a puzzle. Aloof, honest, and . . . gorgeous. And still had that beautiful smile. In all truthfulness, he hadn't been able to get her off his mind since she left the lake.

He found her number and called it. She answered on the second ring. "Tori, this is Scott Sinclair—"

"I know," she said. "Has Ben found our shooter?"

Her low dulcet voice intrigued him. He'd noticed it at the lake. "Scott?"

"Sorry. I got sidetracked. Actually, I'm looking for Zack and wondered if he might be with you?"

"No. Why are you looking for him?"

"He was supposed to go to an AA meeting with me tonight."

"Oh. Hold on a minute, and I'll see if anyone here knows where he is."

Scott heard several voices respond to her question, but he couldn't make out their answers.

"Drew said to try McKay's," she said, her voice sounding troubled when she returned to the phone. "But thanks for trying."

That was what he'd feared. Scott hesitated. "Any chance you'd like to grab a cup of coffee in about two hours?"

"I, ah . . . sure. Maybe you can fill me in about my brother."

He wondered if she could sense his smile through the phone. "I'll pick you up."

"No, I'll meet you there."

"But you don't know where."

"There's only one coffee shop in town unless you count McDonald's, and I don't think you have that in mind."

He laughed. "No. See you at Two Cups."

15

Tori stared at her phone a few seconds after Scott hung up. She'd thought of him several times since she arrived at Erin's, which was about as strange as his call. A memory from the past popped up. Her church was having a Sunday night social, and Scott was new and sitting off by himself.

Nobody would talk to him except Kate Adams—he'd almost been arrested for murder, and then someone had tried to kill him. Tori figured no one knew what to say to Scott—she certainly hadn't. But he didn't have any friends, and she felt sorry for him.

She decided to challenge him to a chess game. He'd looked up at her when she approached him with a chess board, and she'd never forget the smile that started with his full lips and then lit up his face. And then he quickly trounced her in six moves.

Goodness, she hadn't thought about that in years. She pocketed her phone. Tori hadn't expected to hear from him so soon . . . She wrinkled her nose. The call didn't pass the smell test. Sure, he *said* he was checking up on her brother, but why not call Erin or her dad?

Oh, wait . . . the sheriff and Scott had been huddled together when she left the lake. Of course. The sheriff put him up to calling, figuring if Scott paid attention to her, she'd spill what she knew. Tori snorted. If he was looking for information she'd gotten from Drew, they both were wasting their time. Her nephew's mouth was closed tighter than the vault at Fort Knox . . . except Scott had sounded genuinely disappointed when she told him to check McKay's for Zack.

Her brother should be *here*. They'd spent the last hour discussing options for his son, and the least Zack could do was support him instead of hanging out at the local beer joint.

With that thought, Tori walked down the hall to where the family gathered in Erin's den. Drew slouched in a chair, staring at his phone—probably playing some kind of game. Erin hunched over her computer, and her dad stood by the window, worry lines creasing his forehead. If she had to guess, this problem with Drew—or her brother, Zack—had put those worry lines there. Guilt pricked her. If she were honest, she'd probably put a few lines there herself.

Her dad looked much older than the last time she'd seen him and tired . . . no, weary. Watching him stirred her heart. It was a lot easier to be angry at him from Knoxville. Their time together had gone better than she'd expected, maybe because he hadn't tried to apologize again for something an apology could never change. Perhaps they could put the past behind them . . . She wished.

Her phone dinged with a text message, and she glanced at it. A group text from a *Dark Deeds Unraveled* fan club. When another text came in, she muted it and a couple more, her mind on her brother. "Does Zack hang out at McKay's a lot?"

Drew barely looked up from his phone. "Yeah. Even though he told me he wasn't going to go there anymore."

Tori turned to Erin. "Does he need an intervention?"

"You think we haven't tried that?" her sister snapped.

"I didn't know." She tried to not sound defensive.

"Maybe if you came home more often—"

"Come on, girls, don't argue," her dad said. "We have enough problems without being at each other's throats."

Tori opened her mouth to protest but bit back her angry thoughts. "You're right."

Erin nodded. "I'm sorry."

"Me too." She couldn't believe she agreed with her father. "Tell me about Scott Sinclair."

"What about him?" Erin eyed her. "Why are you interested in Scott?"

"I'm not *interested*—more like curious. He was at the lake when I stopped by there." She probably should tell them about the shooting. No . . . they had enough on their plate tonight.

"Not a lot to tell," her dad said.

"Yeah, he just showed up at his brother's place one day around Thanksgiving, recovering from some kind of injury," Erin added.

"What's he been doing all these years?"

"That's the big question that his return stirred, but so far, no one's answered it."

"Why is he interested in Zack?"

"Who knows?" Erin focused on her computer screen again.

"I think Scott worked for the Livingstons in their distribution center back when he first came to Logan Point," her dad said. "Zack would've been his boss."

"He stopped by the house about a month ago," Drew said. "Talked to Dad a long time, and that night Dad went with him to an AA meeting. I thought . . ."

Tori knew what Drew thought—that his dad was going to stop drinking.

"He did stop for a couple of weeks." Drew shrugged. "Then something happened at work, and he started back."

Again, no surprise to Tori.

The front doorbell rang. Frowning, Erin checked her camera feed and jumped up. "Oh my goodness! I forgot the appointment with Richard Livingston and his wife—they want to go over the quote I gave them for a cybersecurity system for the Livingston Oil Corporation."

She turned to Tori. "Would you let them in and get them settled in the living room while I print the quote and grab the files? I meant to do that last night but this thing with Drew distracted me."

That was not normal for Erin. Her sister ran her cybersecurity company from home and was the most focused person she knew. "Of course. I didn't know Richard had remarried."

Her dad chuckled. "Yeah, about five years ago. Kind of took everyone by surprise—we all figured Eli would be the one standing at the altar with the woman."

"Eli's not married?"

"Nope. A couple of close calls, but nothing permanent."

"Why did everyone think it'd be Eli?"

"Richard's wife is maybe three, four years older than Eli. Rumors were that's who she set her cap for when she first hit town, but he wasn't interested. But Richard and Stephanie seem happy—even have matching Cadillacs."

She tucked the information away, hating that she was so cynical, but Tori had seen women like that operate. Sharks. She'd always liked Richard back when she dated Eli in her senior year of high school. "So her name is Stephanie?"

Her dad nodded as the bell pealed again. Tori hurried to the door and ushered them in. "It's so good to see you again, Mr. Livingston."

He took the hand she offered. "I told you a hundred times, Tori, call me Richard. Only people who owe me money call me Mr. Livingston."

"Richard, then. You're looking really fit—you must be hitting the gym regularly."

"Every day."

The man had to be in his sixties, but he didn't look a day past fifty. A golden tan set off his silver hair, and there were remarkably few lines in his face. Tori couldn't help but wonder if he'd had a face lift and maybe even a tummy tuck?

She turned to his wife, and cynicism raised its ugly head again.

The woman *was* much closer to Tori and Eli's age than her husband's. "And you must be Mrs. Livingston." She extended her hand to her as well. "Or do you prefer Stephanie?"

"No one calls me Mrs. Livingston." She shook Tori's hand and gave her a toothy smile that made her eyes crinkle. "Stephanie is fine."

Tori blinked. She'd been expecting someone more aloof, maybe even condescending given the Livingston wealth. She returned Stephanie's warm smile. "Erin said to make you comfortable in the living room. She'll be with you shortly." Tori led the way to the living room. "Can I get you coffee or tea?"

"Oh, coffee would be wonderful," Stephanie said.

"None for me," her husband said at the same time.

"Then none for me, either."

"It's no problem." Tori turned toward the door. "We already have a pot made."

Stephanie brightened. "Well, if it really is no trouble . . ."

Tori hurried to the kitchen and rummaged for a coffee cup that wasn't chipped, finally finding a mug that their local potter, Kate Adams, had made. She looked at the bottom. Yep, there was her KA stamp. She found a tray and a bowl for creamer and sugar packets. At the last minute, she grabbed a bottle of water from the refrigerator and poured it into a goblet before hurrying back to the living room. She wanted a few minutes before Erin joined them to question Richard about Jenny. Maybe he had insight on why she'd been killed. And maybe she'd get a little information on his brother, Walter.

She set the coffee on the table beside Stephanie and handed Richard the water.

"You're a gem," he said, taking the glass. "I advised my son not to let you get away years ago."

Heat crawled up Tori's neck as she sat across from them in a wingback chair, and she wasn't the only one to flush. Maybe there *was* something to the rumor that Stephanie had first set her cap for Richard's son. "How is Eli?"

"I'm still waiting for him to settle down. When I was his age, I'd already started the Livingston Oil Corporation."

She smiled in answer. Nothing had changed about their strained relationship. Eli had always chafed under his dad's thumb. No matter what he did, Richard could have done it better and quicker.

"I'm so sorry about Jenny Tremont's death," Tori said. "I know it was a blow to you all. She'd worked for you quite a few years."

He nodded soberly. "That she had. And this nonsense about Drew being involved . . . surely Ben Logan won't take it any further, but if he does, call me—I know an excellent criminal defense lawyer."

Criminal defense lawyer. The very words sent a chill through Tori. "Thank you, but hopefully that won't be necessary. Do you know anyone who had a motive for wanting Jenny dead?"

"I don't have a clue," he replied.

Tori turned to his wife. "How about you? Do you have any idea?"

Stephanie pressed her lips together, then sighed. "It might've been a jealous wife."

Tori's eyes widened. "What do you mean?"

She dropped her gaze to the coffee cup, then shrugged. "I heard she had a thing for married men."

"Stephanie, that's not true," Richard said. "Jenny was friendly to everyone, married or not. Just because a couple of wives in town got it in their heads that she was after their husbands doesn't make it so."

"I'm just repeating what I've heard at the salon," Stephanie said as the door to the living room opened. They all turned as Erin entered the room.

"Sorry I took so long." She shook hands with Richard and Stephanie. "And thank you for coming here, rather than have me come to your office. With everything going on with Drew, I wanted to stick close to home."

"Where's Zack?" Richard asked. "I understand he called in sick this morning, but I thought he'd be here."

He directed the question to Erin, and Tori waited to see what she would say.

"He seemed to be feeling better when I talked with him midafternoon."

That was news to Tori—Erin hadn't mentioned talking with Zack.

Richard raised his eyebrows. "I noticed a pickup like his at McKay's when we drove by. I thought he'd started going to some AA meetings."

Everyone in town knew that after his wife died, Zack Mitchell had followed in their father's footsteps. Erin shot her a look Tori well remembered from their teen years—time to leave. She stood. "It was good to meet you, Stephanie, and to see you again, Richard."

He stood as well. "Yes, and I hope you'll stop by my office before you leave town. I'd like to discuss the Huey Prescott case with you."

She almost corrected him. That case was resolved, and Prescott had been exonerated. It was now a matter of who murdered Richard's brother. She'd been looking for a delicate way to bring up the subject, and now he'd given her a golden invitation.

"I'd like that very much. How about in the morning?"

"Ten thirty?"

"Perfect." And when she had him one-on-one, maybe he'd talk more about Jenny Tremont.

16

Downtown Logan Point was almost deserted at nine, except for Two Cups. But it was Thursday night, and not much happened around town during the week. Until recently Scott had liked the quiet, but now he was ready to go back to work.

He looked for a red Toyota among the cars parked around the coffee shop and found it midway down the block. With an open parking slot beside it. Good. It would give him an excuse to walk with her when they left.

The thought surprised him. Especially given that if Tori discovered that asking her out had been Ben's idea . . . not that asking her out hadn't already crossed his mind. He just wasn't sure he would've acted on it, given his goal of rejoining the FBI as soon as possible.

Scott'd had his share of dates, but he always made sure his heart wasn't involved. Working undercover was no life for a married man. The few agents he'd known who had married usually ended up divorced. Not all, but most.

He shook the thought off, not believing the direction his mind had gone. But there was something different about Tori. Always had been.

Kate Adams had helped him get sober and encouraged him to attend church and he had, but he'd come close to quitting when everyone his age mostly ignored him. Later he realized it was because they'd all been friends since kindergarten. Tori was the first one who reached out to him. He smiled at the memory of her walking up to him with that chessboard and plopping it down at the table where he sat and telling him they were going to play chess. She'd had no idea that at one time he'd been a Class A player.

He'd almost gotten sidetracked when she'd smiled at him like he was the only person in the room. Otherwise, he would have beaten her in five moves. What he found refreshing then and now was her honesty, something he didn't always find in the women he dated. *Dated? You just reconnected. You don't know the first thing about Tori Mitchell now.*

But he did. Earlier today she'd been cool under fire, literally. And she'd stood her ground with Ben. Besides, he doubted Tori was very different from her podcast persona, and she rocked it there.

He stepped inside Two Cups and scanned the room as soft Dixieland jazz provided a backdrop to the murmur of conversation. His gaze landed on Tori sitting in the last booth facing the door, working on her computer. His usual spot. Maybe they had more in common than he thought.

She picked up her coffee and glanced around. When her gaze landed on him, she pointed to a second cup on the table. Then she smiled, and it turned his world upside down. It was like riding a roller coaster—that sense of floating, becoming untethered from everything. It'd happened in a small way at the lake, but he'd ascribed it to the man taking potshots at them.

In his experience, whatever caused that feeling never ended well, and for a second, Scott didn't move. With a mental shake, he oriented himself and walked toward her. Meeting with Tori was only a job. One he wasn't getting paid for, which made it more a favor. He could walk away any time. He sat across from her.

"I ordered for you," she said and stowed her computer in a case. "Columbian dark roast with two shots of hazelnut creamer."

Scott removed the top. "I never could drink coffee through that little hole." He took a sip. "How'd you know how I take my coffee?"

Tori shrugged. "You just look like that kind of coffee drinker."

He arched an eyebrow, and she laughed. "I asked the barista if you'd arrived and we got to talking. She works days Wednesdays and Fridays and said she could set her watch by your arrival. I almost got you the venti caramel she said you routinely ordered, but I figured it was a little late for that much sugar. She said this was your second favorite drink."

"Thank you." *Set her watch. Routinely. My favorite drink.* The words set off alarms in Scott's head he couldn't ignore. He was getting too comfortable in Logan Point, and while he wasn't undercover, he'd made a lot of enemies in his job. Some of them might be looking for him—in fact, it'd been his first thought when the shooter fired at Tori.

A routine definitely made it easier for anyone to find him, and stopping by the coffee shop after rehab was a routine. But confound it, the way-too-sweet coffee was his reward for the pain he endured at physical therapy.

"I can't believe you got more than two words out of Carla." He was surprised the girl even remembered him—she rarely said more than "thank you."

"Getting people to talk to me is what I do," she said. "How was your meeting?"

"Good. Actually, better than good—one guy got his green coin." She shot him a puzzled look. "Staying sober is hard, and our group gives sobriety coins for encouragement. Green means he's been sober six months."

"That's great." She took a sip of her coffee. "Did you happen to find my brother?"

"Yeah."

"At McKay's, I suppose—Richard Livingston stopped by after you called, and he'd seen Zack's truck there."

He nodded. Her brother's pickup had been parked at the tavern beside two other pickups that Scott recognized as belonging to Zack's drinking buddies, and he hadn't stopped. Wouldn't have done any good, and knowing Zack's buddies, it could've started an argument, or worse.

She sipped her coffee. "Why are you so interested in my brother?"

He thought a minute. "Your brother gave me a job when I needed it." Not for the money it paid, but because he needed the structure of showing up for work every day. "Unfortunately, he's not ready to stop drinking."

"I wonder if he'll ever be ready, but even if he quits, it won't last. At some point, he'll give in to the temptation."

Like her dad. Scott didn't miss the implication in her voice. He'd heard the story of how Clare Mitchell died when the car they were in blew a tire, and Edward Mitchell lost control, overshot a curve, and hit a tree.

Ed, as most people called him, walked away from the accident with few outward injuries or even a drunk driving charge because his blood alcohol concentration was under .08. But the recovering alcoholic's pain was evident whenever he told his story at AA meetings. While he hadn't caused the accident, Ed believed if his reaction time hadn't been impaired by a hangover caused by a drinking binge, he could have kept the car from slamming into the tree.

Scott had heard one reason that Tori never came home was because she'd never forgiven her dad and didn't want to be around him. Scott caught her gaze and held it. "Not everyone relapses."

The lines around her mouth tightened. "What can you tell me about Jenny Tremont's death?"

Before he formed an answer, a man approached their booth. "Tori Mitchell! Is that really you?"

They both turned toward the voice. Tori's eyes widened. "Eli?"

"In the flesh." He turned to Scott and extended his hand. "Good to see you, Sinclair."

"You too, Livingston." Scott shook the man's hand even though he'd just as soon not. Which was dumb. It wasn't Livingston's fault that he always made Scott feel less than for no apparent reason. And that was it—there wasn't a reason in the world for him to feel that way. Scott had a trust fund that probably equaled anything Eli Livingston had, and he was a nice guy to boot.

"Mind if I join you two for a minute?"

Before Scott could answer, Tori said, "Sure."

Scott started to slide over to give him room, but Livingston motioned Tori over and slid in beside her. Okay, he had to admit that Livingston's possessive way of wrapping his arm around Tori didn't sit well with him. But it wasn't like Scott had a claim on her. He managed to keep from grinning when she looked uncomfortable with the action and scooted away from Eli.

Livingston didn't seem to notice. He graced her with a smile, showing off his perfectly even pearly whites, then turned to Scott. "Did she tell you we almost got married?"

Tori gasped. "Eli, you know that's not true."

"Well, it would've happened if you hadn't gone off to college in Knoxville." He turned to Scott. "I gather she hasn't told you we were quite the item in high school?"

Scott shook his head. He couldn't picture Tori with the lanky businessman.

"Oh, that's right," Eli said. "You weren't around then."

"No, I wasn't." Scott had not grown up in Logan Point, and prior to coming to the small town to recover at his brother's house six months ago, he'd only lived in Logan Point that one summer ten years ago. He turned to Tori. "Although I do remember you from that summer. Were you two dating then?"

"No." Tori shot Eli an exasperated glance. "Eli and I had an on-again-off-again relationship all through high school. That summer was one of our off times." She closed her eyes briefly and shook her head. "Eli, you will not do."

"I know." He turned to Scott. "So, what are you doing now? Other than going to rehab for your shoulder."

He knew about that? Oh yeah. This was Logan Point, and everyone knew your business. Except only a few people knew *how* he'd injured his shoulder or that he was undercover FBI. "I'm doing a little of this and that."

"Good work if you can get it." With a flick of his eye, he dismissed Scott and turned to Tori. "What are you doing in town? Oh, wait. For a second I forgot about the mess with Drew. If you need a criminal defense lawyer, I know a good one."

"Your dad said the same thing." She eyed him. "Do you know him from experience?"

He laughed. "Of course not. His son and I attended Harvard together. He became a lawyer, and I went into business."

Now Scott remembered why he was uncomfortable with Livingston. There was no way to have a conversation with him without hearing that he graduated from Harvard. Or that he was Richard Livingston's son, heir apparent to the Livingston Oil Corporation and its many holdings. Not that Livingston did it in an obviously bragging way—it was almost always like this, in passing, but it annoyed him to no end.

Maybe that said more about him than Livingston.

17

Eli's minute had stretched to fifteen. Tori leaned back in the corner of the booth. She'd managed to get him off the subject of their teen years, and they were discussing which team would win the World Series this year. She studied the two men. Eli, blond haired and clean shaven, dressed in a light-blue polo shirt and dress slacks that perfectly fit his lean runner's body. Except somehow she doubted he was a runner.

And then Scott with his dark, three-day stubble and wearing jeans and a short-sleeved black henley that strained against his rock-solid biceps. There couldn't be two men less alike.

She was curious about Scott's tattoos. Why did he choose a mountain road on one arm and a rose on the other? The man was a contradiction.

Tired of their baseball conversation, she leaned forward. "Come on, guys, it's only the middle of May. There's no way to predict which team will even be in the World Series, much less win it. Tell me about Jenny Tremont."

Conversation stopped. You'd think she'd dropped a bomb between them. Tori turned to Eli. "She worked for you. What was she like?"

His mouth tightened, then he held up his hand with his palm toward her. "Jenny didn't work for me—she did the accounting and deposited the cash that Stephanie collected from the convenience stores and laundromats."

Scott leaned forward. "Why don't the managers make the deposits?"

Eli snorted. "You evidently don't know my father. He wants to see the money before it goes in the bank."

"But you knew her," Tori said.

"Not really. It's not like we ran in the same circles," Eli said. "I mean, not meaning any disrespect, but we didn't exactly have the same interests."

How would he know that unless he knew what her interests were? Eli was hiding something, and she *would* find out—extracting information was her superpower. And she wouldn't have to resort to thumb screws or a torture rack. Tori eyed him. "Logan Point isn't cliquish. Did you go to church with her?"

"Not that I know of . . ."

"She went to my church, Faith United," Scott said quietly.

Faith United was the same church her sister attended now. And probably Drew. Maybe that would partly explain the reason Drew was so close to Jenny. It still stung a little that he turned to his mother's friend first after Beth died. Tori and Drew had been tight for years, and she let him down.

But it wouldn't have just been the church connection. What Jenny did for Beth would have made an impression on Drew. He loved his mother and would have bonded with Jenny. More proof he couldn't have killed her.

If only he would talk to Tori about what happened instead of talking around the subject. She looked up as Scott spoke again.

"Jenny worked with the teens, had for years," he said. "She taught a girls' Sunday school class."

That made her heart ache. "Her death will really be hard for those girls."

"I know." Scott's face was grim. "Our youth minister and a

few of the parents who work with the youth were meeting with her class tonight."

Earlier she'd gotten the impression Scott and Jenny were not much more than acquaintances, and now it sounded like he knew her pretty well. Why was he just now telling her? *Maybe because we haven't had much time alone to talk?*

"Enough about Jenny. What have you been doing?"

Tori barely caught Eli's question. "Sorry, I zoned out there for a second. What did you say?"

"I asked what you've been up to since you left the TV station in Knoxville," he said.

"I didn't realize you even knew I was a reporter." Much less that he knew she'd left.

"Of course I did. The whole town knew you were—we don't have many celebrities in Logan Point."

Celebrity? That she didn't aspire to. Never had. The one thing she didn't like about being a TV reporter was viewers recognizing her in public. And that didn't compare to being a *real* celebrity. Tori had seen firsthand the dark side of some celebrities' lifestyles while investigating some of the cases for the podcast. She was perfectly happy with her life like it was.

"I have a true crime podcast," she said. "Do you remember Amy Bradsher?"

"You mean Short Stuff?"

"She's my producer. I don't think she'd appreciate the high school nickname, but yes."

"I don't have the patience to listen to podcasts." Eli frowned. "Do they earn enough money to hire employees?"

She pressed her lips together briefly to keep from snapping at him. Then she pasted on a smile. "Mine does, and Amy is one reason my podcast has been so successful."

She didn't tell him that with over ten thousand downloads a

month and several sponsors, she could hire more than a producer if she needed to.

Scott crossed his arms. "Tori's a great interviewer and investigator. Pretty sure she could hire a whole crew if she wanted to, and she's quite famous in true crime podcast circles—Tori is the one who broke the Prescott case."

Wow. She had not seen that coming. Scott had just scored brownie points, not that he'd been trying, she was sure. He didn't strike her as the type.

Eli snapped his fingers. "Wait a minute . . . I heard my dad talking about some podcaster getting the man who killed Uncle Walter out of jail. Was that you?"

She tipped her head in acknowledgment while Scott took out his phone and a minute later held it up. The screen showed a photo of Huey Prescott walking out of prison with a caption under it: *Wrongfully convicted man walks free due to persistence of podcaster Victoria Mitchell.*

Warmth washed over Tori. To have been a part of Huey Prescott gaining his freedom made all the long hours and low downloads early on worth it.

Eli looked at the photo and then turned to her. "Well, being some kind of investigator doesn't surprise me. You always were nosy . . ."

"I was not!" She narrowed her eyes. "Inquisitive, maybe."

He laughed. "Just another word for nosy."

She laughed with him. "I've been called worse."

"I didn't mean to tease, but you make it easy," Eli said. "Do people call in to your show?"

"I only offered that feature once—last Saturday. Not sure I'll do it again."

Eli cocked his head. "Why not?"

"Sometimes you get weird calls."

"Are you talking about the person who told you to watch your back?"

She turned to Scott. "You listened to last week's podcast?"

He nodded. "I thought you handled the call and the ones after it very well."

"So you thought it was weird too?" Tori asked.

He nodded. "I wonder why he was upset about Huey Prescott being released?"

"I don't know." She stared down at her clasped hands.

"Maybe he thinks Prescott is guilty and you got him off," Eli said. "Did you recognize the man's voice?"

"No. The caller gave the name John Smith, which is suspect, and now I'm not even sure it was a man." Tori looked at Scott. "You heard it, what do you think?"

He thought a minute. "The voice didn't have what I call style—it was flat. Could've been either one."

In her mind she'd made the shift to the caller being a man when in reality she had no way of knowing. Had the caller set the fire? The thought sent a shiver down her spine. And was the caller the one who'd shot at them this afternoon? She definitely thought of that assailant as a man.

If only she'd gotten a better glimpse of the shooter, but when she tried to remember the exact details, all she saw was the barrel of the rifle.

18

"As nice as catching up has been, I didn't mean to stay so long." Eli checked his watch. "I have to meet someone in ten minutes, so pray I can get Carla to make a quick caffè mocha."

Scott laughed. "If you get Carla to do anything quick, let me in on your secret."

Eli rubbed his fingers together. "Money is the secret—I always give her a big tip."

Scott did as well, but not to hurry her—Carla was a single mom struggling to keep a roof over her and her son.

Eli turned to Tori. "When are you going back to Knoxville?"

"I'd only planned to stay in Logan Point two days, but now I'm not sure. It'll depend on what happens with Drew."

"Makes sense."

A shot of something Scott couldn't analyze raced through him when Eli leaned over and hugged Tori.

"If you're still here this weekend, how about dinner?" Eli said.

She hesitated. "We'll see . . . I'll be pretty focused on Drew."

"Well, I'll check out your podcast then."

She pulled a card from her bag and handed it to him. "This will make it easier to find. Click on the tab for the podcast."

"Thanks." He looked past her and frowned.

Scott looked over his shoulder. An older woman stood at the door, scanning the room.

"Isn't that your mom?" Tori asked.

"Yeah, I'm afraid so. If I'm lucky—never mind, she's spotted me." He gave a half-hearted acknowledgment as she approached. "You remember Tori, don't you? And this is Scott Sinclair. My mother, Valerie Livingston."

"Of course I remember Tori." Valerie's gaze flicked over Tori, then her scrutiny moved to Scott. She held out her hand. "It's nice to meet you, Scott. Are you related to Nicholas Sinclair?"

"My brother."

"Really? I would never put you two together."

Scott had the distinct impression Valerie Livingston knew exactly who he was. "I'm the rebel in the family."

He'd met people like Valerie before. People who made snap judgments about others without bothering to get to know them. "But I don't hold it against Nick for being the star."

She surprised him by laughing. "I like you," Valerie said, giving him a big smile.

Maybe he'd been the one to make a snap judgment.

Eli cocked his head. "Did you come for coffee . . . or were you looking for me?"

"Both. I hate to drag you away from your friends, but . . ."

"I'm meeting someone in ten minutes."

"Cancel it. We need to talk. Get me an Americano."

Eli pressed his lips together and narrowed his eyes, but his mother stared him down. He sighed and took out his phone before turning to Tori. "Duty calls . . . but get in touch before you leave town. Maybe we can get together for coffee, if nothing else."

"Sure."

Eli slid from the booth and walked to the counter. Scott turned to Tori. "So, you two were an item in high school?"

"You know how it is in high school, and I guess you could say we were an item." She put air quotes around *item*. "Eli's a nice guy, and we dated, but . . . I don't know. We always had different goals. I wanted to be a TV reporter. He called it a pipe dream, said I should do something like law school or business."

"I'm glad you didn't follow his advice. You've made a difference in people's lives. One in particular—if it hadn't been for you, Huey Prescott would still be in prison."

"Thanks." She dropped her voice. "Another problem was Valerie never liked me."

He'd gotten that impression. "You were competition. I doubt anyone will ever be good enough for her son."

"I never cared enough to figure out why she didn't like me, but that kind of makes sense." She gave him a shy grin. "Oh, and thanks for bragging on the podcast."

"No problem, and I meant every word of it."

A comfortable silence settled between them. Tori drained the last of her coffee and set the mug down. "You know what I've been up to the last ten or so years . . . so, tell me about Scott Sinclair. What have you been doing?"

He'd known this was coming and should've had a cover story prepared, but for some reason he didn't want to lie to her. How much should he tell her?

"You might as well spill it," Tori said. "I'll start digging if you don't, and I'm really good at digging."

He laughed and held up his hands as if surrendering. "Only on the condition that it stays between the two of us."

Her eyes gleamed. "Now you really have my attention."

"You have to agree first—I don't want to hear my name on your podcast."

"That bad, huh?" She grinned. "I promise, now spill it."

"I'm not sure where to start."

"Why not with when you came to live in Logan Point? That's when I first met you."

"That summer wasn't a great time in my life—except it was." When she shot him a question with her eyes, he said, "Remember the opening to *A Tale of Two Cities*—it was the best of times, it was the worst of times? Well, that was my life that summer."

He clasped his hands in front of him on the table. "I'd hit rock bottom with my drinking. I was accused of stalking Taylor out in Washington state. I was a suspect in killing a man. Someone tried to kill me." Scott sighed. "Then Kate Adams introduced me to Jesus, and she got me into church—that's when I met you. She helped turn my life around. I owe her a lot."

"I like Kate." Tori tilted her head, her lips pressed together, then she cleared her throat. "You don't think going into rehab is what turned your life around?"

Scott was an expert at reading people, and she was clearly uncomfortable with his statement about Jesus. That puzzled him. The one thing he remembered about Tori Mitchell when she was a teenager was her unwavering faith. He drained the last of his now-cold coffee. "Rehab would have never happened without discovering who Jesus is."

"I'm glad it worked for you." She stood. "I think I'll grab another coffee."

It was plain Jesus was a subject she didn't want to discuss, and while she went to reorder, he debated with himself about asking her why.

"So, after rehab, what did you do?" Tori asked when she returned.

End of debate. There would be another time . . . he would see to it. Now his internal debate shifted to how much to reveal. The fewer people who knew he was undercover FBI the better. It just surprised him that he wanted to share it with Tori. "I did the usual—went to college, got a degree in criminal justice, joined a weight-lifting club, had a few acting jobs, and then I set out to see the US on my Harley. Got into a few scrapes with a couple of gangs—"

"Wait." She held up her hand. "There is nothing usual about

any of that. Are you saying you've spent the last few years riding around on your motorcycle?"

He nodded.

"And you tangled with gangs? Is that why you have the tats—were you trying to fit in? And how did you get shot?"

Was it lying if he didn't reveal that the acting part was actually his undercover work? He leaned back in the booth and crossed his arms. "Which question do you want answered first?"

She laughed. "Sorry. I know better than to ask four different questions in a row. It's just that you've evidently lived a very interesting life."

He acknowledged her statement with a nod. "I don't deny that."

Tori tapped her lip. "Let's start at the beginning with college."

That was the easy part. "That's when I started working out. By the time I graduated, I'd bulked up to pretty much the size I am now."

The smile on her face after her quick once-over implied she liked what she saw. "Weight lifting?" When he nodded, she asked, "Did you compete?"

Again he nodded. "It kept me busy."

"So you wouldn't relapse."

Knowing how she felt about addicts, he should've known that would be her first thought. "Working out had nothing to do with my addiction. I'm very competitive, and I'm good at what I enjoy doing, so when the weight-lifting coach at the college approached me at the gym one day in my second year, I said yes."

"Oh." While Tori didn't sound disappointed, it was clear that she expected his weight lifting to have something to do with his sobriety.

"Not everyone replaces one addiction with another," he said gently, ignoring the voice in his head that whispered *liar*. He wasn't lying—courting danger wasn't an addiction.

"I didn't—"

"Didn't you? I don't know why, but you have a definite expectation that recovering addicts will eventually fail. Not all do, but it doesn't mean we don't realize the possibility is there."

"How do you stay away from alcohol?"

"You won't like the answer."

She frowned. "How do you know?"

"Trust me."

19

"Now I *have* to know what keeps you from drinking," Tori said. She'd read the statistics, and Scott might be right when he said not all addicts replaced one addiction with another, but a great majority did. A smoker started chewing gum obsessively, a workaholic took up running...

"It's simple. God helps me to stay sober." Before she could protest, he continued. "I can't explain it, so don't ask me to. It's like he took away the desire."

"You don't think you'll ever be tempted to drink again?"

"I didn't say that. I'm no different from any other addict—one drink." He snapped his fingers. "Ten years of sobriety gone. I'd have to start all over again."

"My dad was sober longer than that." Tori shook her head. She didn't want to talk about her dad. "You said you rode your Harley, discovering the US. Why didn't you get a job? You had a criminal justice degree."

He didn't answer right away, and she waited, studying him. Scott might not know it, but he wasn't the only one experienced in reading people—whatever he told her wouldn't be the complete truth.

"I wouldn't exactly fit in the corporate world," he said, flexing his tattooed arms.

She chuckled. "Let me guess... you were looking for something rough and tumble."

"Yeah, and I found it."

"What did you find?"

He studied her briefly, almost like he was trying to make up his mind about something. Then he leaned toward her. "The FBI recruited me to work undercover."

"You're kidding."

"Nope. My first operation involved infiltrating a motorcycle gang, and that led to being a closer—the guy who supplies the guns, bombs, whatever is needed—for a skinhead group in Georgia."

"That sounds dangerous."

"Not as dangerous as traveling around on a Harley as a private citizen." He flexed his muscle. "Seems like when you look like I do, sometimes guys want to prove how macho they are to their girlfriends."

She laughed. Scott was different, all right. "Is that how you got shot?"

"Yeah," he said.

Tori would love to get him on her podcast. "Would you consider letting me interview you?"

"No." Though he said it with a smile, his tone left no doubt that his decision was firm. "I plan to return to undercover work again, and while I can't imagine the people I've dealt with listening to your podcast, if they did and recognized my voice, they would come after you."

"They'd have to stand in line." Though she said it blithely, Tori didn't discount the threats she'd received. On the other hand, she wasn't going to stop her podcasts because of them. Scott tilted his head like he might be rethinking her request.

"Tell you what," he said. "If I can think of a way to disguise my voice and you'll let me script the questions, I'll consider it."

"Deal, as long as we work on the script together." Tori's phone rang. Drew.

"We'll—"

She held up her hand. "Hold that thought."

Tori swiped her finger across the answer button. The screen didn't open. She tried it again. "It's so frustrating when my phone does that. Why doesn't it just give me the option to answer or decline?"

"Because your phone is locked, and if your finger is too dry, it won't slide. Let me try." The screen opened on his first try and he handed the phone back to her.

"Thanks," she mouthed and then spoke into her phone. "What's up?"

"Dad just called. Ben Logan is at the house with a search warrant." Drew's breathless words practically ran together.

"So? There's nothing there for them to find." Why would her nephew sound so panicky? Worry, she understood, but Drew was coming unglued. "Or is there?"

"No! You gotta believe me."

A brick lodged in her stomach. Insisting she had to believe him was a good sign her nephew was lying. Tori closed her eyes briefly. What was in the house that Drew wasn't telling her about? "I'll check it out," she said and hung up.

Scott's brow wrinkled. "What's wrong?"

"Ben Logan is at my brother's house with a search warrant. Did you know about that?"

"I didn't." She eyed him like he was a bug. "Scout's honor."

"Were you a Boy Scout?"

"Cub Scout, but still . . ." He held her gaze. "I promise, I didn't know about a search warrant."

Tori believed him. "Want to go with me to see what it's about?"

"Sure. You look like you could use some backup . . . and a friend."

She hadn't expected that response. Her face flushed as tears threatened to flow. It had been such a long day, and her emotions were all over the place. *Get ahold of yourself.* "Thanks."

She stood and grabbed her computer and followed Scott to the door, nodding at Valerie and Eli in the first booth. Eli caught her eye and started to stand. Tori cringed. He must've read her anxiety. She didn't have time to explain and waved him off and ducked out the door Scott held open. When they reached her car, she eyed Scott's pickup parked beside her Toyota. "Was that an accident?"

He shook his head. "Nope. Luck maybe in finding the spot empty. I'll follow you."

She hadn't realized he'd even noticed what kind of vehicle she drove, but then again, she bet he didn't miss much. She got in her car and fastened the seat belt before she backed out.

A few miles from the house where she grew up, her cell rang, and she glanced at the ID. Eli? She pressed the answer button on her steering wheel. "Hello?"

"Are you all right?" Eli's voice boomed from the speakers.

She turned the volume down. "Yes. Why—"

"You looked upset when you left the coffee shop."

"I was. Ben Logan is searching my brother's house. For what, I don't know."

"That's not good."

"Tell me about it. I'm almost to Zack's house now."

"If I can help, let me know."

"Thanks, but I don't think he'll find anything."

"Call me when you finish, and don't forget I know a good lawyer."

She could've done without him repeating that offer.

"I'll be in touch," she said and turned into her brother's drive, dread settling in her stomach. Tori had grown up in this house. There were a lot of happy memories here. And sad ones. Zack had bought the house after the accident when her dad couldn't stand the thought of living in it. More than once, Tori had wished they'd sold it to complete strangers.

She parked beside the sheriff's truck, and Scott pulled in behind her. Her brother stood under the oak tree in the front yard, his arms crossed, staring at the house. When she reached him, she asked, "What's going on?"

He turned to face her and blew out a hard breath. Tori jerked back. Zack reeked of beer. No doubt about what he'd been doing all evening while they'd been trying to figure a way out of Drew's mess.

Zack didn't seem to notice her reaction and shrugged his left shoulder without uncrossing his arm. "Logan showed up at McKay's and handed me the search warrant, told me I could come unlock the door or he could take it down."

Her brother glanced past her. "Scott," he said with a nod. "Long time, no see."

"Not so long." He softened the words with a smile.

Zach studied him a minute, then rubbed his chin. "Yeah, well, you know how it goes."

They all turned as Wade Hatcher stepped out on the porch. Tori approached him.

"What's with the search warrant, Wade?" she asked.

20

Wade glanced over his shoulder. "Ben's coming. Be better if it came from him."

Ben Logan joined them on the front porch. "Evening, Tori. Scott."

"Why did you need to get a search warrant?" Tori asked. She nodded toward Zack. "My brother would've—"

"Ballistics report came back. The shell casing found at the scene had a partial print on it that matches your brother's fingerprint. And the bullet recovered from the victim's body was a 9mm." He turned a grim eye toward Zack. "Records show a 9mm Beretta registered to you. I have a warrant for it, but I didn't find it when I searched the house."

Zack jutted his chin and glared at the sheriff. "Could be because I don't have it."

Ben stared him down. "You want to explain?"

"Not particularly, since I don't like the way you bulldozed in here accusing me of all sorts of things."

"Ben," Scott said, "Zack's alibi is solid. I checked—he has half a dozen men who say he was at McKay's when Jenny was killed. And surely you don't believe Drew killed her."

"I appreciate your input, Scott, but you should know better than anyone that I have to follow the facts. And the facts point to either Zack or Drew being involved, Zack in particular due to the print on the casing, and . . ." He turned to Zack. "Everyone knew you had a crush on Jenny, but she didn't return—"

"You don't know how either one of us felt."

Ben shrugged. "I want to talk to Drew because Jenny's mobile carrier provided her call log. It shows the last call she made was to Drew and that he called her back after that. So why hasn't he told us that he talked to Jenny that night?"

Her gut clenched. She'd known her nephew was hiding something. "Neither of those prove that Drew or my brother are involved in her murder, especially since Zack has an alibi and no one would seriously believe Drew killed her."

Ben nodded. "That's why I haven't arrested Zack, but it's not unheard of for teens to commit murder."

"Come on, Ben," Tori snapped. "You've known Drew since he was a baby—he's your son's best friend—you know he wouldn't kill anyone."

"I don't want to believe he would, but he knows something." He turned to Zack. "Do you have a key to Jenny's house?"

"Drew and I both have one—she gave them to us in case we needed to get in and she wasn't there."

Tori rubbed her forehead with the back of her hand. She'd stepped into the middle of a nightmare. The humid air clung to her. In the distance a motorcycle with no muffler accelerated, the roar filling the night. It was a nightmare, all right, but not one she could wake up from.

Ben turned to Zack, his tough demeaner softening. "Where's the gun?"

"Told you I don't have it."

"Come on, man. I don't want to take you in, but you're leaving me no choice."

Zack dropped his gaze to the ground, where he kicked at a rock with his boot. Then he shrugged. "A couple of months ago, Jenny thought someone tried to break into her house, and I let her have the gun. It was fully loaded, probably why my print was on the casing."

"There was no gun at her house, either." Ben rested his hand on his holster. "Do you have proof you gave it to her?"

Zack swayed slightly. "Just my word, Ben. It's always been good enough in the past."

Tori tensed as Ben studied her brother, relaxing only slightly when the sheriff gave him a curt nod and took out a small notepad. "Did anyone else know the gun was at her house?"

Zack's mouth turned down as he shrugged. "I don't know who she might've told."

Ben raised the pen from the pad and looked up. "Did Drew know?"

"You'd have to ask him."

"I will." Ben turned to Tori. "Is he at Erin's?"

"You're not going to question him tonight, are you?"

The sheriff gave her a quick glance. "It's as good a time as any."

"It's after ten." She crossed her arms. "He's probably in bed, and if he isn't, my sister is—she has to get up early in the morning."

He started to say something, and she cut him off. "He's not going anywhere, and we all know that Drew wouldn't kill anyone."

Ben glanced toward the house then turned back to Tori. "I expect you to have him in my office by 9:00 a.m. tomorrow. And you might want to hire a lawyer."

That was the fourth time tonight she'd heard a lawyer mentioned.

Zack cleared his throat. "Look . . . no need to bother Drew—I doubt he knows where the gun is, but if he does, I'll get it and hand it over to you."

"Just call me—I'll come get it."

Drew's words echoed in her head. *"I didn't kill Jenny, but I think I know who did."* Did he think his dad killed Jenny?

Before she could process the thought, her cell rang. She started to ignore it, then thought better of it and pulled the phone from her back pocket. Her fingers froze when the ID showed Megan Russell's number.

"I need to answer this." She slid the answer button and put the phone to her ear. "Are you okay?"

"Yes, but you need to be careful."

She walked a few feet away and spoke quietly into the phone. "Can I call you back in just a minute?"

"Sure. I'm not going anywhere."

Tori disconnected and returned to where the men were still talking. "If you don't need me, I'm heading back to Erin's."

"Sure thing, just don't forget—Drew, my office, nine tomorrow morning."

"Do I need to be there?" Zack asked.

She stared at her brother. Of course he needed to be there.

Zack kicked at a rock. "I missed work today because I was sick, and I need to get ready for an inspection at the warehouse first thing tomorrow."

"You need to be there." Ben put away his notebook.

"I'd think you'd want to be there," she muttered, glaring at her brother. She turned toward her car. "I'm out of here."

"Hold on a sec," Scott said, "and I'll follow you."

"You don't have to do that. I'll be safe enough—Erin's house is only a couple of miles away." When he looked doubtful, she said, "I'll be fine."

"Maybe so, but I'll feel better if I know you get home safely."

21

Scott watched as Tori's taillights disappeared. Maybe he should leave now, wait and ask Ben his questions tomorrow. "I'll catch up with you in the morning."

"Wait." Ben held up his hand. "I don't figure I can keep Tori from investigating, so see if she will keep me in the loop."

"I'll try, but I don't know how much influence I have on her." He hesitated. "Did you learn anything about the person who shot at us today?"

He shook his head. "Without a license plate number, it's almost impossible—there have to be hundreds of gray pickups in the area. I did talk with the Knoxville detective, and—" Ben's cell rang, and he checked the ID. "This is Detective Bishop now."

Scott waited while Ben answered. "Logan."

The sheriff listened intently, his face settling into a frown. "If they're divorced, why is there still a joint account?" He listened again. "I see. Okay, thanks for letting me know."

Ben pocketed his phone, and Scott said, "What's going on?"

"Bishop had said he'd call if they got any indication that Calvin Russell was headed this way, and a jointly owned credit card issued to the Russells was used near Memphis a couple of hours ago. Since Megan is in Knoxville, Bishop is assuming her ex-husband used it."

"Why would they have a joint account?"

"That's what I asked, and Bishop said the wife tried to cancel it, but the credit card company said both had to request a cancellation, and the husband refused."

"If he's in the area, he could've been the shooter. I was afraid it was someone from my past."

"Anyone in particular?"

Scott shook his head. "It could be any number of people—I've made a lot of enemies as an undercover agent."

Ben nodded. "The credit card charge doesn't guarantee that the Russell guy was the shooter. Why don't you check with your undercover coordinator and see if there's any word on the street about you having a price on your head?"

"Good idea." He started for his pickup. "Let me know if you get any other information on Russell."

With Ben's assurances ringing in his ears, Scott jogged to his truck and climbed in. Maybe he could catch Tori. Her lead wasn't too much. He kicked up gravel as he sped away from Zack's driveway.

22

Drew paced the bedroom at Aunt Erin's house. He'd about had a heart attack when his dad called and said the sheriff was at the house with a search warrant.

What if they found the secret compartment? If Ben Logan discovered it, he would never believe Drew had found the gun beside Jenny's body. Then there was the money. How would he explain that? He should have turned it in Sunday.

But if he admitted to being at the house and found Jenny dead, no one would believe he didn't do it, especially since he took the gun. And now he didn't know what to do.

Jenny was the only person who understood him. She hadn't thought he was a horrible person when he told her how mad he was at God. She'd responded just like his mom would have.

"I don't know why your mama got sick, but it wasn't God's fault. Cancer is one of those evil things in the world that God hates. Your mom was a believer, like you, and that means she's in a better place. You'll see her again one day."

Drew wasn't sure how he felt about that. Now Jenny was dead. Didn't seem like God had helped her much. Was Jenny killed because of the money or what was in the box? He hadn't opened it yet—probably needed to, but he'd stayed as far away from what was under the floor as he could, like it was a snake that might bite him.

Drew rubbed his face. If only Jenny hadn't died. Could he

talk to Tori? He'd almost come clean with her earlier, then he got scared. No one knew he had the money and the box. If that's what got Jenny killed, and whoever killed her found out he had it, they might kill him and his whole family.

And the money. What was he going to do with it? He'd probably never know where she got it and why. It was hard to believe she'd done something illegal . . . but why else would she hide it?

He sank onto the bed and held his head in his hands. Drew didn't know what to do, and he had no one to turn to.

23

As soon as Tori left Zack's house, she called Megan back. "I can talk now. Are you sure you're all right?"

"I'm fine. I'm worried about you. I told Detective Bishop that Calvin and I have a joint credit card, and gave him the account number and—"

"You're divorced. Why would you still have a joint credit card?"

"Calvin was supposed to sign the papers to cancel it—that was in the divorce papers, but he hasn't. Bishop called earlier to make sure I wasn't in Memphis. Evidently Calvin used the card to charge something at a convenience store there near the state line."

"Are they certain he's the one who used it?"

"Yeah—Bishop just called back while I was waiting on your call—the store has video surveillance, and according to the detective, it was Calvin—he probably didn't think about the store having a camera or that the credit card would be flagged."

Tori gripped the steering wheel. The state line was only fifteen minutes from Logan Point. A call beeped in, and she glanced at the ID. Amy. "Thanks for letting me know. Let me get back to you—I need to catch a call."

"No need to call back. But do keep me updated."

"I will," Tori promised and switched calls. "Hey, what's going on?"

"Just checking on you since I haven't heard from you," Amy said.

116

"Sorry. It's been crazy around here." She glanced in her rear mirror, and headlights flashed in the distance. Probably Scott. "Megan just called." Tori explained what Megan had passed on to her.

"Russell was probably your shooter."

"Good possibility." Something they had discussed when Tori drove from the lake to Erin's house after it happened.

"He had opportunity, motive, and means," Amy continued. "But would he have used a credit card that pinpointed his location?"

"Probably didn't think about it being flagged, and from the research I've done on him, he strikes me as the type to think he wouldn't get caught." She rubbed her head. "If he started the fire or followed me down here, he would have no qualms about harming Erin or Drew." She wasn't putting her family in danger. "I've got to find another place to stay."

"I thought you'd say that," Amy said. "It's another reason I called. Aunt Rainey is in Seattle for the next two weeks, and she insists that we use her house while we're in Logan Point. Since I figure you'll be there this weekend, I'll drive to Mississippi in the morning, and we can set up to record the podcast in her den."

"Great!" Staying at her aunt's house would solve a lot of Tori's problems. She glanced in her rearview mirror. Two sets of headlights flashed in the distance. Hopefully the closer ones belonged to Scott. "What time will you get here tomorrow?"

"Probably by noon."

"Good. I'm tied up early in the day going with Drew to the sheriff's office."

"Why? What haven't you told me?"

Tori quickly filled Amy in on everything that had happened after the shooting.

"If Zack said he loaned Jenny the gun, he did," Amy said.

It didn't surprise Tori that Amy believed Zack. Back when they were in second grade and Zack was a senior, he'd intervened when two bigger boys were picking on Tori and Amy on the playground.

117

He'd been Amy's hero ever since, even if his drinking had left his armor somewhat tarnished. "I hope you're right."

"You know I am. Oh, you received a package today, no return address and the postmark is blurred."

"Did you open it?"

"No, but I will, if you'd like—I'll have to get it."

"Wait. Do you think it could be a bomb?"

"I don't think it's heavy enough for that."

"After someone shooting at me, it might be a good idea to let the police open it."

"I'll call Detective Bishop now."

"Let me know if it's a threat." Tori ended the call then blinked as high beams flashed in her side mirror.

She shifted in the seat to avoid the glare. The vehicle was right on her. It wasn't Scott. He would never ride her bumper. Maybe a truck—she could see headlights and the top of the grill in her rearview mirror, but nothing else.

The image of the rifle pointing at her earlier flashed in her mind. She tapped her brakes, hoping the driver would back off. If anything, the lights came closer, and the S curve where her dad lost control of his car was just ahead.

"Back off," she muttered.

Instead her Toyota lurched forward as the vehicle tapped her bumper just hard enough to make keeping it on the road difficult. She gripped the steering wheel as the car veered to the right.

She was in the curve. One more bump and she would lose control. Tori stiff-armed the steering wheel, waiting for the other vehicle to hit her again. When nothing happened, she glanced in the mirror.

The vehicle riding her bumper abruptly fell back, then whipped around her, its headlights blinding her in the side mirror. Tori slowed and tried to identify her attacker, but she only saw enough to know it was a pickup as it zoomed past her.

Her body turned to mush, and she struggled to navigate her car out of the second curve and onto the side of the road as a second vehicle passed her. *Scott.* He slowed and pulled off the road in front of her. Tori leaned her head against the steering wheel, her energy spent.

Scott jumped out of his truck, ran to her car, and jerked open her door. "You okay?"

She stumbled out of her car and nodded. "You?"

"Yeah. Could you identify the driver of the other truck?"

"All I could see were headlights at first, then when it rammed me, all I could think of was holding my car on the road. Did you see the driver?"

"No," he said, "but it could've been the same truck that was at the lake. As soon as I saw how close the truck was to you, I called Ben and reported what happened. He thinks it might be Calvin Russell."

"Megan said he was in the area." Tori bit her bottom lip. "I don't want to go back to Erin's—what if he knows I'm staying there?"

"Hold on a second." Scott stepped away from her and called someone. A few minutes later he returned. "Taylor and Nick said for me to take you to their house."

She shook her head. "I don't want to put them in danger."

"You won't—they're in California. Besides, they took me in, and no one's found me yet."

"But you're family."

"Some people wouldn't count that as a plus." He grinned at her. "Besides, what're your other options?"

She looked up at the night sky where millions of stars flickered. "I could stay at Rainey Fletcher's house. Amy's coming tomorrow."

Her heart fluttered as he caught her gaze and held it. No one had affected her like this since Michael. *No.* Not happening, especially with a recovering alcoholic.

Tori crossed her arms and tried to resurrect the barrier Scott had somehow slipped past. She couldn't go there again.

Scott eyed her. "Tell me you really want to spend the night in that big old house by yourself."

What choice did she have? It was the only way to keep from involving anyone else in her troubles.

"I promise, you won't be a danger or an inconvenience. The house sits back off the road, and Taylor and Nick have state-of-the-art surveillance. It's one reason I agreed to stay there while I recovered."

Her resolve weakened. Maybe it would be okay. A famous author's house was probably the last place anyone would look for her. And as for the way Scott made her heart race, she'd just have to ignore it. "One night. Tomorrow when Amy gets here, we'll set up in her aunt's house."

He raised his brows. "We'll see. I'll follow you to your sister's house and you can get your things."

"No need. I brought my computer to the coffee shop, and I never unloaded at Erin's—I have everything I'll need."

"Do you always have a backup plan?"

"Yep. Like you, I expect."

He winked at her. "Could be we have more in common than we thought."

Was he flirting with her? If it hadn't been for Michael, Scott would tick all the boxes. Intelligent, kind, trustworthy, strong moral compass, a sense of humor much like her own, and he wasn't hard to look at. Although good-looking wasn't one of her boxes. But she wasn't in the market, especially with him. "I'll text Erin and let her know I'm not coming home."

She followed Scott to the Sinclair home and parked her car in the garage beside his truck.

"You hungry?" he asked when she got out of her car.

"No, but I know I need to eat."

"Well, I'm hungry—I didn't eat before I went to the meeting, and that cup of coffee is long gone." He thought a minute. "There's bread and meat to make a sandwich, and I guess I could settle for that."

The *Pink Panther* theme sounded from her phone. "It's Amy." She answered. "What's going on?" There was hesitation on the line. "Spit it out."

"I called Detective Bishop, and he was concerned. He brought in the bomb squad, and they're here now, examining the package."

Tori glanced at Scott. "Amy, I'm with Scott Sinclair right now. I'm going to put this on speaker."

"Okay," Amy said. "The bomb squad commander is walking this way." A few seconds later, she said, "What did you find?"

Tori heard a gasp. "What is it?" she asked.

"It's a doll . . . with a broken neck."

She wished she could see what Amy was talking about. "What do you mean?"

"It's like a Barbie doll, only someone has twisted the head off."

She gripped the phone hard. "Do not come to Logan Point. It's too dangerous."

Amy grunted. "I figure there's safety in numbers. There's a note pinned to the doll. It says 'mind your own business' and has both of our names on it."

24

This was bad.

"You both need to stay here." Scott took Tori's phone. "Amy, this is Scott Sinclair. You need protection tonight. I'm calling a friend there in Knoxville to come stay with you. When he arrives, ask him what the code is, and if he says anything other than 'It's a lovely day for a stroll,' call the police. Your reply will be 'Only if you're a duck.'"

"Got it."

"No." Tori was already shaking her head. "Whoever's doing this is serious—I'm not risking your life or Amy's."

"We'll discuss it tomorrow." While he understood Tori's desire to not put anyone in harm's way, he wasn't letting her face this alone. Especially since there was a possibility that Scott had brought the danger to her. He hadn't heard any chatter that his location was known, but he wasn't taking any chances with her safety.

"And you're not getting rid of me." Amy's voice rang strong from the speaker. "We're in this together."

"Good," he said. "Talk to Tori for a sec."

Scott handed Tori her phone and took out his own. In less than five minutes, he'd connected with his friend Caleb Jackson in Knoxville and set up the meeting with Amy. "Call me after you make contact."

Once Caleb assured him that he would, Scott disconnected

and turned back to Tori, who was trying to talk her friend out of coming to Logan Point.

"You need to let the police in Knoxville find you a safe house."

"Sorry. I like Scott's solution better."

He admired the determination in Amy's voice. "Thanks," he said. "Caleb Jackson should be there in the next half hour, and he'll follow you to Logan Point tomorrow. We'll be waiting for you at Oak Grove, Nick and Taylor's house."

"No," Tori said. "We're staying at her aunt's house."

"That's not a good idea," Scott replied. "My brother's house is a more secure location. Amy, you need to come to Oak Grove—you know where it is?"

"I do."

"Good. See you tomorrow."

Tori pocketed her phone and eyed him. "Where's that food you were talking about? I'm starving now."

His jaw dropped. Tori Mitchell could go from infuriating to making him laugh in five seconds. He palmed his hand toward the house. "After you—just follow the brick path."

He followed her as she rolled her small bag toward the house, the wheels clacking on the bricks. Once inside, it didn't take him long to lay out the bread and shaved beef from the refrigerator. "I think there are chips here." He opened the cabinet and held up a package. "Or walnuts, if you prefer."

"I prefer." She grinned at him. "Healthier."

He eyed her trim figure. "Don't tell me—you're a health nut."

"You might say that—if eating fruits and vegetables and nuts qualifies. I suppose you like chips and high-calorie desserts."

"Give me a fudge brownie over brussels sprouts any day."

She burst out laughing. "You got me there—so would I."

Her laughter unleashed the tension in his body. In spite of their differences, sometimes they clicked like interlocking puzzle pieces. And that set off a warning in his head.

Tori took a deep breath and slowly released it. "It feels good to laugh. Thank you."

"I'm glad I was able to accommodate." He handed her a plate with a sandwich and a mixture of chips and walnuts, then held up a tomato. "And I have veggies . . . well, technically I believe this is a fruit. Would you like a slice for your sandwich?"

She nodded. Scott sliced the tomato and added half to her plate.

"Some would debate you on whether it was a fruit or vegetable," Tori said. "Either way, I love 'em."

He found himself enjoying being around her. Which wouldn't do. He was going back to undercover work, and that was no life for a married man. *Marriage?* He almost dropped the knife. Where had that come from?

"I love this kitchen," Tori said. "Did Taylor keep the tongue-and-groove floors throughout the house?"

He nodded. "They have some kind of oil on them."

"Linseed." She nodded toward the sink. "Is that the original copper sink?"

"Good question." He handed her a cloth napkin. "I think she kept as many of the original features that she could. I know she and Nick refinished the oak cabinets."

"They're beautiful. So where did you say Nick and Taylor are?"

"Tour for Nick's book that just released."

Tori tilted her head. "Have you ever thought about writing? I bet you have some experiences that would make good stories."

He'd thought about it and promptly dismissed it. "I'm more of an outdoor person. Don't think I have the discipline to sit behind a computer all day."

"I think you'd have the discipline to do anything you wanted to do."

Tori's soft words hung in the air between them, sending a dart straight to his heart. It'd been a long time since a woman had looked beyond his outward appearance.

She caught her breath, and red crept into her face. "I-I mean, you strike me as that type."

The words touched him even more because he was pretty sure she hadn't intended to say them. "It might be true if I *wanted* to write, but one author in the family is enough." He nodded toward the deck. "Do you want to sit outside or here at the island?"

"Outside, if you don't care."

That suited him. It should be safe enough—the house was surrounded by thick timberland that Nick had enclosed with a fence from the road to the lake. A person would have to walk a long way in thick undergrowth and trees to get to the house. "I'll take our plates if you'll bring the glasses of tea."

Scott flipped a switch, and a soft light enveloped them as they stepped outside to the screened-in deck. Once he set their plates on the round table, he pulled out her chair before sitting.

"Thank you." She set their glasses beside the plates.

She sounded surprised, but he didn't comment. They ate quietly, the silence broken only by the lonesome notes of a whippoorwill.

"It's been forever since I heard a whippoorwill." She cocked her ear. "Or a katydid."

"Katydid?" Scott frowned, then nodded. "Oh . . . cicada."

"Yeah, but we never called them that. How far does their property go?"

"They have twenty acres that run all the way to the river and lake. When you add her mother's place, they have a hundred acres."

"I noticed a lot of lights on the left side of the road before we got here. Is it a subdivision?"

He nodded. Tori seemed to not want a lull in the conversation. "Realtors have tried to buy their property, but they don't want to sell."

"Why not? Oh, never mind. I wouldn't sell, either." She picked up a walnut, nibbled it, then raised her head and cleared her throat. "I, ah . . . thanks for all you've done."

Ah, now he understood why it seemed as though she was filling the time with small talk. Tori wasn't used to someone coming to her rescue, and she didn't quite know how to handle it. "Not a problem."

"I'm afraid it is."

"I don't understand." Scott shifted in his chair under the frank gaze of her blue eyes.

"Why are you helping me? What's your angle?"

"I don't have one." He didn't understand why she was suspicious. "Why wouldn't I help? Someone is out to get you, and I can't stand by and let that happen."

25

Scott Sinclair was too good to be true. Most men she knew didn't risk their lives for someone they didn't know. Could he really not have an angle? Once again the lonely sound of the whippoorwill broke the silence.

"So, what's on your agenda for tomorrow?" Scott asked. He checked his watch. "Or rather, this morning?"

Tori leaned back in her chair. A bullfrog croaked somewhere close by. She hadn't heard one of those in years, either.

"You don't have to share your plans if you don't want to."

"It's not that—I just haven't thought that far ahead beyond Drew's interview with Ben Logan at nine."

"You expect me to believe Victoria Mitchell doesn't have a plan?"

"Okay, maybe I'm not sure what I want to do first." It wasn't easy for her to open up to anyone other than Amy. But Scott had been there for her. And having an ally wasn't a bad thing. "After the interview with Ben Logan, I want to question Richard Livingston while I'm waiting for Amy to get here."

"Why?" Scott asked.

She was surprised he didn't know. "Pretty sure the doll has a connection to a podcast series I've done. Two come to mind—Walter Livingston's and the one on domestic violence. I can't investigate Calvin Russell, so . . . since the Walter Livingston case is the one

I'm getting publicity for, and I'm in Logan Point, it makes sense to start there."

He nodded. "That makes sense."

Tori smiled. "Besides, I want to learn more about Jenny Tremont in case Drew or my brother is charged. I figure someone at the Livingston Corporation can give me a better picture of her than I have."

"You could ask me."

She'd forgotten they went to church together. Tori wasn't sure how true a picture Scott had of Jenny—lots of people were one person at church and someone totally different everywhere else. It was one reason she'd quit going. Not the main one, but when you wanted to do something, one reason was as good as another. "Okay, what can you tell me about Jenny?"

"What do you already know?"

He would make a good lawyer. Tori searched her memory bank. "She was my sister-in-law's best friend . . . actually moved in the last three months of Beth's life to help take care of her while Zack worked."

That made her a good person in Tori's mind. "She bonded with Drew. From what Erin's told me, Jenny and Drew were really close—he would do practically anything for her." She thought a minute longer. "That's about all I can think of. What can you add?"

"I admired her."

"Why? You couldn't have known her long."

"That's true . . . but she was one of the first church members who reached out to me when I returned to Logan Point six months ago. She didn't judge my appearance—she even asked if I'd help with the youth."

Scott paused and looked toward the trees. "Jenny had a really sweet spirit, and she really poured herself into the lives of the girls in her Sunday school class."

"So why would someone kill her?"

"Money, jealousy, and vengeance—those are the usual reasons." Scott rattled the ice in his glass and drained what tea was left. "But I don't see where she would fit into any of those."

"Who was she close to?"

"Besides people at church? Drew, maybe Zack." He shifted in his chair. "There *was* a rumor going around that Zack wanted to date her . . ."

Tori had been surprised when Ben alluded to a relationship between Zack and Jenny—she'd no clue her brother was interested in Jenny other than as a friend. "Did he?"

He hesitated.

"So it was true?"

"I don't think so. I asked him about it, and he got huffy. Told me it was none of my business who he dated. When I agreed, he warmed up a little, said it would be like dating his sister—one he could actually talk to without getting a lecture."

She winced. Tori imagined both she and Erin were guilty of that. "He makes it so easy to lecture him," she grumbled.

"Are you judging him?"

"No!" She pressed her lips together. "Maybe. I lost my mother to alcohol. I don't want to lose my brother too."

"Have you ever been to Al-Anon?"

"No. It's not *my* problem."

His raised eyebrows said otherwise.

"It's not," she insisted.

"Al-Anon might help you realize you're not responsible for whether he stops drinking or not."

She stared out at the darkness beyond the deck. Tori didn't feel responsible for making Zack stop drinking. She didn't. "Do you know if Jenny Tremont's house is still a crime scene?"

Scott sighed. "No idea. You'd need to ask Ben."

"If it is, do you think he would allow me to go through it? I might find something they missed."

"Tori, Ben's not going to let you search her house—he wants you to stay out of the case."

"And you know this how?"

He hesitated. "Because if it were my case, I wouldn't want you meddling in it. Besides, he told me as much."

Ben Logan wouldn't be the first law enforcement official to label her investigation as meddling. But every time, she'd discovered something they missed. "Thank you for admitting that Ben put you up to asking me out."

"I'm not admitting anything. He asked me to keep an eye on you after the incident with the shooter. I didn't have to say yes."

But he had, and she should be thankful instead of questioning his motives, especially after he'd scared that truck off earlier tonight. Her mouth twitched. "Thank you."

"That wasn't so hard, now was it?" The twinkle in his eye softened his words. "And you're welcome." He stood. "If you're ready, I'll show you where your room is. It has an ensuite with a shower."

"A hot shower sounds fantastic." Tori stood and picked up her plate along with Scott's. "Thanks for supper."

He acknowledged her thank-you with a nod. "If you'd like, I'll go with you tomorrow when you pick up Drew for his appointment with Ben at nine."

She caught her automatic "I can handle it by myself" response before it got past her lips. Scott was trying to help, and it was possible Drew would open up to him. He certainly hadn't opened up to her.

"How long do you think the meeting with Ben will last?" Tori had an appointment with Richard Livingston at ten thirty, and she needed time to lay out the questions she wanted to ask.

"No clue."

She'd better move the appointment with Richard to afternoon, especially since she wanted to check out the crime scene. "Do you think we could go by Jenny Tremont's house when we finish? I can get a key from Drew or Zack."

He huffed a resigned sigh. "You're determined, aren't you?"

She grinned.

"It'll depend on whether Ben gives the okay."

She didn't respond as she followed Scott into the kitchen. If Jenny's place was no longer a crime scene, Ben couldn't keep her from searching it. She stretched. "I'm calling it a night. Thanks for making all this happen."

"No problem."

A few minutes later, Tori padded into the ensuite and turned on the shower, choosing the massage setting, and she let the hot water beat the knots out of her neck and shoulders. Thirty minutes later, Tori glanced at her phone as she climbed into the queen-size bed. Eli had texted her.

> Are you okay?

She checked her watch. The time stamp on the text was five minutes ago. Why was he texting her this time of night? She texted him back.

> I'm fine. Why?

No way he could've heard about someone trying to run her off the road.

> You were supposed to call me after you went to your brother's.

> Sorry. I forgot.

> Come on, Tori. How am I supposed to help you if you don't keep me in the loop? Were you still with Scott Sinclair?

She gritted her teeth. Same old Eli. That had been their main problem when they were teenagers—he was too possessive. Tori was too tired to deal with Eli tonight.

> I wasn't aware I asked you to help me. Look, I just got home, and I'm tired. We'll talk tomorrow.

He returned a thumbs-up emoji.

> Tell Erin I asked about her.

She hesitated. Knowing him, he was fishing for her location. She tapped on the same emoji and set her phone on the bedside table. It buzzed again.

> Just be careful. You don't really know Scott Sinclair.

> Good night.

Three dots appeared on her phone.

> I don't want you to get hurt. Scott Sinclair isn't who you think he is.

26

Wdyd?

What did you do? At midnight, a text from TJ Logan popped up on Drew's phone. The sheriff's son and Drew's best friend. He'd been dreading a text from TJ now that he was back home from visiting colleges.

Wym?

What do you mean? Drew wiped his hands on his jeans. He knew what he wanted—information on what happened at Jenny's. His dad probably put him up to it.

Yk. H4u.

You know. Here for you.

Tks.

He needed to talk to someone. But not TJ and not in a text. He thumbed another text.

Ttyl.

Talk to you later.

He trusted TJ, but he and his dad were tight. Anything Drew told him would put his friend in a bad spot, and Drew couldn't see him lying to his dad.

His phone lit up. A call from *his* dad. He hesitated. What if the sheriff had found his hiding place? Maybe that's why TJ had texted—no, the sheriff would be banging on the door if that'd happened. He swiped his phone. "Hello?"

"You want to tell me what you and Jenny talked about that night?"

Drew gripped the phone. It was like he'd stepped into a huge bird net, and it was closing around him. "How did you—"

"The sheriff got Jenny's call logs. You should've already told him about the calls. Drew, you should've told me."

Call logs. He hadn't thought about anyone accessing her calls. "Did you kill her?"

"No!" Blood drained from Drew's head, and he stumbled to the twin bed in his aunt's spare bedroom. Rage flared through him. How could his own dad ask him that?

Suddenly he couldn't stop the question that had badgered him since Friday night. "It was your gun. Did you kill her?"

Dead silence followed. Drew hovered his thumb over the end button.

"I can't believe you would even think that." His dad's voice was hard. "Wait a minute. How do you know my gun was used?"

His heart leaped in his throat. "W-what are you talking about?"

"My gun. Earlier tonight Ben Logan said whoever killed Jenny used it or one like it."

"So you're not denying it."

"I didn't know I had to. I gave her the gun months ago when someone tried to break into her house."

"I didn't really think you killed her." His voice cracked. "Maybe she pulled it on her attacker and it went off . . ." The image of Jenny lying on her back formed. No. Whoever shot her did it at point-blank range.

"Do you know where my gun is?"

Drew couldn't admit he'd taken it. But he had a hard time lying. "How would I know?"

"I don't know, but you better have a better story ready when you talk to Ben Logan in the morning."

"In the morning?" Drew couldn't keep the surprise out of his voice.

"Yep. Tori hasn't called you?"

"I dunno. Had my phone silenced. Wouldn't have known you called if I hadn't been looking at the screen." He opened his call log. Three calls and one voicemail from Tori.

"You better get your act together, son."

"Not sure I know how—you haven't exactly been a great example."

Silence stretched between them again. "Drew . . . look . . . I'm sorry I haven't been here for you since your mom—" His voice cracked. A top popped on a can. "I'm going to do better. I promise."

"Yeah, Dad. Sure. Gotta go." Drew ended the call. He would believe his dad's promises when he stopped drinking. And that wasn't happening.

He should've told the sheriff about the call. What else did Ben Logan know? Drew stood and walked to the window and stared out into the dark night. Was it too late to call Tori?

He checked his phone and saw the voicemail again. Drew clicked on it and listened.

"Drew, Ben Logan wants to interview you in the morning at nine. I've already talked to Erin, and she'll make sure you're ready—I'll be there by eight thirty. That way we'll have time to talk before we leave. And don't worry . . . just tell the truth."

"You better have a better story ready." His dad's words rang in his ears. He didn't know what to do. It was too late to call Tori. And what would he say, anyway?

If he told about the money . . . how much trouble would he be in? Couldn't be much worse than it already was. Ben Logan knew they had talked that night. He was on Ben Logan's suspect list, otherwise he wouldn't want to interview him. Drew figured it'd be more like interrogate him. He bit his lip.

If the sheriff found out about the money, would he think Drew killed her for it?

He lay down on the bed with his street clothes on, unable to stop the thoughts. Drew flipped over on his side, but his mind wouldn't shut off.

Whoever killed Jenny had gotten away with murder, and he didn't know how to change that.

27

Swearing filled the night air. Having a tracker put on Victoria Mitchell's car was worth what it cost, but discovering it parked at Oak Grove wasn't good. That place was a veritable fortress—that was the way Nicolas Sinclair had described it in an interview about the changes he and his wife had made to the grounds of the historical house. An elaborate security system, ten-foot gates for the quarter-mile drive, and an iron fence across the front.

If that data drive ever surfaced . . . Jenny said she sent it to Mitchell. But if Mitchell had it, why hadn't she taken it to the police? Unless the podcaster didn't know she had it. Or maybe Jenny was lying, and Mitchell didn't have it at all. Either way Victoria Mitchell had to be taken out.

What if the data drive was hidden somewhere at Jenny Tremont's? The sheriff had searched the house, but he hadn't been looking for a data drive. Chimes from the courthouse knelled the midnight hour in the quiet stillness. At least there was little chance of running into anyone—Logan Point rolled up its sidewalks at dark.

Probably needed to park on the street behind Jenny's and stay in the shadows—it was only a short distance to her house. So far so good. At the door, the key turned easily. It wasn't breaking in if you had a key, was it? Not sure how to explain it if anyone noticed someone was in the house and called Ben Logan. Just have to stay away from the windows.

It smelled like roses inside the house. Jenny's signature fragrance. That was a little spooky. Which room to search first? Her bedroom.

Jenny was a minimalist, and she had very few books or trinkets sitting around. It didn't take long to figure out the data drive wasn't there. Or in the living room. Or the spare bedroom. Or the hall closet.

Where could she have hidden it?

A light flashed in the window as a car pulled into the drive. Had anyone reported seeing someone inside the house? *Stay calm.* Hard to do when your heart was about to jump out of your chest. The back door . . . was it locked? Or even shut?

The doorknob rattled. Yes, shut and locked. Whoever it was didn't try to enter. Probably one of Ben Logan's deputies checking on the house. *Breathe.* Car lights flashed again as the deputy backed out of the drive. As soon as he was gone, it would be time to get out of here.

Besides, the data drive wasn't here. Either Mitchell had it or the kid. Both had to go—it was too risky to chance the drive showing up.

28

The next morning, sunlight filtered through the sheer curtains, waking Tori seconds before the 7:00 a.m. alarm she'd set went off. It took her a minute to remember she was in a guest bedroom at Oak Grove.

She silenced the alarm and took a deep breath, taking in a familiar smell. *Coffee.* Scott must be up.

Eli's texts. Even though she'd dismissed his implication that Scott wasn't on the up-and-up, Eli had created an element of doubt about Scott. Tori didn't know him, not really.

She massaged the muscles in her neck. Scott *had* jumped right on getting Amy to Logan Point with protection. Was it so he could keep tabs on both of them? Amy knew about as much about Walter Livingston's case as Tori did. And then he'd practically insisted on her staying at Oak Grove last night. It would explain why he'd seemed too good to be true. Were there really men out there like him, who wanted to help without asking for anything in return?

And now she had to go downstairs and pretend nothing had changed, that she completely trusted him. If only Eli hadn't put that sliver of doubt in her mind!

Tori pushed the thoughts away and focused on getting dressed. Just before she stepped out of the ensuite, a quick check of her hair in the antique mirror had her sweeping the tangled mess in a ponytail. Seconds later a strand slipped from the band. Frustrated, she found a bobby pin in her makeup bag and pinned it to her head. Then she applied a light touch of lipstick, surprised there were no dark circles under her eyes.

She descended the stairs, making a mental note to call Richard Livingston and change their appointment before she picked up Drew. Correction. Before she and Scott picked up Drew.

Scott turned as she entered the kitchen. "Good morning. How do you like your eggs?"

Tori pasted on a smile, which wasn't that hard—the man cleaned up nicely with a long-sleeved blue shirt and khaki pants. And he'd already shaved. Her breath quickened. There was something about a freshly shaved man.

But what if Eli was right? Was she letting his good looks and easygoing nature blind her? No, she couldn't go there right now. Maybe she could talk to the sheriff about Scott after their meeting, just to get his opinion of him. "I, ah, usually just eat toast."

"That's not enough. Today you're having bacon and eggs and biscuits."

"Biscuits? Did you make them?"

He laughed. "No, they're whop biscuits."

"What kind?"

"You never heard of whop biscuits? You know, whop the can on the side of the stove and it pops open?"

She groaned. "You're not a dad, but that sounds like a dad joke."

His grin spread. "Actually, it's what my dad said every time he made this breakfast."

"So it is a dad joke."

"Yep." He set a plate of biscuits on the table beside the bacon. "And you never said what kind of eggs—how about scrambled?"

"Sure." If she ate anything other than toast it was usually a protein bar, and at least eggs were high in protein. She eyed the flaky biscuits. They looked pretty tempting.

"Butter is on the table. Eggs are coming right up."

Thirty minutes later she sat back in the chair with a cup of coffee in her hand. "Those eggs were great. What'd you do to them?"

"Added cheese. And water—makes 'em fluffy."

"Where'd you learn to cook?" She sipped the coffee and held up the cup. "And make this? It's not bitter."

"A little salt helps with bitterness. And it was learn to cook or starve when I went to college. Found out I liked it."

"Glad someone does." She rubbed the top of the cup handle. Scott was so easy to be around, but no matter how hard she tried, Tori couldn't get Eli's accusations out of her mind.

"You okay?" Scott asked.

She jumped, sloshing coffee on the table. "Oh, what a mess I made!"

He hopped up, grabbed a handful of paper towels, and mopped up the coffee. "It's all right. I'm the one who usually does something like this."

"I'm so sorry."

"Not a problem." He paused with the wet paper in his hand. "You seem . . . distracted."

"Just worried about Drew." It wasn't a lie if it was partly true, was it? She checked her watch. "I think I'll see if Richard or his secretary are in their office so I can reschedule my appointment with him once we finish with Ben."

He cocked his head. "Do I need to reschedule my rehab?"

"No. I'll be fine." Tori didn't want him to hang around after the meeting. "Ben's office is only two blocks from the Livingston parking lot. No one is going to bother me that close to his office, and you need to keep your appointment." And give her space to get her mind settled.

Tori dialed the office number but no one answered. She would call on the way to Erin's house. She pocketed her phone and turned to Scott. "You don't have to go with me to pick up Drew—I can handle getting him to Ben's office."

He gave her a curious look. "But I want to go with you. Drew is a good kid, and he needs someone in his corner since Zack seems to be MIA."

"You got that right. I hope he shows up this morning."

"Me too, but if he doesn't, I thought . . . if we drive separately, maybe Drew could ride with me. I might get him to open up, maybe even tell me what he was doing in Jenny's neighborhood the night she was murdered."

Since Drew had gone silent on her, it made sense to let Scott try and gain his confidence. "Sounds like a plan."

"I know." Scott winked at her as he grabbed his keys from the counter. "And that way if the meeting goes long, I can leave and make rehab at ten."

She agreed and followed him out the door. Ten minutes later, her heart sank when they pulled into Erin's and her dad's Chevy Blazer was sitting in the drive. Tori hadn't figured on having to deal with him.

When Erin opened the front door, Tori jerked her head toward the drive. "What's he doing here?"

Her sister narrowed her eyes. "Really, Tori? He's here for Drew. Not everything is about you."

Tori brushed past her sister without answering. She didn't want to deal with her dad today. She turned around. "Let it go."

"No. You ought to be glad that Dad wants to support Drew. He spent the night here and he's talking to Drew now." Erin glanced toward the road. "Is Scott Sinclair going with us?"

"Yes."

Erin's eyes narrowed. "You want to explain to me why you spent the night with Scott?"

Leave it to her sister to think the worst of her. A small voice whispered, *Aren't you doing the same thing with Dad?*

Tori brushed the thought away. She probably should've explained to Erin last night, but Tori had been so tired. "I didn't think I had to, but if you have to know, someone tried to run me off the road, and I didn't want to endanger you by coming here." She lifted her chin. "Not that it's any of your business, but I slept in a guest room at Oak Grove."

"Wait, did you say someone tried to—"

Tori hadn't meant to say that, but it was too late now. She nodded. "And it wasn't the first time since I've been home that someone attacked me. I didn't want to tell you because we have enough to deal with in Drew's case."

Her dad appeared in the hall doorway. "Did you say someone tried to harm you? Who was it?"

Tori palmed her hands. "I don't know." She took a deep breath and softened her voice. "Can we discuss it later, when we have more time? Ben Logan said to be at his office at nine, and it's almost that now. Where's Drew?"

"In the den," her dad said and then yelled over his shoulder, "Drew! Let's go."

A few seconds later her nephew shuffled into the living room wearing the same pullover and she assumed the same jeans from yesterday. If there weren't dark circles under his eyes, she'd think he wasn't at all worried about the interview. "Don't you have another shirt and pair of jeans?"

Drew looked down at his clothes. "I'm good. Took a shower, and these clothes aren't dirty."

They would have to do. Richard's and Eli's offer to contact an attorney popped into her mind and she glanced first at Erin, then her dad. "Do we need a lawyer?"

"This is Ben Logan we're dealing with," Erin said. "He's not going to try and twist what Drew says into something that isn't true."

Tori hoped that was true. She checked her watch. Eight minutes before they had to be at Ben's office. At least a person could be anywhere in Logan Point in five minutes, and that left three to park and get inside. "Would you like to ride to town with Scott Sinclair? He's going with us."

"Sure. He's cool."

At least that got a positive reaction from her nephew. He'd probably thought Tori planned to grill him on the drive downtown. She turned to her sister. "You coming?"

Erin shook her head. "I have to make changes to the Livingston proposal and get them to Richard before noon."

Rats. Tori had forgotten to call again to change her appointment. Maybe this meeting wouldn't last long. Then she frowned. "Where is Zack?"

"He's not coming," Erin said, her voice tight. "Said there was an emergency at the warehouse."

"And this isn't an emergency?" she snapped. Zack probably had a hangover.

"He thought we could handle it," her dad said and cleared his throat. "Mind if I ride with you? No need to take more vehicles."

Tori swallowed back the instant "Yes, I mind" that wanted to pop out. Why couldn't she do what Erin advised—get past what happened? But how did you change your heart or get back respect you'd lost years ago? *Baby steps, one at a time.* She sighed and nodded. "Good point."

Her dad opened the door and let Drew and Tori go first, then followed them out. "Nice car," he said, opening the passenger door on her Toyota while Drew climbed into Scott's pickup.

"Thanks." She fastened her seat belt, backed out of Erin's drive, and pulled out behind Scott. "I bought it while I worked full-time at the TV station."

"I never have told you how proud I am of you and everything you've accomplished."

It surprised Tori that his words warmed her heart.

"But then you haven't given me much of a chance to tell you anything," he said.

The void left by her mother's death hit her, a pain so deep she ached. "I wasn't the one who messed up."

"You think I don't live with that every day of my life? I wish it'd been me who died that day, not your mom. Maybe if I hadn't had a hangover when that tire blew—"

"What tire?" She didn't remember anything about a tire blowing.

"That's what caused me to lose control of the car."

Why did she not remember that? Had she needed someone to blame so badly that she purposely blocked it? She hadn't been in Logan Point when it happened, and the funeral and the few days she'd spent here afterward were like a distant nightmare. She'd barely gotten her equilibrium back when Michael was murdered. Tori glanced her dad's way. What if the accident wasn't his fault?

"Dad, uh—"

"Watch that pickup!"

With a horn blaring in her ears, Tori slammed on the brakes, and her car skidded through a stop sign. She barely missed the driver laying down on his horn. He flipped her off and gunned his truck around her. Tori was glad she couldn't hear what he was yelling.

She loosened her death grip on the steering wheel and slumped against the seat. She'd almost killed them both . . . and maybe the driver of the truck. It would have been her fault. Her hands shook as she turned toward her dad, who looked as though he didn't have an ounce of blood in his face. "You okay?"

He swallowed hard and tipped his head. "Yeah. How about you?"

"I don't know yet. I'm sor—"

"We all make mistakes, Tori." He squeezed her hand that was still trembling. "But no one died this time."

She held his gaze and managed a tiny smile. "But they could've," she said softly.

"Don't dwell on the negative. I do it enough for both of us."

"Maybe we can change that."

"We'll see, but we better get to the sheriff's office."

She nodded and put the car in gear. A couple of minutes later, she pulled in beside Scott's pickup and climbed out, her legs still shaky.

"What happened? You were right behind me," Scott said.

"I almost ran a stop sign." He questioned her with his eyes. "We can talk about it later. Right now Ben's waiting for us."

She tapped on the window. "Time to go, Drew."

He climbed out of Scott's truck, moving like an old man with his shoulders slumped. Tori would give anything for him not to go through this. She fell in behind. "You okay?"

His answer was a grunt.

"You haven't done anything wrong. Ben will see that. Just tell the truth."

"Tell the truth."

She barely heard him mutter the words under his breath. "That's all you have to do—the truth is something you can tell over and over."

"I didn't kill Jenny."

"I know that."

He rubbed his face. "But what if Ben Logan doesn't believe me?"

29

Dread radiated off Drew like a black fog as Scott followed him into the building. He'd been about the same age when he was a person of interest in a murder case, and Scott totally got the sagging shoulders and slumped gait as they approached Ben's secretary. He nudged Drew with his elbow. "It's going to be okay," he said, speaking only loud enough for the teen to hear.

"I doubt it," he muttered.

The secretary looked up from her computer. "Y'all go on in—Ben's waiting for you."

"Thanks," Tori said.

Ben met them at the door. "Right on time," he said. "Come on in and have a seat."

Drew held back, and he flinched as Scott put his hand on his shoulder. "Go ahead. I promise, it's going to be okay."

Scott probably shouldn't have promised that, but he believed the boy was innocent. He followed them into the spacious room and glanced around. Ben had brought in several straight-back chairs, probably expecting most of the family to come.

It angered Scott that Zack wasn't here, and he wondered how much beer the boy's dad drank after they left him last night. Even if he had a hangover and no matter how busy he was at the factory, he should've been here to give his boy moral support.

"Have you talked to a lawyer?" Ben asked.

"Drew is doing the right thing and coming here to talk to you, so I hope we won't need one." Edward Mitchell leaned forward. "My grandson's done nothing wrong. You know him, Ben. He and your son are best friends."

The look on Ben's face said he'd rather be doing anything other than questioning Drew. "I know, but I have a job to do. Jenny Tremont is dead, and I think Drew knows something."

"Are you going to read him his rights?" Tori asked.

"Drew isn't under arrest, and he's free to leave anytime."

"Then we'll hold off on hiring an attorney, but we can ask for one at any time, right?" her dad asked.

The sheriff nodded and turned to the boy. "I do need to ask you some questions, though."

"I didn't kill Jenny."

"Okay. Why don't you tell me what you were doing near her house about the time she died?"

Drew licked his lips. "You got any water?"

"Sure." The sheriff stood and walked to a small refrigerator in his office and returned with a bottle of water.

Drew uncapped it, taking his time. After he took a long draw, he recapped the bottle. "What'd you ask me?"

Ben pursed his lips as his gaze drew a bead on the teen. Drew shifted in his chair. "I remember now . . . I-I don't know . . . I couldn't sleep. I've had trouble sleeping ever since Mom died. I drove around for a while, then I parked my truck and walked. I wasn't paying any attention to where I was."

"You didn't know Jenny had been murdered when the car almost hit you?"

Drew ducked his head and mumbled something, making Scott wince. Wrong way to look believable.

Ben leaned forward, his hands resting on his desk. "Sorry, I didn't quite catch what you said."

The boy raised his head. "I got scared when I heard the sirens and started running."

"You weren't curious about where they were going?"

Drew lifted his chin. "When you're my age and out that late, sirens mean trouble, and I didn't want any trouble."

"Okay," Ben said, drawing out the word. "Tell me about Jenny Tremont. I understand you hung out at her house sometimes."

The boy chewed his bottom lip, then his shoulders lifted in a careless teen shrug. "She was my mom's friend. Helped take care of her when she had cancer."

"But that doesn't tell me why you liked her."

He swallowed hard. "'Cause she was a good person. She listened to me. And believe it or not, I liked her because she didn't cut me any slack."

His earnest gaze tugged at Scott's heart. The boy needed a friend. No, he needed a father to step up to the plate. Couldn't Zack see what he was doing to his kid?

Ben nodded, encouraging Drew to continue. When he didn't, the sheriff said, "Do you know anyone who wanted her dead?"

"No!"

Ben leveled his gaze at Drew. "You sure?"

The too-quick answer had given him away. The boy knew something, maybe not the person, but *something*.

"I promise, if I knew who killed Jenny, I'd tell you . . . or kill them myself."

"Don't take the law into your own hands, son. Is there anything you can think of that might help us find this person?"

Drew shook his head. "I've told you all I can."

Ben stared thoughtfully at his notes, then he looked up. "Jenny's call records show she phoned you the night she died and talked twenty-two seconds. A few minutes later you called her back and that call lasted only six seconds."

Ben stood and walked around his desk, then sat on the corner across from Drew. "What did you talk about?"

"She, uh, called me sometimes when she couldn't sleep."

"And that's what was wrong that night?"

Drew stared unblinking at Ben. "She—she . . ." He shook his head. "I'm sorry. I don't remember. Everything about that night is messed up in my head. I've told you all I can."

Which meant there was something he couldn't tell? Scott was pretty sure the sheriff had the same thought.

Ben didn't respond right away, then he blew out a breath and stood. "All right, you can go. If you happen to remember something new, call me." Everyone else stood. "Tori, can you stay behind?"

"Sure." She glanced at her dad and nephew before turning to Scott. "Do you have time to run them to Erin's house before your rehab session?"

Scott checked his watch. He had a good fifteen minutes. "You bet."

"You sure?" she asked.

"Wouldn't have agreed if I wasn't. Call me before you head out."

"I will, but I don't think anyone will try anything in the daylight."

"You never know." He turned and shook hands with Ben. "Talk to you later."

Drew and his grandfather followed Scott to his pickup. "I'll ride in the back seat," Edward said.

But Drew was already crawling in the back on the driver side. Scott backed out of the parking space and pointed his truck toward Erin's house.

"Nice wheels," Edward said.

"Thanks." He glanced in the rearview mirror. Drew had his head turned, his gaze glued to the window.

Scott and Edward made small talk on the short drive. He barely had the truck put in park when Drew hopped out. Scott rolled down his window. "Wait up a sec."

The teenager stiffened, but he stopped and turned around. "Yeah?"

"If you ever need someone to talk to, call me."

"Sure." He started to turn around.

"You don't have my number."

The teen's lip twitched, and Scott held out his hand. "Give me your phone, and I'll put it in."

For a second he didn't think Drew would give it to him, but then he held it out. Scott punched his number into Drew's contacts and added it to the boy's favorites. Then he looked up. "Okay if I call my phone? That way I'll have your number."

"Sure." His face said he didn't feel he had much choice.

Once Scott's phone rang, he added Drew's number to his contacts. "Don't forget, anytime you need someone to talk to, call me. I'm a good listener."

For a second, Scott thought the teenager was going to say something, then he nodded.

"If I ever do, I'll call you."

Edward came around to the driver's side as Drew walked toward Erin's house.

"He admires you—thinks you're cool with your tattoos," Edward said. "Who knows, maybe he'll reach out to you."

"I'll text him soon and see if he wants to hang out, maybe grab a bite to eat. Food always makes it easier to talk."

"I hope he agrees—he needs someone to listen to him. I've tried, but he thinks I'm out of touch with what's going on in his world. So, thanks for wanting to help," he said and walked to his car.

Maybe if Scott told Drew more of his background, of what had happened to him when he was Drew's age, he could gain his trust. Because it was going to take a lot of trust before the boy told Scott what he was hiding. He climbed out of his pickup.

"Drew," Scott called before the teenager reached Erin's front door. He turned around and waited for Scott to approach him.

"Yeah?"

"I wondered . . . after I finish with rehab, I'm planning on going fly fishing. You ever fly fish?"

Interest sparked in his eyes. "A little."

"Maybe you'd like to give it a try again?"

Drew's interest turned to suspicion. "Why?"

"What do you mean, why?"

"You hardly know me, so why would you ask me to do something with you?"

"I know you better than you think. We do go to church together, and I help out with the youth group."

Drew crossed his arms. He wasn't buying. Scott tried again. "I've watched you with the other kids—you and TJ are friends . . . and I know how you cared about Jenny. She was my friend too, you know. But, hey, if you don't want to go, that's fine."

The teenager dropped his gaze. Indecision warred in his face. Scott was about to give up when Drew looked up. "Okay, I'll go with you on the condition you don't grill me."

Scott held his hand up in the Scout's salute. "I promise I won't bring up Jenny's name unless you do."

"You were a Scout?"

What was it with everyone having trouble believing he could've been a Boy Scout? "Cub Scout. Does that count?"

Drew laughed, a sound Scott hadn't heard from him lately. "I kind of find that hard to believe too."

"Why?"

"Somebody said you were in a gang . . . that you made someone mad and they shot you."

Ahh. He'd seen the looks from people, even at church, and he could understand to a point. He had tattoos, and he didn't talk about his past. When people didn't know the truth, they usually made up something that fit their suspicions.

"Is that what you believe?"

Drew considered his question, then shrugged. "Maybe. Did you get shot?"

He had to tread lightly here. He didn't want to lie to the boy, but the truth could get Scott killed if word got out he was in Logan Point. "That part was true."

"Who'd you make mad?"

"That's the part I don't want to talk about." The timer on his watch dinged. "I have to get to rehab. You want me to swing back by here and pick you up? I have an extra fly rod, and I'll be happy to show you how to use it."

"As long as you stick to our agreement not to grill me."

"Deal. I'll be back in an hour."

30

Tori turned to Ben Logan after the door closed behind Scott, Drew, and her dad. The sheriff made an imposing figure as he stood behind the desk, his feet planted and his hand resting on his gun. "So, what did you want to talk to me about?" Tori asked.

Ben crossed his arms. "I just want to make sure you don't get involved in Jenny Tremont's case."

"I'm not making any promises. My nephew's reputation is at stake here, and I can't have people whispering that maybe he killed her when we both know he didn't."

"Don't make me arrest you for obstruction of justice."

She held up her hands. "I promise, I'm not going to interfere with your investigation. I have one of my own I'm working on."

"The Prescott case?" He sat in his chair and motioned for her to sit as well.

"That case is old news." Tori sat as he indicated but on the edge of the chair. She didn't have much time before her appointment with Richard Livingston since she hadn't been able to change it. Plus, she hadn't written out the questions she wanted to ask. Thankfully the office was within a three-minute walk of Ben's office. She'd have to use that time to figure out her strategy.

"It's actually the Walter Livingston case," she said. "And since his murder happened in Memphis, it won't affect you at all."

Ben leveled a serious gaze at her "Make sure that's the one you focus on."

"Of course." As long as he didn't arrest Drew or her brother. Tori tilted her head. "But I do wonder if you have an opinion on who killed him?"

"Afraid I can't help you there. I was just a kid when that happened. My dad was sheriff, but he's been gone five years now." He rubbed his jaw. "Although my mom might remember something about it. Stop by and see her—she'd love that."

"I'll try." Tori had always liked his mother, Marissa, but as a kid, she'd been terrified of his dad. He always seemed so stern.

Ben cleared his throat. "You might want to be careful being out alone. Were you able to identify the vehicle that bumped you? Or who was driving?"

"Afraid not. Even with a moon, it was too dark, and if it was the guy who shot at us, the dark tint on his truck would've hidden him. I do believe it was a truck, though."

"I'll turn your question on you—do you have an opinion on who's after you?"

She thought a minute then blew a breath through her lips. "I wish I had just one opinion."

"Care to lay them out?"

She checked her watch and made a decision. "I'd rather ask you about Scott."

"Scott?" The hint of a frown crossed his face. "What about him?"

She picked at a hangnail on her thumb. "I heard he got into some trouble with the law. Is that true?"

"Have you asked him?"

Tori blinked. He wasn't going to tell her? "Not yet."

"Then I suggest you do."

"You're saying I can trust him?"

"Depends on what you're trusting him with."

He was talking in riddles.

"I will say, Scott is very good at what he does. Now, back to my question. Who might be after you?"

"I'll have to make it fast since I'm meeting Richard Livingston in"—she checked her watch—"ten minutes. At least two people—Calvin Russell, whoever killed Walter Livingston, and anyone else I might've ticked off."

"Russell is the obvious choice. He's in the area based on his credit card use, and from what the Knoxville detective said, he isn't happy with you."

"Yeah, but he has a sister in Memphis, so he could be in the area legitimately. And I don't think he knows where I'm from. I've never talked about it, even when I discussed Huey Prescott's case, and I don't see him having the savvy to do the research."

"I wouldn't underestimate him—he's avoided being questioned since the fire. As for the people you may have made mad, does any particular case come to mind?"

She made a whistling sound as she blew out a breath through her mouth. "Two maybe . . . this past year I conducted an investigation into a drugstore selling outdated drugs, and there was a case involving a slumlord who refused to bring his apartment building up to code—there was a fire, but thankfully no one died. Both of them have their hands full right now dealing with prosecutors, so I don't see them coming after me. As for Walter Livingston's case, we don't know who we're dealing with—"

"But if Walter's killer lives in Logan Point, he or she knows you and what kind of car you drive."

"Yeah." She checked her watch again. It was something to think about. "I need to leave for my appointment."

"How are you getting there?"

"I thought I'd walk—it's just a couple of minutes away." That way she could clear her mind.

"You're kidding, right?" Ben shook his head and stood. "You're not. Come on, I'll drop you off, and I expect you to call when you're finished."

"I have my own car—I can drive myself."

"I'll feel better if I take you."

She started to protest but then realized he was right—after all, they were just discussing who wanted her out of the picture. "Thanks. I'm not used to depending on others—I didn't get that gene, and I'm not sure how long it'll take me to adjust."

Tori followed Ben to his SUV and climbed in the front seat. The driver's side almost looked like the cockpit of an airplane. "Nice setup. Why did you use a paper notebook last night when you have that electronic one?"

He laughed. "You can teach an old dog new tricks but you can't make him use them. I'm old school—a pen and paper are much easier to carry around. And I remember what I write with a pen more than what I type."

"I outline my podcasts by hand," Tori said. "Then put them into the computer while I can still read what I wrote."

"I know exactly what you mean. I have to enter my notes into the computer ASAP." He pulled into the Livingston parking lot.

A white Escalade was parked in the spot next to the door. Probably Richard's, or it could be Stephanie's. "Thanks for the ride, but really, I would've been fine walking."

"Maybe. Be sure to call when you're ready to go back for your car."

She made a face at him. "Okay."

After Tori got out of the vehicle and approached the door, she waved at Ben, who still idled in the parking lot. He nodded, and the SUV rolled toward the exit. It surprised her how comforting his concern was.

After taking a minute to compose herself, she stepped into the role of interviewer. Most of the time she had a list of questions in her head or on her phone, but so much had been going on, she hadn't had time to put anything together. Plus, she wanted information on two fronts—the recent Jenny Tremont murder and Walter Livingston's from years ago.

Tori squared her shoulders and entered the building through

the glass double doors. She'd worked here as a file clerk the last two summers of high school, and if she remembered correctly, Richard's office was down the hallway on the right. She rounded the corner and smiled when a middle-aged woman looked up.

"May I help you?"

"Mrs. Curtis?"

"Yes?" She peered over a pair of black-rimmed glasses.

Tori couldn't believe Donna Curtis was still here as Richard's office manager. She'd seemed ancient when she trained Tori, which made her want to chuckle—the woman was probably early fifties, which was no longer ancient to Tori.

"I have an appointment with Mr. Livingston." It didn't occur to Tori to refer to him as Richard, not in talking to Mrs. Curtis.

"And you are?" The secretary removed the glasses, pulling a strand of salt-and-pepper hair from her low bun. It was the style she'd worn ever since Tori had known her. She finger-combed the strand back in place while she waited for Tori to answer.

"Victoria Mitchell."

Mrs. Curtis slipped the glasses back on and squinted, then her eyes widened. "Tori! I hardly recognize you. And you say you have an appointment with Richard?"

"At ten thirty." She didn't know if she was more shocked that Mrs. Curtis had called him Richard or that she didn't know about the appointment.

"That poses a problem—he just left to meet the mayor for a cup of coffee." The secretary frowned. "You're sure he knows you're coming?"

At this point Tori wasn't sure of anything. "We talked last night at my sister's house."

Donna tapped her cheek. "Could Valerie Livingston help you? She's part owner of the company."

Tori had no intention of speaking to Valerie. "My appointment is with Richard."

"Hold on." She took out her cell and sent a text. Seconds later there was a return message and she looked up. "Oh, I'm sorry. He forgot and will return immediately."

"No, tell him to take his time. I'll wait—I have something I can work on until he returns."

"Have a seat and let me text him your message—I think he had a matter he wanted to discuss with the mayor." A minute later, the secretary turned to her, beaming. "He asked if you were all right with waiting thirty minutes?"

"Of course." There were a lot of things she'd rather do with the next thirty minutes than to cool her heels in the waiting area. However, she really did want to find out what he could tell her about Jenny . . . and maybe about his brother. If she could pin him down today, it would go a long way with her research. Tori took out her phone to check her email, but before she could open the account, Mrs. Curtis cleared her throat.

"How did you know Huey Prescott wasn't guilty of killing Walter?"

Tori thought a minute. "There were several reasons. Have you listened to my podcast, Mrs. Curtis?"

"Some of them." She smiled. "A lot of folks around Logan Point listen in—you're quite the celebrity here. I caught Saturday's podcast, and please, call me Donna."

Wow. She never thought Mrs. Curtis would ever ask her to call her by her given name or that she listened to her podcasts. "You should check out some of the older podcasts. You can tell by the titles what the subject is."

"I'll do that."

Tori hesitated. "Maybe you can help me . . . if you listened to last week's podcast, then you know I'm digging into Walter Livingston's death. How well did you know him?"

She leaned away from Tori. "Walter was my boss, but he was

also my friend. Such a good man. Terrible thing that happened to him." Donna pulled a tissue from a box and dabbed her eyes.

Tori let the silence stretch while the secretary composed herself. "Were you romantically—"

"Good heavens, no," she said, her eyes wide. "I was already married to Mr. Curtis, and Walter was a gentleman. He wouldn't have gotten involved with a married woman."

"I gather he never married."

"No. He . . ." She checked the hallway before she leaned toward Tori and lowered her voice. "The woman he loved married someone else."

"Really?" Her research had never uncovered that little gem. "Was she someone local?"

Footsteps sounded in the hallway, and Donna's face flushed. She shook her head. "Forget I said that—I shouldn't have . . ."

Tori turned as Richard Livingston approached the desk.

"You made it back sooner than you thought." Donna smiled brightly. She handed him a Post-it note. "That's the only message you have except one from Stephanie, cancelling your lunch date again."

Tori caught the note of . . . satisfaction . . . or was it I-told-you-so in the secretary's voice.

Richard frowned. "Did she say why?"

"No."

He gave a brusque nod and motioned for Tori to follow him. At the door, he turned back to his secretary. "What time is your lunch break?"

"I, ah, haven't decided. Eleven thirty, probably."

"Well, let me know so I can get someone to cover the desk."

"Oh, sure."

Tori wondered if Richard caught the disappointment in his secretary's voice. She glanced at him. No. He was totally obtuse to the fact Donna, married or not, was in love with her boss.

Maybe Donna could use a sympathetic ear.

31

Tori followed Richard into his spacious office and glanced around. A soothing blue color had replaced the drab gray walls she remembered, and plantation blinds covered the windows instead of heavy wine-colored drapes. She eyed the bold abstract painting over the sofa—that was new as well, since she definitely would've remembered it.

Tori turned to him. "You've redecorated."

Richard flicked his gaze around the room and shrugged. "Stephanie said it needed updating." He nodded toward the colorful abstract. "I haven't gotten used to *that* yet."

Tori tilted her head, studying the painting. "I like it."

He sat behind his desk that hadn't changed. "You would. You're young," Richard said dryly and motioned for her to have a seat.

She sat in the chair across from him. It didn't take a detective to figure out all might not be well in paradise. Tori hoped she was wrong. She'd liked Stephanie in spite of her initial misgivings that she might be interested in Richard for his money.

Her gaze went to the photos on the wall behind him. Large, beautifully framed individual portraits of Richard and his brother, Walter. Both of them handsome men, and judging by their age and clothing, the photos must have been taken several years before Walter was killed.

"I see you still have those." She nodded toward the portraits.

He followed her gaze. "Again, Stephanie. She thought we ought to keep them."

Richard's voice was flat, unemotional. Puzzling. He'd asked her here to discuss the case, but maybe he'd had second thoughts. With some people, Tori danced around a subject before asking the hard questions. She didn't think that would work with Richard Livingston. "What—"

"Where—"

She should've waited another few seconds. "You go first."

"Okay." He leaned forward and rested his hands on the desk, interlocking his fingers. "Where do you stand on the Prescott case?"

"Are you talking about your brother's case? Because the Prescott case is solved. He did not kill your brother and is a free man trying to restart his life. Right now he's trying to find his daughter, who would be in her late thirties now."

He slowly nodded. "I heard the interview. His ex-wife won't reveal the daughter's location?"

"She's dead. Cancer."

A small wince crossed his face. Richard leaned back in his leather chair and steepled his fingers. "Are you 100 percent sure he didn't kill my brother?"

"Yes. And so is the judicial system."

He sighed and looked out the window before turning back to her. "Then the Memphis police will be looking for whoever killed him. Hopefully."

She nodded. "And I plan to help find him . . . or her, in any way I can."

His brow lowered. "You think it could be a woman?"

"Why not? Was your brother involved with anyone at the time of his death?"

"No."

"You seem sure of that."

He shrugged. "I knew my brother."

"Do you know if he had enemies?"

"Of course he did. You don't get to where we were in the business world without making enemies, but the police never followed up that angle."

"No, they thought they had their man in Huey Prescott after a tip to their hotline accused him of the murder."

"Well, his prints *were* found in my brother's condo, and Prescott had prior drug arrests—which didn't do him any good at the trial."

Both had been a problem—Prescott didn't remember ever being in the condo. But he didn't remember a lot of things from that time due to the drugs.

Another problem had been a burglary ring working Walter's neighborhood just prior to his death. Prescott had admitted to being involved in the ring so it was possible he'd broken into Walter's condo.

"The police never looked at anyone else," she said, "mainly because they believed Prescott did it even though he didn't have gunshot residue on his hands or clothes."

"It was days later when he was arrested for Walter's death. The residue would've been long gone."

It was clear Richard didn't believe in Prescott's innocence. She leaned forward. "He didn't do it."

"Yeah, so you say."

"Why do you doubt it?"

"Because if he didn't do it, the killer is still out there."

She studied Richard. His matter-of-fact attitude about his brother's death could be because of the twenty-two years since it happened. "Tell me about your brother. My research shows he was instrumental in starting the Livingston Oil Corporation."

Richard's lip twitched. "Yeah, he put the up-front money in, but it was my hard work and long hours that kept us afloat. I'm the one who ran the oil company and dealt with the wholesalers. He just collected deposits from the laundromats and convenience stores until Val took part of the load. Walter was the pretty face of the business."

Maybe Richard harbored a little jealousy?

"Sorry." He waved his hand in a dismissive gesture. "That sounded petty, but he would've been the first to tell you he didn't like to roll up his sleeves and do the hard work—he was into wearing expensive suits and driving BMWs. My brother liked to project the image of a successful businessman with the Midas touch."

Tori rarely remembered Richard in anything other than the style he wore today—stone chinos paired with a long-sleeve shirt with the sleeves pushed up almost to his elbows. He wore the younger style well. Again, she had the impression he worked out—no belly, and while she couldn't see his biceps, judging from his broad shoulders, he had decent muscles.

His wry chuckle drew her attention. "What?"

"He would hate what I'm wearing. Would say I'm dressing too young, but in today's business world, youth sells."

Richard had caught her checking him out, and there was that slight undertone of sibling rivalry again. "Do you have any opinions on who might have killed your brother?"

"Other than Prescott? That question has kept me awake at night since the state indicated they planned to release him." He leveled his gaze at her. "You've studied the case. Who do you think did it?"

She sat back in the chair. "Someone who had a lot to gain from his death."

"I'm sure you already know I gained control of the company at his death, but it wasn't me."

"Did anyone else gain from his death?"

"My ex-wife, Eli's mother."

"Valerie?" Tori had known her all her life. "I don't see her killing Walter. She's too . . ."

"Refined?" He snorted. "That's what most people think. I happen to know a different side of her—she'll do *whatever* it takes to get what she wants."

That, Tori knew from experience, but she still didn't see her shooting Walter. "I suppose. I've heard you really never know someone until you share an inheritance with them."

"Or a divorce." Bitterness oozed from his voice.

"How did Valerie gain from Walter's death?"

"He left her 20 percent of his shares."

"But you retained control of the company?" Tori made a mental note to set up an appointment with Valerie.

"Yes. And to change the subject . . . how did Drew's interview with Sheriff Logan go?"

"You knew—"

"You should know not much happens around here that I don't know about."

"The meeting was brief—Ben didn't arrest him." Although Tori didn't believe Ben bought Drew's story any more than she had. Tori sighed. "I don't see how anyone could think Drew would kill Jenny. He loved her like a mother."

"Jenny was special," he said.

"Exactly how long had she worked for you?"

"Ben asked me that the other day, and I had Donna look it up. In June it would've been eight years."

"Do you mind if I take notes?"

"Not at all."

Tori could easily remember what Richard had told her about Walter, but she wanted to make sure she took everything down that he said about Jenny. She took a notepad from her purse. Like Ben, she was old school, mostly because people were suspicious of tablets—they were afraid you were recording them. "Everyone liked her?"

He nodded. "She was a great asset, although this past year, she was preoccupied with something."

"Did you ask her about it?"

"No. She was a very private person, and it didn't affect her job performance. I learned a long time ago, if it's not broke, don't fix it."

"Was she close to anyone here?"

He thought a minute. "Donna, maybe . . . and Valerie."

She jotted the names down, pausing on Valerie's name, surprised that Jenny had counted her a friend. Tori had never known Valerie to befriend anyone, but maybe she'd changed in the last few years. "What exactly was Jenny's job?"

"Bookkeeper—she had an accounting degree and tallied the receipts for the laundromats and convenience stores against the deposits. But she did more than that. She kept us straight with the government, both state and federal—the woman was brilliant."

"Where was her office?"

"Down the hall in Walter's old office."

Immediately Tori's mind went to the dark side. What if Jenny had discovered something in Walter's office that pointed to his killer? "Could I take a look?"

He questioned her with his eyes. "The police went over the room already. There's nothing to find."

"I figured they had, but I'd still like to see it—a person's space tells a lot about them. I'd like to know what Jenny thought was important. In fact, I'd like to see her house too."

"I can't help you with the house, but if you want to see her office, Donna will show you where it is." He punched in a number on his phone and asked his secretary to join them.

Donna entered the room seconds after he hung up. "Yes, sir?" Richard explained what Tori wanted. "Right now?"

"Unless you have something else you need to do," Tori said.

"No, it's fine." Donna checked her watch. "I have plenty of time before lunch."

"Thank you." Tori smiled at her. Earlier, the secretary had been about to tell her something when Richard arrived. If she invited Donna to have lunch with her, perhaps she could ferret out whatever it was. She started to invite her but something held Tori back. No, she would wait until they were alone.

She stood and held out her hand to Richard. "Thank you for seeing me today. Perhaps I can drop in again, maybe discuss what I learn, if I learn anything?"

He stood, and his somber gaze held hers, then he took her hand. "Prescott's release blindsided me, but I definitely want to stay in the loop."

"Of course." Her heart faltered, and she hoped it didn't show in her face. Something about the way Richard spoke . . .

Keep your friends close but your enemies closer. The quote from Michael Corleone in *The Godfather* rang in her mind. But why?

32

At eleven, Scott bypassed his usual after-rehab venti caramel at Two Cups and drove to Erin's house. Even before he'd asked Drew to go with him, he'd decided not to stop by the coffee shop. Routine was what often blew your cover.

Instead he stopped at a convenience store and picked up a couple of sandwiches, a few snacks, and drinks even though he had his doubts that Drew would actually go until he pulled into Erin's driveway. The teenager was waiting on the steps. He jogged to his truck and hopped in the passenger seat.

"What kind of rehab are you doing?" he asked before Scott even got out a hello.

Deflect and divert. Great tactics if you were afraid someone was going to ask questions you didn't want to answer—the boy might have a career in undercover work. Scott flexed his right hand. "Trying to regain the use of my hand again."

"Why'd someone shoot you?"

Scott pulled out of Erin's drive and took a left. In undercover work, sharing personal information was one way of gaining a target's confidence, even when the personal information wasn't true. Maybe a half-truth would work here. "I got involved with the wrong people, and they thought I crossed them."

"Did you?"

"Depends on how you look at it."

"What does that even mean?"

"Sometimes people ask you to do something that goes against what you believe in, and you have to decide if you're going along with them. Either way there can be bad consequences."

"That's the truth."

Scott had hit a nerve, but there was a time to talk and a time to be quiet, and this was a time to let silence settle between them. The silence lasted all the way to the lake. Scott parked and opened his door. "We have to walk from here."

They climbed out of his truck, and he handed Drew the tackle box. "I'll carry the rods."

Drew glanced around the back of the truck. "Don't we need waders?"

"Nope. I'm practicing my hand-eye coordination, and you're just learning. Where we're going there aren't any trees for your line to get snagged on. And be careful with the tackle box—it has our water in it . . . and lunch."

Scott led Drew around the edge of the lake until they reached a bank of large angular rocks that controlled erosion. It was a good hundred yards from where he'd been casting yesterday. "Like I said, nothing here to get your fly caught on . . . unless you hook a rock."

He spent the next half hour taking Drew through the basics of fly fishing and managing the line. "You sure you haven't done this before?"

"A couple of times . . . TJ likes to fly fish, and he tried to show me."

"You learned more than you thought," Scott said. That or the boy was a natural. "Are you two *good* friends?"

"He's my best friend. TJ doesn't act like the sheriff's son at all." Drew's face turned beet-red. "I mean, he doesn't do bad stuff, he just . . ."

"He's a regular guy?"

"Yeah!" Relief showed in his face.

"Well, I'm glad you have a good friend, someone to hang out with and talk to." Scott pointed to a log about forty feet from shore. "See if you can land your fly in front of the log."

Drew's fly overshot the log. Scott took his time, concentrating on where he wanted to put the fly before casting. When it landed way right, he ground his teeth. A baby could've done better than that. How long was it going to take him to gain accuracy with his left hand?

"Dude, you missed it by a mile. Have you tried using your right hand?"

"No." Scott rolled his shoulders, trying to release tension. "The muscles in my right shoulder and my hand don't work right, and it looks like they never will. The physical therapist thought fly fishing with my left hand would be a good way to gain accuracy."

"Don't think it's working."

"Tell me about it," he muttered. "How about a water break?"

"Sounds good—it's getting warm here."

Thankfully the sun ducked behind a cloud, and they found a comfortable spot on the rocks. He handed the teenager a bottled water and a pack of cheese and crackers. Scott leaned his elbow on one of the flat rocks as a boat raced by, sending ripples to the shore in its wake.

"My brother Nick and I used to go fishing when I was a lot younger than you are."

"He the one who taught you how to fly fish?"

"Yeah." Scott broke open the cellophane and took out a cracker, and Drew followed suit.

"He and his first wife, Angie, raised me until I got too smart for my own good." Scott tossed a cracker to a gull that had landed near him. He told Drew about the trouble he'd landed in when he was a teenager and ended it by saying, "By the time I was your age, I thought I didn't need anybody, including God. That I could handle anything that came my way. And the alcohol numbed the pain for a while, but it always came back."

"That sounds like my dad."

"Yeah. Losing your mom knocked him for a loop. Right now he's treading water, trying to keep from going under."

"That's the way I feel. Any second now, I think I'm going to drown."

"I hope you don't follow his path."

Drew grunted. "Tried it and all it did for me was to make me sick. Jenny about read me the riot act."

Scott chuckled. "I can see her doing that. I wish it'd made me sick—would've saved me a lot of grief."

Drew uncapped his water and chugged it. "Jenny kept me on the straight and narrow after my mom died. She was always there for me. And now . . . all I want to do is catch whoever killed her."

The way he said it sent a chill through Scott. "That's understandable, but if you know something that will help Ben Logan, you need to tell him."

Drew froze, then he glared at Scott. "You said we wouldn't talk about Jenny."

"I don't think I brought her name up." Scott eyed him. "But if you want to talk about her, I'm here to listen."

Silence answered him as Drew stared toward the lake. The boy was scared, and he didn't trust Scott. He had to change that. "You know why I got shot?"

The boy's head shot up. "You said you made someone mad."

"That's just part of it." Scott leveled his gaze at Drew. "This is just between you and me—I'm an undercover FBI agent, or I was until I got hurt."

Drew's eyes widened. "You're a—"

"Yep. I had infiltrated a motorcycle gang out West that was involved in drugs, and the operation went south when a new member from South Carolina recognized me. They meant to kill me, but my team got there in time. God and my team are the reason I'm here today."

Scott didn't share the part about Andy getting killed. Thinking about it all the time was hard enough, talking about it even harder.

Drew cocked his head at Scott. "I get how your team helped, but how does God figure in it?"

Scott smiled. "My team just 'happened' to be at the right place at the right time . . ." He touched where the bullet entered his body. "And the bullet missed an artery by millimeters."

"Yeah, but he let you get shot."

Drew was looking for answers. Scott floated a quick prayer before he nodded.

"Like he let your mom get cancer," he said quietly.

The boy nodded.

"So why did I survive but your mom didn't? Why did she have to die so young and leave you behind?" The boy didn't have to ask the question—it was on his face. Plus Scott had the same question for months after Andy died. "I don't know. It's the same question I ask when people I care about die. When my mom died, I was so angry at God I yelled at him."

"You?"

"A wise woman told me that I might as well since he already knows," Scott said with a smile. "After that, I learned that this life isn't the end, there's a life beyond what we know, and your mom is experiencing that life now. And God's watching over both of us."

"What about your arm—what if it doesn't get better?"

He nodded at the fly rod. "I'm working on shooting proficiently with my left hand."

Drew jutted his chin. "Why doesn't he just heal you? What if you never learn how to use your left hand? And your right one doesn't get stronger?"

"Then he has another plan for me, even better than the one I envision."

The teenager looked doubtful.

"God is big enough to handle anything, even our disappointments. Besides, even though I'm injured, I'm still pretty good at my job." Scott held Drew's gaze. "Good enough to keep you safe if you want to talk about Jenny."

33

Drew's stomach twisted in a knot. Could Scott really keep him safe? Tori too? And maybe find the person who killed Jenny? Drew picked up a rock and tossed it toward the water. "How well did you know Jenny?"

Scott leaned back on the rock. "Probably as well as I know anyone at church. I admired her and always figured she was one of those what-you-see-is-what-you-get people."

"Yeah. Jenny was always straightforward, and she never put on airs. I don't know what I would've done without her when Mom died. Last week she came over to the house and made sure I had clean clothes. Dad too." Drew picked up another rock and ran his thumb over the rough surface. "She changed this last year, but I don't think anyone else noticed it."

"What do you mean?"

"Something seemed to be bothering her, but she wouldn't tell me what it was. Said it was an adult thing." He chewed his lip. "She called me that night. Asked me to bring something to her."

"Bring what?"

Drew turned and stared out toward the water. There were no boats out there now, and the lake was flat, but he knew beneath the placid waters the current could grab you and pull you under.

"Drew?"

"She'd put something in a secret place I showed her and wanted me to bring it to her. The thing is . . . When I looked where she told me, there was all this money. Bundles of hundred dollar bills."

"What?" Scott sat up straight. "Are you sure?"

"I know what money looks like."

"Sorry, it's just I don't understand."

"You and me both." He turned to face Scott. "Where'd she get it? I can't believe she did anything illegal," he said, his voice cracking.

"That's what you were doing in her neighborhood, taking the money to her?"

Drew nodded. "We were supposed to meet at this house she'd been taking care of, and I was going to ask where she got it, but she never came. So I walked to her house."

"Was she dead when you got there?"

"Yeah," he whispered. Drew closed his eyes, remembering the scene, and shuddered. "I never got a chance to ask her."

He felt Scott's hand on his shoulder. "I'm sorry. That was a bad thing for you to go through. Why didn't you tell Ben Logan?"

Because Ben would ask if he found his dad's gun at the house, and he would've known Drew was lying if he said no. His heart raced. "I couldn't."

"I don't understand."

"I-I just can't." He looked at Scott. "What if Jenny was killed because of the money? They might kill me and my family."

"Not if you turn it in. Where is it?"

"In a safe place." He had to move the gun before he told anyone where he'd hidden it.

"Drew, you need to—"

He froze, knowing what Scott was about to say. "No, you promised you wouldn't tell anyone."

"You know Tori is investigating Jenny's shooting because she's afraid you might be arrested. What if she stumbled into this person and—"

"But I don't know who it is." He wished he hadn't told Scott anything. Drew pressed his thumb against the sharp edge of the rock, drawing blood. What if Tori crossed paths with whoever Jenny got the money from? The person might hurt her . . . or worse.

"Maybe Tori and I can work together and solve this."

Drew wished he could believe Scott, that they could solve it. But Jenny's murderer had killed once . . . it wouldn't bother them to kill again.

34

Tori followed Donna from her boss's office down another hallway and waited while the secretary unlocked the first door on the right.

"The police went over the office—took them two days, so I don't think you'll find anything new."

"I mostly want to get a feel for Jenny."

"She was a good person." Donna checked her watch. "Well, I'll leave you to it."

"Thanks." She hesitated. "I shouldn't be long here . . . Hey, would you like to join me for lunch?"

Donna tilted her head and raised a questioning eyebrow.

"I wanted to talk to you a little more about Jenny." And the Livingston brothers. Tori gave her a hopeful smile. "I'll be happy to buy your lunch."

Donna hesitated, then shrugged. "I suppose it would be okay, although I don't think I can add anything to what I've already told the sheriff."

"I probably won't ask the same kind of questions Ben asked. Where would you like to eat?" Somewhere quiet, preferably.

"Do you like Asian food?" When Tori nodded, Donna named a Japanese restaurant two blocks over.

"That sounds good. I don't have my car. Would you want to walk with me?"

"I'll meet you there. I need to run a couple of errands after we eat." She handed Tori the key to the office. "I'll be at my desk when you finish."

Tori stepped inside the room and glanced around, startled to see a photo of Zack, Beth, and Drew on Jenny's desk. She'd known they were close, but Tori hadn't expected Jenny would have their photo on her desk.

She swept her gaze around the rest of the room, noting it hadn't had the same update as Richard's. Pine paneling gave the room a dark vibe, and the books on the bookshelf looked like the same ones that had been there when Tori worked at the company. At least the red curtains were gone, replaced with plantation blinds, and the paintings were similar to the ones hanging throughout the building. Something about the room bothered Tori. She scanned it again, trying to put her finger on the problem.

Then she saw it. Jenny had spent at least eight hours a day in this office, five days a week, for eight years, and other than the photo, there was not one thing that said anything about who Jenny Tremont was.

Why hadn't she put her stamp on the room? *Curious.* Tori opened the file cabinet and flipped through the few files in the drawers. Nothing there. Evidently she did everything online.

Tori sat in the leather chair, imagining herself as Jenny. There would probably be a spreadsheet on the computer screen. She jiggled the mouse, and the screen came to life, requiring a password to access the files. A password she didn't have. Did Donna know what it was? Tori would ask when she returned the key.

She opened the side drawers in the desk. Everything was neatly organized, pens, notepads, paperclips . . . just like she would expect of an accountant. Tori frowned. Except there were no snacks in the desk—who worked without snacks?

Tori tried to open the bottom drawer. Locked. If Ben's deputies had searched the desk, why didn't they leave the drawer unlocked?

Should she try to get it open? Richard had given her permission to look through the office . . . which included the desk . . .

Using the bobby pin from her hair, she jiggled the lock open. A folder lay in the bottom, and she picked it up. Ancestry Line was on the label. Tori had heard of the DNA testing company.

She opened the folder. Inside was a printout of a receipt and a website along with a sheet of paper. Evidently Jenny had submitted her DNA to the site. Tori examined the paper that was mostly doodling. Daisies, a sketch of a cat, Mother = HT. Father = HP? A little lower she'd written *Aunt* with a question mark.

Her heart rate kicked up a notch. She drummed her fingers on the paper, wishing there was a report, but it would be on the website.

There wasn't time to look up the site, and while she had her account number, she didn't have Jenny's username and password. She snapped photos with her phone. When she picked up the folder to return it to the desk drawer, a note fluttered out. Looked like it might be the username and password. She quickly photographed the paper.

"Excuse me, but what are you doing in Jenny's office?"

Tori gasped and jerked upright. She tensed even more when she saw that the demanding voice came from Valerie Livingston, Eli's mother . . . and Richard's ex.

"You startled me," Tori said. She stuck the note in the folder and laid it in the drawer. Then she took a breath to calm her nerves. "Good to see you again."

The woman barely nodded. "You didn't say what you're looking for."

"Nothing in particular," she said lightly. "I'm just trying to get a feel for who Jenny was."

Valerie snorted. "You won't find it here. She came in and worked her eight hours and went home. You aren't inserting yourself in *Jenny's* case, are you?"

Like she had Huey Prescott's case? Hostility oozed from the woman's pores. "If you're referring to Huey Prescott, what's your problem with an innocent man being set free?"

The look she gave Tori said it all, even if she was too refined to voice it. "You seriously have no idea how much trouble you've stirred up for the Livingston family with this Prescott case?"

"Why don't you tell me?"

Valerie fisted her hands on her hips. "Every member of the family except Eli and Stephanie will come under scrutiny for Walter's death, and the company will take the hit."

"You believe his killer lives in Logan Point and has something to do with Livingston Oil Corporation?"

Valerie's breath hitched. "I never said that. I have no idea who killed him. But now the whole sordid mess will be reopened."

Tori shook her head, trying to clear it. "What part of the case qualifies as sordid? My research didn't find anything that would tarnish Walter Livingston's reputation."

"We all have our secrets," she said softly. "Even you, Tori Mitchell."

Her cold words sent a shiver down Tori's back. "That's where you're wrong, Valerie. I'm an open book."

"Really? You seemed awfully cozy with Scott Sinclair last night."

"I barely know the man. We were simply having a cup of coffee."

Valerie glared at her. "Why don't you go back where you came from?"

"I will as soon as Jenny's murderer is found."

"I hardly think Ben Logan needs your help to solve the case."

"I'm not trying to help him, just looking for someone other than my nephew as a suspect."

"I heard he was a person of interest." She turned to leave.

"Do you know anyone who would want Jenny dead?" Tori called after her.

Valerie turned around, a sly smile on her face. "I can think of at least one. Stephanie. She and Jenny had words the day she died. I told Ben Logan about it, but I see he hasn't arrested her yet."

"I think he has to have a little more motive than an argument."

"We'll see." She pursed her lips. "Oh, and don't get any ideas about Eli. You blew your chance with him a long time ago."

Tori dug for a reply, but she came up empty. It was probably for the best. Women like Valerie Livingston had to have the last word.

Valerie gave Tori a fake smile. "Nice to see you again."

"I'm not interested in your son," Tori said to Valerie's retreating back in spite of her resolve, then she clamped her mouth shut to keep from saying more. Why in the world did she let the woman get under her skin?

35

Tori sat at the desk a few minutes longer to give Valerie time to put distance between them. What she'd like to do was get into Jenny's computer and look at her Ancestry Line account, but Tori didn't know the password to the desktop. It would have to wait until she got back to Oak Grove to her own computer. She locked the office and walked around the corner to Donna's desk just as Stephanie Livingston approached from the other hallway with a folder in her hand.

"Tori," Stephanie said. "Did you and Richard have a good meeting?"

"We did." Tori handed the secretary the key.

"Did you find what you were looking for?" Donna asked.

"Somewhat," Tori said. "I found that there was very little of her personality in the office."

"I know," Donna said. "Whenever I tried to get her to add a few touches to the room, she always said she wasn't into decorating."

That was putting it mildly. "Was she into genealogy?"

"Isn't everyone?" Stephanie asked. "Why do you ask?"

Tori shrugged. "I came across a note that gave me the impression."

"Actually, she was," Donna said. "She never knew her father, and sometime back she submitted her DNA to one of those ancestry sites. Thought she might find a relative, or even him possibly."

"I didn't know that." Stephanie handed Donna the folder she still held. "Richard said you would know what to do with this."

Donna flipped through it. "I'll take care of it."

"And I'll get back to work."

"Wait," Tori said. "Valerie said you and Jenny had words the day she died. Is that true?"

Stephanie's face flushed. "I don't know where Valerie got that. We did discuss a problem with the deposits, but it was nothing."

"Oh?" Tori said.

"I don't think it's anything I should discuss with you," Stephanie said. "I told the sheriff about it . . . and I have to get ready for the meeting with your sister about her security measures."

Tori hoped she hadn't messed up her sister's chances of selling them her software program.

Donna checked her watch as Stephanie turned and walked toward Richard's office. "Do you still want to go to lunch?"

Tori was torn between getting into her computer to check out Jenny's DNA profile and seeing what she could learn from Donna. She opted for lunch—Donna seemed inclined to talk to her now, and she might not be inclined later. "Lunch sounds good. Do you know the password to Jenny's computer?"

"No, our IT guy reset it Monday. I can email him and request it after lunch."

Now that Tori had the information for the ancestry site, there was no rush—doubtful there was any personal information on it anyway. "Thanks."

The secretary grabbed her purse. "You said earlier you were going to walk, but you can ride with me and I could drop you off at your car after we eat."

"Thank you. I left my car at the sheriff's office, if it's not out of your way."

"You must like to walk," Donna said.

"It's good exercise." She saw no need to tell her Ben had dropped her off.

Ten minutes later, they settled in a booth at the half-empty restaurant and gave the waitress their orders for the daily special. "And bring me a cup of your strongest coffee," Donna added.

"Just iced tea for me," Tori said.

When they were alone, Donna closed her eyes and took a deep breath and released it. "Some days just call for something a little stronger than tea, but it's too early in the day for anything other than coffee."

Tori watched as the other woman unwrapped her utensils and placed them side by side on the napkin. "I hope I'm not the cause of your distress."

"Not really. Losing Jenny has been hard. She was my friend as well as a good bookkeeper. We'll have to replace her, and that means I'll be training someone new." She shuddered. "Not my favorite thing to do."

They both sat back as the waitress placed a cup of coffee on the table and then set a glass of tea in front of Tori. "Be right back with your orders."

Donna added creamer to her coffee and lifted the cup to Tori's glass. "Cheers—if it weren't the middle of the day, I probably would've asked for something *much* stronger."

She clinked her cup to Tori's glass, took a long sip, and sighed as she set the cup down. "Just what I needed. Unlike most people, coffee calms me."

"Me too," Tori said.

Donna's eyes widened. "I knew there was a reason I liked you—kindred spirits and all that."

They both laughed. Donna sipped her coffee again and leaned forward. "Please keep what I said earlier about Walter to yourself—Richard would be very unhappy to know I was talking out of school."

"He won't hear it from me, but you didn't say anything negative about him or Walter."

"Maybe not, but Richard is a very private person," Donna said and lifted the cup to her lips again.

Tori nodded her agreement. "Unfortunately, with the new developments in his brother's case, people will be inquiring. That's one reason I'd like to learn as much as I can about Walter. I think I can help solve the case."

The other woman stilled, then set her cup down with a thump. Donna's body language flipped like a gymnast as she crossed her arms and her eyes narrowed.

"You probably can," she said coolly. "But I wouldn't broadcast it. Not everyone wants that case reopened."

"I know. I've already had threats on my podcast, and I figure they're related to Huey Prescott's case." Among others.

"Did you ever stop to think it might've been better to let sleeping dogs lie? It's not like Prescott was an innocent—he had a record."

"But not for murder." She'd struck a nerve, much like she had with Valerie. The question was, why? Tori studied the other woman. She'd interviewed enough people to know, like the song said, when to hold 'em and when to fold 'em. "Tell me more about Jenny."

Donna frowned. "Do you think the two cases are related?"

"No. Why would I?"

"You switched subjects very quickly."

Tori shrugged. "You didn't seem comfortable with the subject of Walter. Did anything seem to be bothering her lately?"

After weighing the question, Donna nodded.

"Jenny never knew her dad," she said slowly. "From what I can gather, they never married, then he got in trouble with the law right after she was born. Went to prison for a few years. She and her mom moved to a small town north of Memphis. From what Jenny said, her mother refused to talk about him, wouldn't even tell her his name.

"She stopped asking about him because her mom cried every time she brought it up. Jenny thought she had plenty of time, but then her mother died the summer Jenny graduated from high school. She'd been on her own ever since."

Tori had heard the part of the story about Jenny's mother from Zack's wife, Beth. Jenny and Beth had met at the University of Memphis and became best friends. About eight years ago, Beth had connected Jenny with the personnel manager at Livingston, and he'd hired her on the spot. Then when Beth's health failed her, Jenny was right there with Tori's sister-in-law all the way to the end.

Tori tried to remember if Beth had ever mentioned Jenny's mother by name. If she had, Tori didn't remember. "Do you know what her mother's name was?"

Donna scrunched her eyes together. "Hope . . . I think that's what it was. Anyway, a while back Jenny decided to try and find her dad, and she sent in her DNA to one of those companies."

That was the receipt Tori found, and she was anxious to log in to the account and check it out. "Had she found him before she died?"

"I don't know. I asked her about it once, and she acted uncomfortable, so I didn't ask again." Donna paused for the waitress to refill her coffee before she continued. "Jenny's case is the one you should be investigating, not Walter Livingston's."

Tori wiped the condensation from her glass with the napkin. "Can I ask you something?"

"Sure." She grinned. "Not sure I'll answer, though."

"Memphis PD has Walter's case on the back burner because they lack the personnel to investigate a twenty-year-old cold case. Why is it no one wants me to investigate it?"

"Probably because it'll stir everything up again."

"Like . . ."

"That Memphis office, for one. There was a big row between Richard and Walter when he opened it. They probably weren't on speaking terms when he died."

"So there was bad blood between them?" Tori had been surprised when the police hadn't looked closer at Richard in the original investigation.

"I didn't say that." Donna stared down at her coffee. "There was always a healthy rivalry between the two brothers that people sometimes misunderstood." She looked up. "And that's exactly why I don't think anyone should be investigating it. Ripping the murder open again is going to reopen all the sibling rivalry, and besides, after twentysomething years, I don't think his murder can be solved."

"You've known them a long time?"

Donna looked up and pressed her lips together for a second. "I've known Walter and Richard since I was a teenager. They're like family." A blush filled her cheeks. "Okay, I'll admit it—there's something about the Livingston men. I even had a crush on Walter when I was a silly teenager."

Donna seemed to be warming up again. "Did he return your interest?"

"No. He only had eyes for—" She clamped her mouth shut, pressing her lips together then wagged her finger. "You're devious."

"I've been called that before." Tori raised her eyebrows. "You know I'll keep digging until I discover who he was interested in, and you have the opportunity to make sure I get it right."

She kept quiet while Donna picked up the creamer and stirred it in her coffee. "Okay, but you didn't hear it from me."

She almost said Scout's honor. Scott would've laughed. "I'm not in the habit of revealing my sources."

"Walter . . ." Donna took a breath. "He was engaged to Valerie, and—"

"Wait, are you talking about Eli's mother . . . Richard's ex-wife?"

Donna nodded.

"What happened?"

"Richard is what happened." She shook her head. "Like I said, Walter and Richard were so competitive when they were younger, and this time Richard wanted what his brother had, namely Valerie. And he was more charming than Walter."

Tori had seen that side of the man. "That doesn't exactly surprise me."

Donna grunted. "He would've been better off if he'd left her alone—the marriage lasted less than ten years. But it was long enough for her to get a slice of Livingston Oil Corporation."

Tori mulled over what she'd learned. "Did Valerie and Walter get along after the broken engagement?"

"Surprisingly, yes . . . or maybe not so surprising. He probably saw Valerie for who she was and was thankful he'd dodged a bullet." Donna clamped her hand over her mouth. "I shouldn't have said that."

Tori leaned closer to her. "For the record, I agree that Valerie can be hard to get along with. How did Walter handle her getting shares in the business?"

"It didn't affect him—they came out of Richard's half."

"So, for a while Walter had the controlling shares in the company?"

She nodded. "They'd been equal partners, and after Richard and Valerie's divorce, he had 50 percent at the time of his death with Richard and Valerie having 25 percent each. Of course, when Walter died, his shares went to Richard, and he got control of the company."

Interesting. Walter's death put Richard in the catbird seat as far as the company was concerned. "Is Valerie very hands-on at the company?"

"Oh yes." Donna finished off her coffee. "She still manages the laundromats."

But not the oil company or convenience stores. "Do Valerie and Richard get along now?"

"I wouldn't say that." She fell silent as the waitress put their food in front of them.

"Chopsticks?" the waitress asked.

"Not me," Donna said.

"Please." Tori separated the disposable chopsticks and lifted a piece of chicken and a few noodles from the plate and into her mouth. She looked up to find Donna staring at her.

"How did you learn how to do that?"

"Practice." Tori grinned. "I was determined that two little sticks would not defeat me."

Donna chuckled. "That's kind of the way I am with Valerie. The only reason I never have words with her is because no matter what she says, I agree—drives her up the wall." She stared at her empty cup. "I wish Jenny had taken that route with her."

Tori leaned closer. "What do you mean?"

"Let's just say that sometimes Jenny didn't agree with Valerie's bookkeeping methods, and Valerie didn't like that—" Donna's eyes widened, and then she closed her mouth. "There I go again—Valerie is my boss."

"I won't repeat it, but I imagine she can be hard to deal with."

"You said it, not me." Then she lowered her voice. "Sometimes you could hear her yelling at Jenny all the way to my desk."

36

They had just finished their meal when Donna's cell rang. She pulled it from her purse. "Richard," she said and punched the answer button. She listened intently and checked her watch. "I have a couple of errands to run, but I'll have it done by the time you get back from lunch."

Donna folded her napkin and laid it beside the plate. "I hate to eat and run, but Richard needs some research completed for a contract he's working on."

"I've enjoyed our discussion."

"Me too . . . But I do wish you'd drop your investigation into Walter's death. Nothing good can come of it."

"I wish I could, but I don't think it's fair that a man spent twenty years behind bars while Walter Livingston's killer walked around free."

Donna held her gaze, then stood. "I guess you have to do what you have to do, but if I were you, I'd be watching my back. And thanks for lunch."

"You're welcome . . . and don't worry, I always watch my back." For more reasons than Walter Livingston's investigation.

By the time she paid for their meal and stopped off at the restroom, Donna was long gone. A text chimed on her phone. Amy. She was an hour from Logan Point. That would give Tori time to get home and check out Jenny's Ancestry Line account.

Wait. She didn't remember the code to get past the gate. Tori quickly called Scott, but it went to voicemail. She exited the restaurant and hesitated. Ben said to call him and he would come pick her up . . . reluctantly she scrolled to his number and pressed call. Since it wasn't quite twelve thirty, maybe he would be at lunch and wouldn't hear the phone. When it went to voicemail, she grinned. She'd tried.

Tori started walking the three blocks toward the sheriff's office where her car was parked. Instead of hurrying home, she could run by Jenny's house and at least walk through if she could get a key from Drew. She called her nephew, and it went straight to voicemail as well.

Where was everyone? Last time she'd seen Drew, he was with Scott, but where were they? Her dad probably knew . . . She brushed that thought off. Calling him would be a last resort. She tried Scott again and was ready to hang up when he answered. "Hello? I don't . . . recept . . ."

"Where are you?"

". . . Lake."

She pressed the phone closer to her ear like that would help and stepped off the curb to cross the street.

Spinning tires screeched behind her.

Tori glanced over her shoulder and screamed.

A dark car hurtled toward her.

For a second she froze.

Run!

Not enough time to make it across. Tori wheeled around and dashed to the curb.

The car grazed her and sent her sprawling face-first on the asphalt. The last thing she remembered was grasping for her phone as it slammed against the street.

Tori didn't know how long she was out, but someone was asking her a question. She focused on their lips.

"Are you all right, Miss?"

"Yeah . . ." she mumbled. Concerned blue eyes surrounded by a mass of wrinkles bored into hers before dizziness made her close her eyes again. But she'd seen enough to think the grizzled man with gray streaking his beard wouldn't hurt her.

"Let me sit up." Tori groaned when she tried.

"Don't move. An ambulance is on the way," he said. "You took a nasty blow to your face—gonna have a shiner for sure."

Sirens wailed nearby. From the sound of it, the police were on their way too. She lifted her fingers to her swollen cheek and winced. "Were you driving the car?"

"Me? No way. I heard you scream and caught the back of the vehicle as it raced away. Didn't you see it?"

"No, it came out of nowhere. Did you get the tag number?"

"Sorry. I don't see too good, and it happened so fast."

That was an understatement. Where was her phone? She'd been talking to Scott. He must be frantic. "Do you see my phone?"

"I'll see if I can find it, but you have to stay put. Okay?" She agreed, and he stood and searched for her cell. "Here it is."

Tori examined it. It looked to be in one piece. She tapped the screen. Nothing happened. She tapped it again. No! It couldn't be dead. What if she'd lost the photos of Jenny's username and password to the Ancestry Line account? Sirens approached as she tried to reboot her phone.

An ambulance rolled to a stop in the intersection. She dropped her phone in her lap and pressed her hands to her ears until the siren died and EMTs descended on her. Along with Ben Logan.

"I thought you were going to call me," he said.

"I did. It went to voicemail."

Ben stepped back and let the emergency medical techs tend to her. Once they assessed her, and she agreed to let them transport her to the hospital, he approached again.

"I'm glad you're going to get checked out," he said. "But you might want to let Scott know you're all right—I have two frantic messages from him."

She checked her phone. Still black. "I think my phone died when I dropped it. Do you mind letting him know?"

"Will do, and I'll stop in at the hospital and get your statement."

"I can give it to you right now—I didn't see who hit me. I wasn't expecting anyone to try and run me down, and it happened so fast I didn't see the driver and can't identify the vehicle other than it was a vehicle." She winced as they settled her on the gurney. "Would you give me a minute and please raise my head before you transport me?" she said to the EMTs. It scared her that she couldn't remember anything about the vehicle that could have killed her. She turned back to Ben. "I don't know why I can't describe what hit me."

"What do you remember?" Ben asked.

She leaned back on the gurney. "Leaving the restaurant where Donna Curtis and I ate, calling you . . . trying to call Scott and Drew."

He jotted something in his notebook. "Maybe you need to drop the Livingston case and the domestic violence case as well and let the authorities handle them."

Tori leveled her gaze at him. "The Livingston case is a cold case at the bottom of probably thousands of others just like it, and if I don't investigate it, who will? And there is no domestic violence case—all I did there was encourage an abused wife to get help."

"Tori . . ." He stretched out her name.

"Is Jenny Tremont's house still an active crime scene?"

He did a double take. "What? That has nothing to do with Walter Livingston's murder."

"I don't know about that. I've been asking questions about Jenny, and she worked in Walter's old office. What if she discovered something linked to his death? Maybe that's why someone tried to run me down—they're afraid I found something."

"Now I know you need a brain scan."

She mustered a smile. "If it's such a harebrained idea, then you won't mind if I look around her house."

He stared toward the heavens before he answered. "I haven't released it yet."

"Come on, Ben, I'm good at finding things other people miss. Please?"

He shook his head. "Oh, all right. I was going to release it today, anyway. We returned everything that wasn't evidence, including her laptop since we didn't find anything pertaining to her murder on it. But I don't have the key with me."

She could get a key from Drew or her brother. And if her phone had totally died, maybe the username and password to Jenny's Ancestry Line account was somewhere in the house.

37

The antiseptic smell of the hospital followed Scott as he stepped inside the ER room where Tori lay propped up in the bed. He'd slipped through the ER doors and bluffed his way to her room by acting like he was supposed to be there.

"You've had a concussion," the doctor was saying. He stopped, and they both looked toward him.

"Sorry, didn't mean to interrupt," Scott said. He got his first full look at Tori's injuries, and anger outpaced the relief that she was not any worse than she was. But at least she was alive.

"I was finished," the doctor said, turning his attention back to Tori. "But I hope you'll reconsider and stay overnight for observation."

She was slowly shaking her head, and Scott agreed. It'd be too easy for whoever ran Tori down to reach her in the hospital—look at how easily *he'd* gotten into her room. "I'm a trained EMT," Scott said. "I'll watch her and make sure she takes it easy."

Tori's lips pinched. "I don't—"

"If you're dead set on leaving, that's an excellent idea," the doctor said.

She looked as though she wanted to argue the point, then Tori's shoulders slumped and she caught Scott's eye. "Thank you."

"You're welcome. It'll be easier to keep you safe at Oak Grove." It wasn't like the Tori he'd come to know to give in so easily.

Either this last incident had really scared her or she had a hidden agenda. If it were the latter, he'd have to keep really close tabs on her. Especially after he shared what Drew had told him. And the hospital wasn't the place to do that.

"Over-the-counter pain medication should suffice for your pain." The doctor put his stethoscope in his coat pocket. "Use ice packs on your face for the next twenty-four hours, then you can alternate with heat."

"How long before the swelling goes away?" Tori asked.

"At least a week," Scott answered for the doctor and smiled at the "I didn't ask you" look she shot him. "I've had experience."

"He's right . . . you already have a beaut of a shiner," the doctor said.

The automatic blood pressure cuff inflated, and the doctor frowned as it registered her blood pressure. "It's a little high, but that's normal after what you've been through. That said, I'll be back to check it one last time before you leave."

"Drew is in the waiting room," Scott said once they were alone.

"Good. Does it really look as bad as the doctor implied?"

"Pretty much," he said. "You haven't seen your face yet, but at least it's only on one side."

"Now you're a comedian," she said.

He swept his hand and followed through with a bow. When he straightened up, she was laughing, and he joined in with her. There hadn't been many women in his life that he could joke around with without them thinking he was flirting. And maybe he had been, but then their feelings had been hurt when they learned Scott was only interested in friendship.

At least romance was one thing he didn't have to worry about with Tori. He was a recovering alcoholic, and she would never have a romantic interest in him. Scott hadn't expected that to bother him, but it did.

Maybe it was better this way. It wasn't that he hadn't had girlfriends, but his relationships never ended well. A relationship took time, and for the past seven years his career had been his life—there hadn't been time for anything else.

What if he had to give up the FBI? He had no idea what he would do. Not that he needed the money, but he liked having a purpose.

Scott could always volunteer at Walls of Jericho, Nick and Taylor's camp for at-risk youth, but he wanted more structure than volunteering would afford. And it wasn't the same as making a difference by fighting evil.

"Earth to Scott. Come in, please . . ."

He blinked. "Sorry."

"Where were you?"

"Just thinking about my career."

Concern laced her face. "How did your rehab go?"

"Like usual. I'm not making much progress."

She studied him. "If the FBI doesn't work out, you could always become a bodyguard."

"Right." He almost laughed. "You saw me at the lake. I'm sure the world would beat down the doors to hire someone who can't hit a billboard from twenty feet."

"You'll get better."

"I wish, but thank you for the encouragement." Scott squeezed her free hand. "Can I take a closer look at the damage?"

Tori removed the ice pack, and he examined her face and winced.

"You're not making me feel better," she said.

He leaned over, breathing in her soft, clean fragrance, and with a light touch, he traced her swollen cheek. Her face was hot where the ice pack hadn't touched it. "Does it hurt much?"

"Not like it did. When I hit the ground, it jarred my teeth." She gave him a crooked smile. "I think the ice has numbed it now."

Scott hadn't met many women as gutsy as Tori. Her cheek had to be hurting, and she was passing it off. "The cuts aren't deep. They'll heal quicker than the swelling," he said softly.

Their eyes connected, and his breath caught in his chest. His gaze traveled down to her lips. The air between them shifted, but that didn't compare to the way his heart pounded. It was like someone pulled a switch.

A rap at the door had him jerking back as Erin entered the room.

She fisted her hands on her hips and stared at him. "How did you get back here when they wouldn't let me when I first arrived?"

38

Tori slowly pulled her gaze away from Scott, whose face had turned a bright shade of red. What had just happened? The better question was, what would've happened if her sister hadn't come into the room?

Nothing. *Liar.* Tension still filled the room. Scott had been about to kiss her, and she'd wanted him to. Thank goodness she wasn't hooked up to a heart monitor. Was her face as red as his? She grabbed the ice pack and laid it back on her cheek.

Tori didn't know which was worse: the pain in her face or dealing with a man she wasn't certain she could trust. She swallowed hard. It wasn't only Scott, it was dealing with feelings she'd shut down since Michael died. Did she even want to open her heart again?

"I'm waiting for an answer," Erin said.

"I'd kind of like to know that myself," she said, glad for the distraction.

Scott muttered something as he stood by her bed with his arms folded across his chest.

"I'm sorry, I didn't understand you."

He had the decency to look uncomfortable. "I might've walked in with another person. And it's all the more reason you don't need to stay overnight."

"Would someone tell me what's going on?" Erin said. "What happened?"

Scott turned to her. "Ben told me she was walking from the Japanese restaurant to his parking lot, and someone tried to run over her."

"What?" She jerked her head toward Tori. "Why? Did you see who did it?"

"I don't remember the car, much less the driver, and I don't know why."

Erin slowly sat in the chair by her bed. "I don't understand . . ."

"I told you earlier today that someone had tried to run me off the road last night . . . I thought it had something to do with one of the podcast cases I'm working on, but now I'm not so sure."

"Then what were you doing walking down the street by yourself?" Erin looked up at Scott. "I'm assuming she wasn't with you."

"You got that right." Scott glared down at Tori. "Care to explain yourself?"

Tori glared right back at him. Where was the guy who'd been about to kiss her? "First, would one of you raise the head of the bed so you're not towering over me? It's manual—I can't do it myself."

His features relaxed and he did as she asked. "Is that better?" he said.

She nodded. "Thank you, and now, sit down—you're still towering over me. It's intimidating."

He huffed but pulled a chair beside Erin and sat down. "Look, I'm sorry if I sound abrupt, but when you called and all I heard was a scream, and then I couldn't get hold of you . . . Well, I probably lost a good three years off my life. What were you thinking, strolling around Logan Point by yourself?"

"I didn't mean to worry you, or anyone else," she said, glancing at her sister. "And I wasn't strolling. I'd had lunch with Donna Curtis, Richard's secretary, it was a pretty day, and I tried to call Ben, but he didn't answer. I never dreamed it wouldn't be safe to walk back to the sheriff's office parking lot where I left my car. I was in downtown Logan Point in the middle of the day, for Pete's sake."

He leaned toward her. "But it's Friday, and the businesses near that restaurant close at noon if they open at all. It's practically deserted."

"What kind of business closes on Friday?"

"An IT company bought up several of the office buildings," Erin said. "They have a four-day week. And there's a clinic there that closes at noon."

"No wonder the restaurant wasn't busy."

Erin's phone rang, and she glanced at the screen. "It's a client. I better take this."

"Go, you have work to do. Scott will be taking me to Oak Grove, anyway."

Erin stood and held up her finger as she answered her phone. "Can you hold, please?" She muted her phone and leaned over the bed, giving Tori a hug. "Be careful." Then she winced. "The skin around your eye is already turning black, but don't worry, I have concealer that will take care of it." Then Erin turned to Scott. "Take good care of her—I don't have another sister."

Tori could tell that her sister was shaken up. "Don't worry. The doctor said the CT scan showed no brain bleed, and X-rays showed no broken bones in my face."

"But you're an adrenaline junky, always have been," Erin said. "Please, think before you do something."

"Okay." Enough lecture. "Go take care of your client."

"Call me later, once you get settled."

The timer she'd set on her watch dinged just as Erin walked out the door, and Tori removed the ice pack again. From the way Scott looked at her, the bruising must be worse. "You already told me it looks awful."

"And it'll probably look a lot worse before it gets better." Scott chewed his bottom lip. "It's a wonder you weren't killed."

"Thank you for being concerned, but it'll heal. And I'll definitely be more careful anytime I'm out alone."

"That won't be happening anytime soon."

"You're not my keeper." Tori said it as gently as she could.

An emotion she couldn't identify crossed his eyes. "I know that, but I *will* protect you."

The implication was "or die trying." Tori took her time replying and mustered as much confidence in her voice as she could. "You can't put me in a gilded cage. I have a job to do."

"I understand that, but you're not doing it alone. I'll help you, but first you have to get over this." He waved his hand toward her face.

"There's nothing to get over. I'm fine." This was not the time to tell him her plans to search Jenny Tremont's house.

"You are not fine. Your eye is swollen shut, and tomorrow you'll probably be so sore you won't be able to move."

She didn't doubt that, not that she would let him know. A hesitant knock on the door kept her from having to respond. "Come in," she said.

The door opened, and her dad stuck his head inside the room. "Okay if I come in?"

"Might as well, it's like Grand Central around here."

"What?"

"There've been a lot of people in and out," Scott said.

"Gotcha. I won't stay long, but I wanted to see for myself that you're okay." He glanced toward her face and cringed. "Does it hurt very much?"

At least he didn't tell her how bad it looked—she was getting tired of that. "Probably not as bad as it'll hurt tomorrow."

He approached the bed. "Can I get you anything? You can stay at my house if it's too noisy at Erin's."

"Dad, you have a one-bedroom apartment."

"You can have the bedroom—I'll sleep on the sofa."

Unshed tears stung her eyes. Tori rubbed her hand over the thin sheet on the bed. She'd have to be blind not to see how hard he was trying. Could they start over? Build a relationship?

"Thanks, but I'm not putting you in danger. Did you see Drew?"

"I did, told him I'd take him home when I left, but he said he wasn't leaving until you did."

Scott's cell phone rang. "It's Amy."

Amy! She'd forgotten to call her. Tori hoped she wasn't at Oak Grove looking for her. "Can I talk to her?"

While Scott answered, her dad said, "I'll go, but if you need anything, just call me."

She connected with his gaze and nodded, swallowing hard at the hope in his face.

He gave a little wave and walked to the door. Suddenly the good memories of the dad she'd grown up with bombarded her. They'd been the all-American family. She'd believed her dad hung the moon until . . .

Her stomach clenched. If he hadn't relapsed, her mom would still be alive. But was that true? "Thanks," she called after him.

He stopped. "You're welcome." He looked as though he would say more, but then he turned and closed the door behind him.

Tori twisted the sheet in her hand. Why did life have to be so complicated? She heard Scott say her name and shifted her attention to him.

"She's right here." He handed Tori the phone.

"Where are you?" Tori asked Amy over the phone.

"I'm at this huge house and no one's home," Amy replied. "When will you get here?"

"As soon as the doctor releases me."

"What?"

She quickly explained what had happened.

"You want me to come to the hospital?"

"No. I should be there soon."

"Good. I'll tell Caleb."

"Caleb?"

"Scott's friend who followed me from Knoxville?"

Tori would've head-slapped herself if she wasn't so tender. She'd totally forgotten Scott had arranged for his friend to escort Amy. Maybe she *should* stay for observation. No. Not after the way Scott got into her hospital room so easily.

Besides, she had too much to do, and that included recording the podcast tomorrow night. Tori looked up as the doctor entered the room. "The doc's here—maybe they're about to release me."

She disconnected and handed Scott his phone. The doctor walked to the bed and pressed a button on the monitor, and the cuff on Tori's arm inflated. She focused on breathing in and out slowly and mentally lowering her blood pressure. It was a trick she'd learned a long time ago.

"That's much better," he said as the cuff deflated. "It looks like you're good to go, but if nausea or headache occur, don't wait to see if it gets better—return immediately."

"Don't worry, we will," Scott said.

A few minutes later, he went to get his pickup while the nurse wheeled her toward the lobby, where Drew waited. "You don't have to stay with me," she said to the nurse. "My nephew is here, and Scott will be right back."

The nurse nodded. "If you need anything, see the aide behind the desk."

"I will." She turned to Drew. She wanted a few words with him before Scott returned, but before she could say anything, he took one look at her and said, "You look awful!"

"Thanks." She gave him a black glare with her good eye. "Just what I needed to hear."

Eli Livingston stepped from behind a column. "Drew's right. You do look awful."

Her jaw dropped. He was the last person she expected to see at the hospital. "What are you doing here?"

"I had a meeting with the hospital CEO about the fuel contract for the ambulances and saw Drew when I was leaving. He said you were being discharged so I waited with him to make sure you were okay."

"Thanks. As you can see, I'm fine."

"I don't know about that." Eli moved her wheelchair away from Drew, then he knelt until he was even with her. "I didn't expect to see Sinclair with you."

She flinched at the accusation in his voice. "It's complicated. And it's none of your business who I'm with."

He looked over his shoulder toward the door before speaking. "While he's gone, I want to tell you what I found out," he said as if he hadn't heard her. "I got my dad to call some of his drug enforcement sources—that motorcycle gang Scott was a part of? They're involved with the cartel. You have to get rid of him."

Evidently Eli didn't know everything, since he didn't know Scott was an undercover FBI agent. "Listen to me." She waited until he focused on her. "You don't have a clue about what's going on, so drop it. Scott's a friend, and I don't appreciate you bad-mouthing him."

"Are you involved with Scott Sinclair?"

"No. It's none of your business even if I were." They weren't teenagers anymore, and she wasn't walking on eggshells around him, dreading an interrogation if someone of the opposite sex talked to her. He'd even been jealous of her friendship with Amy. "He's helping me with security."

From the look on his face, it was the wrong answer. "You could've asked me for help."

"It isn't that simple."

"It never is with you."

She crossed her arms. "I appreciate your concern, but just go."

Eli stood and jammed his hands in his pockets as he narrowed his eyes at her. "I heard you were poking around in Jenny's office. Did someone try to run you down because you're looking into her murder?"

39

Scott parked in the pull-thru and hopped out of his truck. He hoped Tori didn't give him any flak about going straight to Oak Grove. He strode through the entrance to the lobby and frowned. Drew was leaning against the wall, and Eli Livingston was talking to Tori. How did he even know . . . of course. It was Logan Point. There probably wasn't anyone in town who hadn't heard about the accident . . . that wasn't an accident. She looked exhausted.

"Everything okay?" Scott asked.

"Yeah. You remember Eli . . ."

"Of course." When Eli held out his hand, Scott automatically held out his right hand. He managed not to wince when Eli gripped him in a bone-crushing handshake. What had Tori said to Eli that had him trying to prove his strength? He turned to Tori. "Your carriage awaits."

"Thanks."

She even sounded weary. Scott caught Drew's eye. "You ready?"

When the teenager nodded, Scott wheeled Tori through the electric doors. "Good to see you again," he said to Eli over his shoulder.

No one spoke until he pulled out of the pull-thru. "Sorry about Eli," Tori said. "I don't know what his problem is."

Scott knew, but to voice it would sound . . . petty.

She leaned back in the seat. "Can we stop and pick up cold packs and maybe a heating pad on the way to your house?"

"Sure," Scott said even though he'd wanted to drive straight home. Taylor probably had those items, but he had no idea where they were stored. "And once you're settled at Oak Grove, Drew and I can come back to town for your car." He looked in the rear mirror. "You two good with that?"

The teenager nodded, and Scott glanced at Tori.

"I guess that's the simplest way to get my car," she said.

He gunned his truck a few miles over the speed limit toward the drugstore. The sooner they got home, the better. Scott kept a check in his mirrors for anyone following them. A motorcycle came into view in his side mirror, and his heart jumped into high gear.

"Where are you going?" Tori asked when he made a right turn.

He hadn't thought she was paying attention to his driving. "Just making sure no one is following."

She turned and looked out the back window. "I don't see anyone."

"We're good." At least Scott hoped they were as he made a left turn to get back on the drugstore route. He kept a check in his mirrors to see if anyone took the cyclist's place. No more motorcycles, but he couldn't shake the feeling that someone was watching them as he turned into the parking lot of the drugstore. Tori had her eyes closed, but he didn't think she was asleep.

"I'll go in and get the stuff," Drew said. He'd been quiet in the back seat, and in fact he'd been withdrawn ever since Tori had called and all they'd heard was a scream.

Once the teen returned with the items, Scott headed to Oak Grove.

"Drew . . ." He glanced at him in the rearview mirror. They had at least ten minutes of uninterrupted time before arriving at the house. "Is it okay to discuss what we talked about?"

The teen turned and stared out the window.

"Is that a yes?" Scott asked.

"What are you talking about?" Tori asked.

"Drew has something to tell you." Scott made a left turn onto the road out of town.

"Do I have to? You said—"

"We decided bringing Tori into it was for the best."

Drew glared at him in the mirror. "You decided."

"Would someone tell me what's going on?" Tori said.

Scott waited. He'd told Drew he would keep what he told him in confidence, but . . . he glanced in the mirror again. Drew looked as though he'd bit into a lemon. "It could be dangerous for Tori if she doesn't know—she could walk into a risky situation without realizing it. You don't want that."

"All right," the boy said through a tight jaw. "Jenny asked me to bring her something the night she was killed."

As he related the details, Scott listened to see if Drew deviated from the story, and except for a couple of minor points, he repeated it word for word.

"Where did she get the money?" Tori asked.

"I don't know, and I never got a chance to ask."

"Why did you agree to take it to her?" Tori asked.

"Because Jenny was good to Mom. I don't know what we would've done without her. I didn't even think about saying no." He blew out a hard sigh. "Maybe I should've called Ben Logan when I found the money . . . if I had, Jenny might still be alive."

Jenny had put Drew in a hard place. "It wasn't your fault," Scott said. "And it might not have done any good."

He was having a difficult time reconciling the person who worked with teenage girls at church with the one who had hidden what was probably illegal money. Not that he knew for sure, but what other explanation was there? Jenny didn't make the kind of money to sock away huge sums of it.

Scott glanced in the rearview mirror again. His heart jumped in his throat. Was that the same motorcycle that had been behind them before?

"Where is this money?" Tori turned to look at her nephew. He didn't answer, just chewed on his thumbnail. "Drew?"

"I'll get it and bring it back when we pick up your car."

Scott kept his focus on the bike in the distance and let Drew's evasion go unchallenged. Once they got to Oak Grove, he'd call him on it. He glanced in the mirror again. *Where did the bike go?*

Scott checked the side mirror. No motorcycle. Heat flushed his face. Was he seeing trouble where there was none? Sometimes that was as bad as ignoring a threat. Nevertheless, he would call his coordinator and make sure his location hadn't been compromised and also let him know Tori and Amy might need protection. He pulled into the gate at Oak Grove and keyed in the code.

"What did you just put in?" Tori asked. "I couldn't remember it earlier."

He told her and she tried to open her phone and groaned. "I hope this thing isn't dead. I had some really important photos on it."

"Even if it's dead, you should still be able to access your photos—you do have them set to upload to the Cloud?"

She gaped at him. "The Cloud! Yes! Of course, they're programmed to upload—I can access them through my computer." Then Tori bit her lip. "What if they didn't upload right away? That happens sometimes."

"We'll just have to hope for the best." Scott had barely parked when the front door to the house flew open.

Amy ran to the passenger door and threw it open. "Are you okay?" she asked as Tori eased out of the truck. "You look . . . like you can use a hug."

Tori held out her hand, stopping Amy. "Make it an easy one. Please."

"Yeah," Scott added. "She's pretty sore."

He climbed out of the pickup, and Drew scrambled out behind him, his face drawn. Scott stopped him. "You okay?"

He shrugged. "I don't know."

"It's going to work out, Drew." Scott patted his shoulder.

"I hope you're right."

"I am and we'll get it once we pick up Tori's car, and then we'll decide what to do."

"Sure."

Scott watched as the teen stopped and asked Tori if she needed help. When she shook her head, he hurried toward the house. Drew said the right things, but his voice said his heart wasn't in it. If he had a chance to bolt, he might. Just then Caleb Jackson ambled out the door. Scott would get him to keep tabs on Drew.

"Hey, man," Caleb said and approached Scott with his hand out.

"Good to see you," he said, shaking his friend's hand. Caleb had had Scott's back more than once. "Thanks for following Amy down here."

"Anytime." A wicked grin stretched across Caleb's face as he turned and watched Amy help Tori into the house. "You never told me she was a knockout."

Scott shot him a look. "Don't get any ideas—she's out of your league."

Caleb clutched his chest. "You wound me. Besides, I've changed my ways."

Scott raised his eyebrows.

"Promise. Cross my heart and hope to die."

That made Scott laugh. The former FBI undercover agent was a good man, but he was also a maverick. Not to mention a player when it came to women, and Scott didn't want Amy to get hurt.

Caleb crossed his arms. "How about you—I saw the way you looked at Amy's friend just now."

Heat flamed his face. Was he that obvious?

"Most people wouldn't notice, but I know you, so don't try to tell me you don't have feelings for Tori Mitchell."

Caleb must have read his mind, but Scott wasn't admitting anything. "You mind staying here while Drew and I pick up Tori's car?"

"You're changing the subject . . . but the pleasure's all mine."

"Don't get so caught up with Amy that you let Tori out of your sight."

40

"Thanks. I'm good now," Tori said once they were in the living room. She really hadn't needed Amy's help to get in the house, but it felt good to have someone to lean on even if she found herself wishing it had been Scott.

She hadn't been able to get Scott out of her head since he almost kissed her. This wouldn't do. Tori couldn't afford to lose her focus. She took a deep breath and erased him from her thoughts.

"Are you all right?" Amy asked.

"Someone tried to kill me—of course I'm not all right." She hugged her arms to her waist. "I'm sorry. That was uncalled for. How about you, are you okay? You just drove all the way from Knoxville."

"Eh . . ." She waved off Tori's concern. "I'm fine, maybe tired, but at least no one has tried to kill me."

"Which I'm glad for. Now we have to figure out which case my attempted killer is connected to."

"You have a few to choose from. By the way, while we were waiting for you to get here, Caleb and I checked out the basement, and it'll be perfect to record the podcast tomorrow night. And I spoke to the director of the safe house where Megan is staying, and she agreed to be your guest on the podcast tomorrow night with Megan."

"Super." Tori could always count on Amy to stay on top of the podcast, but was that a spark in her eye when she mentioned Caleb?

They both turned as Scott and Caleb entered the living room. Yes, Caleb definitely brought a spark out of Amy.

"Once I put your ice packs in the freezer, would you like me to get your computer from the guest bedroom?" Scott asked. "That way you can find your photos while Drew and I go back for your car."

"That would be great."

"What photos are you talking about?" Amy asked and Tori explained. A minute later Scott returned carrying her computer with Drew in tow.

"We'll be back in half an hour," he said then turned to Caleb. "Come on, and I'll show you the security system."

As soon as Scott left, Tori pulled Drew aside. "Do you know Jenny's Ancestry Line login information?"

"What are you talking about?" Drew lowered his voice to match hers.

There went that hope. If her photos weren't in the Cloud, she'd have to get back into Jenny's office. "Never mind. I need the key to her house."

"Why?" he asked.

"I might find evidence that points to where that money came from—something the sheriff's deputies probably weren't looking for." And speaking of the sheriff, they needed to bring him in the loop.

"No!" His whisper was frantic. "Somebody probably killed Jenny for that money—it's too dangerous for you to go there."

"What could be dangerous about going to her house?"

"The same thing that was dangerous about you walking down the street today. Whoever killed Jenny may be watching you." He crossed his arms. "I don't have the key with me, anyway. It's at the house."

"Get it while you're out."

Scott returned with Caleb. "If you're ready, Drew."

"Just a sec." Drew turned toward Tori. "You got to promise me you won't keep digging into Jenny's murder."

"We'll discuss it when you return."

That and other things. Scott called Drew again, and he followed the two men, who were probably discussing last-minute instructions on how to keep Tori still. She grabbed her phone and stood.

"What do you need?" Amy asked. "I can get it."

"I was going to charge my phone—but I just realized my charger is in the bedroom. I don't think I can make the stairs just yet."

"I saw a charger in the kitchen along with pods of Lady Grey. How about a cup? Scott said to help ourselves to whatever we needed."

Tori normally preferred coffee, but the hot tea appealed to her. "That sounds good. I'll bring my computer."

Amy grabbed the computer. "You bring the phone, I'll take the computer."

"Thank you." Tori didn't like being treated like an invalid, but she *was* moving slow. In the kitchen, she plugged in the phone, hoping the fall simply drained the battery, but it didn't light up. Disappointed, she left it charging anyway.

While Amy made tea, Tori booted up her computer and checked her iCloud account. "Rats."

"What?"

"None of the photos I took at Jenny's office uploaded to the Cloud. I really need that Ancestry Line username and password."

"You took a photo, so you saw it." Amy handed her a steaming cup of tea.

"Yeah."

"Close your eyes and visualize it."

Tori did as Amy suggested and tried to picture the scrap of paper, but hitting the pavement with her face had somehow clouded her brain. "I'm pretty sure Jenny T was the username, but the password was numbers . . . and you know how I am with those."

Amy laughed. "Too bad I didn't see it, because you're definitely a words person, not a numbers one. All you can do is try."

Tori pressed her fingers to her temples and winced. Even her left temple was touchy. She concentrated again on remembering and wrote down her impression. Then she typed in the address for the DNA site. When asked to log in, she typed in *Jenny T* then the numbers for the password. *Invalid.*

Amy looked over her shoulder as Tori stared at the screen. She was pretty sure the username was correct, but maybe she transposed a number. She tried another one. It was incorrect as well, and there was only one more attempt before the site would shut her out.

"Why don't we go back to her office and get the original?" Amy asked.

What was wrong with her? That should have been her first thought when the phone died.

"I'd like to see where she spent eight hours a day, anyway," Amy said.

Tori checked her watch. Four thirty. "I'll see if anyone is still there." She called Donna. "Is there any way I can get into Jenny's office again?"

"Whatever for? I mean, you were just in there this morning."

Tori froze. She hadn't thought about an excuse.

"Oh, never mind," Donna said. "If you can get here in the next fifteen minutes—"

"I'm on my way." She disconnected the call and turned to Amy. "Come on. We're going to the Livingston offices."

"Excuse me?"

Tori looked around. She hadn't heard Caleb come back inside. "Look, I really need to get something from Jenny's office. You can come with us or stay here. Your choice, but I'm going." She returned his intense gaze without budging.

"Scott said you were a hard case."

"Yeah, well, he's probably right."

He cocked an eyebrow at her. "I figure you'll go one way or the other. Come on."

"Thank you." She couldn't believe her ears and wanted to do a fist pump but doubted he would find it amusing.

"But just so you know, I'm calling Scott to tell him where we're going."

Bummer. She grabbed Amy and walked around him toward the front door. "Tell him on the way."

Ten minutes later, Tori climbed out of Caleb's SUV, wincing as her tightening muscles made it hard to walk.

"You sure you're up to this?" he asked.

She gave him a quick nod. "I'll be fine."

Tori hobbled behind Caleb with Amy bringing up the rear. Caleb held the door open for them and then followed them down the hall to the reception area.

Donna gasped when she saw Tori's face. "What happened?"

"I kissed the asphalt." She was a little surprised that Donna hadn't heard that someone tried to run her down less than two blocks from the office building. She introduced everyone, then asked, "When did you get back to the office?"

"Later than I meant to—one of my errands took longer than I expected, and Richard wasn't too happy the report he'd asked for wasn't ready." She took a key from her desk. "You have ten minutes before I lock up—everyone else is gone."

"It won't take me that long."

"You two go ahead. I'll keep Ms. Curtis company," Caleb said.

She smiled at him behind Donna's back. He was handy to have around—she'd worried the office manager might check on them, and now that problem was out of the way.

With Amy on her heels, Tori hurried to Jenny's office and unlocked the door. While she made a beeline to the desk, Amy walked around, examining the room.

"No personal photos," she said, tapping the tongue-and-groove paneling with her fingers.

"I noticed that."

Amy moved to the bookcase and browsed through a couple of the books on the shelves. Tori sat behind the desk. She hadn't locked the bottom drawer where she'd found the Ancestry Line information and pulled it open. Her breath stilled. She looked up. "The folder is gone."

Amy turned and stared at her. "What do you mean, gone? Are you sure you're in the right drawer?"

Tori stared down into the empty drawer. "I think so."

A quick check of the other drawers confirmed that the folder had indeed disappeared. "Why would someone take it?"

"Why indeed? Makes me think it's related to why she was killed."

"I agree, or it wouldn't have been stolen. We have to get into that account."

"Could the login information be at her house?"

"I hope so." Tori crossed her arms. "And that means Jenny's house is my next stop as soon as I get a key."

41

Drew leaned over to open the door handle when Scott pulled in behind Tori's Toyota at the sheriff's office. He was anxious to get in her sports car and hightail it home to make sure no one had found his hiding place.

"I'll follow you to your house so we can get the money," Scott said.

Drew hesitated. He needed to move the gun before showing Scott where the money was. Maybe he could get Scott to wait downstairs while he retrieved it.

Scott started to say something else when his cell rang. "Hold on a sec, Caleb is calling." He answered, and his eyes widened. "You're doing what? . . . I'll meet you there."

He ended the call and shook his head. "I can't believe it. Tori is at Jenny's office."

"Sounds like her. Did he say why?"

"Something about files." He looked uncertain. "Maybe you better go with me."

"I'll be all right to swing by my house and pick up the money." When Scott hesitated, Drew shrugged. "No one knows that I have it—I'll grab it and meet you at your house. I'll be fine."

"You know the code to the gate?" When he nodded, Scott put his truck in gear and drove away.

Drew climbed in Tori's Toyota and pulled out of the parking lot, turning in a different direction. Halfway to the house, he couldn't shake the feeling someone had eyes on him. Which was crazy. No one knew about the money Jenny had hidden. He checked his rearview mirror but didn't see anyone.

A few minutes later, he pulled into the driveway and parked out front. In his bedroom, he grabbed his backpack and went to the closet. Once he had the secret compartment opened, he stared at his dad's gun. Should he take it, maybe give it to the sheriff?

No. He'd seen enough cop shows to know the killer would've wiped the gun clean. The gun would point right back to his dad, and Drew knew in his heart his dad hadn't killed Jenny. Instead, he tucked the gun in the compartment bottom and then placed the money in the backpack.

The small box was the last thing. Drew wanted to open it before he left just to see what was in it and laid it on the floor. He stuffed a pair of jeans and a couple of T-shirts on top of the money. When he was satisfied that if someone looked in his backpack, all they would see were his clothes, he picked up the box and untied the cord around it. Inside was a black thumb drive. He held it up. Did he have time to boot up his dad's old desktop computer and see what was on it?

A step on the stairs creaked, and Drew froze. He knew that sound—it was the board on the landing at the bottom of the stairs. He tried to swallow, but the inside of his mouth had turned to cotton.

Someone was in the house.

No time to put the money back, but he stuffed the thumb drive back in the box and laid it beside his dad's gun. After closing the compartment, he covered the floor with his dirty clothes. What should he do with the money? Drew grabbed the backpack and shoved it under his bed. There were enough other boxes that maybe if anyone looked, they wouldn't notice it.

Drew eased to the door and listened for footsteps. Total silence except for blood pounding in his ears. He let another five minutes pass. No sounds came from the stairs. Tension eased from his muscles, and he blew out a deep breath. Nobody was here but him.

Drew couldn't believe he'd gotten so spooked. He ran his tongue over his lips, which felt as dry as his mouth. He had to have some water. Cold water.

He descended the stairs, still a little spooked, but it was plain the house was empty. He couldn't wait to get away, the sooner the better, but he'd have to go back and grab the money he'd told Scott he would bring. He hurried to the refrigerator and pulled out a bottle of water and uncapped it.

Just as he raised it to his lips, something pressed into his neck. "Don't move."

A voice that sounded just like Darth Vader almost made Drew's heart stop. "Wh-what do you want?"

"Just shut up."

Drew couldn't tell if it was a man or woman—the person must be using something to alter their voice. Sweat trickled down his back. "You can have the money."

The words flew out of his mouth before he could stop them. But the person's mechanical breathing and the eerie voice spooked him. He squeezed his eyes shut and took a deep breath to calm his heart. Didn't work. He was afraid his chest would explode.

"Nobody said anything about money."

He groped for words. "Uh, I . . ." He took another deep breath. "Look, I can pay you. Just let me go."

"We'll talk about that later. Right now we gotta go."

The guttural words were slow and precise. The gun pressed harder against his neck. "Listen carefully. Leave your phone on the counter, walk out the back door to the car in the driveway, and get in the trunk. Don't try running unless you want to die. You do what I say and you'll live."

Chills raced over Drew. The assailant prodded him with the

gun, and Drew did as he was told. He walked toward the door, careful to keep his gaze down. As long as he couldn't identify the person, maybe he'd get out of this alive. "W-what are you going to do with me?"

"We're going someplace where no one will find you, and you're going to call your aunt. You better hope she'll think you're worth saving."

The weird voice had Drew straining to understand. "What do you want with her? What'd she ever do to you?"

"She ruined my life. Everything was fine until she got involved."

Drew clenched his jaw. No way was he going to lure Tori to her death. Maybe it was time to rely on someone besides himself. Scott had said God was big enough to handle anything. Maybe it was time to trust him.

42

"Why do you have to get into Jenny Tremont's house?" Scott asked as he entered the room.

Tori jumped and then gingerly turned toward him. "You scared me—I wasn't expecting you here."

"Obviously." He crossed his arms. "What are you looking for?"

Before she could answer, voices sounded outside the office, and Donna stuck her head in the door. "If y'all are done, I'd like to get out of here."

Tori picked up her bag. "We're finished."

Once they were outside, Scott pulled Caleb aside while Tori waited with Donna while she locked the building. "Would you take Amy back to the house? I need to talk to Tori."

"Sure, man." Then Caleb grinned and elbowed him.

"What?" Heat crept into his face. Scott had a few choice words for Tori and didn't want an audience. She'd had no business leaving the house, not in the shape she was in.

"You don't know?" Caleb stared skeptically at him.

"What are you talking about?"

"I'm telling you—I see the way you look at her."

"You have it all wrong. We're friends, if even that." Scott couldn't, *wouldn't* let himself have feelings for the petite blond.

Or was it too late? Something inside him wanted to protect her, something that went beyond anything he'd ever felt.

"Keep telling yourself that," Caleb said. "But I'll be happy to take Amy back to the house."

While Caleb walked Amy to his car, Scott stood in the same spot, trying to wrap his mind around how he felt about Tori. Caleb had to be wrong.

"Is Amy riding with Caleb?"

"What?" He hadn't seen her come up. Tori repeated her question. "Yeah."

He opened the passenger door on his pickup, and Tori climbed in. Scott didn't say anything while she fumbled with the seat belt.

"I know you're upset," she said, pausing with the strap in her hand. "But I believe Jenny's ancestry report is important, and the photos I took weren't in the Cloud. Can we just go by my brother's house and get a key to her house and skip the lecture?"

He opened his mouth and closed it, swallowing his "what were you thinking" speech. "We'll skip the lecture," he said, not bothering to soften his tone. "Just buckle up so we can leave."

"I can't get the seat belt to work."

He frowned and leaned across to find the problem. His heart pounded as her perfume teased him, reminding him of how close she was. Close enough to kiss.

"Your shirt is caught in it," he said gruffly. "There, I got it."

Scott straightened up, his gaze colliding with hers. How he wanted to take her in his arms. He jerked back. He couldn't afford to go there . . . not until Tori's assailant was caught.

Scott closed her door and jogged around to his side and climbed into the pickup. He glanced at Tori. The stunned look on her face said she'd been affected by their nearness as much as he'd been. His hand shook as he pushed the start button and pulled out onto the street. "I'm not sure going to Jenny's house is a good thing. Ben Logan isn't going to like you meddling in his case."

"I'm not meddling."

"Care to explain what you would call it?" He glanced over at her, and she had the grace to blush.

"When I first saw the ancestry report, I felt like it was important. Now that it's missing, I believe it's tied to Jenny's death, maybe even Walter Livingston's."

"You felt, you believe—I don't think Ben Logan will buy into your reasoning. You heard him last night—he goes by fact."

"He said I could go through the house."

"Really? When?"

"When they were loading me in the ambulance after I gave him my statement."

Scott rubbed his jaw. It wouldn't take long to get to Jenny's house from here. He sighed and took out his phone and handed it to her. "Call Drew," he said. "He can meet us there with a key."

She took his cell, punched in a number, and waited while it rang. "Come on, Drew. Answer." Tori frowned. "It went to voicemail."

He made a left turn.

"Where are you going?"

"To your brother's house—can't get into Jenny's house if we don't have a key."

He tried not to smile as she beamed at him.

"Thank you! You won't regret it."

He doubted that was true. "You want to call Ben and let him know? His number should be in recent calls."

She tapped the number and put it on speaker.

"What's going on, Scott?" Ben said.

"Afraid it's not Scott. It's me, Tori, but he's with me. The accident fried my phone so I'm using his."

"O-kay." His tone of voice indicated *and* . . .

"I found a file when I was in Jenny's Livingston office, and now it's missing. I thought Jenny might have duplicate information at her house, and since you said it was okay to go through Jenny's house, Scott is taking me."

"What kind of file?"

"She'd submitted her DNA to a site and gotten a report back. The file had her username and password."

"Why would anyone take that?"

"I don't know," Tori said. "That's why I want to access it—Jenny probably has a file with the same information at her house. We're picking up a key at my brother's house."

"I don't have a problem with it as long as you keep me in the loop."

"That's what we're doing," Scott said. Tori disconnected from the call just as he turned on the street where Drew and Zack lived. He nodded toward her car. "Looks like Drew is still here. You want me to run in and get the key?"

"Please. And see if he'll go with us. He might know where she would keep a password."

Scott turned. His gaze dropped to her full lips. Tori bit her bottom lip, and desire to kiss her flamed in his chest.

"Man, you got it bad." Caleb's words hit him like a splash of ice water. "Uh yeah. I-I'll do that."

Was that disappointment that flashed in her pretty face? Did she feel the tension between them? He was pretty sure she did. He hadn't felt this way since . . . ever. But now wasn't the time.

Scott reached for the door handle. "I, uh, noticed you didn't go in last night, but didn't you grow up in this house?"

Tori stiffened. "Yeah, I grew up here. Too many ghosts."

He nodded. "I'll go find Drew."

Scott climbed out of the truck and jogged to the front porch. He climbed the steps and rapped on the screen door. The wooden door was open, revealing an empty hallway. Scott opened the screen and stuck his head inside. "Drew, you here?"

Silence answered him. He glanced back at the Toyota. The teen should be here. He stepped inside the house. "Drew?" he called.

Scott stopped at the foot of the stairs and called again. When there was no answer, he took the stairs two at a time and stuck his head inside the first room next to the stairs. He wasn't sure which room was Drew's, but probably not this one with frilly curtains and a white quilt on the bed.

The next bedroom looked more like a teenager's with clothes strewn on the floor, but it was empty as well. And he wasn't in the last bedroom, either.

Scott hurried down the stairs to the kitchen. His heart sank when he saw Drew's phone on the counter.

The boy would not have willingly left his phone behind.

"What's taking so long?" Tori's voice came from the front, and Scott turned and hurried down the hall.

"I thought you were going to wait."

"I changed my mind. Is Drew here?"

"No, and he left his phone behind."

43

A cold chill seeped into Tori's veins and spread. Drew would never leave his phone behind. "Did you look upstairs?"

"I did. He's not there, either." Scott's voice was grim.

"I want to search his room."

"I'm coming with you." There might be something in the room that would give them a clue to Drew's whereabouts.

"I can do it—you're in no shape to climb the stairs."

"In shape or not, I'm coming with you."

Reluctantly, he turned and she followed him to the stairs. Her mind was a jumble between worrying about Drew and processing what happened just moments ago in the pickup. Once again, Scott had been about to kiss her.

Tori brushed the thoughts away. Even if he kissed her, it didn't mean he wanted a relationship. She didn't do relationships, anyway.

Before she started up the stairs, she turned and scanned the home she'd lived in until she went away to college. Tori hadn't been in the house since her mother's funeral, and in seven years, it didn't look as though Zack had changed anything in the house.

Everywhere she looked, a picture or vase or piece of furniture triggered memories of her mother. Some even included her dad. With a start, she realized they'd been happy here.

Tori climbed the stairs, fatigue attacking her legs, either because of the memories or the accident. Didn't matter, she couldn't quit. Tori pushed herself to keep up with Scott. She couldn't let him know she was less than 100 percent. Who was she kidding? She was nowhere near that. And if Scott knew, he would call Caleb to come get her, and Tori was bound and determined to search Jenny's house.

But first they had to figure out where Drew had gone. At the top of the stairs, she got her breath while Scott stepped inside her nephew's room. Seconds later, Tori joined him. She scanned the bedroom, looking for clues to Drew's whereabouts.

She checked his closet. There were no gaps on the hangers so he hadn't taken anything. She stepped back and swept her gaze across the floor.

A narrow black strap was barely visible from under the bed. Could it belong to a book bag? Tori dropped to the floor and peered under the bed. Boxes and dust bunnies . . . and a backpack that looked like it was stuffed full.

"What are you doing?" Scott asked.

"Just looking." She pulled the backpack from under the bed and unzipped it. A pair of jeans and two T-shirts lay on top, but beneath the clothes were packs of money bound with rubber bands. Tori sat back on her heels and looked up at Scott.

"Looks like you found the money."

She nodded. "But why would he leave it here, under the bed? Why didn't he take it with him, wherever he went? And my Toyota is still sitting in the driveway. How did he leave?"

Scott picked up the backpack and set it on the bed. Then he extended his hand to Tori. She hoped he didn't notice that she winced as he helped her to her feet. She blinked as Scott dumped the money on the bed. "How much do you suppose is here?"

He held up one of the packs that had a sticky note under the rubber band with writing on it. "This says $10K."

She examined the note. "It's not Drew's handwriting."

Scott counted the packs. "There are ten bundles, and if each has 10K, I'd say this is at least a hundred grand."

"What was Jenny Tremont doing with that kind of money?"

"That's a good question. Unfortunately, the only person who can tell us is dead." He took out his phone. "It's time to call Ben."

Tori agreed and followed Scott down the stairs as he talked to the sheriff. There had to be answers somewhere, and she figured they would find them at Jenny's house. Scott ended the call as they entered the kitchen, and Tori reached for her phone only to remember hers had died. "I need to use your phone again."

"For?"

"To call Zack. He might know where Drew is, and he has a key to Jenny's house."

"Do you think he knows about the money?"

"I doubt it, not with it being in Drew's room."

He handed her his phone. "Good point. Zack is in my contacts. While you talk to him, I want to check out something."

She gave him a puzzled frown. "What—"

"Let me check out my theory first. Be right back." He turned and hurried out the back door.

As Tori sat at the kitchen table, she couldn't help thinking how many meals she'd eaten in this room and at this scarred old table that had belonged to her grandmother. For the first time, she regretted the years she'd stayed away from her home. They had been a close family until her mother's death. And now Zack was drinking and she was bitter. Only Erin seemed to be trying to hold them all together. She owed her sister an apology. Dad too.

She might not be quite ready for that.

"Did you get him?"

She jerked her head up as Scott came in through the back door. "Just finding his number."

Tori quickly scrolled through Scott's contacts, noting that he listed everyone alphabetically by last name. A person's phone told a lot about them. Like Scott might not look like he was organized, but he was.

She found the number and called it. After the fourth ring, she was about to hang up when Zack answered with "What do you need, Sinclair?"

"This isn't Scott, it's me, Tori. Have you seen Drew?"

"No. Thought he was with you. Why?"

"He's missing."

"Try TJ Logan. He hangs out with him a lot."

"Thanks. One more thing. I need a key to Jenny Tremont's house. Can I borrow yours?" Silence answered her. "Zack?"

"What are you looking for?"

It occurred to her that he might know something about the DNA report. "I saw a report in her office from a DNA company that Jenny had an account with. Do you know anything about it?"

"The DNA thing . . . she was looking for her father because her mother had refused to answer her questions. It always bothered her that she didn't know who he was. I encouraged her to do it, but later, whenever I asked what she learned, she'd brush me off."

"Do you know if she had a copy of the report at her house?"

"Probably. She was meticulous about having copies of everything, but if it's at her office at Livingston—"

"It's gone."

"You're kidding. Why would anyone at Livingston be interested in that?"

"Good question. The key. Can I come pick it up?"

"No need to. It's hanging on the hook over the washer. Got a green collar on it."

"Thanks, bro."

Tori disconnected and turned to Scott. "The key is over the washer, and Zack thinks Drew might be with TJ."

"I hope so."

When he returned with the key, she asked, "Did you discover what you were looking for?"

"I'm afraid so." He fished his handkerchief from his pocket and unfolded it to reveal a small black box.

A tracker. "Where did you find it?" Tori was pretty sure she already knew.

"Under your rear bumper. I think someone has Drew, but I think they intended to take you."

44

Drew's head slowly cleared except for a buzzing sound. He was in a straight chair. His arms ached and he tried to move them, but they were tied behind his back. He had a faint memory of being in the trunk of a car and a rough cloth rubbing against his face each time the car hit a pothole.

At least the cloth was gone and he could breathe. He inhaled and wished he hadn't. Something had died in here. If his hands were free, he'd clap his hand over his nose and mouth to keep from throwing up.

Drew searched the room, his gaze landing on a dead rat covered in flies. That explained the buzzing. Nausea boiled up from his stomach again.

And his head—it was like a curtain over his mind. A thought surfaced . . . walking, a rough cloth over his head, climbing into the trunk of a car, almost falling . . . something pricking his arm. The person had been nervous. Probably hadn't given many shots. He took a deep breath through his mouth, trying not to inhale the scent of death again.

Why had he been kidnapped? What was it the kidnapper said? Something about Tori . . . a memory was just out of reach . . . *the data drive*. The kidnapper wanted it. Drew should've given it to Ben when he had the chance, and if he escaped from this mess, that was the first thing he'd do.

Escaping was the problem. He scanned the room, steering clear of the corner with the dead rat. The dusty wooden floors didn't look like they'd been swept in months, maybe years. Cobwebs hung from the water-stained ceiling. The water had dripped on the walls, leaving strips of wallpaper curled away from the Sheetrock.

No one had lived here in a while. An old, remote house. Around Logan Point that could be anywhere.

He tried to think how long they'd driven so he could calculate where he might be, but it was no use. The shot had quickly knocked him out. And it didn't matter where he was if he couldn't get free.

Drew's mouth was so dry he could barely swallow. "Hey! Can I have some water?" he yelled.

The house was deathly quiet. Had the kidnapper left him alone? He yelled again, his voice echoing through the empty house. Was he going to die of starvation? Maybe that's what happened to the rat. Drew shook his head to clear it and turned toward the dingy window. Even though the sun was low, it was still daylight, so probably no one had missed him yet.

Or was it the next day?

Drew flexed his muscles and wiggled his hands. The zip ties dug into his skin. Tight was good—it would make it easier to break them. And he wasn't stiff enough for it to be the next day.

He braced his feet and stood. Those squats he'd been doing came in handy. At least he wasn't tied to the chair.

Drew walked around, loosening his muscles. Through the dirty window all he could see were trees. They must be on the back side of nowhere. He backed up to the door and tried to open it. Locked.

He turned and faced the door. The wood looked old. If he were loose, he could easily break it down, but first he had to get his hands in front of him.

He crouched down and worked his hands over his hips, the plastic digging into his skin. He didn't remember it being this hard when he and a bunch of his buddies had been goofing around one day and practiced getting out of zip ties.

Sweat ran down the side of his face. He'd gotten his hands to his thighs but no way could he get his legs through his arms, not in this position. Drew took a breath and dropped to the floor, a cry escaping his lips as pain shot up his arms. He lay on the floor for a few minutes, getting his breath back. What if the kidnapper returned? Drew renewed his efforts and worked his hands toward his feet.

No matter how hard he tried, he couldn't get them over his shoes. They had to come off. Once he had his shoes off, he worked his hands over his feet.

With his hands in front of him, he took a minute to catch his breath and loosen his shoulders—he'd almost pulled them out of their sockets. Drew examined the ties. Good. They weren't police zip ties, just everyday run-of-the-mill ones.

He untied his sneakers, his stiff fingers fumbling with the laces that he'd tied in a double knot this morning. When they were loose, he threaded one lace through the zip tie and tied it to the other shoelace. He slipped his feet back in his sneakers and pumped his legs, sawing the plastic.

The ties dug into his wrists, sending pain to his elbows, but he kept moving his feet. The zip ties popped apart. Drew wanted to dance, but instead he lightly massaged his wrists, trying to restore feeling in his fingers.

The hum of a motor caught his ear, and he cocked his head toward the window. Tires crunched on gravel, disturbing the dead silence.

No! His kidnapper was back.

Stay and fight, or escape? No-brainer. The gun the kidnapper had held on him was real. But which way to go? A car door closed to his left, solving that problem. He turned to the window and pushed against the bottom frame, moving it an inch. The back door slammed and footsteps tromped through the house.

He slid his fingers under the opening. Using the last of his strength, he strained against the windowsill. With a screech, the dry wood broke free, and the window slid up. Drew climbed out and raced for the woods.

45

Possibilities flew through Tori's mind. That Drew was even missing wasn't one she wanted to contemplate. Or that she'd been the target. She handed Scott his phone back. "Call Ben."

While he phoned Ben, she drummed her fingers on the table, trying to ward off the exhaustion creeping over her. Every muscle in her body hurt, but she couldn't stop now. If someone had taken Drew, it was her fault. She should've left investigating Jenny's death to the professionals. Walter's as well.

"Okay," he said after disconnecting. "Ben's coming and he's calling his son on the way to see if he knows where Drew is. And he was a little put out we hadn't told him about the money."

"But we didn't know about it until just a few hours ago."

"I know," Scott said. "He also said that if TJ doesn't know where Drew is, Ben will make a few calls to see if anyone's seen him before he puts out a BOLO or starts a search party."

BOLO. *Search party.* "Maybe he's with one of his other friends."

"I hope so, but either way, Ben's almost here. He's called his crime scene techs to meet him."

A few minutes later, a car door slammed, and Tori jumped up. "Maybe that's Drew."

She raced to the back door just as Ben rounded the corner of the house. She stepped back so he could enter. "I thought maybe you were Drew."

"Afraid not, and TJ hasn't heard from him all day."

She walked back to the table and sank into the chair. "How about some of the others?"

He shook his head. "No one's heard from him. My deputies have started canvassing the neighborhood." Ben turned to Scott. "Where's the money?"

"Upstairs in Drew's bedroom. You want me to show you?"

"Not yet. Wade's at the courthouse waiting for Judge Mathis to sign off on another search warrant for the house and one for her bank records. I'd rather wait until he gets here."

Tori frowned. "You haven't examined Jenny's bank records?"

"We have. And her account matched the bank statements we found at her house. I always check with other banks in the area to make sure there are no other accounts floating around and found one a couple of hours ago. She had a lockbox at another bank. That's the one we're getting a warrant for."

Ben rubbed the back of his neck. "The thing is, Jenny's bank statements showed she was living paycheck to paycheck, even overdrawing some months. If she had all that money, why didn't she use it?"

"Maybe she hadn't had it long," Scott said

"Could be. Does Drew know where it came from?"

"He said he didn't," Scott said. "And I believe him."

"Did you find a will?" Tori asked.

"No—we're hoping one is in this lockbox." Ben glanced toward the table. "Is that the tracker you found on Tori's car?"

Scott pointed to the table. "I wrapped it in a handkerchief."

"Good. We'll dust it for prints and then put it back under the bumper."

"So they won't know we found it?" Tori said

Ben nodded. "Whoever put it there is keeping close tabs on you. And they're dangerous."

Tori locked her fingers together. Who wanted to keep tabs on her, and why? Her eyes widened. "Last night and today—whoever tried to kill me knew where I was!"

"You're probably right—so that means the tracker has been there since sometime before last night." Ben took out a notepad. "We need to figure out when exactly it was put there."

"Could it have been before you left Knoxville? Maybe by the guy in the gray truck who shot at us?" Scott asked.

Tori considered his question. "I don't think so. I saw the truck a couple times on the interstate. I'm pretty sure now it was Calvin Russell following me. If he'd tagged me with the tracker, he would've hung back and located my car once I got here."

"Then it was probably put on after you arrived." Ben wrote that down.

"Maybe, but do you think Russell would hang around a small town like Logan Point where he'd stand out?" she asked. "I think the tracker is linked to something else—either Jenny Tremont's murderer or—"

"Walter Livingston's." Scott turned to Ben. "I know I'm here unofficially, but I am an FBI agent if you'd like my help."

"I'd just as soon not have the FBI here officially, but unofficially—I'll take it."

"Good. Email me Jenny's case files, and when Tori and I get back to Oak Grove, we'll sit down with Amy and organize what we know about her murder, probably bring in Walter's case as well, just in case they're connected some way."

"Texting my secretary now," Ben said.

Tires crunched on the gravel drive, and he looked up.

Tori half rose. "Maybe it's Drew."

"It's probably Wade with the warrants."

Tori checked anyway, and he was right.

His chief deputy entered the back door, and Ben said, "I'll need you two to clear out of here while we process the house."

"We could go to Jenny's house and see if we can find a copy

238

of the DNA report or her password to the account," Tori said. "Something tells me that profile is important."

Scott nodded. "Since we can't do anything here, I agree." He turned to Tori. "Are you ready?"

"You want to show me where the money is before you go?" Ben said.

"You'll let me know if you hear anything at all from Drew?" Tori said.

"You know I will."

Tori waited downstairs while Scott showed Ben and Wade to Drew's bedroom. When they returned, she followed Scott to his pickup, and ten minutes later, they slowed in front of a neat, craftsman-style house and turned into the drive. Pink azaleas bloomed in the front yard under a huge oak tree, and white peonies lined the side yard. Jenny had put a lot of work into the yard. Quite a contrast to her office. Tori's heart ached for Jenny's senseless murder.

"Wonder what will happen to the house?" Scott turned into the drive.

"Good question," Tori replied. "I don't think she had any family, at least not around Logan Point."

Scott pulled his truck to the back of the house, and they entered through the back door. Zack had mentioned that Jenny was meticulous, and the great room and kitchen proved it even though fingerprint powder covered everything.

Nothing was out of place, and the countertops and tables were uncluttered. But like her office at Livingston, there was nothing about the room that said "This is Jenny." No photos, no whatnots . . . it had the same sterile feel of her office. So unlike her yard. Strange.

In the den, Tori glanced down at the floor and quickly looked away from the bloodstain where Jenny had died. "Why hasn't this been cleaned up?"

"Like you said, she doesn't have any family here," Scott said. "I'll check and see if there's a crime scene cleanup company nearby."

"I'll pay for it." From what she'd learned so far, Jenny Tremont would have been horrified if she knew the floor hadn't been cleaned.

"No, she was a friend of mine—I'll pay."

Tori cocked her head at him. Scott Sinclair was truly one of the good guys. "You're a good man, Charlie Brown."

His eyebrow quirked. "Even though the tree always eats my kite?"

"Even though." She smiled at him. Scott's gaze scorched her, and she ducked her head. One smoldering look from his brown eyes sent her heart to the moon and back. She wanted to fan herself. Maybe it was time to start living again, even date. Not that Scott had asked.

Tori mentally shook her head. What was she thinking? They were here to find a report or login information, not for her to swoon over Scott. "Ben said he returned the computer. I wonder where he put it?"

"Probably in her office?"

She had no idea which room that was and walked down the hall, checking each one. Two bedrooms, a bath. The last door opened to an airy room with an L-shaped desk and the laptop. "Bingo."

Scott stepped into the room behind her and looked around. "Where should we look first?"

"Zack thought Jenny probably had a copy of the report somewhere in her house. Maybe it's in a file on her computer."

"See if it's password protected."

Tori sat at the desk and booted up the computer. No such luck. "It is. Maybe the report is in a file or on the desk somewhere."

"I'll check the file cabinet. You look on the desk."

She tried to imagine herself as Jenny. Where would an organized person store passwords? Tori sifted through the desk drawers. Nothing that looked like a copy of an ancestry report or a list of passwords. She turned to look at Scott. "Finding anything?"

"I think she kept receipts for everything she'd ever bought in the top drawer. The second one holds monthly bills and insurance policies. Haven't gotten to the other two."

Tori turned back to the desk just as Scott's cell phone rang. "It's Ben." He put the call on speaker.

"Did you find Drew?" Tori asked.

"Not yet, but my people are still canvassing the neighborhood—it's just that Zack's house is at the end of the road and all the houses are on two-acre lots with a lot of trees between them," Ben said. "I was checking to see if you'd discovered anything."

"Nothing so far," Scott answered.

She swiveled the chair around and stared at the computer that might hold the key she was looking for. "How did you access Jenny's computer?"

"I didn't—my IT guy did. I'll call and get back to you."

No telling when that would be. She searched the desk again while Scott and Ben's conversation faded into the background. She lifted the pencil holder, thinking Jenny might've stuck a list under it. Nope.

Tori had scanned the monthly desk pad calendar on the L extension, but she examined it again. A few notations of appointments but nothing that looked like passwords or usernames.

If only those photos she'd taken had uploaded to the Cloud, she could've used her computer to access the ancestry report. She lifted the calendar to look under it, and a yellow Post-it fluttered to the floor. She'd missed that the first time. Tori snatched it up, hoping it was the password she was looking for.

"I think I found it," she yelled. Her fingers shook as she typed in the number on the Post-it. Seconds later, the home screen opened up.

"I'm in." She looked over her shoulder and grinned at Scott.

"I'll call you if we discover anything," he said to Ben and hung up. "See if you can find that report or a list of her passwords."

Tori was already scanning Jenny's files.

46

Scott moved a chair beside the desk and sat beside Tori. Just like in the pickup, her light floral scent wrapped around him. Clean smelling. That's what it was. And very intoxicating.

He watched as she opened file after file. "Try searching for a key word, like the company name or even DNA," he suggested.

"I did. Nothing came up."

"Do you remember the username you saw at the office?"

She nodded. "I think so."

"Try it and see if anything pops up."

Tori typed in *Jenny T*, and ten files appeared. She groaned and clicked on them one by one. He was about to despair of finding the passwords when Tori clicked on the seventh file. Her eyes widened. "I think this is it."

He leaned in closer to the computer and tried to ignore the way her nearness increased his heart rate. "That looks like a whole list of passwords that aren't even in order. Why didn't she lock the file? Anyone could've found this."

Tori shrugged. "Most people don't think about someone hacking into their home computers."

"Do you see anything that resembles the DNA login?"

She scrolled down the list of usernames and passwords. "I'm pretty sure the username is Jenny T . . . but she used that a lot and she didn't always identify what the username was attached to. Like that one." Tori pointed at a line on the screen. "It's just initials, probably in a code only Jenny knew."

"Sort the list alphabetically—that'll group all the Jenny Ts together."

Tori did as he suggested and stared at the screen again, then ran the cursor down each row, stopping at the next to last row. "That might be it," she said.

"Let's try it."

Tori highlighted the password and copied it, and then she typed in the ancestry page. When the page appeared, it asked for login information, and she typed in *Jenny T* for the username and then pasted the password she'd found. They both held their breath when she hit enter.

The ancestry website opened up to Jenny Tremont's profile page. "O-kay! Where to first?"

He stared at the tabs. "Now that we can get in, why don't we go back to Oak Grove and research the site there? Ben said he emailed Jenny's case file, and I'd like to read it."

"Amy can help me with the ancestry site—she's good at this sort of thing."

"I'll call Ben and let him know."

Tori glanced at the laptop. "Ask if we can take the computer with us."

He nodded and quickly dialed the sheriff, putting him on speaker. "Have you heard from Drew?"

"No," Ben said. "Did you have any luck with the computer?"

"We got into the ancestry site and decided to return to Oak Grove to do our research. Tori wants to take the computer with us. She'd like for Amy to go through it."

"My IT specialist didn't find anything of importance on it."

Tori spoke up. "Then you don't mind?"

"Since I've unofficially invited you into the case, I guess there's no harm in you looking through it. I'll drop by your place later."

Tori grinned at Scott.

"Good deal," Scott said into the phone. "See you at the house."

"Wait—I think you need to get Tori a phone ASAP," Ben said before Scott could disconnect. "Just in case."

"I agree. See you in a bit."

Scott hung up and slid the phone in his back pocket. He turned and caught Tori chewing her thumbnail. He couldn't imagine how she felt.

She dropped her hand, wiping it on her pants leg, but the concern in her face remained. "Someone took him, didn't they? And Ben thinks I need a phone in case the person who took him tries to get in touch with me."

"You need a phone, but don't borrow trouble yet."

"We both know Drew wouldn't voluntarily go off without his phone. It's attached to his hand." Tori looked up into his face. "Earlier when you found the tracker, you said someone took Drew by mistake. What did you mean by that?"

He didn't want to tell her what he was thinking.

Her eyes widened. "Collateral," she said softly. "But what could I have that they want?"

"Maybe it's not what you have, but what they *think* you have."

"And we won't know what that is until they contact me."

"I'm afraid so." He stood. "You ready to go? There's a phone store in town. We should be in and out in thirty minutes."

She grabbed the computer. "Put this password in your phone—I don't want to take a chance of losing it."

Forty-five minutes later Scott escorted Tori out of the phone store and opened the truck passenger door. The rep had downloaded everything in the Cloud from her old phone onto the new one and even connected her watch to the phone.

"I added a locator service and sent you an invite," Scott said once they both were settled in his truck. "Accept it and make sure your 'share my location' is turned on."

Tori saluted. "Yes, sir." A minute later she said, "Done. Does this mean I can tell where you are as well?"

"Yep."

She was quiet as they drove, probably worrying about her nephew. A few minutes later when they pulled into the driveway at Oak Grove, Caleb's vehicle was in the driveway. Scott hoped Drew was here in spite of knowing that Caleb would've called if that were the case.

"Maybe he's here," she said and scrambled out of the pickup as soon as he put it in park. Amy opened the door before she reached the porch.

"Have you heard from Drew?"

Amy shook her head. "I was hoping you had news."

"We don't."

This had to be killing her. He squeezed Tori's shoulder. "Ben will find him."

Her chin quivered, then she straightened her shoulders and handed the computer to Amy. "This is Jenny's. Can you look through her files? See if you find anything that will help us find Drew or understand why he was taken."

"You bet." She hugged Tori. "I've been praying."

Tori muttered something he didn't catch before she followed Amy into the house. Scott was right behind them, and the rich aroma of onions and garlic reminded him he hadn't eaten anything since sharing the cheese and crackers with Drew. "Something smells good," he said.

"I made spaghetti for dinner while I was waiting for you," Amy said. "I hope that was okay."

"Perfect. Where's Caleb?" he asked.

"In the kitchen." Amy nodded down the hallway.

"Good. We need to do some brainstorming, and I need some coffee."

He strode to the kitchen, where Caleb was making coffee and a spaghetti sauce simmered on the stove. Looked as though it'd be a bit before they ate, so he grabbed a protein bar from the cabinet.

"Figured you'd want some caffeine," Caleb said with a grin. "And while the three of you discuss the cases, I'll walk the perimeter and make sure no one has accessed the back side."

"I don't think anyone can gain entrance to the property from there, but it won't hurt to check."

A few minutes later, Tori and Amy gathered in the kitchen with him. He sipped the coffee, letting the hot liquid explode on his taste buds. Nick and Taylor definitely knew their coffee. "We need some notepaper . . . Nick probably has some around here, but it'd be in his office—in the basement."

"I have some, and I printed out information on Livingston Oil Corporation," Amy said. "Be right back."

Scott remembered Tori telling him that Amy was always prepared. When she returned, she handed them each several sheets of printed paper. He flipped through them. Amy had printed out bios of the four Livingstons as well as the Livingston Oil Corporation annual state filings.

"Very good. Why don't you take notes." When Amy agreed, he said, "Let's get down everything we know about Walter Livingston's death and Jenny Tremont's."

"You think the two are related too," Tori said.

"I don't know. Let's look at that." He turned to Amy. "Let's make notes about Walter first. Who was working or had anything to do with the Livingston Company twenty-two years ago when Walter Livingston was killed?"

"His brother, Richard," Tori said. "At Walter's death, he gained control of the company."

"I thought they were equal partners," Scott said.

"They were until Richard and Valerie divorced," Tori said. "She got half of Richard's shares, making Walter the major stockholder."

"Richard gained from his death. Put that down," he said to Amy. "How about Valerie? Did she benefit in any way?"

Tori nodded. "According to Donna, Walter left part of his shares to her in his will. Which puzzled me—she and Walter were engaged for a time before she threw him over for his brother. If it'd been me, I would've been done with her."

"Maybe he wanted to keep the shares in the family?" Amy said.

Tori frowned. "Why not give them to Eli?"

"Maybe Walter was still in love with her," Scott said. "Who controls the company now?"

"We had to do some digging since the company isn't publicly traded," Amy said. "But according to the Mississippi Secretary of State business registry, Richard has controlling interests, even with the shares Walter left to Valerie."

"Put that in the notes . . . and that we need to interview her," Scott said.

Tori laughed. "Have at it—I doubt she'd even talk to me. Remember at Two Cups?"

Scott did. Valerie definitely had her claws out when they ran into her at the coffee shop. "Do we need to dismiss Valerie as a suspect?"

Amy paused her writing. "What would her motive be?"

"She wouldn't need one," Tori muttered. "But don't write that down."

Scott noticed Tori checking her phone again. "Nothing from Ben?" he asked when she looked up.

"No. How about you?"

He glanced at his phone and shook his head. "Sorry." He was at a loss for what else to say.

Tori took a deep breath and released it. "Okay, who else?" Silence fell in the room. "Come on, y'all, we have to figure this out."

Scott cleared his throat. "Besides Richard and Valerie, there's Donna."

Tori nodded. "And Eli would've been too young."

"I never knew Walter, but I know most of these people," Scott said, "and it's hard to see any of them killing him, even Valerie. Moving on to Jenny. Do you know of any enemies she had?"

"None that I can find, although according to Valerie, Stephanie and Jenny had words at work the day she died. Stephanie downplayed it, though. And Donna indicated Valerie and Jenny argued a lot." Tori looked at the notes she'd made. "Here's what I have—Jenny was in Walter's old office, she'd submitted her DNA to an ancestry site, and the night she was killed, she asked Drew to bring a package she'd hidden at his house."

Amy stood and stretched. "I get why she probably hid the money at Drew's house—no one would think to look for it there. But how? If Drew is telling the truth and there's no reason to think he's not, wouldn't they have seen her bring it in?"

"Drew said she still came over to the house to make sure he had clean clothes to wear," Scott said. "That means she was in and out of the house often, probably when they weren't there—it'd be easy to slip it in. But maybe it's not about the money. Drew was at the house the night of the murder. He found Jenny's body. Maybe he found something else."

"But what?" Tori asked.

"I don't know," Scott replied. "But I'm sure there's something he held back."

47

Drew barely made it to the timberline when he heard yelling coming from the house. He thought about stopping to see who came out, but that would be a stupid move. He needed to get as far from the house as possible and then figure out where he was.

As he dodged limbs and brush in the dense woods, Drew tried to remember the different road surfaces they'd traveled now that his head was clearer. Except there was little to remember after being injected with some kind of drug. He did remember they had been on pavement. He must've been totally out of it when they reached the house because he had no memory of a gravel road.

Drew jumped over a log and kept running. His lungs cried for more air. A cramp in his leg almost sent him to the ground. Ahead was a huge oak tree. If he could make it to the tree, he could rest . . .

Drew finally made it to the giant oak and slid to the ground, feeling the rough bark on his back. He listened for sounds that his kidnapper had found his trail, but the woods were quiet; not even a bird twittered. He just needed a few minutes, then he would push on.

Drew rested his head against the trunk and tried to remember . . . bits and pieces came back to him. He was pretty sure they'd crossed a bridge, but since he'd been tied up and blindfolded in the trunk, there'd been no way to know if it was the river or the dam they crossed . . .

How had the kidnapper gotten him inside the house? Drew weighed a hundred and sixty pounds and he would've been dead weight. That date rape drug he'd heard about. That was probably what he'd been injected with and why he had no memory.

He struggled to his feet. There was no need in trying to remember something that wasn't there. He had to keep moving. But which way should he go?

Maybe he should walk back toward the house and see if his kidnapper had left. At least that way he could travel parallel to the road instead of wandering the dense woods around him where even the sun didn't penetrate the canopy of leaves. It was getting dark too. He turned and hesitated.

Which way was the house? He'd been so intent on getting away, he hadn't paid attention to direction or landmarks. He turned, looking for broken branches, footprints . . . anything that showed how he got here. A twig snapped behind him, and Drew froze. Before he could move, hard metal pressed against his neck.

"Don't turn around." Instead of Darth Vader, the voice was low and raspy.

"I-I won't." His mouth was so dry, he could barely get the words out. "What do you want?"

"I want you to walk back to the house without giving me any trouble. Now start walking—and don't forget I have a gun pointed at your back."

Drew did as he was told, but he wasn't going back. That house reeked of death, and if he returned, it'd be him who was dead next. But how could he get away with the kidnapper holding a gun on him?

A low-hanging branch slapped him in the face, stinging his cheek. He grabbed the next limb and slowed down as he pulled it taut. When he was certain the kidnapper was right behind him, he let it fly. He didn't wait for the scream that followed and took off running again.

"Stop!"

He ignored the command. A bullet whizzed by his ear so close Drew felt the heat. Another shot and pain burned his thigh. He stumbled and face-planted the ground.

The kidnapper kicked him in the side. "You're almost more trouble than you're worth. You know I could've shot you in the back instead of your leg."

"But then you couldn't get me back to the house."

"You're a real smart one, aren't you."

The kidnapper had forgotten to disguise his voice . . . but Drew didn't recognize it.

"Good thing you're worth more alive than dead," the man said. "But you pull another stunt like that, and so help me, you'll walk with a gimpy leg the rest of your life." Drew felt the gun on his back. "Now, get up."

Pain rocked his knees as he clambered to his feet and limped toward the house. "Don't put me in that room with the dead rat."

The only answer he got was a grunt.

"Inside," the kidnapper said when Drew stopped at the back door. "And don't turn around."

Drew stumbled into the kitchen, and the kidnapper prodded him with the gun into another room. Must've been a dining room at one time. He almost turned when wood scraped across the floor.

"Sit in the chair and put your hands behind your back."

A chair, that's what the scraping was, but thank God they were in a different room. He winced as zip ties dug into his skin. "What do you want, anyway?"

The person pulled a rough burlap cloth sack over Drew's head. "In due time. Sorry about the hood, but this way I don't have to worry about you seeing me."

After the first breath, Drew made himself take short, shallow breaths—that first one almost made him gag from the mildew and stink.

"Your aunt has a data drive I want, and in a few minutes you're going to call her, and if she wants to see you alive again, she'll bring it to me." His kidnapper fell silent for a few seconds.

"I'm not calling my aunt."

Pain rocked his head as the kidnapper slammed the gun against his skull, and a wave of nausea worse than before rolled through his stomach.

"You don't call her and I'll kill your whole family."

"Why do you want my aunt?"

"Because her meddling is ruining my life."

His head throbbed. Drew closed his eyes, trying to come up with a way out. But there wasn't one, unless . . . "Look, I'll give you the money you gave Jenny. I have all of it. Just leave my aunt out of it—she doesn't know anything."

The kidnapper didn't respond. Was the person even still here? He strained to hear movement, but the only sound he heard was his heart pounding in his ears. Then he felt the pressure of the gun barrel against his head again.

"I want the money, and I want the data drive. So, one more chance. You blow it and you're dead. Do you understand?"

"Yes," he whispered.

Silence filled the room for more than a minute. Sweat ran down his face. He wanted to rub it away on his shoulder, but with the pressure of the gun against his temple, he was afraid to move.

"We're calling your aunt."

"She doesn't have a phone—you broke it when you tried to run her down."

"I don't know what you're talking about."

Now who was lying? Drew should never have admitted to having anything. He jerked his head toward the sound of someone pressing phone buttons.

"When she answers, tell her where the money and data drive are. Then tell her to get them. If you don't do it, I'll find her and kill her. And maybe your dad for good measure. That's after I kill you."

Drew's heart stuttered. He didn't know what to do, except pray.

48

Tori shuffled the pages Amy had printed out. There was nothing negative on any of the Livingstons. Her phone rang and she grabbed it. The number wasn't one she recognized, but it could be whoever took Drew. She tried to swipe the Slide to Answer button, but the feature didn't respond. "Not again!"

The papers had made her fingers dry. She tried swiping once more as hot tears welled in her eyes. "Why won't it work!"

"Let me try it." Scott took the phone and swiped across the screen. The ringing stopped, and Tori snatched it back. "Hello!"

No one was there. She looked up. "What if it was Drew?"

Amy said, "If it was about Drew, maybe they'll call back. Just make sure your phone isn't locked."

What else can go wrong? Tori knew better than to ask that question. She opened the setting on her phone and set the auto lock to never.

Amy opened Jenny's computer. "While we're waiting, send me the password to the computer and the Ancestry Line login information."

That was better than sitting here staring at her phone. She turned to Scott. "You send it. I don't want to take a chance on missing another call."

Scott tapped on his phone.

"Got it. I'll start on it now," Amy said. She moved to the far end of the table and booted up the computer.

Tori's phone beeped. "It's a voicemail. Maybe they left a message." She clicked on the message and gasped. "It's Drew!"

She hit replay on the message and put it on speaker. *"Tori, please pick up the next time I call."*

"Hit call back and see if it'll go through," Scott said.

She tried it, but the call went straight to an automated voicemail.

"He said he'd call again."

Scott was trying to calm her down, but it wasn't working. Tori paced the kitchen. Amy looked up from the computer screen. "Did you notice Jenny received this report over a year ago?"

She stopped pacing. "What?"

Amy pointed to the date that was April of last year. "And she corresponded with an aunt listed under her father's line."

"You're kidding," Scott said. "Did Jenny find out who her father is?"

"I'm pretty sure she did. The aunt's name is Aubrey Williams—"

"Aubrey Williams? Huey Prescott's sister? That means—"

"Huey is Jenny's dad."

Tori was confused. "If she knew about him, why doesn't he know about her?"

"I'm assuming the aunt never told him," Amy said. "According to the messages in her file, when the aunt discovered Jenny worked for Livingston Oil Corporation, she didn't trust her and accused Jenny of being in the Livingstons' pocket. I bet she never told Huey about Jenny."

"Oh, man," Tori said with a groan. "That's why he's still looking for her, and now she's dead. I wonder if Aubrey is aware of that?"

"Possibly not." Amy glanced at the computer screen again. "The only message other than the first one that Aubrey responded to was six months ago. It was kind of heated—Jenny wrote that as soon as her father was out of prison, she planned to contact him, and Aubrey wasn't happy. Jenny didn't respond. Maybe she was waiting for him to be released."

Tori paced again, letting her mind sort out the new information whirling through it. Two years ago an interview with Aubrey Williams for the Knoxville TV station had started the wheels turning that resulted in Huey Prescott being released.

She'd hired a private investigator to examine the case, and his report refuted every argument the prosecutor laid out at the trial. The story intrigued Tori, so much so that she'd followed up on the private investigator's reports and found more proof that Huey Prescott had been wrongly convicted.

In the TV interview, Aubrey Williams had been adamant that someone at the Livingston Corporation had killed Walter Livingston. She'd been so outspoken against the company that part of the video was cut.

Tori stopped at Amy's chair. "You were the videographer when I interviewed the aunt. Do you remember the section the producer cut?"

Amy looked up from the computer. "I'd forgotten that. Let me think . . . It was something about the Livingstons . . . someone's alibi didn't hold up."

Tori snapped her fingers. "That's it! And the police brushed her off when she tried to get them to revisit the case. In the interview, Aubrey accused the police of taking a bribe to not involve the Livingstons. She was convinced someone at the company killed Walter Livingston and said so. She wasn't very happy when that part was cut, either."

"The piece did run too long," Amy said, then she kind of grinned. "But I think the producer would've cut it anyway. In my opinion it detracted from the overall piece. Especially since Aubrey Williams had no proof anyone at the company was the killer."

The question that kept nagging at Tori returned. *Where did Jenny get the money in the backpack?*

"That's the same thing I've been asking myself," Scott said.

"I didn't realize I'd said that aloud. But, what if Aubrey Williams passed on her suspicions to Jenny, and she somehow found proof that implicated someone at the company?"

Scott cocked his head. "You think Jenny was blackmailing someone?"

"I don't know. Sometimes talking out my thoughts helps me see things clearer." Tori paced again, still talking. "That was a lot of money we found, and Jenny got it from somewhere."

"Who has that kind of cash?" Amy asked.

She could think of a few. The Livingstons, for sure—with the convenience stores, fuel stations, and laundromats—they dealt in a lot of cash. Tori blew out a deep breath. She was good at hunches, but this one had more holes than Swiss cheese.

Her cell phone rang, and her heart kicked into overdrive. "It's the same number."

"Put it on speaker," Scott said.

This time an answer or decline button popped up and she punched answer. "Don't hang up, Drew! I couldn't get to the phone to answer the first time."

"Tori. You gotta help me." His voice cracked. "He's holding me out at—"

The line went dead.

"Drew!" Every muscle in her body tensed, and she gripped the phone like it was a lifeline.

Scott pried it from her hand. "They've hung up."

A text dinged on her phone, and she grabbed it from him. Tori opened it and groaned. "The kidnapper wants a data drive. And I have until three tomorrow afternoon to come up with it. The kidnapper will call me at that time and tell me where to bring it or Drew dies." She punched in a text.

No idea what u r talking about.

A reply was instant.

> I think you do. The kid knows but won't tell.
> 3 tomorrow.

"How can I find something when I don't know where to start?" She held up her phone. "Can Ben trace this?"

"Probably only to a general area," Scott said. "It sounded like Drew isn't being held in town, and there aren't a lot of cell towers out in the county to triangulate a call. But Ben can try. I'll call him."

She nodded and paced the kitchen while he contacted the sheriff. When he finished, she said, "What'd he say?"

"He's going to try."

Trying wasn't good enough. "The text said they'll kill Drew if I don't find this data drive. Did anyone record the call?"

"I did." Amy laid her phone on the table and hit play.

Tori sank into the chair next to her, and the room fell quiet as they all leaned toward the phone. The stress in Drew's voice broke her heart. He'd lost so much in his young life. And now this.

"Drew didn't say what he was supposed to," she said.

Scott nodded. "He was trying to tell us where he was, and like I said, it doesn't sound like it was in town."

Tori's phone rang, and she snatched it from the table. Not Drew, but Megan Russell. She answered. "Is everything all right?"

"Did the Knoxville detective call you?"

The worry in Megan's voice put Tori on high alert. "No, but my phone's been dead. What's going on?"

"Calvin is in Logan Point. He used that credit card again to buy gas and beer there."

What if Calvin had kidnapped Drew? He blamed Tori for Megan leaving him, and he might think it was a way to get revenge. "Do you think your husband is capable of kidnapping?"

"He tried taking the kids before, but why are you asking that?"

She quickly explained what had happened. "The kidnapper wants a data drive that I have no clue about."

Megan gasped. "Are you talking about a flash drive?"

"I'm assuming it's a storage drive. Why?"

"When I was with Cal, I used to write out everything in a journal, and he found it one day. Beat the living daylights out of me. After that I started writing the journal on my computer and saving it to a flash drive."

49

Scott listened to Tori's side of the conversation, wishing she'd put it on speaker. But what he heard didn't sound good.

"Thanks for letting me know," Tori said and hung up.

Scott raised his eyebrows. "What's wrong?"

"Sorry I didn't put it on speaker . . . didn't think of it, but that was Megan Russell. Her ex used the credit card here in Logan Point." Tori walked to the refrigerator. "Where did you put the ice packs?"

"In the freezer side," he replied. "What else did she say?"

Tori pulled an ice pack out and pressed it to her face before returning to the table and sitting down. "Megan kept a journal detailing Cal's abuse on a flash drive. She also said he'd tried to kidnap his kids so there's that history—he's a definite possibility for whoever took Drew."

Amy shook her head. "Why would Russell kidnap Drew when you're his target?"

Scott looked at Tori. "Maybe Russell tracked your car to Zack's house, thinking it was you. When it turned out to be Drew, he probably panicked and then decided to use him as bait."

"You think Russell put the tracker on my car?" Tori said.

"He's the only player I can identify so far." Scott walked to the kitchen window and looked out. It was almost dark. It looked as though they wouldn't be finding Drew today.

Tori laid the ice pack on the table and stood and paced the kitchen. Scott wanted to take her in his arms and smooth the worry lines from her pale face. He stiffened. Not something he could act on. Scott needed to keep his head in the game if he was going to keep her safe and get Drew back.

"But I have no idea where to even look for a data drive. Ben Logan searched the house, and if it or the money in that backpack had been out in the open, he would've found both. Drew must have hidden it somewhere other than the house." She continued to pace back and forth.

"Tori, you need to rest," he said.

She rubbed her palms on her pant legs. "I can't. Not until we get Drew back."

"You have to. You've had a lot happen today." He took her hands. "You're in pain, stressed, exhausted, and that's when mistakes happen."

"It's not your nephew." She pulled her hands away and hugged her waist. "You don't understand. I should've been there for him."

"Scott's right." Amy walked to where they were and wrapped her arms around Tori. "You need to take a break and at least eat," she said. "There's not one thing you can do tonight. Maybe if you give it a break, something will come to you, but right now you can't even think straight."

Thank you, Amy.

At first Tori didn't respond, then she nodded slowly. "I know you're right, but it seems so wrong not to do something."

Tension eased from Scott. "I promise, you'll feel better once you have food in you."

"Yes," Amy agreed. "I'll put the pasta on and make a salad."

During dinner, Ben called with the disappointing news that the call and texts had pinged off a tower, but the area was too broad to pinpoint an exact location other than it was in Bradford County.

Later Caleb went upstairs to make phone calls. Scott cleared the table and loaded the dishwasher while Tori watched as Amy searched Jenny's computer.

"I can't find anything here that relates to a data drive," Amy said, "but I've found a couple of spreadsheets that make no sense. I need to study them more, but I don't need any distractions."

"In other words, you want us out of the kitchen?" Scott said with a smile.

"Something like that." She gave Tori a pointed glance.

"Okay, I get the message." Tori walked to the back door. "I think I'll sit on the patio for a bit."

"Good idea," Scott said. At the door he gave Amy a thumbs-up. "We'll be out here if you need us."

50

Tori walked away from the house to a brick wall at the edge of the patio. The moon was barely rising. She turned toward the west where it was inky black except for stars twinkling like diamonds.

All around them katydids and tree frogs trilled their unique songs. Soon a whippoorwill joined their chorus with its lonesome call. Was it the one they heard last night, still calling for its mate?

Had that just been last night? Tori sat on the ground and leaned against the wall. Scott sat down beside her. In the dim light, she barely caught his profile.

"God's creation." He pointed toward the sky. "Did you ever see anything so beautiful?"

"It is amazing, isn't it," she replied softly. Peace flooded her heart in spite of her worry about Drew. Was this what her mom had talked about when she said God was big enough for any adversity life threw at her? Scott hummed a tune, one she'd heard before but couldn't place until he began to softly sing.

"I see the stars, I hear the rolling thunder . . ."

She closed her eyes and raised her face to the night sky and let the rich timbre of his voice as he sang the words to "How Great Thou Art" wash over her. When he finished, Tori blinked back the tears that had formed. It'd been years since a song touched her that way even though she knew why he'd sung it. Just like her mom, Scott wanted her to trust God.

But could she trust him with Drew? The peace she'd experienced just a moment ago fled as everything in her resisted letting go. She focused on Scott instead. "I didn't know you could sing like that."

"There's a lot you don't know about me."

That was the truth. And she wanted to know more.

"One day I'd like to show you a Colorado night sky," he said.

She gave him a curious glance. "What were you doing in Colorado?"

He was quiet a minute, and she waited. He'd said little about his life before he came back to Logan Point other than he worked undercover.

"This isn't the right time to talk about it, but I know you've felt the . . . electricity between us," he said quietly. "And once we get Drew back, I'd like to see where our relationship can go."

Her heart stilled. He wanted a relationship with her. Tori couldn't deny she was developing feelings for Scott, but doubt assailed her. She hadn't loved anyone since Michael, hadn't wanted to open herself up to that kind of risk. *Michael would've wanted you to embrace life again, not bury yourself in work.* The words Amy spoke just a few days ago.

Embracing the possibility of a relationship with Scott would be like stepping off a cliff. No, more like a leap.

And then there was his alcohol addiction. Did she want to open herself up to that kind of worry? That he would relapse like her dad?

But he made her feel alive again.

"I . . ." She lifted her gaze to him. "I'd like to see too."

He took her hand. "For that to happen, there are a few things you need to know about me and my faith. You may not feel the same once you know."

"I won't know until you tell me."

"I never told you the details of when I was shot."

"I'd like to hear them."

He didn't start right away, instead looked up at the sky again. Then he dropped his gaze and turned to her. "I'd been working undercover for the FBI at least five years, still trying to bust skinhead motorcycle gangs. This particular case a DEA agent was working undercover with me. When my cover was blown, and I was wounded, my team arrived and saved my life."

Heaviness wrapped around her. "The DEA agent?"

"He didn't make it. Andy was my best friend."

His voice was so low, she had to strain to hear him.

"Oh, Scott." Tori bit her lip. "I'm so sorry." Neither of them spoke for a minute. "How did you get past that?"

He pulled a blade of grass beside the walkway and stuck it in his mouth, chewing on it. "Part of me never has. Not a day goes by that I don't think about Andy. Another part of me is thankful God was looking out for me."

"So why wasn't God looking out for your partner?"

"I wish I knew how to answer that question. But I do know that since that night, I've looked at death differently. Andy knew he wasn't going to make it. But he also knew Jesus. The last thing he said was for me not to feel guilty because I survived—he was going to a much better place."

Heaven. A place everyone wanted to go, but most didn't want to die to get there. What made his partner different? She raised her gaze just as a bright streak raced across the sky. Tori caught her breath. It was the first shooting star she'd seen since she was a kid. What was that rhyme . . .

"Star light, star bright, first star I see tonight," she recited softly. "I wish I may, I wish I might . . ." She frowned.

"Have the wish I wish tonight," Scott finished for her. "But you can't depend on a wish."

"I know."

"You *can* depend on God." She felt him turn toward her. "Tell me how you can look at that sky and not believe in God?"

"Oh, I do believe in him—that sky did not randomly happen. I just don't believe he's ever answered my prayers. He didn't save my mother when I pleaded with him in the hospital after the wreck. And I didn't even have time to pray for Michael—he died at the scene of the robbery."

Scott stilled. "What are you talking about—you've never mentioned anyone named Michael before."

And she hadn't meant to mention him tonight. Tori pressed her lips together. In fact, she rarely discussed him with anyone other than Amy, and Tori wasn't sure she wanted to share that part of her life with Scott.

Silence dropped between them like a dark cloud. "I'm sorry," he said. "You don't have to talk about him if you don't want to."

Tori wanted to look at him to see if he was for real. The fact that he wasn't pressuring her made her feel safe. She drew her knees up and wrapped her arms around them. "It happened right after my mom died. Michael and I met at the University of Tennessee my freshman year and we'd gotten engaged two days before he died. I'd only told Amy about it because I was pretty well estranged from my family after Mom's funeral, except for Drew.

"Michael had a scholastic scholarship, but money was tight, and he'd gotten a job at a convenience store near the campus working from eleven at night until seven in the morning. A kid strung out on drugs held up the store, and when he didn't get enough money for his next buy, he shot Michael dead."

For a second quiet surrounded them, then Scott released a breath. "I had no idea. I'm so sorry."

"Me too." Tori unfolded her legs and stood. She'd known too many deaths. It was why she didn't have pets. After Michael, Tori decided she wasn't opening her heart up to anyone, man or animal, again. It was too painful.

She had jettisoned friends left and right . . . except for Amy. Amy had been her friend since grade school, and she refused to abide by Tori's new rules.

"I really am sorry."

"Thanks." She hadn't heard him stand, but he was beside her. The night air was cool, and she rubbed her arms. His cell phone buzzed. "You better answer that."

"It's a text—I'll check it in a second. Look, I know how hard it is to lose someone you care about. After Andy was killed, I would've lost it if it hadn't been for God. He—"

"Stop!" She whirled around. "I don't want to hear it," she cried and fled to the house.

Tori had believed once that God was enough . . . until he wasn't. God could've kept Michael and her mother from dying. But he hadn't, and she couldn't trust that he would protect Scott.

Scott dared people to shoot him, for heaven's sake.

51

Scott's cell buzzed again as he stared at Tori's retreating back. If only she could understand that God was in her corner. He jerked his cell from his pocket. "This better be important," he muttered.

Howard Wilson's name showed on his phone. His undercover coordinator. There was only one reason he would be texting—it wasn't safe to talk. Suddenly Howard's name flashed on his caller ID. It must be really bad if he was now calling. Scott jabbed the answer button. "Sinclair."

"We need to meet. Now." The clipped tone was terse even for Wilson.

"What's happened?" Scott gripped the phone. He knew better than to question his coordinator, but why couldn't Wilson, just once, open a conversation with the weather?

"We have intel your location has been compromised."

The motorcyclist from earlier today. Scott hadn't recognized him, but that didn't mean the rider wasn't part of the gang.

"Where do you want to meet?" He choked the words out as his mind raced. If they had intel on his location, they knew about Tori, that she was staying with him at Oak Grove.

If she got hurt, it'd be his fault.

"Meet me at McKay's."

"McKay's?" He looked around to make sure no one had heard him. If Tori thought he was going to McKay's, she would think the worst. Something was going on with her anyway—Eli Livingston had probably sowed seeds of doubt in her mind about him. Scott lowered his voice. "Why there?"

"It's less than five minutes from where you are . . . and I'm already here."

"OK, I'll see you in ten."

"Make it eight."

Easier said than done. He needed to get backup from Ben and time to explain to Caleb what was going on. Scott called his friend. "You upstairs?"

"No, walking the perimeter."

"Could you come back to the house? My handler called, and I'm meeting him ASAP."

"Be right there."

He disconnected and texted Ben, requesting a couple of deputies to drive by the house.

He pocketed his phone and hurried to the kitchen to let Amy and Tori know he was leaving. They were nowhere to be seen. He checked his watch. It'd been a long day. Tori had probably retreated to her room . . . and Jenny's laptop was gone so Amy probably had as well. He quickly texted them both that he was leaving.

His fingers hovered over his phone. This couldn't have happened at a worse time. He wanted to tell Tori how much she meant to him. Instead, he typed *"I'll be back as soon as I can."* Then he added *"DON'T LEAVE THE HOUSE."*

Scott hurried to the gun safe and grabbed his Glock 19 and a couple of magazines. With his gun locked and loaded, he jogged to his pickup just as a text chimed on his phone. Tori.

I don't know where you think I'd go.

Scott groaned. She was still upset, and he didn't have time to respond. Howard was waiting for him. And no telling who else.

Eight minutes later he parked at McKay's and checked out the parking area. One good thing about McKay's—the parking lot was fairly well lit. Even so, there were shadows where evil could hide, but as far as he could tell, there were no motorcycles. He'd half expected the gang to be here. Zack's vehicle was here, though. His son was missing and he was drinking instead of looking for him? Scott had hoped he'd finally wised up.

Scott entered the dark tavern. Friday night was in full swing, which could be bad if the motorcycle gang showed up. Cigarette smoke created a haze as couples danced to Hank Williams Jr.'s "All My Rowdy Friends." Once his eyes adjusted to the lighting, he scanned the crowded room for his coordinator.

Howard sat in the back corner with his back to the wall. And to his right was an exit door—that might come in handy. Judging by the white shirt, black pants, and a jacket thrown over the chair beside him, his coordinator must have come straight from the regional office in Memphis.

The guy screamed FBI. At least he'd loosened his tie and rolled up his sleeves. No sidearm in view, which meant he was conceal carrying, probably in his pants pocket.

Scott paused at the bar and nodded to the bartender.

"What can I get for you?"

He would prefer water but doubted a freebie would go over well. "Iced tea with lemon."

The bartender looked at him over his glasses. "You kidding me?"

"Nope. If you don't have tea, I'll take a Coke."

"One Coke coming right up."

While he waited, Scott felt a presence at the bar and turned.

"Surprised to see you here," Zack said.

"That goes two ways."

"I'm not drinking, if that's what you mean. And neither are my friends. They want to help find Drew."

"That right?" Scott couldn't keep the skepticism from his voice.

"No, really. Smell my drink." He held out his cup "We thought somebody here might know where Drew is."

He didn't smell alcohol and hoped Zack was telling the truth. "Any luck?"

"Nah. We're heading out soon. Gonna ride the back roads, see if we see anything that don't look right."

"If I hear anything, I'll let you know," Scott said as the bartender set his drink on the bar. He paid and took it to the table where Howard waited and sat to his left so he could watch the front door.

His coordinator tapped his watch. "You're a minute late."

"Sue me." He grinned. Sometimes the man could be a pain, but he'd been good at keeping Scott safe until his cover was blown. "Good to see you again . . . I hope."

Howard made a face. "Memphis police picked up J-Dog two days ago for felony possession of a controlled substance. We were notified two hours ago, but he'd already made bail and disappeared. Oh, and good to see you again."

J-Dog. The name made him sick, and he took a swig of the Coke. Scott should've known that if there was a price on his head, J-Dog would come after him. He'd been the head of the Iron Wolves when Scott's cover was blown, and J-Dog had vowed to track him down and kill him. Looks like he'd found Scott. But J-Dog hadn't been the rider on the motorcycle he'd seen when they were driving home from the hospital. Scott turned and scanned the room. "Know how many are with him?"

"No." Howard crossed his arms. "MPD said he put up the full bail—five thousand."

"How'd he get such a low bail?"

"Overcrowding at the jail. Have you seen him?"

He turned back to Howard. "I saw someone on a cycle earlier, but it wasn't him," he said and described the man.

Howard took out his phone and scrolled. "This him?"

Scott studied the photo of a wiry man with a scraggly white beard. "Pretty sure it is."

"He goes by Blade. Usually runs with four other members."

Out of habit, Scott turned and swept his gaze over the crowd again. If the motorcycle gang showed up here, it wouldn't be good. "So, we're probably looking at six in total?"

"I hope that's all." Howard shrugged. "At least a backup team will be here in the next couple of hours. They're coming in from a job in St. Louis. You have anyone at the house with you in case they decide to attack?"

"Caleb Jackson."

"He's a good man, but that won't be enough until the team gets here. I'll join you and we can offer Tori Mitchell and Amy Bradsher protective custody, if you'd like."

Oh, he'd like all right, but he doubted Tori and Amy would accept. Scott checked the room again and groaned when three rough-looking men in leather jackets entered. He recognized them as part of J-Dog's gang. "Looks like we have company," he said softly.

An uneasy silence rippled through the crowd, but when the men sauntered to the bar, most conversation resumed. Howard jerked his head toward the exit, and Scott nodded. As much as he would love to take the motorcycle gang down, someone would get hurt if they initiated it inside McKay's.

Howard grabbed his jacket, and they eased the door open and slipped out of the room. The fresh air was a welcome relief from the smoky bar. Their feet crunched on gravel as they walked in the dim light around to the front of the building.

"Where're you parked?" Scott asked. The skin on the back of his neck tingled. He didn't like being in the dark.

Howard pointed toward a white SUV. "You?"

"Three spaces over—the red pickup."

"I'll follow you to your house," he said and Scott nodded.

Seconds later, two men materialized on their left, cutting them off from their vehicles. Howard and Scott kept walking. Scott quietly pulled his Glock from his back holster and glanced at his friend, catching a glint of steel in his hand. He also caught a glimpse of another biker on their right.

"Target at two o'clock," he murmured. "When they get closer, you take the one on the right, then come help me out."

"Gotcha," Howard said softly.

The two to the left stood with their feet spread, and one smacked a lead pipe in his hand. "I thought my boys would smoke you out."

Scott flinched at the raspy voice. He would recognize J-Dog's voice anywhere. Beside him, Howard planted his feet.

"Drop the pipe," he ordered.

J-Dog laughed. "I don't think so."

A force slammed into Scott from behind, knocking him down. *The men from inside.* They'd let the three in the parking lot distract them.

Another gang member tackled Howard, and he pitched forward, his gun skittering across the dirt.

A steel-toed boot came at Scott, barely missing his ribs. He grabbed the foot, flipping the man backward. Blade. Scott jumped to his feet.

J-Dog came at him with the pipe. Scott head-butted him just below the rib cage, and the gang leader went down, sucking for air. He grabbed J-Dog's pipe and came around swinging, connecting with another member of the gang.

The blessed wail of an approaching siren was music to Scott's ears. They had to hang on a few minutes more. Out of the corner of his eye, he saw that Blade had sprung to his feet and waved a knife in one hand. A man dashed out of the shadows toward the biker, tackling him.

Someone grabbed Scott from behind in a bear hug while another biker barreled toward him with brass knuckles. Scott leveraged his weight and executed a double kick and made a solid connection with the man's chest. His attacker stumbled back before going down.

The man holding Scott pressed his meaty arm across Scott's windpipe, blocking his air. He kicked at the man's knees. His assailant roared as he pulled back, squeezing Scott's throat tighter. White dots appeared in his vision. In a last-ditch effort, he slammed his fist into his captor's groin.

With a howl, the man dropped his hold and fell to the ground, writhing. Scott sucked in air. A shadow moved in his peripheral vision, and he wheeled around, his hands fisted, ready to take on the next attacker.

Flashing blue lights raked the night sky as cruisers converged on the parking lot and deputies spilled from their vehicles. It was over. He looked to see what had happened with Blade, and his eyes widened. The biker was out cold, and Zack stood guard over him.

"Thanks, man," Scott said when he reached him.

"You looked like you could use some help."

He high-fived Zack as a deputy cuffed the biker, and then Scott looked for Howard. His coordinator held his gun on one of the motorcycle gang. J-Dog.

Scott stalked to the gang leader, and Howard tossed him a flex-cuff. "You want to do the honors?"

"Gladly." He nodded at J-Dog. "Hands behind your back."

J-Dog narrowed his eyes, then complied. "How's that pretty little friend of yours?"

"Shut up."

"You might want to make sure she doesn't stroll down the street again."

Scott jerked the zip tie cuffs tight. "That right? You're admitting to attempted homicide?"

"Naw. Just giving you a friendly bit of advice."

"That'll be the day." Scott stared the motorcycle leader down. "If so much as a hair on her head is damaged, I'll come after you." Then he grinned. "Expect I won't have to go far. Jail is just ten minutes away."

52

Tori jerked awake. What woke her? Bathroom break, that's what. She padded to the bathroom, but once she was back in bed, sleep eluded her. She checked her watch. Only midnight? Tori closed her eyes.

Drew. Where was her nephew? And how were they going to get out of this mess if she didn't know where this supposed data drive was? Years ago, when she had problems, she went to her mother ... who always sent her to the Bible looking for answers, telling Tori that it was good therapy.

After her mother's death, she'd walked away from God. No, not walked. She'd run.

Maybe she needed to try a little of that Bible therapy again. Tori had seen one in the room earlier. She sat up and turned on her lamp. A quick scan of the room located it on the dresser, and she retrieved the leather-bound book.

She opened the Bible to the page where someone had left a bookmark. It was a psalm, and one of the verses was underlined. *"When I am afraid, I put my trust in you."*

Tears filled her eyes. The verse sounded just like her mother. She missed her so much. Her mom would know what to do about Drew. She flipped to the New Testament—Matthew. Again, a verse was underlined. *"Ask and it will be given to you; seek and you will find; knock and the door will be opened to you."*

That was the verse her mom *always* sent her to. It was the one Tori had turned to when her mom was in the hospital. *"Ask and it will be given to you..."* Well, she'd asked and her mom died anyway.

A thought struck Tori. How would Mom feel about the way she had turned from God? She almost closed the Bible. But the thought wouldn't leave. Her heart demanded an answer.

What was it Mom always said? God will never leave you. That he was as close as you want him to be. "God, are you there?" she whispered.

Of course he didn't answer... except, a tiny bit of peace crept into her heart. "I'm... sorry I..." Tori gently touched her face, wincing when her fingers brushed the swelling. Maybe God had kept her from dying today.

"Lord, I don't know if you'll even listen to me, but I need help. Mom... and Scott... they both say you know what's going on. If you could help me find Drew or what the kidnapper wants, it would go a long way helping me to believe you again..."

She closed the Bible and leaned against the headboard with her eyes closed. Waiting. After a few minutes, Tori sighed. Nothing. Just like she expected. She turned off the light and tried to go back to sleep.

She had almost nodded off when her eyes flew open. Of course. How had she forgotten the secret hiding place in her old bedroom? She'd shown it to Drew way back when she babysat him at the house. But it'd been so long ago.

If he had the data drive, that's where it would be. Tori didn't want to wait until morning to find out. Scott could take her. Wait—he'd texted that he was leaving and for her to stay at the house. She hadn't heard him return, but that didn't mean he hadn't. Maybe he was asleep.

She pulled on her robe, cinching it at the waist before she hurried down the hall to his bedroom. A faint light shone under the door. She tapped lightly.

No answer. "Scott? she said softly as she eased into his bedroom. The room was empty, the bed not slept in. Where was he? Maybe he was walking the perimeter with Caleb. He'd put that locator on her phone, and it would show if he were on the property. Tori grabbed her cell and opened the app.

She frowned. No . . . Scott couldn't be at McKay's. Ha! Of course he could. He was an alcoholic. She'd known it was just a matter of time before he relapsed.

Just when she needed him too. Tori took a deep breath. She'd have to make it happen herself, which wouldn't be a problem if she had wheels. Her car was still at Zack's. If she woke Amy for her keys, she would try and talk her out of leaving—same with Caleb. She'd just have to walk.

Tori closed the app and noticed an unread text from Eli. The time stamp put it two hours ago.

> I know it's late and you may already be asleep . . .

Maybe he was still up. She needed someone to talk to.

> I'm awake.

Three dots appeared below the text. He was texting her.

> I really want to help.

Three more dots.

> You've always been special to me.

Her mind raced. Eli would take her to Zack's house. She could meet him at the gate, and that way she wouldn't have to tell anyone who would try to stop her.

What if the data drive had information that would help her figure out where Drew was? And she wouldn't be by herself—Eli would be with her . . . Her mind made up, she texted him.

> Can you pick me up? I'll meet you at the road in front of the house.

He texted a thumbs-up.

Tori pulled on her jeans and a sweatshirt and slipped her feet into her sneakers. She checked to see if Scott was still at McKay's. He was. Had he been planning to go there earlier?

But why now? What had been his trigger? Surely not their argument?

Tori set her jaw. Hadn't she always said once an addict, always an addict? One excuse was as good as another. She didn't know why she was so surprised or disappointed. No, she knew why—Tori had actually thought Scott was different.

With her bag over her shoulder, Tori crept down the stairs and eased out the front door. Hopefully, Caleb was asleep and not outside standing guard. She didn't see him and jogged toward the road. A car approached from the west and she held her breath until it slowed and stopped at the gate. Eli.

He lowered his window and grinned. "Would you like a ride, ma'am?"

She laughed and hopped in his SUV on the passenger side.

"Where to?" he asked as he pulled away from Oak Grove.

"My brother's house."

"Zack's?"

"Yeah. For once I hope he's at McKay's and not at home."

He glanced over at her. "Why do you want to go to your brother's?"

"I want to get something."

"And it couldn't wait until morning?"

She eyed him. "If you don't want to help me . . ."

"It's not that. I'm just curious about what's so important that you'd ask *me* to help when you've all but ignored me since you met Scott."

"I told you before, it's complicated," she said. "I thought of something I wanted to check out and then I couldn't sleep, but I didn't want to disturb anyone. When you texted that you were up, it was like confirmation."

He turned on the road to Zack's house. "You still haven't told me what you're looking for."

"It may be nothing at all. Just drop me off in front of Zack's house."

"I'm not leaving you, not with someone obviously out to hurt you, even if you won't tell me the details." He turned right at the end of the road. "And don't tell me it's complicated."

Tori sighed. "But it is."

"Don't you think it's time to tell me what's going on? Or is Scott Sinclair the only one allowed to know?"

Heat blazed her cheeks. "Come on, Eli . . . it really is complicated. Yeah, someone is out to get me . . . Drew is missing, a friend's ex-husband is threatening me, Scott is—" She didn't want to go there. "I don't even know where to start. And we don't have time for me to fill you in."

He blew out a breath. "Okay. Check out whatever it is at your brother's, then maybe you can tell me what's going on."

"Yeah," she said as he pulled into Zack's driveway and parked. She pulled her key ring from her bag, glad she'd never removed the key to the house she grew up in.

"I don't see Zack's pickup," Eli said.

"He's probably closing McKay's down. Why don't you stay here and text me if he drives up?" She held his gaze while he studied her. "Please."

"Since you asked so nicely . . ." He winked at her. "I hope you find what you're looking for."

So did she. And if she did, she was texting the phone that Drew's kidnapper called her on and offering it in exchange for her nephew.

53

Tori moved to open the door.

"You sure you don't want me to come with you? I really do want to help."

Her chest tightened. Eli's insistence creeped her out. Asking him to bring her . . . what was she thinking? He never did anything unless it benefited him.

"Thanks." She sucked in a breath and forced her lips into a bright smile. "But this is something I want to do by myself."

"If you change your mind, text me, and I'll be right there."

"Sure." Why hadn't she waited for Scott?

Because he was at McKay's.

Tori climbed from his SUV before Eli could insist on accompanying her. She half jogged to the steps and walked up to the door, the key in her hand. Except Zack had left the door unlocked. Only in Logan Point.

In her old room, Drew's now, she made a beeline for the closet and dropped to her knees, brushing aside a pile of her nephew's dirty clothes that covered the door to the secret compartment. Tori stared at the floor. It'd been years since she opened it . . . where was the spring?

"Oh, wait." With a groan she stood and searched Drew's desk for a knife to trigger the spring. Paper clips, pens, staples, even a desktop computer, but no knife. She scanned the room, searching for something thin and sharp. Her gaze landed on her purse. Nail file. She opened the bag and pulled out her travel case.

Once she found the nail file, Tori returned to the closet and used it to trigger the spring. The door popped open, and she stared at the small box in the bottom of the compartment. Did it hold the answer to all their questions?

Maybe she should call Scott. She yanked her phone from her pocket and checked his location first. Tori ground her teeth. He was still at McKay's. Probably having a high old time with her brother. She punched his number, and it went to voicemail. *Okay. He doesn't want to be bothered.*

She pocketed her phone and reached for the box. Wait. There might be prints on it. Her trusty bag came in handy again as she fished several tissues out. The box rattled when she lifted it from its hiding place.

The data drive. Heaviness released from her chest. Tori used the tissue to lift the top of the box. *Yes!* Nestled inside was a small black storage device.

She glanced inside the compartment again. For a second, she didn't breathe. Was that a gun?

Tori used more tissues to lift the gun from its hiding place. *"I didn't kill Jenny, but I think I know who did."* Drew's words that first day when she talked to him. Drew must've found the gun at Jenny's house and hid it because it belonged to his dad.

She laid the gun back in the compartment. Tori would deal with it later. She turned back to the data drive. Did she have time to boot up Drew's desktop and see what was on it? She would make time.

A text sounded on her phone, and Tori glanced at it. Eli. She ignored it and booted up her nephew's computer, praying it didn't need a password to unlock it.

She breathed easier when it opened to his home page. Tori popped the drive into the USB port and opened it. She frowned at the list of files, all of them encrypted. At least the date each file was created showed, and the oldest was more than twenty years ago.

Another text chimed. Eli again. This time she read it.

> Hurry up or I'm coming in.

What was the deal with him? Tori didn't want him seeing what she'd found and quickly texted that she was coming. She saved the files to Drew's computer, but before she ejected the drive, Eli sent another text.

> Two minutes.

Tori gritted her teeth, returned the data drive to the secret compartment, and closed it. She held a bargaining chip now—the data drive had to contain evidence of something illegal, and she wasn't dumb enough to just hand it over. If whoever had Drew wanted it, they would have to release him first. Ben would cover her on the exchange, and they could get the kidnapper.

She opened her text app, and her fingers hovered over her keyboard. If Scott was drinking, he would be of little use to her. *But what if he's there but not drinking?* Tori tried to ignore the small voice in her head. Huffing, she checked the location app again.

Still at McKay's. That place should be closing soon. She narrowed her eyes and texted Ben Logan.

> Found the data drive. Need your help. Contacting kidnappers for exchange.

She hesitated and added:

> Meet you at Oak Grove. Scott is at McKay's. Tell him if he's sober enough.

After wavering briefly, she added Scott to the text. That ought to do it. Then Tori found the text from Drew's kidnapper and sent another text.

> Have data drive. Will exchange it for my nephew.

Tori glanced back at the closet. The bare floor looked as though it had a neon arrow pointing at the secret compartment, and she grabbed a few articles of Drew's clothing and tossed them over the spot.

When she exited the house, Eli was leaning against his SUV, scrolling or texting on his phone—Tori couldn't tell which. "Sorry it took so long."

His head jerked up, and he closed his hand over the phone and quickly slid it in his pocket.

"You're awfully nervous."

"I didn't hear you come out. Did you find what you're looking for?"

"Yeah."

"Can I see it?"

Before she could formulate an answer, a text dinged and Tori took out her phone. "Hold that thought."

She opened her message. It was from Scott.

> Whatever you are thinking, don't do it.

She stared at her phone. He didn't sound drunk.

> I found the data drive. What are you doing at McKay's?

> Too much to explain in a text. Please return to the house. Ben and I will take it from there.

She wanted to see this through to the end and hovered her fingers over the keyboard, formulating a response.

"Give me your phone." Eli's cold, threatening voice stopped her.

"Why?" She looked up and froze. He held a gun pointed straight at her heart.

54

Scott slapped his coordinator on the back. "You weren't half bad," he said with a laugh. "Maybe if you got out in the field more often, you'd get to 100 percent."

Howard worked his jaw. "I think I'll keep my present job. And if you don't need me any longer, I'm headed home."

"Me too, but I need to see someone first." Scott scanned the parking lot for Tori's brother and located him talking to Ben Logan. He jogged to where they stood. When he reached them, Scott held out his hand to Zach. "Thanks again for helping us. You said earlier that you were here to ask about Drew. Did you learn anything from anyone in the bar?"

"Naw. Nobody's heard anything, but the guys inside are ready to beat bushes, looking for him."

"We'll handle it," Ben said.

Zack crossed his arms. "It's not your son that's missing. We already figured out he's not being kept anywhere in town. We're going to hit the back roads and before you ask, I haven't had a drop to drink." He jerked his head toward his buddies. "And neither have they."

"Might not be a bad idea to let them," Scott said.

Ben's jaw muscle worked furiously, then he relaxed. "As long as you're not armed, and I mean even hunting rifles, and you contact me if you find *anything* that looks suspicious."

Zack studied the ground, then raised his gaze and nodded. "We can do that."

Scott hoped he was telling the truth, but in a way he didn't blame the man for doing anything he could to find his son.

Zack turned and walked toward a group of men waiting just outside the bar. Ben shook his head. "He's as bad as his sister. Did you get a text from Tori?"

Scott's stomach dropped. He yanked his phone from his back pocket. There was a missed call and a text. He quickly read it.

He blinked and shook his head to clear it. Tori seriously thought he was drinking? And she was going to contact the kidnappers? He looked at Ben. "What is she thinking? Once they get that data drive, they'll kill her. Drew too."

"She only said she was contacting them," Ben said.

"But if they wanted to make an immediate exchange, she'd probably do it."

Scott quickly sent her a text, then he checked her location. "She's at her brother's house." But how did she get there? Scott checked the box in the location app for him to be alerted if she left her brother's house, then he quickly called Caleb and put it on speaker. "Is Amy's car there?"

"Let me check the camera feed." A few seconds later, Caleb came back on the line. "Yeah, why?"

"Tori is at her brother's, and I don't know how she got there. Can you check the camera feed that covers the gate and road and see if you can tell when she left and how?"

Seconds later Caleb groaned. "A little after midnight, she walked to the road and slipped through the small opening between the gate and the fence. Looks like someone picked her up."

Ben leaned toward the phone. "Can you tell who was driving or the make and model?"

Caleb took a few seconds to respond, then he said, "Too dark to identify the driver. Hold on while I zoom in on the vehicle."

Scott clenched and unclenched his hands. Tori didn't trust him, not if she'd assumed he was drinking. Just when he'd finally acknowledged she might be the one. No might-be to it. He'd *wanted* her to be the one. But without trust, they could never have a relationship. He rubbed the back of his neck. Even more important, she didn't trust God, and they definitely weren't on the same page when it came to faith.

"The video is too dark to identify the vehicle," Caleb said. "But let me keep working with it."

Scott's locator app trilled. "Tori's on the move," he said. "Hopefully headed toward Oak Grove. I want to see what's on this data drive she's found."

"So do I," Ben said. "I'll meet you there."

Ten minutes later, Scott keyed in the code at the gate, and Ben followed him to the house. Caleb met them at the front door. He looked beyond Scott. "Where's Tori?"

"Isn't she here?"

Caleb looked worried. "Hasn't shown."

They hurried inside and met Amy coming down the stairs.

"What's going on?" she said. "Tori isn't in her room."

"I know. She was at her brother's."

Scott paced the foyer while Ben filled in the other two. "She's supposed to be returning to Oak Grove."

"I can't believe she left without telling me," Amy said. "I need some coffee."

As they walked down the hallway, Scott checked his phone again. What was going on? "She's stationary again not far from the last time I checked."

In the kitchen Ben turned to Amy. "Do you know anyone she might call to take her somewhere?"

"Erin, maybe . . . but she would've asked me first." She looked at Scott and grimaced. "Unless she thought I would try and talk her out of going anywhere."

Scott turned around. "I'm going to Zack's house."

"Call her first," Amy said.

He punched in her number and waited until it went to voicemail. "She's not answering," he said. "I'm going to Zack's now."

55

"Tori..."

She couldn't look away from the gun. "Why are you doing this?"

"Hand over what you found."

"Excuse me?"

"You heard me. Jenny said she mailed you a data drive."

Her eyes widened. "I don't know what you're talking about."

"That's what I figured. Jenny was pretty smart. This house made a perfect place—no one would think to look for it here. So if she didn't send it to you, she either gave it to your nephew to hide or hid it herself. That's what you found, right?"

"I didn't find anything—"

"Stop lying. I know it was there—Drew admitted as much."

"Drew told you he had a data drive?"

"Not exactly. He told me he found money Jenny had hidden—I figure she hid the data drive with the money."

"You figured wrong. I thought maybe it was here too, but it wasn't."

"You're lying!"

Her cell rang. Scott. Tori tried to answer, but Eli knocked the phone from her hands. She lunged for it, but it skittered down the gravel drive. He jerked her back. "I don't want to hurt you, so don't make me. Now give me your hands."

"No!"

He twisted her arm behind her back, and pain shot through her shoulder. "Give me your other hand, or I'll break your arm."

When she didn't immediately respond, he pulled her hand higher, bringing more pain. Tori quickly complied.

Once her hands were secured in ties, he said, "Now we're going inside and getting that drive."

A faint *wee-oo-wee-oo* raised her hopes that the police would get here before he killed her or took her somewhere else. He jerked his head toward the siren and swore. Then he opened the passenger door. "Get in."

Seconds later Eli climbed in on the driver's side and gunned the motor. Tori slammed against the door when he did a U-turn and barreled down the drive.

Even though she'd hit the side of her face that wasn't bruised, it'd been hard enough to send pain shooting to the left eye. Tori righted herself. "You sure you want to do this? Scott will hunt you down."

"Shut up." He gripped the steering wheel. "You just couldn't keep your nose out of it, could you? You had to mess everything up."

"I only wanted to get my nephew back. Why did you take him?"

"It was supposed to be you." Eli raised his hand, and she thought he was going to hit her. "Just shut up."

When he turned away from town at the end of the road, her stomach twisted. If he'd turned toward Logan Point, there would've been at least a chance of someone seeing them. This direction led to secondary roads that would allow him to disappear into the countryside.

Eli hit a pothole, and a sharp pain knifed her shoulder, bringing tears to her eyes. She gritted her teeth. Crying was not an option.

"Can you at least put my hands in front of me? My arm is killing me," she said, her voice breaking.

Eli didn't respond, and in spite of her vow, tears ran down her face. After a while, he sighed and pulled over. "Turn toward the door."

Was that remorse in his voice? She'd meant something to him once, at least Tori thought she had. Maybe Eli was remembering those times. She turned and lifted her hands away from her body, and pain shot through her shoulder again. The binding tightened, then released.

"Put your hands in front of you."

"Give me a second to get the blood moving again." Tori massaged her arm, barely feeling her fingers work the muscles.

"Hurry up."

"I'm sorry—I can't move my arm." She cried out as he pulled her hands out in front of her. "You don't have to be so rough—"

"Enough!" Eli jerked her hands together and secured them with another zip tie.

Tori took a deep breath and waited for the pain to subside. She'd managed to cross her hands when he tied them, but was it enough? Was this how her life would end? She wasn't ready to die. She needed to make things right with her dad. Erin. And Drew . . .

It's not your time. Tori stilled. She didn't hear the words as much as she felt them. Her mom had always said Jesus would never leave her. Was he reassuring her? Hope filled Tori, clearing her head and giving her strength. Maybe if she connected with Eli, she could still reach that boy she remembered. He *had* tried to make her more comfortable. And if they sat here long enough on the side of the road, maybe someone would come along and see them.

He must have had the same thought because he suddenly gunned the motor. The SUV shot forward back on the road, slamming her against the seat. With a groan, she straightened back up.

"I wish you'd warn me next time."

Eli didn't respond and she glanced at him. The glow from the dashboard cast enough light to see that he was coiled tighter than a spring ready to snap. "You don't have to do this." Tori kept her words soft.

"That's where you're wrong. I'm in too deep to stop now."

"Too deep into what?" Not that she really expected him to tell her, but if she could get him to talk, she could figure out what he had planned. Maybe even the why. Evidently his silence meant he wasn't cooperating.

"What happened to you?" She held up her arms. "This isn't you."

That got a response, but not what she was hoping for as he shot a withering glare at her. "You have no idea who I am."

"Then tell me who you are. And why are you doing this? Why have you been trying to kill me? Can't be for the money. You're a Livingston—you're set for life."

He barked a laugh. "You'd think. And actually I am, but not from anything dear old Dad gives me. Nothing I ever did was good enough for him, no matter how hard I tried."

"Okay. I get it. You and your dad don't get along, but why are you involving me? And my nephew?"

He exhaled sharply. "Because you got caught in an unfortunate set of circumstances. Jenny said she mailed you a data drive. Couldn't take a chance she was bluffing."

Why would Jenny say something like that . . . unless she was bargaining for her life. Tori gasped. "You killed her."

He shook his head. "Not me."

She didn't believe him. "Just like you're not going to kill me."

Eli ignored her and made a sharp right turn onto a gravel road. She bit her lip to keep from crying out as she fell into the door again. "Where are you taking me?"

"You wanted to see your nephew." He gave her a sarcastic smile.

Wait . . . if Eli was with *her* . . . "Who's with Drew?"

"You'll find out soon enough."

At least he didn't say Drew was dead. But that meant there were at least two of them. She should've known Eli wasn't the brains behind all of this.

The jarring beams of the headlights revealed nothing but a dense forest. She slumped against the seat. Her phone was gone. Scott would never find her this deep in the woods. The hope she'd clung to just minutes ago was slipping away.

No. I'm not dying tonight.

Tori dropped her gaze to her wrists. She'd crossed her hands when Eli cuffed her, but did she create enough space to escape from the restraints? She tried to straighten her hands, but the ties dug into her skin. Wiggling free would be impossible without Eli noticing.

Her gaze landed on her watch, and she caught her breath. It was synced to her phone. Tori closed her eyes, praying Scott would think to check her watch location. She opened her eyes. Could he even do that? If there was a way, Scott would find it.

They reached a Y in the road, and Eli followed the right side and then turned on a crooked lane a few hundred yards from the split. She pressed back into the seat and leaned toward the console, trying not to lose her balance again.

The SUV lights swept across a dark wooden structure with a half-opened door and windows that looked like vacant eyes. A strong wind could blow it down.

Her eyes widened. Another vehicle was parked to the side. A white Escalade. One she'd seen just this week.

"Why is your father's SUV here?"

"It's not his." He pulled next to the Escalade and killed the motor. Eli turned to her, his eyes dead. "And he's not my father."

56

Scott bolted from the kitchen and out the front door to his truck.

"Wait—my deputies are leaving McKay's," Ben said. "They'll meet us there. Ride with me."

Scott switched direction and headed toward Ben's SUV. Five minutes later they pulled up to Zack's house with Ben's siren going full blast and his deputies on their way.

"The app says she's here." Scott climbed out of the vehicle.

"It says her phone's here," Ben said, joining him. "See if you can ping it."

Scott tapped the device locator, and a faint beeping sounded near the road. He jogged toward it with the sheriff on his heels, but it was hard to pinpoint the location. "Do you see it?"

"Not yet—it's too dark." Ben shined his flashlight along the edge of the drive.

The beeping stopped, and Scott kicked at a clump of dirt. The phone shouldn't be this hard to find. He pinged it again.

"Over here," Ben said, pulling on a pair of nitrile gloves.

The phone was face down in the drive. The sheriff picked it up and bagged it. "Someone ran over it."

Scott was surprised it had even pinged.

Three of Ben's deputies pulled in and climbed out of their vehicles. Scott remained where he was as the sheriff joined them. Where could Tori be? Scott's cell rang. Caleb. "What do you have?" he asked.

"Not much. I was able to enhance the video enough to see that it's a light-colored SUV. Can't tell the make or model, but at least you'll know generally what to look for."

"Thanks." Scott disconnected and joined Ben and explained what Caleb had told him. "Do you know anyone who owns a light-colored SUV?"

"You say an SUV? That eliminates Erin—she has a Civic." Ben rubbed his jaw. "Eli has a light tan Infiniti. Richard Livingston has a white Escalade. I think Stephanie has a matching one . . . and Valerie has a black Lexus."

"Let's start with Eli." He'd never trusted the man.

Ben made the call, and after a few seconds, he pocketed his phone. "He doesn't answer, but he could have his phone turned off. Let's drive to his house."

Scott agreed. All the Livingstons lived in the same high-end neighborhood where the houses backed up to a lake. But if Eli kidnapped Tori, they weren't going to find her at his house. "How much property do the Livingstons own?"

"I'm not sure," Ben replied.

Scott opened his text messages. "I'll get Amy to locate any property Eli owns in the area other than his house."

He sent the text, and seconds later she texted back that she was on it.

It was only a short drive to Eli's two-story colonial-style house, but it seemed to take forever. The house was dark when they pulled into the drive, and Scott was out the door as soon as Ben stopped. They hurried to the front door, and Ben rang the doorbell and then knocked.

"He's either not here or ignoring us. Can you tell if his SUV is in the garage?" Scott asked.

Ben shook his head. "No window, and I can't break in without a search warrant, and I have no probable cause for one. Let's check the back."

They jogged to the back of the house where there was a door to the garage. A door with a window. Ben shined his light through the glass. Empty.

"Where would he take her?" Scott asked.

"If he took her. And I don't know."

"Do Richard and Stephanie still live next door?" When Ben nodded, he turned toward their house. It was dark as well. Scott checked his watch. Hardly seemed like 3:00 a.m. "Do we check with them?"

"I doubt they would know anything, and I hate to disturb them this time of night."

"You mean morning? Can your deputies put out a BOLO for Eli's car?"

"Already done. But you know, we may be blowing this out of proportion. For all we know, they could be having a good time somewhere."

"No way." Scott jutted his jaw. "She's too worried about Drew. How long would it take for you to get her call logs?"

"Who does she have her phone service with?"

He told him.

While the sheriff called the carrier, Scott checked with Amy to see if she had any information on property Eli owned in the county.

"I've found several. Do you want me to text it or email?"

"Email it." Scott gave her his email.

Ben slid his phone in his pocket. "I talked to the carrier. It'll take a few minutes to access her records. Has Amy found anything?"

He nodded. "She's emailed a list."

"Great," Ben said "Let's go to my office. I have a big county map—we can pin the properties he owns and decide where to go once we have an idea of the bigger picture."

Scott opened the list and stared at how many there were. How would they ever decide which place Eli might have taken Tori? She could be dead before they found her.

57

Tori stared at Eli. "What do you mean, he's not your father?"

"Do I have to draw you a map? What part of that don't you understand?" Without waiting for an answer, he climbed out of the SUV and slammed the door and then walked to her door and opened it. "Get out," he said, motioning with the gun.

The first step was a long one. "I need your help."

She thought Eli was going to refuse, but then he held out his left hand. "Just don't get any ideas of trying to escape. Your nephew tried it, and I don't think he'll try it again."

"If you hurt him—"

"You'll what?" His mouth twisted. "I don't think you're in any position to threaten anyone. Now get inside."

Tori's shoulders slumped. There was nothing she could do if he'd hurt Drew—past, present, or future. At least not in her power. She straightened her shoulders. No matter what Tori faced inside the house, her mom was right—she wasn't alone. God was with her.

He gripped her arm as they climbed the rickety steps to the porch. At the top, she stumbled on a loose plank. She fell, jerking from his grasp, and rolled onto her back. Eli staggered, his arms flailing to get his balance. Tori kicked at him with both feet, connecting with his knees.

He screamed and grabbed his knees as he fell. The gun clattered to the floor. With her hands still zip-tied, Tori scooped it up and pointed it at Eli. "Get up."

He moaned. "I can't, you broke my kneecaps."

"I don't think so. I didn't kick you that hard. Now get up!"

He glared at her before he rolled over and used the porch rail to pull himself up.

"Where's Drew?"

"Inside." He spit the word out.

"Who else is in there?"

"Why don't you go in and see."

His cockiness made her want to kick him again. She was pretty sure someone was inside waiting for them . . . the zip ties dug into her wrists, but she wasn't about to let Eli near her with a knife. Once she had Drew free, he could help her get loose.

"I have a gun on Eli," she yelled. "Whoever is in the house, come out or I'll use it."

At first there was no response, then feet shuffled toward the door. Drew appeared first. She couldn't see who stood behind him. "Are you all right?"

He shook his head, like he was trying to warn her. Then Stephanie Livingston stepped where Tori could see her. Not Richard. Tori had forgotten the couple had matching Cadillacs. The woman held a gun near Drew's head.

"You can let Eli go now," Stephanie said.

"I don't think so. Why don't you release Drew?"

"Let's cut to the chase. You won't shoot Eli—you're not that kind of person. But I am. And unless you want your nephew to die in the next minute, lay the gun down and come inside." She pressed the gun to Drew's temple as if to prove her point.

Tori stared into Stephanie's hard eyes. The woman would pull the trigger and not think twice about it.

"Okay. Don't shoot him." She moved the gun away from Eli, and he snatched it from her hand.

"Inside," he growled.

Tori stepped through the doorway into a dark room and followed Drew and Stephanie down a hallway. A faint light spilled from under a closed door. Stephanie nudged Drew to open it. Once he did, she shoved him inside and told him to sit down. Then she motioned for Tori to follow.

"Sit there." Stephanie pointed to a chair beside Drew, facing the window. "Tie her to the chair."

Once Tori was secured, Stephanie stuck her gun in her waistband. "Where's the drive?" she asked. "And what took you so long?"

"Got here as soon as I could, babe."

Eli had avoided the subject of the data drive. And *babe*? That plus his tone suggested familiarity, like they had a close relationship. "So, you two . . ."

The other woman laughed. "It's a business deal."

It didn't appear to be totally business, at least on Eli's part. Tori glared at him. "How could you do this to your dad?"

"I told you, he's not my father. Dear old Uncle Walter was my dad. Of course, I didn't know until I submitted my DNA to a site, and, well, let's just say Jenny wasn't the only one surprised when she found out who her father was."

What a messed-up family. But despite Eli's sarcasm, the information had hurt him.

"And since you are so interested in who killed Walter, it was my father," he said, putting the last word in air quotes. "I understand he was livid when he discovered my mother's unfaithfulness. With his brother, no less."

Richard killed Walter? And let Huey go to jail for it? "I suppose you have proof."

"Enough reminiscing, you two." Stephanie turned to Eli. "Give me the drive."

Eli's face reddened. "She claimed she couldn't find it, and then we had to beat it because the cops were coming."

A string of expletives spewed from Stephanie's lips, then she shook her head and paced the room, muttering. "I should've taken care of it myself."

While the woman ranted, Tori scanned the room. There had to be a way out of here. The room was small, maybe ten by twelve feet with a battery-powered lantern in the middle of the floor. One window. One door. Something in the corner . . . She frowned. Then she blinked. It looked like a body. "Who is that?"

Stephanie stopped in front of Tori. "I see you've discovered my cousin, Cal. I thought he'd be useful since he lived in Knoxville, and he had an interest in keeping tabs on you. Then he got fire-happy, which would've been fine if he hadn't bungled the job. Our problems would've gone away if he'd managed to burn your studio down with you in it."

"Is he . . . is he dead?"

"Not yet." The cold words sent a chill through Tori. She was dealing with a true sociopath. She glanced at Eli. Make that two.

Stephanie turned on her partner. "He's as bad as you. Why didn't you go with her into her brother's house?"

"I wasn't ready to reveal my hand. I thought she'd bring the drive out with her, but then she said she couldn't find it."

"You *thought*." She waved the gun. "We have to get that drive and destroy it."

"Jenny's dead, and if she can't find it," Eli said, jerking his head toward Tori, "maybe it'll never surface."

"Don't tell me you believe her?" The corner of Stephanie's lip curled. She shook her head. "The drive has proof that we—"

"Not we," Eli snapped. "You."

She glared at him. "You're in this just as deep as I am."

He palmed his hands. "No. I'm only taking what's mine, or will be one day."

Stephanie let out a huff. "Not if Richard discovers that you've been embezzling funds from the company."

Eli shrugged. "Then I'll be happy with my mother's part. You're the one who got too greedy and hooked up with money launderers."

"You were happy to take their money. You think they're going to just let you walk away? Especially if we don't come up with that drive?"

"Why did you keep records anyway? That was plain stupid."

"It was for insurance to use against the cartel if they ever got too unreasonable." She turned back to Tori. "I want the location of the drive, and I want it now."

"I didn't find it." She stared Stephanie down.

"There's more than one way to find out." Stephanie walked to Drew's chair and held the gun to his head. "You know where the drive is, don't you?"

Drew shrank back.

Tori strained against the rope binding her to the chair. Stephanie had killed once to cover up her illegal activities. She would have no problem killing Drew. "He doesn't know anything."

"I think he does."

Tori's heart almost stopped as Stephanie's finger tightened on the trigger.

58

Scott paced the floor in the conference room at the sheriff's office. Another couple of hours and it'd be daylight. He stopped in front of the map where Ben sorted out the different properties Amy had sent. Eli owned property with his mother and individually, and it was painstakingly slow. There had to be a quicker way to find Tori.

A text dinged from his phone on the conference table. He reached for it, and his watch lit up. Scott froze with his hand halfway to the table.

"Ben, I think I know a way to find her!"

The sheriff turned from the map. "How?"

"I never looked at the locater app again after we found her phone, but when we bought Tori's phone, I had them sync the watch with it." Scott snatched his phone and opened the app. "It'll show her location even if she doesn't have the phone with her."

He tapped on Tori's name and frowned. "Doesn't give an address, but can you tell the location?" He handed the phone to Ben.

The sheriff tapped the phone screen to zoom out, then he turned to the map. "I bet that's the Wallace old homeplace." He pointed to a spot he'd circled on the wall map. "Right here."

"How sure are you?"

"Ninety percent." He looked at the phone again and pointed

to another circle close by. "Or it can be here. Either way, the two properties are adjacent to each other. Let's check them out."

As they rushed out of the office, Ben called Wade Hatcher to round up the rest of the deputies and meet them at the Wallace property. "Come in silent and no lights," he said.

He and Ben were thinking alike. If Tori was being held against her will, sirens could make Eli panic and maybe kill her so she couldn't testify against him. "How long will it take to get there?" he asked as they jumped in Ben's vehicle.

"Winding country roads . . . probably ten, fifteen minutes."

Scott gripped the armrest and sent up a silent prayer that they were on the right path and that they would get there in time.

After ten minutes that seemed like an hour, he said, "How much farther?"

Ben turned onto a narrow gravel road. "We're not far from where we'll leave the car and hike in."

He pressed his lips tight to keep from telling Ben to hurry. A few minutes later the sheriff pulled off the road onto an even narrower one and parked. "We walk from here, but give me a second to see where my deputies are."

Wade Hatcher was closest at five minutes out. Ben gave him instructions to follow the lane to the house, but unless he heard shots fired, to come in quietly. Scott hoped there would be no gunfire. Then Ben grabbed what looked like an oversized black marker from a box behind the driver's seat. A flash-bang. The disorienting grenade with its blinding flash and 180 decibel sound could come in handy.

With the moonlight guiding them, they walked single file down the road until they rounded a curve and a vacant house with two SUVs parked out front came into sight.

"Eli's SUV," Ben whispered and pointed to a tan Infiniti. "I imagine the Escalade beside it belongs to Richard or Stephanie Livingston."

They approached the house cautiously. Near the porch, they stopped and Scott cocked his head. Voices filtered from a room on their left. They veered to the left side of the house.

A dim glow emanated from the dirty window, and the voices were much plainer.

"I'm not telling you where the data drive is until you let Drew go."

Scott's stomach lurched. That was Tori's voice.

"You don't hold the cards here, honey. I do."

He recognized Stephanie Livingston's voice. She was near the window. If her back was to them, he could sneak a peek through the glass. He started to raise up when a man spoke.

"Tell her where it is, or she'll kill him."

Scott caught Ben's attention. "Eli," he mouthed. There were at least two of them.

Silence followed, then the woman said, "Either you tell me where to find it or I'll blow your nephew's kneecaps off."

A twig snapped behind them, and both men whirled around. Wade. Ben nodded to his chief deputy. "Where are the others?" he whispered.

Wade held up five fingers. Five minutes out.

They didn't have five minutes.

59

Stephanie pointed her gun at Drew's knees.

"He's just a kid," Tori pleaded. Her hands were almost free. Tori stilled as Stephanie switched the Glock back to her, the crazed look in her eyes almost as scary as the gun. Tori turned away, shifting her gaze toward the window. Was that movement? It was gone so fast she didn't know if it was real or wishful thinking.

"Then tell me what I want to know."

When she didn't answer immediately, Stephanie swung the gun back to Drew.

Everything froze. The hazy room. Stephanie's face, determination stamped in it like granite, her finger on the trigger, the gun just inches from Drew's knees. Her nephew's eyes wide, mouth open. The body against the wall. Eli looking away.

Suddenly the zip tie popped, and Tori lunged at Drew's chair. The blast from Stephanie's gun reverberated in her ears. The heat of the bullet seared the side of her head as she shoved Drew's chair over. The rope binding her loosened and she shrugged out of it.

Her ears throbbed as she spun around and grasped Stephanie's wrist. The gun fired again. Tori slammed Stephanie's hand down onto the floor, but she stubbornly held on to the weapon.

The room exploded in a bright flash of light, blinding Tori before a deafening boom rocked the room. Acrid smoke burned her nose and throat.

What happened? Tori blinked, only seeing white spots. Stephanie jerked from her grasp, and Tori blindly dove for her. "No!"

The door flew open.

"Hands where I can see them!" She just barely heard Ben's voice over the ringing in her ears.

Her vision cleared, but it took a second to register that Scott had kicked the gun from Stephanie's hand. Tori climbed to her feet and staggered as deputies swarmed into the room.

"I've got you." Scott scooped Tori into his arms. "You're safe now."

"Drew—"

"He'll be okay. Wade is cutting his zip ties. Everything is going to be fine."

Tori rested her head on Scott's chest as he carried her outside. The wail of a siren reminded her just how narrowly she and Drew had escaped death. If Scott hadn't shown up when he did with Ben . . . Guilt swept over her. He'd risked his life to save her even though she'd accused him of drinking. She had to apologize, even though he would probably never forgive her, and she wouldn't blame him. "Scott . . . I'm sorry—"

"Not now. We'll talk later." He set her on a solid part of the porch. "Ambulances are almost here for Drew and Eli."

"Eli?"

Scott nodded. "He was shot."

The gun had gone off while she and Stephanie were struggling over it—the bullet must've hit him. "Is he bad?"

"It's a shoulder wound. Do you know the identity of the other man who was shot?"

"Calvin Russell."

"Russell?" Scott said. "Why's he here?"

"I don't know . . . he was Stephanie's cousin."

Flashing red lights announced the arrival of the ambulance, and Scott left her to show the EMTs where Eli and Calvin were.

Once Tori gave Ben her statement and the EMTs checked her out, Scott drove her to the hospital to check on Drew. Amy and the rest of the family met them in the ER.

"Now that this is over and there's no danger," Erin said, "you can come back home. And you're welcome too, Amy."

Tori nodded. It was time to start mending fences.

60

SIX DAYS LATER

Tori parked in front of the apartment building. She had a wrong to make right with her dad. She stepped out of her Toyota and walked to his apartment.

The door opened before she rang the doorbell.

"Tori! I'm so glad you're here." He tilted his head, looking puzzled. "But aren't you coming to the party later?"

"I am, but I didn't want an audience for what I have to say." The excitement in his voice laid another layer of guilt on her. "Can I come in?"

"Of course. I'm sorry."

He moved back, and she entered his apartment. "It looks really nice."

"Thanks. Join me for a cup of coffee?"

"That sounds good." She followed him to his small kitchen and sat at the counter while he made their coffees. "I listened to your podcast with Huey Prescott the other night. He's an amazing man."

"You did? And yes he is." While the podcast had been bittersweet, it seemed to bring closure to the man. Tori had been amazed to hear him say that while he was hurt that he never had a chance to talk to his daughter, he'd forgiven everyone involved, including Stephanie.

"Did I hear right?" Her dad set her cup down in front of her before he took a seat across the counter. "The DEA took the money Drew found and discovered traces of heroin on it?"

"Yeah. Once Ben's IT guy broke into the encrypted files on the data drive and found the offshore accounts, Ben theorized Stephanie was laundering money through the convenience stores and laundromats for the drug cartels."

Her dad shook his head. "I never took her to be that kind of person."

"I didn't, either. Guess that's what greed will do to you." She sipped the coffee. "This is good." Almost as good as Scott's. Would she ever get a chance to make things right with him?

"How is Eli, anyway?"

His question diverted her from thoughts of Scott. "He's been released from the hospital. Once he learned Stephanie had told Ben that Eli was the mastermind behind the crimes, he blew up and confessed to everything."

"So no honor among thieves?" her dad said with a hint of humor.

"I guess not. He claimed she made a play for him. Evidently Stephanie wasn't happy in her marriage to Richard, but she'd signed a prenup saying she got nothing if they divorced. Once Eli confided in her that Richard wasn't his father, she convinced him he would never inherit Richard's part if he found out—knowing her now, that was a veiled threat and he knew it."

Her dad shook his head. "Hard to believe. What was the trigger for Jenny's murder and for Stephanie to go after you?"

"Jenny implemented a new system and caught the difference between what the managers reported they gave her and what was actually deposited. Ben isn't sure how Jenny got hold of the information on the data drive, but his IT guy found an identical file on Stephanie's computer. In his confession, Eli claimed Jenny told Stephanie she'd mailed the data drive to me—that's what got me in their sights." Thinking of Eli's cold eyes when he held the gun on her sent a shiver down Tori's spine.

"It's sad, but what a complicated web she wove, all for money." He looked thoughtful. "Which one of them killed Jenny?"

"Eli claims he had nothing to do with her death. Of course, Stephanie is denying she had anything to do with it, but she practically admitted it the night we were kidnapped." She sipped the coffee again. "Plus, Ben found video footage of Jenny on Stephanie's computer—proof she was watching her. With Eli's testimony, there's enough evidence for the DA to charge her with Jenny's murder." She still wasn't sure they had the right person, but that might never be known. Just like they might never know who murdered Walter.

"How did this guy who kidnapped Drew get involved?" her dad asked.

"Calvin Russell?" She shook her head. "He was Stephanie's cousin, and she knew his history with his wife. She used it to get him to kidnap me."

"Stephanie told you this?"

"No. She threw him under the bus, said kidnapping me was all his idea. Once Russell recovered enough for Ben to question him, and he heard her claims, he turned on her. Confessed his part in shooting at us at the lake and trying to run me off the road and Drew's kidnapping. He'd put a tracker on my car and followed Drew, thinking it was me. After he realized his mistake, Calvin thought he could use him as leverage, and he was right. But it was his downfall too."

"But how did he get shot?"

"According to him, he and Stephanie got into an argument and she shot him."

"She's one evil woman," her dad said. "Thankfully it's all over now."

Her gaze landed on a photo hanging on the wall. The picture

of the whole family at the lake had been taken years ago. She stood and traced her finger over each person. A happy family in a happy place.

Tori squared her shoulders and turned to her dad. "But all of this isn't what I came here to talk about." Her throat tightened, and she swallowed. "I'm sorry for the way I've acted since Mom died."

"It's okay, honey. I understand."

"How? I blamed you for her death, and you never said a word."

"Maybe because I blamed myself too. Everyone told me it wasn't my fault, but I kept thinking if I hadn't felt so bad, I could've reacted faster and your mom would still be alive."

"You don't blame yourself anymore?"

"Not that so much as I've accepted I can't go back and change it."

"Well, I want to go on record and say I don't think the outcome would be any different if you'd been stone-cold sober with no hangover. Sometimes an accident is just that—an accident."

"Oh, honey . . . thank you."

He held out his arms, and she went to him with tears in her eyes. How she'd missed this. He patted her back, and she squeezed her arms around his waist. Just like when she was a kid.

Once she had her emotions under control, she stepped back. "Thank you for forgiving *me*."

"I did that a long time ago." He smiled. "Now where's that young man that's been hanging around? I haven't seen him this past week."

She bit her lip. Tori had apologized to him for accusing him of drinking, and he'd forgiven her, but then he'd disappeared. "Neither have I. Could be that I've messed that up royally too."

"I don't think so. I saw the way he looked at you at the hospital. That man loves you."

It's what Tori's heart told her too. "I just don't know if I'm ready to take that step. I thought I'd go to the lake to try and figure it out."

Her dad stared at her. "Do you regret what you had with Michael?"

Tori didn't regret one minute of time that she had spent with him. "No . . . I'm just not sure I can do it again."

"Would your life have been better if you'd never known him?"

She didn't have to think twice about that. "Of course not."

"Would you do it all over again with him?"

"Knowing I was going to lose him?" Would she? "I don't know. That's what I'm going to the lake to figure out."

He hugged her again. "I'll be praying for you."

"Thanks . . . I need it."

Half an hour later, Tori turned into the road that led to the lake. After parking, she walked down to the oak where she and Scott had taken refuge from the shooter. That day seemed like a lifetime ago.

Crazy man, risking his life to save someone he didn't even know. She sat down at the base of the tree, and a breeze from the lake cooled her face. Could she risk loving someone again? For years she'd told herself it wasn't worth the pain she'd gone through when Michael died.

Michael with his brown eyes so much like Scott's and a heart that knew no bounds. He'd loved her as fiercely as she'd loved him. Tori closed her eyes.

Until she met Scott, Tori had been satisfied with the new normal she created, and it hadn't included falling in love. New normal. Once she'd blithely used the phrase to refer to anything that was different. Michael's death so close to her mom's had taught her the true meaning, and she didn't like it. Yet her heart yearned for more. Scott had awakened feelings she thought long dead.

Her dad's question ran through her mind . . . and in her heart, Tori knew the answer. She settled against the huge oak and let her mind drift, the heat making her drowsy.

"Hey, you okay?"

The soft words jerked Tori awake. She opened her eyes and stared into Scott's dark ones. Was she dreaming? He held out his hand and helped her to stand.

No, not dreaming.

"I didn't mean to startle you."

"Not your fault. I must've fallen asleep." She inhaled a breath to calm her racing heart. "How did you know where I was?"

"Amy. Actually, Amy told me you were going by your dad's and he told me you would be here."

"Oh." She toed the dirt with her shoe.

"Hey, your black eye is about gone."

"Yeah." Tori touched her cheek. "I missed you."

"I missed you too." Scott brushed away a strand of hair the wind had blown across her face, then gently traced his finger along her jawline. "Actually, I missed you a lot."

She closed her eyes and leaned into his touch.

"Dance with me," he said softly

"Here? Now? There's no music."

"We'll make our own."

Scott held out his arms, and she stepped into them. He drew Tori close, humming "Moon River" in her ear. As they swayed in the shade of the tree, she'd never felt so cherished, even with Michael.

Scott stilled, and Tori raised her face to his, recognizing the desire that matched her own. He bent his head, hesitating, and then he brushed his lips against hers, as if asking permission. With a moan she pressed into his arms.

In that second, sounds faded. Nothing mattered except being here. Kissing Scott. When his lips captured hers, she lost herself in the moment, matching his passion. Seconds, or maybe hours, passed . . . fears of both past and future faded. Only the present mattered.

When he released her, she rested her head on his chest.

"I'd like to do that again sometime," he murmured against her hair.

"Anytime, mister."

"Good. That means I made the right decision."

She raised her head to look at him. "What do you mean?"

"It's why I haven't been around. I had meetings in Virginia . . . and I turned in my resignation."

Her eyes widened. "What?"

"Ben offered me a job and I accepted."

Tori was quiet for a moment as she absorbed the news.

Scott smiled at her. "So do you think we could go on a real date?"

Tori grinned. "I think that could be arranged."

He tilted her face toward him. His lips were so close to hers. "Are you sure? I'm not Michael, and I'll always be a recovering alcoholic . . ."

She didn't hesitate. "I'm sure."

"Do you mind if we start this off with a kiss?"

"I thought you'd never ask." Tori slipped her arms around his neck.

ACKNOWLEDGMENTS

On February 5, 2014, my first book, *Shadows of the Past* (Logan Point series), released. It was one of the greatest thrills I've experienced, and it kicked off a career in writing that has been a joy when I wasn't pulling my hair out. The next eleven years would bring seventeen more novels and five novellas. I want to thank Revell for giving me this wonderful opportunity and for allowing me to return to Logan Point with *On the Edge of Trust*.

Over the past twelve years I've worked with the best editors—Lonnie Hull DuPont, Rachel McRae, and Kristin Kornoelje. I never met a suggestion I didn't like . . . eventually. Seriously, my editors wanted the best possible book released, and they helped me develop books that have won numerous awards and accolades. Thank you.

Early on, the marketing team of Karen Steele and Michele Misiak fell in love with my books and steered them in the best marketing direction. After Michele went on to Baker Book House, Brianne Dekker, then Lindsay Schubert came on the team and were both outstanding. And the artistic team—I can't say enough good things about the covers of my books—the artistic designs have been beautiful. Again, thank you.

My first agent, Mary Sue Seymour, was amazing, and when

she went to be with the Lord much too soon, Julie Gwinn took over. In the following ten years, Julie and I became good friends. I'm thankful for the hard work they both did to help me place my books with a wonderful publisher.

I am so thankful for my family who has supported me through these years of writing. Your support and love have encouraged me and kept me going.

And last but not least, thank you to my readers. Thank you for reading my books and sharing wonderful reviews and telling others by word of mouth.

Most of all I thank Jesus, my Lord and Savior, for the creativity he gifted me with and the discipline to stick with it.

Read on for an excerpt
from Patricia Bradley's

SHADOWS OF THE PAST

Available now wherever
books are sold.

1

Death unfolds like a budding flower,
Tentatively, sweetly.
Unfurling in majestic power.
Until then, my love . . . until then.

Black roses last week, now spidery words scrawled on a scrap of paper with "Meade Funeral Home" printed across the top. Someone was stalking her, and they wanted her to know it.

Taylor Martin sucked in a sharp breath and tried to ignore the icy shiver traversing her body.

He was here.

Hair raised on the back of her neck. She turned in a circle. Heavy clouds hung low, shrouding the tall firs with their mist. An air ambulance waited in the clearing to lift off for Seattle as soon as Beth Coleman's vitals stabilized. Only a few members of the search and rescue team remained at the crime scene, packing their gear.

Whether he was one of the men who came out to comb the woods for the kidnapper and his victims, or he'd simply followed her here to this remote area southwest of Seattle, it didn't matter. What mattered was that he'd been close enough to touch her, to put the note in her pocket.

To kill her.

An artery in her temple pulsed. He had to know she volunteered her profiling skills to the Newton County Sheriff's Department.

A puff of wind brought a light fragrance. Old Spice. The scent her dad had worn. She frowned, seeking the source of the aftershave, but only encountered Dale Atkins striding toward her. The leathery-faced sheriff was her advisor and, tonight, her chauffeur. It wasn't him—Dale was a Grey Flannel man.

Perhaps the stranger with him? Her gaze flicked over him, barely registering the broad shoulders, plaid shirt, and jeans. No, too young for Old Spice. She looked past him and realized the scent had dissipated.

Had she imagined it?

The sheriff touched her arm. "You're white as a sheet."

She held up the scrap of paper. Old Spice tickled her nose again. She sniffed it and made a face. Aftershave lingered, potent. Another piece to add to the puzzle.

"Taylor, what is it?"

"This was in my coat pocket." She shoved the paper at him. "Someone wants me dead."

Dale scanned it, his eyebrows pinching together in a frown. "How did it get there?"

"I don't know." Taylor wrapped her arms across her stomach.

He tore a sheet from his notebook and folded it into a pouch before putting the note inside. "Have you worn your jacket all day?"

"Not all day." Her teeth chattered, and she ran her hands up and down her arms. "Lunchtime. I took it off then. Slipped it back on when the helicopter arrived for Beth Coleman."

Dale took off his black cap with "Newton County Sheriff" across it and smoothed his gray hair. "Could it have been in your pocket awhile?"

"No." She fisted her hands. "I haven't worn the jacket since it came from the cleaners."

"Are you sure?" He waved his hand at the expanse of Douglas firs. "We're—"

"I know where we are. In the middle of a logging road a hundred miles from nowhere." She caught her breath as heat crawled up her face. This was not like her. "I'm sorry. Can I see the note again?"

Taylor unfolded the pouch and studied the words. The cadence and the words reminded her of a student in her victim profiling class—the Goth student who'd been popping up in odd places, like the pharmacy and the jewelry store. The one she figured had left the anonymous boxes of candy on her desk and then the flowers.

The black roses were what made her zero in on him—they matched his black hoodie and black jeans and black hair—black everything—but she'd dismissed it all as a student's crush. But candid photos and now this note were not things she could just dismiss. "Scott Sinclair has been following me, and a couple of his papers had notes like this doodled in the margin."

The stranger stiffened. "I don't know what's in that note, but Scott wouldn't hurt anyone."

The words shot from his mouth, his Southern accent zinging Taylor, reminding her of how syllable by syllable her ex-fiancé had hammered her drawl away. For the first time, she really looked at the man who stood shoulder to shoulder with the six-foot-one sheriff. Around her age, maybe a little older. Thirty at most. And with the saddest, most beautiful hazel eyes she'd ever seen.

Taylor took in the planes of his face and wondered whether he fought a losing battle with his beard each day or if the five o'clock shadow was deliberate. Either way, he carried it well. But he didn't look like law enforcement, which was what Taylor assumed he was when she had seen him with Atkins earlier. Up close, she realized he wore his hair too shaggy for a cop. More like a lumberjack. Probably with the search and rescue team.

She cocked her head at him. "And you know this, how?"

"I'm sorry," Dale said. "I should have already introduced you two. Nick Sinclair, Dr. Taylor Martin from Conway University. She found the link between the kidnapper and the Colemans."

The sheriff put his hand on her shoulder. "This young lady is well known in the field of victomology and teaches a pilot class at the university. She aims to be the best profiler in the country one day. Personally, I think she's already the best."

Taylor's cheeks blazed at the sheriff's high praise. But she wasn't that young. She'd be twenty-nine in exactly one month, June seventeenth. She looked away, catching sight of the air corpsman as he slammed the helicopter bay shut. She hoped Beth Coleman made it to Seattle.

Dale chuckled. "She doesn't like me bragging on her, either."

She shrugged. "It's not really about being the best, just doing my best."

He nodded toward the stranger. "Nick is a writer."

Taylor almost snorted. "Researching a book, I suppose."

"No. I'm looking for my brother. Scott Sinclair."

■ ■ ■

Maybe Nick's tough love campaign with his alcoholic brother had been all wrong. He tried to wrap his mind around the accusation this Dr. Martin had leveled at Scott. Kind of hard when the woman had taken his breath away. Not that he hadn't noticed her statuesque beauty when he first arrived at the crime scene earlier in the afternoon.

She had the kind of beauty found in high-class fashion magazines—raven hair pulled into a silky ponytail and cheekbones most models would kill for. But it'd been the startling blue eyes that drew him in like a boy to candy. Right now, they were flashing lightning bolts at him. Just like Angie's when he'd rubbed her the wrong way. "What do you have against my brother, anyway?" The private investigator's report hadn't indicated bad blood between Scott and the professor. Only that he'd taken a couple of her courses.

"Nothing." She tapped the pouch. "This sounds like something he'd write."

His brother a stalker? No way. "Do you mind if I read it?"

"You've got to be kidding. This is evidence."

"What does it say, then?" He didn't blink under her intense scrutiny.

"It's a poem," she said finally. "'Death unfolds like a budding flower, tentatively . . .'"

She could quit reading any time. The poem sliced through his memory with the precision of a laser. *Unfurling in majestic power* . . . "You say it's on a funeral home's letterhead?"

"Yep."

Was it possible . . . no. Scott would never hurt anyone. But he had still lived at home when the verses first appeared in one of Nick's short stories. Nick licked his lips, his conscience prodding him to reveal the words were his. "This poem—"

Three hundred yards away the helicopter screamed to life, drowning out his voice, and the moment of confession passed. He turned toward the chopper, blinking against the wind that whipped his body. Less than a minute later a steady *whop-whop* filled the air as the orange chopper lifted with the victim.

When the noise abated, the sheriff cleared his throat. "Be a miracle if Beth Coleman makes it to Harborview alive."

"Yeah." Even though he wasn't from the Seattle area, Nick had heard of the level-one trauma center. He said a silent prayer as the chopper disappeared over the tree line. Taylor, he noted, said nothing, her blue eyes unreadable.

A deputy called to the sheriff, and with a nod, Atkins pocketed the note and left them.

Taylor stuffed her hands in her pockets. "So, why are you here looking for your brother?"

"Because he's the only family I have left, and I haven't seen him in almost three years." Not since he showed up drunk at Angie's funeral.

Her expression softened. "I'm sorry about that, but why here? At this crime scene?"

"Oh." He'd misunderstood her. "I didn't intend to come to the crime scene. I had a lead Scott was in Newton, and when I stopped by the sheriff's office this afternoon to discuss it, Sheriff Atkins wasn't in since he was here, but I overheard the dispatcher give directions to one of the search and rescue teams, and I sort of tagged along, thinking I might get a chance to talk with the sheriff."

"But you stayed. And it's almost eight o'clock."

The beautiful professor had noticed him. A pang of guilt tempered the pleasure from that knowledge. Then the undercurrent of her words nailed him. "Okay, so you were right. I figured out pretty quickly the sheriff doesn't know where Scott is, but I was here, and I thought I could help . . . and I don't often get a chance to do research like this."

She rested an elbow on one hand and tapped her finger against her jaw. "Okay, that explains why you're here today, but what took you so long to look for him? You said he'd been missing for three years."

"I didn't say he was missing." He flushed. He didn't know this professor, and he certainly didn't want to air all his problems with his brother. Or that he'd been practicing tough love, hoping Scott would hit rock bottom and reach out to him. Except it hadn't worked, and recently he'd felt an urgency to locate his brother. "I . . . had cut off contact with him and lost track of where he was living. I only engaged the investigator recently." He stiffened at her questioning gaze. She was waiting for why, but why was none of her business.

"I see. Well, if you find your brother—"

"Dr. Martin!"

A man hurried toward them holding his small daughter tight against his chest. The sheriff had identified him earlier as the victim's husband, Jim Coleman. Nick's gaze shifted to Taylor, and the naked longing in her eyes rocked him. A knife twisted in his heart. He'd seen that look before in his wife's eyes when she'd talked about wanting children.

"Thank you, Doctor." Jim grasped Taylor's hand, pumping it.

"Nothing to thank me for—just doing my job." Taylor nudged a rotted branch with the toe of her shoe. Dank spores blew over the rotting leaves, filling the air with their musty scent.

Jim hugged his daughter closer. "No. You're the only one who believed me. You saved my daughter and my wife."

Little Sarah blinked open her eyes and pulled her thumb from her puckered lips. "Will Mommy be okay?"

The child's chocolate-brown eyes stared up at Taylor, her brows knit together. Alarm darted across the professor's face. "I—"

"I told you, honey. She'll be fine." Coleman smoothed a strand of blonde hair from her eyes. "She's going to the hospital . . . I promise. They'll make her all better."

It was plain Taylor didn't want to mislead the child, but as Sarah continued her doe-eyed gaze, Taylor sucked in a breath. "I'm sure your daddy's right."

"Thank you," he mouthed, then nodded and hurried to his car.

"You did the right thing," Nick said.

Taylor exhaled a long breath. "I don't know. What if she doesn't make it?"

"She could definitely use a miracle."

This time there was no mistaking Taylor's pursed lips.

■ ■ ■

Taylor stared at the ground, seeing the image of Beth Coleman lying in the wet leaves, blood staining her cashmere sweater. Miracle? That meant she'd have to pray, and if she thought it'd do any good, she would. It wasn't that she didn't believe in God or that she didn't believe he answered prayers for some people. He just didn't answer hers.

"Sorry to have to leave you, but I have work to do." She turned to walk up the hill where Dale was wrapping up the investigation. "If you find your brother, call the sheriff, please," she called over her shoulder.

"Wait, I'd like to discuss Scott with you."

Something in his voice halted her. What was it he'd said? *He's the only family I have left.* She glanced at the third finger on his left hand. A wedding band. The sad eyes. "Your family, what happened to them?"

"What?" Nick took a step back.

Taylor rubbed the burning in her neck. She was too tired to be standing here having this conversation with Nick Sinclair, and it wasn't like her to be so direct, but something about Nick made her want to know. Besides, it was too late to take back her question. She lightened her tone. "You said Scott was all the family you have left. What happened?"

He kicked at a dirt clump, and mud smeared across the toe of his cowboy boot. "My wife . . . died over two years ago, my parents a long time before that. I have to find Scott."

Their deaths explained his acquaintance with grief. And she understood grief. It also explained why he felt he had to find his brother. "I have to finish up here, but if you want to stop by the university tomorrow, we can talk. Just call me first."

She rattled off her cell number, then wondered if she should have. It might be an invitation to disaster, given the way her heart kicked up a notch when he looked at her with those eyes.

He jotted her number on a card and snapped a short salute. "Yes, ma'am."

As Taylor walked the short distance toward the command center, a coroner's hearse crept along the logging road with the kidnapper's body. His suicide meant no answers to some of her questions about why he kidnapped Beth Coleman and her daughter. A shadow crossed her heart. She half halted, the skin on her neck prickling.

Someone was watching her.

She scanned to the left. One of the men who'd helped with the search ducked his head. She started toward him, noting his longish hair and camouflage hunting jacket. As she got closer, his fingers flew over his phone. Texting. Not stalking her.

Just peachy. Was she destined to suspect every scruffy male who glanced her way? Taylor retraced her steps.

"Ready to take me home?" she asked when she found Dale.

"Give me a minute with Zeke."

"Sure." As long as Taylor didn't have to deal with the prickly Zeke Thornton. Dale's chief deputy challenged her on every idea she came up with, always asking *why*, and if she was honest, he probably made her better. But he could be so irritating.

Taylor leaned against the sheriff's cruiser as the minute stretched into forty-five, and the gray twilight turned into nighttime dark. The kind of dark where you couldn't see your hand in front of your face. The kind of dark that made her think of her dad. The kind of dark she hated.

Finally, Dale returned, and Taylor slid into the passenger side and fastened her seat belt, inhaling the stale odor inside the aging patrol car that had seen too many cups of coffee and onion-topped burgers. Thoughts of her dad lingered. Tomorrow she would delve again into her search for him, but at this point, all she had was a cold trail that was getting colder.

Dale's voice cut into her thoughts as he pulled the Crown Vic onto the highway. "You did a good job today. You worked that crime scene like a pointer hunts quail. You didn't give up."

"Yeah, but with Ralph Jenkins's death, we can only guess why." Still, the sheriff's words soothed the aches in her body. At times she felt like a bird dog on the hunt, sniffing through evidence, looking for the connection between victim and assailant hidden beneath the surface 75 percent of the time. Today her instincts homed in on the father's past and scored a direct hit. Except, something bothered her about the case, but nothing she could put her finger on. She sighed. It was probably that she couldn't question the kidnapper.

"I wish Coleman had told us sooner about that wreck fifteen years ago." The kidnapping and shooting appeared to be Jenkins's revenge for the death of his wife and girls in an accident that hadn't been anyone's fault.

"Well, you were dead-on right."

Yeah, she had great instincts when it came to other people. So why was finding her father so difficult? And on more than one level. She unwrapped a lemon drop, then popped it in her mouth, the candy tart on her tongue. Her cell phone rang, and she glanced at the ID. "Do you know anyone with a 901 area code?"

"Not off hand," Dale said.

She answered, putting the phone on speaker. "Martin."

"Dr. Martin? This is Nick Sinclair. Scott's brother."

"Yes?" She should have known giving him her number would prove to be a mistake.

"I know it's late, but I'd really like to talk to you about my brother tonight."

"I'm busy right now. And I don't want to discuss him over the phone." She checked her watch. Nine-thirty. She never went to bed before midnight, anyway, and this might be an opportunity to get information on Scott. "However, I'll be home shortly, and I can give you thirty minutes."

"That'd be great. I won't stay longer than that, I promise."

After giving him her address, she hung up and turned to the sheriff. "Can you hang around?"

"Sure. I have a couple of questions for him myself."

Taylor slipped the phone in her pocket. What could be so urgent to Nick Sinclair that he couldn't wait until tomorrow? She thought of the poem. Could he have slipped it in her jacket? No, he hadn't been around for the other "presents." "What's your take on the poem. Do you think it's Scott Sinclair?"

"Possibly. What's more important is why you think it's him."

"I didn't until I received the black roses. I had no clue who was sending me candy." In late March, every week a box of Godiva chocolates had been placed on her desk. No one ever saw the gifter, but Taylor figured one of the male students had a crush on her. That happened sometimes with a student and a professor. Then in late April, the black, long-stemmed roses appeared.

"Those roses sure fit that strange getup he wears," Dale said. "What do the kids call it? Goth?"

"Yeah." Scott always showed up in class wearing a black T-shirt under a black Nike jacket with a hoodie, black jeans, and black tennis shoes. And jet-black hair.

"Those photos, though. They put a different slant on the situation, and now this note really changes it. I'll bring him in for questioning again."

The photos had arrived right after the roses. Shots of her shopping, jogging, at the pharmacy, at a ball game, Taylor doing everyday tasks. Just knowing whoever took the pictures lurked that close sent a shiver through her body.

Dale had questioned Scott after the photos arrived, but the only connection to him had been the black roses, and even that had been tenuous. Several stores in the area sold the flowers, and none of the clerks identified Scott. With no concrete evidence, the sheriff couldn't hold him.

"I can usually size someone up pretty quick, and Scott Sinclair didn't strike me as dangerous," Dale said.

"Same with me. He was always somewhat shy, especially in those first classes last fall. Turned beet red when I asked him about the candy and roses. Mumbled something about not knowing what I was talking about. But then he dropped my class."

The sheriff turned his blinker on and made a right turn. "The thing is, no one saw him at the crime scene. How did he get the note in your coat?"

Taylor had asked herself that same question over and over. And came up blank. "He could've changed his look, and there were a lot of volunteers." She picked at a hangnail. "Maybe it wasn't him. Could've been anyone, even someone at the cleaners."

"I'll check that tomorrow. It also could be connected to a past case, even before you came to Newton." Dale drummed his fingers on the steering wheel. "You've helped to put away a couple of pretty bad guys, and criminals have long memories and bigger grudges."

"Sometimes I think I should have stayed in my nice, safe classroom."

"You have a cop's heart, Taylor."

She didn't know about that. Her thoughts chased around in her head. "The paper doesn't actually have my name on it. Maybe it's just a sick joke."

"We're going to check it out. Until then, you need to be extra careful."

Taylor intended to do just that. She swayed against her seat belt as the sheriff turned onto Rainey Road and picked up speed.

Dale rested his hand on the armrest between their seats. "Um, how're you doing? About, you know—"

"Fine." Taylor clipped the word off, then softened her voice. "I *really* don't want to talk about Michael."

Silence rode with them for a mile before Dale reached and patted her arm. "You were too good for him. You're young. Give it time."

She turned and stared though the window at the dimly lit houses whizzing by. Her biological clock ticked off another day every twenty-four hours. Of course, women bore children into their late thirties and early forties now. Which was fortunate, given her history with men. But that history made dreams of having children, the white picket fence, and the fairy-tale ending rather unlikely. The image of little Sarah Coleman in her dad's arms sent an ache through her chest.

The front tire centered a pothole, jarring her.

"Sorry, didn't see that." He cocked his head toward her without taking his eyes off the road. "There's something I tell my girls. At the right time, God will bring the right man into your life, but you have to wait for his timing."

"Let it go, Dale." Like God even cared. "I'm not looking for anyone."

Nick Sinclair's face with his day-old beard surfaced in her mind. *No.* He would be the last person she would ever date. Too good-looking, like Michael. Not that he'd be interested in her—she'd just accused his brother of stalking.

They neared her winding driveway, and the car slowed, then turned beside her mailbox. "If you'll let me out here, I'll pick up my mail." Taylor unbuckled her seat belt. She'd rather get her mail now, before he left. After getting out, she poked her head back in the car. "Go ahead, I'll walk."

Dale's brows knit together.

"Climbing back in just isn't worth the effort," she said.

"Make the effort. We've just been talking about someone stalking you. And, it's pitch-black. Not even a moon."

"Come on, it's not like you're leaving me—you'll be at the end of the drive. Besides, you won't be here tomorrow night when I get in from the university." Taylor tried to laugh, but the sound stuck in her chest. She wished she'd never told him how she hated the dark. She straightened her shoulders. Time to face the monster under the bed. "I need to do this."

"Sorry." He shook his head. "You don't have to get back in the car, though. I'll just drive slowly ahead of you."

High winds moaned through the pines in her yard as she fished a penlight from her purse and pointed the beam toward the ground. Taylor retrieved several envelopes from her box, almost losing them in a gust of wind loaded with the threat of rain.

The tiny light flickered then came back to life, cutting a narrow swath through the darkness between her and Dale's cruiser ahead.

Her feet crunched on the loose gravel, the only sound other than the wind. She focused on the bouncing light until she rounded the curve.

Dale parked and climbed out of the cruiser. He jerked his head toward her house. "Why didn't you leave your porch light on?"

Hadn't she? Taylor tried to think back to when she left. She remembered now, the bulb had burned out. "I meant to replace the bulb this morning, but I forgot."

They climbed the steps, and Taylor fumbled in her purse for her key. "You don't have to do this."

"Did you forget Nick Sinclair is dropping by?"

She slapped her head. "It's been a long day."

"It wouldn't matter if he wasn't coming." His face cracked into a grin. "I do it all the time for my girls. We get together for dinner, and afterward I go in and check out their apartment. Make sure it's secure—it's what dads do."

The words echoed in her empty heart. For a second, she envied Dale's daughters. She unlocked the door and let him go ahead of her.

"Where's the light switch?"

"I'll get it." Taylor followed him into the house. A strong odor of Old Spice filled her nose as she flipped on the living room light.

Nothing. Her flashlight cast an eerie circle on the far wall, then flickered and snuffed out. Taylor swallowed a cry and shook the light. Her heart hammered against her ribs. The light twitched on again, a faint shaft in the dark.

"Get out of here." Dale shoved her toward the door. He barked into his shoulder mic. "I need backup, 302 Rainey Road. Now!"

He unsnapped his holster and pulled his gun. Footsteps scuffed somewhere to her left. Before she pinpointed the direction, a bone crunched and Dale yelled. His gun spit flame, and a deafening roar boomed in the enclosed space. Gunpowder burned her nostrils.

"Dale! Where are you?" Taylor swept the dim light to her left.

He lay crumpled on the floor. A man whirled toward her with a pipe in his hand, his face hidden by a hood, a Nike emblem on his jacket. The flashlight flickered off again. *No! Stay on!*

Darkness pressed in on Taylor. She couldn't move. Old Spice threatened to smother her.

Air whooshed overhead. She jerked back, kicked, and slammed into soft tissue.

"Umph."

Taylor dropped to the floor and scrambled for Dale's gun, her fingers probing under his body. Blood pounded in her temples. The gun wasn't there. He groaned. Had to get him out. Her breath ragged, she stood and tugged at him.

The pipe sliced the air again. She ducked—not low enough. Pain slammed down the side of her skull then her shoulder. White light pierced her vision, splintering into a thousand points ringed with darkness. Taylor staggered, grabbing air. Strength flowed from her body. She fought the black fog filling her head.

Patricia Bradley is the author of the Pearl River series, as well as the Natchez Trace Park Rangers, Memphis Cold Case, and Logan Point series. Bradley is the winner of an Inspirational Reader's Choice Award, a Selah Award, and a Daphne du Maurier Award; she was a Carol Award finalist; and three of her books were included in anthologies that debuted on the *USA Today* bestseller list. She makes her home in Mississippi. Learn more at PTBradley.com.

Meet
Patricia
BRADLEY

PTBradley.com

- **f** PatriciaBradleyAuthor
- **X** PTBradley1
- **◉** PTBradley1

Be the first to hear about new books from Revell!

Stay up to date with our authors and books by signing up for our newsletters at

RevellBooks.com/SignUp

FOLLOW US ON SOCIAL MEDIA

@RevellFiction

A Note from the Publisher

Dear Reader,

Thank you for selecting a Revell novel! We're so happy to be part of your reading life through this work. Our mission here at Revell is to publish stories that reach the heart. Through friendship, romance, suspense, or a travel back in time, we bring stories that will entertain, inspire, and encourage you. We believe in the power of stories to change our lives and are grateful for the privilege of sharing these stories with you.

We believe in building lasting relationships with readers, and we'd love to get to know you better. If you have any feedback, questions, or just want to chat about your experience reading this book, please email us directly at publisher@revellbooks.com. Your insights are incredibly important to us, and it would be our pleasure to hear how we can better serve you.

We look forward to hearing from you and having the chance to enhance your experience with Revell Books.

The Publishing Team at Revell Books
A Division of Baker Publishing Group
publisher@revellbooks.com

Revell